TO ROUSE LEVIATHAN

TO ROUSE LEVIATHAN

MATT CARDIN

Featuring two collaborations with Mark McLaughlin

Hippocampus Press

New York

Publication History: See p. 373.

Published by Hippocampus Press
P.O. Box 641, New York, NY 10156.
www.hippocampuspress.com

Cover art by Michael Hutter, octopusartis.com
Cover design by Daniel V. Sauer, dansauerdesign.com.
Hippocampus Press logo designed by Anastasia Damianakos.

First Edition
1 3 5 7 9 8 6 4 2
ISBN 978-1-61498-270-8 (paperback)
ISBN 978-1-61498-271-5 (ebook)

There is here involved [in the phenomenon of weird supernatural horror fiction] a psychological pattern or tradition as real and as deeply grounded in mental experience as any other pattern or tradition of mankind; coeval with the religious feeling and closely related to many aspects of it.

—H. P. Lovecraft, "Supernatural Horror in Literature" (1927)

[The] antecedent stage [of "religious dread" or "awe"] is "daemonic dread" . . . It first begins to stir in the feeling of "something uncanny," "eerie," or "weird." It is this feeling which, emerging in the mind of primeval man, forms the starting point for the entire religious development of history.

—Rudolf Otto, *The Idea of the Holy* (1917)

The completest religions would therefore seem to be those in which the pessimistic element is best developed.

—William James, *The Varieties of Religious Experience* (1902)

Let the day perish on which I was born. That day—may it turn to darkness. Let gloom and deep darkness claim it. Let the blackness of the day terrify it. Let those sorcerers who place a curse on days curse that day, those who are skilled to rouse Leviathan.

—Job 3:3, 4, 5, 8

Contents

PART ONE
DIVINATIONS OF THE DEEP

Now when the sun was going down, a deep sleep fell upon Abram; and behold, horror and great darkness fell upon him. Then God spoke.

—Genesis 15:12-13

He made darkness his hiding place.

—Psalm 18:11

Preface: Divining the Darkness

The Hebrew scriptures tell us that when God began to create the world, "the earth was a formless void and darkness covered the face of the deep" (Genesis 1:2). The English word "deep" is a translation of the Hebrew word *tehom,* which many scholars have speculated is a cognate of the Sumerian *Tiamat.* In the Babylonian creation epic known today as *Enuma Elish,* Tiamat is described as a deity of darkness and watery chaos that was slain by her children, the Babylonian gods, who then used the halves of her body to create the world: half for the sky, half for the earth.

In light of the possible connection between Sumerian mythology and the Judeo-Christian scriptures, the presence of the primeval "deep" in the Genesis creation story takes on a decidedly sinister aspect. As with Tiamat in the Babylonian story, in Genesis *tehom* is a primeval chaos that is fashioned by an anthropomorphic deity into an ordered cosmos. As in the Babylonian story, the primeval chaos of Judeo-Christian scripture is not completely done away with. It is merely . . . subdued. It continues to exist in the background of Hebrew thought, eventually becoming associated with the depths of the ocean. At one point Yahweh even allows *tehom* to reclaim the cosmos: in the story of Noah and the flood, the waters come not only from above but from below: "In the six hundredth year of Noah's life, in the second month, on the seventeenth day of the month, on that day *all the fountains of the great deep burst forth,* and the windows of heaven were opened" (Genesis 7:11). Thus, the flood was not just a flood, but an *unmaking*, a temporary return of the earth to its original formless state.

For a certain type of person, this all raises the question of whether God is truly the final power in the universe. Since the deep existed with God from the beginning, is it not possible to conjecture that it is at least as powerful as he? In light of the link between the Hebrew and Babylonian creation stories, is it not possible to speculate still further that *tehom*, like Tiamat, *predates* God? That God is perhaps the *offspring* of the deep? If these speculations are accurate, then God is living on borrowed time, and we are left with the disturbing conclusion that both he and his world—the world we take for granted, the ordered world of life, light, and logic—are merely foreground to a background of death, darkness, and derangement. Eventually, inevitably, the great deep will rear its monstrous head and reveal to God and to us the true nature of our universe and our selves.

There exist a few scattered souls who claim that we can glimpse this reality even now, while the charade is still up and running. We encounter the deep, so they say, in the dark mysteries of life: in horror, pain, nightmare, disillusionment, and death; in the places where light and reason seem to be absent, or to have only a precarious foothold; at the seams of the universe, where sometimes a thread comes unraveled and a ray of darkness shines through, and the light does not overcome it. But to seek such glimpses is always dangerous, and to ask such questions is to court the ultimate disaster, for we can never know in advance what form the answers will assume. We can only know that they will arrive as the unexpected, the uncanny, and the inconceivable. And there are, after all, so very many ways, both witting and unwitting, that each of us attempts to divine the deep.

An Abhorrence to All Flesh

No longer mourn for me, when I am dead,
Than you shall hear the surly sullen bell
Give warning to the world that I am fled
From this vile world, with vilest worms to dwell.
                              —William Shakespeare

Wretched man that I am!
Who will rescue me from this body of death?
                              —Romans 7:24

1

It seemed a harmless enough invitation, and in fact a welcome surprise, when my friend Darby called to summon me to a party at his brick mansion just beyond the city limits of Terence, Missouri. By his description I understood him to be planning another one of his "famous" parties that had played so large a part in our early years together.

"Wine, women, and song," he announced as the program for the evening's festivities. Even through the curious crackle of static in the earpiece of the telephone, I could hear the calm, assured attitude of my old college buddy coming through, and I secretly rejoiced that he had at last seen his way clear of the funk into which he had fallen upon our graduation eight years ago.

"When did your parties ever involve wine or women?" I said. "They were always more beer and bachelors, as I recall."

"And so it may be again," he cheerfully replied, apparently unruffled by my good-natured jibe. "You will be there, won't you, Todd? It simply wouldn't be the same without you."

"You can count on it," I told him. "An invitation from a gentleman of your stature must be counted an honor."

He laughed out some pleasantry and we hung up, leaving me to marvel at the unexpected revolution in his mood. After having heard nothing from him for—God, how long was it? Three years! And then to have him call and announce a party just like it was old times? I could hardly force myself to wait patiently for the night after next to arrive. Surely we would spend the evening indulging in another of those wide-ranging and wildly colorful conversations that had always been such a heady joy to an intellectual dabbler like me.

As I pondered this pleasing prospect, I wandered from the den to the kitchen in search of an easy dinner. A moment's idle rummaging through the refrigerator turned up a covered dish near the back of the top shelf that contained a generous portion of the casserole that I had prepared and partially eaten two days ago, so I slid it into the oven and soon sat down to a hot meal at my cheap dining table.

I chewed the first bite obliviously, hardly tasting the food at all as fantasies about Darby's party flickered through my brain like mental movies. There I sat, expounding on literature and film and philosophy while the other guests eagerly asked for more. There Darby stood, half-annoyed at the way I had stolen his spotlight. Then a hideous taste invaded my mouth, and my gorge rose with the threat of vomiting. My fantasies popped like soap bubbles as all my attention flew back to the immediate reality of my kitchen, and the casserole, and the revolting lump of vileness on my tongue. I spat the offending mouthful into a napkin. Closer examination of the pulpy mass revealed an entirely inappropriate maggoty presence, and I must have run at least two gallons of water down the sink as I retched and drooled and wondered just how it was possible for the damned things to hatch and grow in a refrigerated environment, or for them to emerge still wriggling and writhing from a hot oven.

2

The next evening I made my preparations for the party with as much care as possible. Having attended so many of these gatherings in the past, I knew the conversation would most likely escalate or, as was sometimes the case, degenerate into an informal contest of wits, a good-natured but increasingly heated competition to determine who could display the greatest erudition—not in terms of depth, of course, but of breadth. It was at times like these that I most enjoyed my own dilettante style of learning. The old phrase "jack of all trades, master of none" most certainly described me, with my smattering of knowledge from many different fields of inquiry. And a good thing it was, since I could never know for certain what topic Darby would choose as the centerpiece for the evening's conversation.

At such times I was also the most smugly happy with my own library. The larger of my two bedrooms served as the repository for most of my books, but the evidence of my bibliographic obsession also adorned shelves, desks, mantels, and tables throughout the house. These volumes represented many enjoyable years of impulse buying at numberless bookstores, especially second-hand ones. I often took pleasure at the thought of what this diverse collection might say about my character, intellect, and depth. I was also fully aware that it was this bit of unrepentant narcissism that led me to anticipate the imminent gathering with Darby and his friends so eagerly. After all, where else could I expect to find a captive audience (nobody left one of Darby Cole's parties until it was made clear that permission had been granted by the host) that would act suitably impressed at the extent of my literary sagacity?

I seated myself comfortably on the brown sectional sofa in the den and spread out a stack of books before me—paperbacks, hardbacks, clothbound, leather-bound—culled from the nooks and crannies of the house. Subjectwise, they centered around the broad field of knowledge that was of greatest interest both to Darby and to me: religion. For starters, I flipped through a few pages of my worn leather copy of the Bible. The familiar stories, and especially the bizarre and dark aspects of the Judeo-Christian deity that flickered past my eyes in scattered verses, were enticing as always. But I soon wearied of biblical matters and moved on to an introductory college survey text on anthropological approaches to the study of religion. The Holy Scriptures of the Christian church were so deeply ingrained in my psyche that I had no need to brush up on them. Were they not a part of my cultural inheritance, a component of my very blood and bones?

But I soon wearied of this book as well, and so I turned to another, and then another. It was a behavioral pattern of virtually geologic antiquity in my life: I passed glibly from book to book and author to author, gleaning a term here, an idea there, storing them all in memory as best I could, attempting to erect a façade of learning. And all the time, the November night outside my windows grew blacker and colder, while the incandescent light of my lamp burned white and harsh.

Presently, I noticed that I had developed a headache. Rubbing my weary eyes, I glanced at the ersatz antique pendulum clock on the wall and saw with surprise that it was only 12:30 in the morning. From the throbbing in my head I would have sworn I had already spent the entire night hunched over a book. Closing the current volume, whose title I had forgotten, I rose to get a glass of water and try to walk some of the stiffness out of my back and neck.

As I passed from the den into the hallway, and then to the kitchen, I thought I heard a noise behind me: a tapping sound, maybe, like someone thumping a finger on the window back in the den. I retraced my steps with a dose of unease, since the thought of finding someone crouched outside my window in the dark, watching me read in the glow of my lamp, was anything but comforting. But when I switched off the lamp and peered through the single high, narrow pane into the gloom, I saw nothing but the moonlight shining through the nearly denuded branches of the great oak tree in my backyard. The patterns of silvery white light appeared disconcertingly serpentine on the carpet of fallen leaves.

After that, I chose to leave the lights off and retire. Once in bed, I was plagued all night by the half-understood ideas of a dozen different writers as they twined their way through my dreams in various symbolic guises. When I woke in the morning to the sound of the garbage man carting away the trash from my curb, a phrase from one of those dreams, a fragment of an unremembered reading from the night before, remained caught in my consciousness. Even after I got up, showered, ate breakfast, and sat down to my day's work, it still echoed over and over to the rhythm of my breath. Strangely enough, I could not speak it or remember its exact words. It had something to do with loathing, and something to do with flesh. A semi-subconscious mantra, it seemed.

All that day as I worked at my typewriter, I found myself glancing down from time to time and wondering why I felt such a strange disgust at the sight of my hands, my fingers, my skin, and especially at the thought of the flesh and bones beneath.

3

The long driveway to Darby's house was cloaked with a scattering of late autumn leaves that only a few weeks ago would have made a festive carpet of crimson and gold. As it was, they formed a brittle dead reminder of the dying season. Even through my closed windows I could hear them crunching beneath the tires.

I counted one, two, three cars already parked in front of the house, which squatted sphinxlike under the starry firmament. I could see soft-edged shadows moving inside the yellow glare of the arched window facing the drive. This was the window to the great room of Darby's massive mansion. The indistinct outlines of the shadows reminded me of something I couldn't quite recall. Something unpleasant. My headlights slashed across the brick exterior of the house as I turned to park among the other vehicles, and one of the shadows in the window moved and then coalesced into the silhouetted form of a man: Darby, peering out to see which of his guests was arriving late.

I waved at him as I made my way toward the front door, and he waved to me and then backed away into the room. The smell of burning hickory logs wafted down from the high chimney as I ascended the stone steps.

The door opened before I rang the bell, and there was Darby, trim, smiling, wearing a cream-colored sweater and holding a drink in a beautiful crystal tumbler.

"Todd!" he cried, beaming his brightest smile and offering me his hand. "Wonderful to have you here! We had begun to wonder whether you were going to grace us with your presence after all." His grip was firm but his hand was cold.

"Like I told you, it's impossible to refuse an invitation from Darby Cole." I stepped inside the blue-carpeted entryway and removed my coat as he shut the door. "Besides," I added, "the others are even more tardy than I am."

"There are no others," he said as he deposited his drink, which appeared to be a vodka, on a small glass-topped table, and took my coat. "This is an intimate gathering, not one of those awful, noisy affairs from our college days."

"You shock me, Darby!" I feigned horror while he hung my coat in the closet. "A Darby Cole party with fewer than thirty guests? What about your reputation?"

"What about it?" He shrugged, shut the closet door, and picked his drink back up. "I'm not as concerned with image as I once was. Now come and greet the others."

He led me down the long hallway to the great room, where I was briefly overcome with nostalgia as I observed the familiar scene: the oak paneling, the hardwood floor, the massive oriental rug, the fully stocked bar in the southeast corner, the fire blazing in the fireplace, the vaulted ceiling that seemed as remote and mysterious as a cavern at twilight.

"Everyone," Darby announced, "this is Todd Whitman, one of my oldest and dearest friends, and a long-time regular at these get-togethers." *So treat him with the proper damned deference,* his tone seemed to imply. I liked that.

I smiled and introduced myself to a man and woman who appeared to be about Darby's and my age. The man was dark-haired and somewhat overweight, while the woman was blonde and trim. And quite attractive. I imagined Darby must have his eye on her, if indeed he hadn't already laid a bit more on her than that. They said their names were Barbara and Jim.

Next was another stranger, a professorial-looking gentleman who rose from a plush, velvet-covered chair near the window and offered me his hand while nodding vigorously. "Walter Snyder," he announced himself.

Last was a familiar looking man, again Darby's and my age, who stood blinking before the fireplace. When I introduced myself by name, he seemed puzzled. "I'm Mike," he said. "Mike Dugan." For a minute I drew a blank. Then the memory of our long acquaintance rushed back upon me. Ah, yes, Mike. Mike Dugan. The hanger-on. I apologized and shook his hand, and laughed and tried to make a joke of it. But even though he and the others laughed with me, I knew that my long-standing opinion of him—that he wasn't worth remembering—had just been embarrassingly revealed.

"Well," Darby said, "now that we're all here, let's enjoy some refreshments." He walked behind the bar, rummaged through several cabinets and refrigerators, and in a matter of minutes produced an astonishing array of food and drink: cheeses and breads, cold meats and fruits, coffees and juices, and of course the perennial wines and liqueurs.

"You've outdone yourself this time, Darby!" I exclaimed as I examined a shockingly luscious out-of-season strawberry. No matter that he took credit for preparing this repast when I knew full well that his housekeeper and cook were responsible for it. What did I care if the others thought him a more competent host than he actually was? I was here to be intellectually stimulated, not to ruin my friend's charade.

But alas, it soon began to appear that my desired stimulation was not likely to be forthcoming, and that the charade was the entire substance of the evening. The food, yes, was excellent. I drank my wine and nibbled my fruit and waited for Darby to begin the expected conversation in his usual masterfully underplayed way. But on this particular evening he seemed less interested in playing the role of Socrates than that of socialite. He laughed and joked with Barbara and Jim about some matter known only to the three of them. By eavesdropping, I gathered in a roundabout way that some relative of theirs had been friends with an uncle of Darby's whom I had never heard of.

When this conversation grew boring to me in approximately thirty seconds, I crossed the room and tried to engage Mr. Snyder in a discussion of anything interesting. He had returned to his velvet-covered chair by the window and was eating a bit of chicken in silence. I asked him what line of work he was involved in and was disappointed to learn that he was not a professor but a librarian. Hoping at least to enjoy a discussion of good books, I mentioned several authors and titles chosen deliberately to impress him. But even though the man was courteous and pleasant almost to the point of artificiality, I soon realized that his close contact with books did not entail a healthy acquaintance with their actual contents. Apparently, his idea of good reading was to spend an evening grappling with the most recent issue of *Reader's Digest*. I let him know in no uncertain terms what I thought of *that* particular rag, and the conversation was effectively ended.

As a last resort I considered striking up a conversation with Mike. But when I looked at him standing in front of the fireplace, gazing vacantly into the flames and swirling a half-empty glass of juice in his hand, I recalled far too many past attempts at extricating myself from gallingly inconsequential and interminable chit-chat with him. Better to risk a discussion of *Reader's Digest* with the mousy Mr. Snyder than one of Mike's ephemeral excuses for a dialogue. And yet I still couldn't stomach the thought of such a wretched exchange.

Feeling blocked at every turn, I glanced past Mike to the bar and saw Darby still bantering with his wholesome new friends. When I heard the grandfather clock in the corner strike eight o'clock, I began to conspire how I might worm my way out of the situation and beat a hasty retreat. The jumble of ideas with which I had stocked my mind the night before was going stale with every passing moment. I began to feel sick at my stomach, and another headache seemed imminent.

But then Darby raised his voice and looked my direction, and I realized he meant for me to hear what he was saying.

"Why yes, I *am* interested in such matters. And so is my friend Todd."

The hint wasn't lost on me. "And what might that be?" I called, striding rapidly across the room.

"Barbara was just telling me about the church she and Jim attend," Darby said. He turned to her and asked in his sweetest tone, "Now, what did you call it, dear?"

"The Temple of Jehovah," she replied, turning to look at me with big brown eyes. I couldn't help wondering what Darby might have said to her about me while I wasn't listening. Good things, I hoped.

"Todd is a freelance writer," Darby said as he refilled my glass with red wine. "He's been published in some fairly well-known magazines. Where did you finally sell that piece on cats, Todd?"

My jaw tightened as I tried to speak in a voice calculated to reach only the three people in front of me. *"Reader's Digest."*

"A marvelous little story!" Darby exclaimed. "I don't remember exactly what it was about. Something about cats. But that's not why I thought Todd would be interested in your religious faith. You see," he continued, stepping out from behind the bar to rest his hand on my shoulder, "Todd here is researching a book he plans to write on fringe religious cults in the United States, and I just know he would be fascinated to hear what you have to say about your own unique brand of Christianity."

I stared helplessly at these two strangers and wondered how Darby could have managed to insult all three of us so thoroughly in just one stroke. Jim looked edgewise at Barbara and then back at me, while she simply stared at me with an expression of open suspicion. Darby walked behind the bar and poured himself another drink. I could tell he was immensely pleased with himself.

"Well," I began, and my voice was so gravelly that I had to stop and clear my throat twice. "Yes, I suppose I would indeed be interested to hear about your faith. If you feel like talking about it, that is."

"What kind of book are you writing?" Barbara asked. Her eyes were hard as stones.

"Oh, it's nothing very special." I hemmed a bit as I tried to formulate a response. What could I possibly say about my long-planned, much-bragged-about, never-written book? "I guess it's just a layman's look at the new sects cropping up outside the religious mainstream in this country." I glared at Darby to emphasize the deliberately polite phrasing I had used, and he grinned back at me.

It was obvious that my careful description had not softened Barbara a bit. "Our church," she said with more than a hint of haughtiness, "is not something that just 'cropped up,' Mr. Whitman. We have a history that stretches back over two thousand years."

In spite of myself, I felt a tug of familiar annoyance at her all-too-trite appeal to a buried historical validation. It was something that I simply couldn't let pass unchallenged. "Yes," I said, "I'm sure that's true in some form or other. But virtually all splinter groups claim a long history, as if *they* are the pure form of the parent religion. Surely you can point to a date, a founder, a place where the Temple of Jehovah got its name?"

Before she could answer, Darby clapped his hands together. The sound shot through the stuffy air of the great room like the report of a pistol, and I nearly choked on my drink.

"If we're actually going to talk about this," he said, "let's move out by the fire where we can relax and the others can join in." With that, he picked up a glass in each hand—one filled with cranberry juice and the other with red wine—and delivered them to Mike and Mr. Snyder, respectively. Barbara and Jim and I moved out by the fireplace while Darby returned to the bar for his own drink. Soon we were all seated in various expensive chairs, except for Mike, who perched on the hearth, and Darby, who stood directly in front of the blaze like a master of ceremonies.

"You were saying?" he asked me.

I cleared my throat again. "I was just asking Barbara about the immediate origins of their church." I felt uncomfortably histrionic in my mannerisms and expressions, and I had the rotten suspicion that Darby had planned this scene from the beginning. I cursed him silently as I drained my glass. The last mouthful tasted so sour it set my teeth on edge.

"The 'immediate origins' are noble," Barbara said. Jim sat mutely beside her, and I noticed for the first time that they were both drinking water. "In fact, Darby knows something about them. Or at least he should." She looked to Darby for confirmation, and he nodded, still smiling.

"I know a bit about it," he said, "but only a trifling amount. My uncle never really explained anything in detail. I'd love to hear your own account."

"My knowledge is only second-hand," she said, turning back to the rest of us. "Grandfather died before he could tell us the story himself. He was a great man, a world traveler, a preacher: a man of God. He loved to see people come to a saving knowledge of the truth. Once when he was in the Holy Land, he met someone who told him things, certain forgotten stories from Christianity's past. Grandfather thought and prayed about these things, and he received a revelation from Jehovah about the church. He had a new insight into the Bible, and he realized that the true church had almost been lost over the long years since our Savior ascended to His Father in heaven. When Grandfather returned to America in 1948, he founded the very first Temple of Jehovah in Fillmore."

I knew of Fillmore, of course. It was a nonentity of a little town situated just thirty miles east of Terence. But how had I never heard of the Temple of Jehovah—a cult so geographically near and tantalizingly bizarre?

"Who was the mysterious Middle Eastern man, the one who

spoke to your grandfather?" This unexpected question came un-expectedly from Mr. Snyder, who was listening to everything from the recesses of his great chair and watching us all with bloodshot eyes. I suspected his wine was going right to his head. He couldn't have had more than a couple of glasses, but I would have bet money he was more thoroughly inebriated than he had been in many a year.

"I'm not sure of that," Barbara said, smiling at him. "Grandfather never even mentioned his name. He was a member of some old church, an ancient Christian group located in Jerusalem. Or was it somewhere in Egypt?" She frowned slightly as her mind worked to dredge up the long-buried memory. "I really don't know. Isn't that odd?" She turned to Jim, but he shrugged and offered no help.

"Actually, the fabled theological interloper was from Cairo. *Old* Cairo. He was a member of an ancient sub-cult within the Coptic church that believed itself to be the inheritor of the one true Christian faith." It took me a moment to realize these words were issuing from the mouth of my friend Darby. I stared at him dumbly, thunderstruck, but my own amazement must have been minuscule next to Barbara's.

"How do you know that?" she gasped. Darby offered her another charmer of a smile, and a look of comprehension crossed her face. "Your uncle?"

"Yes, my dear. My uncle's acquaintance extended not only to your grandfather, but to his Egyptian friend as well. In fact, my uncle was even present for the famous conversation that eventually proved to be the genesis of your church."

Barbara's eyes were all but glowing with excitement, but I simply couldn't keep out of the conversation at that point.

"Darby," I said, butting in as Barbara was already opening her mouth to speak, "what exactly did your uncle *do* in the Middle East? If memory serves, you were always vague about that."

He nodded. "A fair question. He was involved in the oil trade. He made our family fortune."

This answered a long-standing question for me. When I had first realized in college that Darby came from a fabulously rich family, I had asked him where the money came from, and he had answered simply, "Business." Another probe or two had shown that no explanation was forthcoming, so I had dropped it. Strange that he would choose this particular night, all these years later, to reveal the source of his family's wealth.

Barbara could contain herself no longer. "What was his name? What did he tell Grandfather? How did they meet?" She nearly tripped over her tongue in a desperate burst of enthusiasm.

"His name," Darby said, "was Anwar. But before I elaborate on the famous conversation, why don't you explain your church's beliefs more fully to Todd and my other guests? I have the feeling this would be of great interest to them." He fixed me with his eyes and then walked over to the bar for another drink. I recalled that he had always been able to put away alcohol like it was water. As for me, I was really beginning to feel my wine, and I knew that I would soon have to excuse myself for a visit to the restroom.

"We believe the true message of Christ has been distorted over the centuries," Barbara said. She was still speaking rapidly, still charged with excitement from Darby's revelation. "He never meant to start a religion that would leave behind his Jewish heritage. The church we see today is more pagan than Christian. It has forgotten the true nature of God. In the Temple of Jehovah, we recognize this truth and make a point of living up to the standard Jesus set when he said, 'I came not to destroy the law, but to fulfill it.'"

I asked her, "And how precisely do you do that?" This part of her speech was wearisome. In fact, her whole routine was as old as Christendom itself, with all its long centuries of crackpot prophets and reformers 'rediscovering' the true faith.

"We call God by His true name, for one thing," she said, flaring at me. "When God told Moses His name was 'I Am That I Am,' this revealed His true nature. The God of the Jews is our God as well, and we should address Him by the name He gave."

"Well," I said, "I'm afraid you've bought into a long-standing misconception. The ancient Jewish name for the deity is written Y–H–W–H in the Hebrew scriptures. There are no vowels in written Hebrew, just consonants. And since the Jews believed 'the Name' was so sacred that it could only be uttered by their priests, and then only once a year on a high holy day, the exact pronunciation has been lost to the ages."

"The name is Jehovah," Barbara asserted with confidence. "That's what Grandfather learned from the Egyptian man. From Anwar."

"Most scholars think it's probably pronounced 'Yahweh,'" I continued, "but nobody's sure. The word 'Jehovah' is artificial, the result of arbitrarily interpolating the vowels from another Hebrew word—'Adonai,' meaning Lord—into the tetragrammaton."

"The *what*?" Mike asked. I had almost forgotten him. He was sitting on the hearth to the side of Darby, looking bored and sleepy.

"The tetragrammaton," I repeated. "That's the technical term for the four-letter Hebrew name for God." I smiled inwardly. This was turning out to be more pleasant than I had expected.

Barbara was staring at me with an expression of intense dislike. A pity. But she was married anyway.

"You'll have to forgive Todd." Suddenly there was Darby, riding gallantly to the rescue. "He really doesn't mean to insult you. He's just passionate about certain matters when he knows a little bit about them. And believe me, he knows a little bit about a lot." He looked at me and smiled, and I winced at what I knew was coming.

"The 'Whitman Sampler,' I used to call him." He said it with obvious relish. There was a ripple of laughter across the room, and I felt my face flush. Damn him, anyway.

Somehow the conversation stalled at that point, and everyone returned to the small talk that had so marred the early evening. Darby asked Mike if he would "be a chum" and add more wood to the fire, which Mike cheerfully did. I figured he was probably thrilled to have a task on his own level. The logs were old and dry, with rough pits and holes marring their surfaces, and as I watched him pitch them into the flames, I wondered idly what might have happened to cause this rather grotesque appearance.

Mr. Snyder spoke up and began describing some upcoming event at the Terence public library, and I took the opportunity to excuse myself. Down the hall, first door to the right, yes, Darby, I remember. When I flipped the light switch, one of the bulbs above the vanity flashed, gave a delicate *pop!* and went dark. As I relieved myself in the remaining half-light, I examined the room and found that nothing had changed. Same gold-trimmed, pearl-handled faucet controls. Same decorative soap dishes, same candlesticks, same expensive thick towels. I almost had the feeling that I was urinating in the middle of a museum gallery.

When I returned to the great room, Barbara, Jim, and Darby were all promising to attend the upcoming library event, whatever it was. Barbara, I noticed, deliberately avoided looking at me as I retook my seat. This at least allowed me the luxury of looking more closely at her rather full breasts—as they appeared beneath her tight pink sweater—but, other than that, I had no desire to stay any longer. For me, the party was over.

I tilted my head back and stretched my arms and shoulders. The firelight threw writhing shadows up the walls and into the high recesses of the vaulted ceiling. Darkness licked hungrily at the flickers of golden-brown luminance on the taupe paneling. As I watched, the darkness seemed to gain ground. Hadn't Mike just added more wood to the fire?

I knew I had had too much to drink. It was high time to head home, before I had to stay the night. But then, unexpectedly, Barbara and Jim were rising from their chairs and bidding everyone goodnight. Hadn't Barbara wanted to hear more about her grandfather's famous conversation with the Egyptian? I rose unsteadily and bade them farewell. They barely acknowledged me. Darby saw them out while Mike, Mr. Snyder, and I stared at each other with nothing to say. I dropped heavily into my chair and strove to clear my mind of the moist fog that was rapidly filling it.

Darby returned a moment later and headed for the bar yet

again. "More, anyone?" he called.

"None for me," I replied, as did the other two. Then, suddenly, Mike was rising from his perch on the hearth and saying it was probably time for him to go as well. I shook his hand, and he shook Mr. Snyder's hand, and then Darby saw him out, leaving me alone with the old librarian for the first time. The gray-haired man sat quietly in his plush chair by the window and held up his wine glass to examine it by the light of the fire. The blood-colored liquid cast a murky red glow across the contours of his face, and I blinked. His body seemed to fade in my vision, while the image of his face still hung in the air. For an instant I had the impression that I was looking at a red mask, which hovered in mid-air before the black double panes holding the night at bay behind it. A shadow of a smile seemed to flicker across its lips.

Then Darby re-entered the room and the illusion passed. *Definitely* too much to drink, and also too much delay in my departure. I rose again and began muttering my excuses for leaving so early. What time was it anyway? A glance at the grandfather clock showed it to be ten o'clock, straight up. The chimes started to sound even as I looked.

"Do you think you can stay a bit longer?" Darby asked me. He had stepped up to the fire and was gazing into its glowing depths. Something in his manner suggested he might have a sincere desire for my company, and sincerity being an uncommon attitude for him, I had to wonder what he might be wanting to tell me.

"I may not be able to drive home at all if I don't do it now," I said.

"Then stay the night." He said it without looking away from the fire. "You know I have the space." He sat down on the hearth and sank into himself. His shoulders wilted, and he looked like nothing so much as a forlorn little boy.

I hesitated. I told myself to be reasonable and leave while I still could. Then I took a breath, opened my mouth, and acquiesced—not to my own better judgment, but to his request. It had been a bizarre evening already. Why not go for broke?

"Thank you," he said in a quiet voice.

4

And we sat there. At first I thought we might have our own re-laxed conversation now that the others were gone; that we might catch up on old times, laugh about old college antics; that I might berate him for manipulating and humiliating me earlier. But we simply sat there, I in my stuffed chair and he on the brick hearth, while the clock ticked away the seconds.

Seconds became minutes. Soon the clock chimed the West-minster first quarter, and still we sat in silence. The clock chimed the half hour. And then the third quarter. If I had been sitting there sober, I would have long since been fidgeting and trying to make conversation. But with the aid of my wine, I was uncom-monly able to sink into a semi-trance state of temporal flow. My eyes drooped, the orange glow of the fire filled my head, and time glided by like steel blades on ice.

When the clock chimed eleven, I awoke and realized Darby had said something. I asked him to repeat himself, and my voice came out as a croak.

"Do you want to know the real story of my uncle's acquaint-ance with that old preacher, and with the Egyptian?" he asked. For a moment I hadn't a clue what he was talking about, but then the memory resurfaced, and I nodded, still in a daze.

He started to speak, and it was in a solemn tone, with no trace of his former jovial mood. "It was in 1944, during the war. My un-cle's business interests in the Middle East were threatened. He was my great-uncle, actually, my grandmother's brother. He was very young and very stupid, and he managed to arrange an illegal passage for himself to Cairo for the purpose of meeting with one of his business associates and discussing how best to protect their investments. As fate would have it, he made the trip from the United States with a stranger, a young American preacher who was traveling to the Middle East for his own reasons. This preach-er eventually fathered a daughter, who went on to give birth to two of my guests this evening."

He would have gone on, but the significance of this last

statement suddenly struck me. "Wait. Wait a minute. Do you mean to say that Barbara and Jim are *siblings*?"

"Of course." He gave me a quizzical look. "When did I say otherwise?"

I just shook my head and indicated for him to go on. The fact that I had so badly misinterpreted that portion of the evening's social dynamic truly bothered me for some reason.

"My uncle," he said, "and their grandfather talked a lot during the steamship voyage. It seems that Richard—that was their grandfather—had some very peculiar theological ideas that piqued my uncle's interest. He was always ragingly curious about such matters. They became friends, of a sort, and when Richard met Anwar, my uncle was present.

"I think the meeting with Anwar wasn't accidental. I think it was the purpose of Richard's trip. He was a queer bird, from what my uncle told me about him. However strange he may have sounded from Barbara's description tonight, I think the reality of his company must have surpassed it. My uncle said he was always talking about something he called 'the truth hidden in flesh.'"

"What in the world could that mean?" I mumbled. My voice sounded like it issued from the hollow bottom of a bucket, and the bucket was my head.

Darby smiled faintly and looked at me askance. "I thought you might be interested. Let me show you something." He left the room for a moment, and then returned carrying a book. As he approached my chair, I glanced toward the window and experienced a jolt of surprise to see Mr. Snyder still seated in his chair. I had completely forgotten about him. With head drooped forward and chin resting peacefully on his breast, he appeared to be sleeping.

Darby followed my eyes, and gave a dismissive wave. "Never mind him. He's been out for a long time." He set the book in my lap, and I saw that it was a huge, black, leather-bound Bible with gold letters impressed into the cover. They said simply "Holy Bible."

He retook his seat on the hearth. "That belonged to my uncle. He marked several passages that he remembered from conversations with Richard. Look up Leviticus, chapter ten, verses one and two."

The binding of the ancient tome creaked as I opened the cover. The title page predictably announced it as the Authorized Version. I flipped to the named passage and found it underlined in trembling black ink. "Read it aloud," Darby said, and I opened my mouth, but then hesitated, feeling an inexplicable reluctance to speak the words with Mr. Snyder present, even in his somnolent condition. After a moment, I simply stuffed this feeling to the back of my mind and did as Darby had requested.

"And Nadab and Abihu, the sons of Aaron, took either of them his censer, and put fire therein, and put incense thereon, and offered strange fire before the LORD which he had commanded them not. And there went out fire from the LORD and devoured them, and they died before the LORD." I looked up at him and waited for him to explain his interest in this passage. It was obscure, yes, hardly the usual pulpit fodder for your typical Sunday morning worship service. But other than that I saw nothing particularly compelling about it.

"Fire from the Lord," he said softly. "For nothing more than a bungled offering. Look up Numbers, chapter eleven, verse one." I dutifully did so and read it aloud.

"And when the people complained, it displeased the LORD: and the LORD heard it; and his anger was kindled; and the fire of the LORD burnt among them, and consumed them that were in the uttermost parts of the camp."

I had barely finished with this passage when he named another for me to read, and then another, and still another. The stately Elizabethan phrases began to roll off my tongue more easily the more I read, their dignified cadences contrasting strangely with the grotesque subject matter.

"Numbers 16:31–35. And it came to pass, as he had made an end of speaking all these words, that the ground clave asunder that was under them: And the earth opened her mouth, and swallowed them up, and their houses, and all the men that appertained unto Korah, and all their goods. They, and all that appertained to them, went down alive into the pit, and the earth closed upon them: and they perished from among the congregation. And all Israel that were round about them fled at the cry of them: for they said, lest the earth swallow us up also. And there came out fire from the LORD, and consumed the two hundred and fifty men that offered incense.

"First Kings 18:38. Then the fire of the LORD fell, and consumed the burnt sacrifice, and the wood, and the stones, and the dust, and licked up the water that was in the trench.

"Exodus 3:2. And the angel of the LORD appeared unto him in a flame of fire out of the midst of a bush: and he looked, and, behold, the bush burned with fire, and the bush was not consumed."

By this time my head was humming with death and flames and burnt flesh. I looked up at Darby and saw him watching me closely.

"How do you think it would feel to be that bush?" he asked. I stared back at him without comprehending. "To be burned by fire and yet not consumed," he explained. I reflected for a moment and then shrugged, having no idea what he wanted from me.

"From his new preacherly acquaintance," he said, resuming his former storyline, "my uncle learned a deep secret of the Jewish God. Or at least, what Richard himself took to be a deep secret. The God who created the world, who created life and flesh in Genesis, also implanted within that life the possibility of corruption. He made the possibility of decay, dissolution, putrefaction. As a matter of fact, *that is the truth found in flesh*. This phenomenon we call 'life' is merely negative entropy, a rottenness held temporarily in abeyance by the power or principle known to the ancient Jews as Yahweh, and known to us simply as God. Death, the grave, the riddling of these soft bodies by gnawing worms, is simply the inevitable transition between things as they are now and things as they are in reality. Life and health are themselves unnatural."

He paused, slightly out of breath, and looked to me for a response. I passed a hand across my face and sucked in air sharply, as if waking from a dream. "And you really believe this?"

After an almost imperceptible pause, he laughed a bit too loudly. "Well, *Richard* certainly believed it. And so did my uncle, eventually. You see, when the two of them encountered the Egyptian Anwar in old Cairo, my uncle thought it was mere chance, and he was greatly impressed at the way Richard's occult theology corresponded to Anwar's ideas. As I said earlier, I now suspect that Richard and Anwar had been carrying on a long correspondence, and that their meeting was hardly accidental. But they must have deliberately kept this from my uncle. Whatever the case, my uncle was sucked into this strange world of occult Christianity, and when he died a short time later, he had bequeathed a huge portion of his fortune to Richard for the advancement of the newly formed Temple of Jehovah."

"Darby." I said his name with gravity, cutting him off. He stopped and looked at me.

"Darby—what does this have to do with anything? Why are you telling me all of this?"

He shut his mouth and studied my face for a moment. Then he turned to look into the fire again. After a few minutes of silence, I began to fear that I had upset or offended him.

"We've been friends for a long time," I said in a softer tone. "When you fell into that depression, or whatever it was, and fell out of contact for all those years, I was truly worried about you. I didn't even know where you were. I did try to keep in contact, you know."

He remained silent, as if he hadn't heard me.

"Where were you?" I finally asked.

After a moment he spoke. "Would it matter if I told you I was overseas trying to save the family fortune?" His voice was like deadwood. He turned to look at me, and I couldn't understand the anger in his eyes. "Would it matter at all?"

"Where were you?" I repeated.

"Egypt," he replied, with eyes as hard as Barbara's.

I was at a loss for words to mollify him. "Look," I finally said, "regardless of what differences we've had over the years, you were my closest friend. And you still are, as far as I'm concerned."

He turned his face to the side, and the fire behind him made his profile a silhouette tinged with burning gold. "Are you saying you forgive me?"

"I'm saying I missed you."

Then he turned toward me again, and the room seemed to darken. "Don't say that." His voice was a whisper, almost a hiss. "Sincerity sets it free. *Insincerity* is a wall of protection."

"Sets *what* free?" I asked. A throbbing pinpoint of fear began to make its presence known at the base of my neck.

"Don't you understand?" He rose to his feet and took a step forward. "In Anwar's theology, God is actually *kept out* of the world by the artifice of religious practice. God created this world from chaos, created life from slime, and now He has to be kept separate from His creation in order for anything at all to survive. God, Yahweh, whatever you want to call it, is the Truth with a capital T. And when absolute Truth breaks through into this world of lies. . . ." He left this thought unfinished.

"Now wait," I said, struggling to speak reason to him. "It's only a myth. Your uncle was foolish for believing it, remember?" Mr. Snyder suddenly emitted a loud snore, and I nearly sprang from my chair in fright.

"There's a lot more to it than what you just read," Darby said. "Throughout the Bible. Wars. Plagues. Bloodshed on a scale that can still horrify even here in the aftermath of the bloodiest of all centuries. The tale of Truth breaking through into the world of flesh. Fire from the Lord, the cleansing fire that burns away the false to reveal the true nature of all it touches. And when it touches flesh itself. . . ." Another thought gripped him before the current one could finish. "It's described as a plague, too. Surely you know that? Look up Numbers, chapter sixteen, verses forty-six and forty-nine."

"Darby—" I tried to find words to calm him, but the attempt only excited him more.

"Look it up!" he snarled. When I still hesitated, he sprang forward, snatched the book from my grasp, and ripped open the pages. Bits of gilt-edged paper fluttered to the floor as he read.

"For there is wrath gone out from the LORD. The plague is begun. . . . Now they that died in the plague were fourteen thousand and seven hundred." He began turning and ripping pages faster and faster, whipping himself into a frenzy as he found passage after passage to support his delusion.

"And the first angel went, and poured out his vial upon the earth; and there fell a noisome and grievous sore upon the men which had the mark of the beast, and upon them which worshipped his image. And this shall be the plague wherewith the LORD will smite all the people that have fought against Jerusalem: their flesh shall consume away while they stand upon their feet, and their eyes shall consume away in their holes, and their tongue shall consume away in their mouth. And they shall go forth, and look upon the carcases of the men that have transgressed against me: for their worm shall not die, neither shall their fire be quenched: and they shall be an abhorring unto all flesh."

This last phrase struck a strange chord in me, as if I had recently heard it: "an abhorring unto all flesh." A cold rumble of nausea washed through my gut as I struggled to recall why the speaking of those words should affect me so strongly.

As I wavered helplessly in my confusion, Darby began to calm down. His feverish tirade of quotations stopped, and he looked strangely at the Bible he was clutching with white-knuckled fingers. For an instant I thought he was making to fling it into the fire. But then he simply laid it on the hearth and stepped away.

"What really scares me," he said after a moment's silence, "what really gets under my skin on long nights in this damned house, is that the ancient Jews saw no division between the body and the soul. It's all so easy to read these plagues and sufferings as metaphors of spiritual corruption. But to the Jews, a corruption of the soul and a corruption of the body were the same thing. It's such a *carnal* religion, all blood and bones and sweat and semen." He looked at me. "You don't know how my uncle died. How he was when we found him." I thought he would go on, but he simply stared at me with eyes that gleamed.

"Do you believe in family curses?" he asked. I had no answer. "I do," he said. Then he turned to look out the window, with Mr. Snyder still napping in front of it, and I had a sudden insight into him that almost brought tears to my eyes. There he stood, in the middle of the great room of his mansion, in the midst of the collective possessions of at least three generations. He had no surviving family, no parents or siblings, just servants and so-called friends like the ones at tonight's party. (Like me?) Also, he had the memory of a religion-crazed uncle to torment him on lonely nights. For the first time in our many years of friendship, I realized that he was probably the loneliest person I had ever known.

The clock clicked, whirred, and began to play the full hour. Twelve chimes. We looked at each other.

"The guest room is fully made up," he said. "Upstairs and to the left. You remember."

"What about Mr. Snyder?" I asked. We both regarded him still sleeping peacefully with his wine glass resting between his legs.

"He'll sleep until morning," Darby said.

Out of nowhere, a question surfaced in my mind, a question that seemed unaccountably important. "Where did you meet him?" Darby, who had been heading for the hallway, stopped.

"At the library. He stepped up and asked if I needed assistance. I still don't know why I invited him to the party." He paused and his brow furrowed as he recalled the incident. "Come to think of it, he sort of invited himself. Now, how did he know that I was having a party?"

Another question came to me, and once again it seemed of burning importance, even though I could think of no significance to it. "Darby, what position did the Egyptian man hold in his church? What did he actually *do* for them?"

He looked directly at me with an absence of expression so complete that it looked forced.

"He was their librarian."

5

I awoke from black dreams of a titanic struggle whose outlines fled from memory the instant I tried to reflect on them. I had been watching two enormous, shadowy shapes poised opposite each other, waiting to clash in battle, and I had known in a wordless but definite way—definite *because* it was wordless, with a certainty beyond knowledge—their true nature and the reason for their imminent clash. But upon waking, this all fled to the back of my brain, leaving me with just the opaque image of towering opponents shaped like mountain peaks.

I was disoriented in the darkness, and I sat bolt upright with a sudden fear that I might still be dreaming. But then I remembered the party, with its strange conversation and disturbing conclusion, and I lay back down on the comforter where I had fallen asleep in my clothes without turning down the sheets. Darby's dislike of digital clocks left me with no way of gauging the time on that moonless night, and I felt somehow unmoored, adrift in an eternal nocturne.

I must have dozed off again, for the shrieks startled me out of the beginnings of yet another nightmare. My body froze with shock as a series of blood-curdling screams began slicing through the oppressive night air. I stumbled off the bed and groped my way to the door even as they grew louder.

In the upstairs hallway the sound seemed to be coming from below. Nothing on earth should have been able to experience the sustained agony expressed by that voice, and I nearly tripped twice as I flew down the curving staircase, through an arched opening, and down a hallway toward a door that stood ajar.

It was the door to Darby's room.

Screams like hell, screams like death and flames and impossible horror, exploded from behind that oblong barrier. I looked down and saw flashes of a strange luminance spilling out from beneath the edge of it, and as if in a dream, I watched my hand reach out to push it open. The door swung back to reveal a scene that my eyes and mind could not adequately encompass.

A humanoid mass thrashed and writhed on Darby's canopied bed, staining sheets and pillows and mattress with blood and pus from a constellation of ruptured boils riddling its meaty form. Twined about it and winding their way in and out of these gaping holes were scores of thick, white, ropelike strands. As I watched, one of them snaked out of a hole in the figure's abdomen and wrapped its entire segmented length around a convulsing leg. Cold white flames wreathed the body, burning and sizzling the raw flesh without consuming it. A sudden jet of flame darted up from the foot of the bed, drawing my uncomprehending eyes to yet another figure.

Something standing or hovering. A black shape, ropes of fire leaping out of its depths. So dark. Cut from the natural shadows of the room. Darker than darkness. A hole in the night. A hole in darkness itself. A howling void. The end of everything.

I was screaming at it. My voice shouted insanely at it to stop, stop, stop! And when the shape seemed to notice me, when it seemed to turn toward me while its tormenting flames still shot out to caress the corrupt form on the bed, when it seemed to look deep into my eyes—I saw a face like a red mask hovering in the air, a mask with the shadow of a smile still playing on its lips.

I fled. I ran, stumbled, crawled down carpeted hallways, through darkened doorways, across tiled floors, past china cases and bookshelves and paintings and other empty remnants of a life that had now passed out of existence with a finality greater than death. At last I found the front door and burst out into the chill November night, where the screams still polluted the air. I raced to my car, fumbled for the keys with trembling hands, turned the ignition, slammed the gears into reverse. A moment later I was kicking up gravel and whipping fallen leaves into an inferno as I roared away from the house that had once belonged to my friend Darby.

Even as I flew down the darkened streets leading into Terence, my ears still rang with the distorted shrieks of a creature that had come face to face with its creator, a creature that now writhed and danced on puppet strings of white fire in an agony of eternal putrefaction.

6

In the ensuing weeks, I freely answered a great many questions that were posed to me by law enforcement officials from various levels of the local and national bureaucracies. It was easy, because the great lie at the center of my responses was completely concealed by the truthfulness of the many minor details. I truly did not know where Darby had disappeared to, nor what, in a practical sense, had become of him. It was easy to say that I had attended a party at his house, drunk a bit too much, and spent the night in one of his guest rooms, only to awaken and find him gone the next morning. Easy, because nothing seemed out of the ordinary when the police went to the house to investigate. There were no signs of forced entry, no signs of a struggle. According to the housekeeper, there were no signs of missing clothing or suitcases.

(No signs of a burnt, bloody mess in the master bedroom.)

He had simply vanished with the proverbial lack of a trace. In the end, law enforcement agreed that I had no real bearing on the case, and so I was cut loose and left to drift in my perpetual shock. I later heard the F.B.I. was looking into a possible connection between Darby's disappearance and the unnamed business he had been conducting during his overseas visits, but I knew they would discover nothing conclusive.

I continued to try to write. I tried to go on with my life as it had once been. But I soon began to notice a disturbing trend in my work: I could no longer lie. Especially on mornings after the worst of the nightmares that now disrupted my sleep, I simply could not generate the false persona that was necessary to any form of writing other than private journaling. My columns, my reviews, my essays were now impossible, for I found that I could write nothing but words and phrases appropriate only to a madman's diary.

Twice I gave in to my need for answers. Once was in the month of December, when I saw posted on a telephone pole an advertising flyer for a special program at the Terence public library. The flyer said the program would deal with a recent archaeological discovery in the Middle East. At the library, I looked around desperately for a pretty blonde woman and her dark-haired brother, but neither was present. I also kept an eye out for a smarmy gray-haired man who claimed to be an employee, but I found it thoroughly unsurprising when he was nowhere to be found, nor when the staff claimed never to have heard of him.

Then, when I took my seat among the folding metal chairs along with the dozen or so other library patrons in attendance, and when the elderly female volunteer introduced the archaeology professor from the local university, and when the lights went down and the professor began to present a slideshow about an ancient library in the old part of Cairo, a library found buried under a section of the current city, a library that might once have belonged to a hitherto unknown sub-cult within the Coptic church—when this happened, I rose and exited with a wave of nausea in my gut and a faint sound of shrieking in my ears.

The only other time I gave vent to this need for answers was a month later, deep in the frozen depths of a bitter January. I was driving east on Interstate 70 on some now-forgotten errand. The iron gray sky lowered with the threat of impending snow. I switched on my headlights and saw illumined in their beams a green road sign announcing "St. Louis 140 miles, Fillmore 2 miles."

Two miles later I exited, turned right at the top of the off-ramp, and soon found myself driving through what might have passed for any anonymous Missouri town in the no-man's land separating Terence from St. Louis. Sagging houses and storefronts looked as if they had been cut from a single bolt of colorless cloth. The entire town was on the verge of collapsing from sheer exhaustion. The attendant at the town's single gas station, which still displayed a sign offering full-service fill-ups, pointed me in the direction I asked, and within ten minutes I found myself parked in the woods outside of town, in front of an old wood-frame building that looked as if it might cave in upon itself at the faintest hint of a breeze. I could just make out the faded letters painted above the front door. They said, "Temple of Jehovah." I tried to work up some private humor at the thought that Darby's uncle's money had obviously not gone very far, but the attempt failed utterly. A crow barked out its raucous cries from the branches of a nearby tree as I forced open the door.

The temperature inside was no warmer than outside. The church looked as if it had been closed for decades. Ancient pews held a thick carpet of dust, and the tall windows lining either side were blackened with what looked like soot. An old wood stove was planted in the center of the building, right in the middle of the aisle. The flooring creaked dangerously as I skirted the squat iron structure.

At the front of the church stood an altar, a simple, unadorned wooden structure like those found in small churches around the world. I looked at it with fascination, although I couldn't have articulated what drew me to it. Then I looked up at the pulpit, which bore a crudely formed wooden cross that was shaped more like a capital "T" than the conventional symbol.

Before I knew what I was doing, I was kneeling at the altar. In this unfamiliar posture of supplication, I silently asked myself what I had expected to find there. An answer? A hope? The company of two people who had at least been present at Darby's final party? In the deathly silent atmosphere of that abandoned church, where reality held its breath, I could almost believe I had merely dreamed the entire incident.

When I looked back down at the altar, I was gripped by a sudden compulsion to feel it with my bare hand. I removed my right glove, reached down, and brushed my fingers lightly across its pitted surface.

The touch of the frozen wood seemed to bring me out of a trance. I quickly rose, replaced my glove, and exited the church. The crow still cried out from the bare branches of the tree as I started my car and drove back toward the interstate.

The skin of my hand began to peel three days later. I was sitting in my den attempting to read a light novel, but I could not concentrate because of an insistent itching in my right palm.

When I finally went to examine the problem in the harsh light of the bathroom, I saw a faintly darkened circle edged with white, dying skin. At first I tried to remedy it with lotion, but it quickly became apparent that this was no ordinary dermatological condition. During the next three days my entire hand scaled over with a raspy layer of dead skin that flaked off in thick white strips. Eventually the whole outer layer was gone, and still the hand burned with an agony of itching. Then it started again, and then again and again, in cycles of increasing frequency, until the skin was sloughing off daily. It became difficult to shake the delusion that the flesh of my right hand was struggling to rip through its garment of skin, as if it were trying to shout at me, "Here I am! The *real* you!"

One morning I noticed the dark spot on my palm had ruptured and become an actual hole, a tiny moist opening at the center of a brownish purple ring. As I looked at it more closely, a fat white shape poked its tip out, struggled to squeeze its bulk through the opening, and then dropped squirming to the floor. The screams I heard erupting from my throat sounded strangely familiar.

7

Now I understand. How simple. No distance between body and soul. No "spirit" here and "flesh" there. The worms have taken over completely, in the food, in the furniture, in my library.

Yesterday I opened one of my books and found it completely eaten away, but I could read a new Word in the contours of the pulsating mass that had replaced the text.

Today when I looked in the mirror, I paused too long and saw beyond my mask to the truth. The strange part is, I felt no surprise.

Now I know where the worms come from.

Notes of a Mad Copyist

The secrets of the hoarie deep, a dark
Illimitable Ocean without bound,
Without dimension, where length, breadth, and highth,
And time and place are lost; where eldest Night
And Chaos, Ancestors of Nature, hold
Eternal Anarchie, amidst the noise
Of endless warrs and by confusion stand.
            . . . this wilde Abyss,
The Womb of nature and perhaps her Grave.

              —Milton, *Paradise Lost*

1. THE LIFE HID WITH CHRIST

It all began, as nearly as I can tell, with a boundless longing for spiritual transcendence. I was possessed by such a longing from earliest childhood, so it was natural that I should invest my life in the formal pursuit of divine union. When the revelation of darkness began to occur in the third decade of my life, I was in my sixteenth year as a monk in the Abbey of Mont-Saint-Michel. There could hardly have been an environment more conducive to the nurturing of my spiritual sensibilities, nor a duty more favorable for the exercising of my innate endowments. I had spent the greater part of those sixteen years hunched over a tiny wooden table, copying the words of the Holy Scriptures onto the thick leaves of a parchment tome from a hoary exemplar.

There were half a dozen of us employed in the dim, dusty scriptorium of the abbey. Our stations were arranged opposite each other in severe rows against the clammy stone walls. We presented a supremely pious appearance in our monkish array:

crowns shorn, robes rough, feet bare, fingers ink-stained and raw. Only rarely did we speak to each other. We had taken no vow of silence, but our task was so serious and sacred, and our focus so intense upon the duty we were privileged to fulfill, that it seemed we had added an unspoken rule to the explicit rule of the order: Do not defile the Word of God with your own words. Let your speech and thoughts be pristine mirrors of the divine Speech and Thought. And so, having nothing of our own to communicate that seemed worthy to compete with God's own words, we remained silent. For days and weeks on end, the only sounds to break the silence of the scriptorium were the moaning of the wind through granite hallways and the scratching of pens on parchment.

The abbot would appear at the end of each session, like a pale gray wisp of smoke, to glide silently through our midst; to pause, look over our shoulders, and examine our work. And he would praise us for our progress in this sacred endeavor. "The mind of Christ," he would say, and lay his withered old hand on a brother's bald pate. "Allow the mind of Christ to be formed within you. Allow Him to guide you in the transmission of the sacred Word."

And I would thrill to his praise, his kindness, his touch. His hand was so gentle, his wisdom and compassion so renowned throughout the order, that I felt rarely privileged to be his son in the Lord. Perhaps due to the extent of my love for him, I strove, as I saw it, harder than all the others to know the mind of Christ. I wanted to know what my master knew. I wanted to see with Christ's eyes, to know with His mind, love with His heart, and record His Word with His own hand.

Even though I knew it was sinful to take pride in my own progress, even though I recognized such pride early on as the bane of my spiritual aspirations, still I sometimes allowed myself to reflect on how pale were my brothers' spiritual attainments next to my own. I glanced furtively at them as we worked together, and I noted their laxity, their secretive yawns, their irritable expressions on those bitter cold mornings when it seemed as if the wind were determined to scoop the entire monastery up from its precarious perch on the mountain shelf and hurl us all to a craggy death. My brothers were merely doing what was expected of them, out of a sense of duty, or worse, out of fear of reprimand, whereas for me it was a labor of love. I felt as if the words were burning bright and golden within me as I copied them from the exemplar. Sometimes I was overcome by such transports of rapture as should have been the privilege of no mortal man. At odd intervals, unexpectedly— sometimes in the dead of night as I lay alone within my cell, sometimes when I was engrossed in my scribal duty, sometimes, most perilously, during Matins or Vespers—it seemed as if a well were opened up in the depths of my soul, out of which came surging such sweet delights that I felt my flimsy human frame could not contain them all. I never spoke of this to anyone, and I was obliged to take great pains to conceal these occurrences.

At the time everything began to change, I had passed many long, contented years in the monastery, sustained by the secret hope that I was progressing with unique rapidity toward a grand fulfillment of the metaphysical longing that had first compelled me to join a holy order. Little did I know that the culmination of my longing would reveal to me a new and unexpected Word that would swallow everything I had devoted my life to serving.

2. THE SEED OF CORRUPTION

When the first evidence of something extraordinary made itself known, I was very nearly unaware of it. I had long since grown accustomed to passing my days like any other monk, with my life arranged according to the outline of the Divine Office. I arose from my pallet in the icy darkness of early morning, unrefreshed after four hours of sleep, to attend Matins. I washed with the brothers in the common basin and ate with them around the common table. I diligently put to use the prescribed hours of public and private prayer. And while the others tended the garden or minded the goats and pigs or washed the scullery, I took my place in the scriptorium with my fellow copyists and labored to preserve and propagate the written Word of God. In quantity, it was a life no different from that of any other monk. But in quality—in the hidden, internal aspects, which are visible only to Him who looks upon the heart instead of the outward frame—I far surpassed them all in depth and scope of passion.

The change first began to appear in my scribal work. I recall looking back over my efforts at the end of an otherwise uneventful day of copying, and noticing with shock the errors that had crept into the margins: a wobble here, a smear there, several uncharacteristic loops and swirls jutting out from the beginnings and endings of lines. My breath caught in my throat, and I must have emitted an involuntary groan, for the abbot was behind me in a flash. I had not heard him enter, although I knew it was the usual time of day when he trod lightly among us to examine our work. My blood froze as I felt his gaze sweep over my shoulder and across the page. My failure was unprecedented, and I could not guess how he would react. But I was astounded when he merely placed his hand upon my head and whispered a blessing.

The feeling of an anticlimax, of something momentous having occurred, and of my having been too obtuse to comprehend it, hounded me for the rest of the day. It lay so thickly upon my heart that I felt smothered by its weight. When at last I collapsed onto my rough pallet in my solitary cell, I stared up through the window at a waning gibbous moon and fancied I could hear the abbot's blessing still murmuring in my ear. Presently, I felt as if his words had descended to my heart, where they continued to murmur their approval of my efforts. Soon afterwards I drifted into a sleep more profound than any I had ever known.

I awoke the next morning with a powerful sense of remoteness, and with an odd sensation of coolness in my breast. It was not an unpleasant feeling, but more like a balm having been applied to a burning wound. For several minutes I lay there trying to divine the nature of the change. When I closed my eyes, I gained the impression of a second heart having been born within me. It was a heart made entirely of light, but of a strange sort that appeared as a luminescent darkness rather than a warming glow. My sense of imminent insight had never been so powerful, and yet its fulfillment hovered just beyond my grasp.

Of course I was ecstatic at the thought that I might have experienced divine illumination while I slept. But I feared to say anything to my brothers, lest this phenomenon prove to be other than what I hoped. Something about it seemed awry; the dark radiance of the new heart within me was colder and more piercing than the light I was accustomed to encountering in my religious service to God. It was also more thrilling, in a way I could not pinpoint. By the time I finally arose a bit later than my accustomed time, my joy had become tempered with anxiety, and I was anticipating the ritual of the daily schedule with a comforting sense of security.

My disappointment was severe when I found I was denied this small comfort. Instead of providing reassurance, the discharge of the Divine Office had never seemed so appallingly restrictive. My thoughts kept turning all throughout the day to the errors I had committed in my copying. While we read the morning hours, bathed, and ate, I felt distant and distracted, and afflicted by a growing restlessness. When at last we dispersed to our specialized endeavors at midmorning, I rushed to the scriptorium under the sway of an impulse I could not understand, and flung open the covers of my book with a sense of exultation.

With the pages laid out before me, I could see there was no evident reason why I should be gripped by such an acute sense of excitement. The errors were simply errors, nothing more, the mere product of wandering attention. I knew that I should feel properly contrite, and yet the inappropriate sense of excitement still gripped me in total opposition to the facts of the situation. The new heart swelled within me at the sight of the strange markings, and before I knew what I was doing, I had seized the quill and was about to start writing without any conscious notion of what I would write.

Of course it was my training that called me back to myself. I froze right before the tip of the quill made contact with the page, and then sat for many long minutes collecting myself. There was something happening inside me, some transformation that filled me at once with joy and confusion. At the moment, its primary outward expression was a perverse and nagging desire to alter the sacred work with which I had been entrusted. Except for a few meditative thoughts at the start and end of a day's work—perhaps a quick reflection on the passage being copied, perhaps a prayer to God for guidance of the hand in its task—no copyist was ever supposed to write freely, using nothing but his own thoughts as a guide. And yet I felt that if I but loosed my hand, I could fill a thousand books with original words and still not have begun to exhaust the ocean of ideas struggling to emerge from my pen.

At last, with an effort of will aided by many long years of inner discipline, I forced myself to focus upon the exemplar, and not the new thoughts boiling like a storm in my spirit. I was partway through the Gospel of St. John, and I hoped that I might regain a sense of calmness and equanimity by letting my thoughts be molded to the writings of the disciple whom Jesus had loved. Still, I felt a sharp pang of regret as I dipped the quill into the inkpot and began to copy the words of the Scripture.

Shortly before it was time for the abbot to enter, I set down the pen and scanned back over my work. Again there was that sensation of my breath being squeezed off inside my throat, as I slowly understood what had happened without my being aware of it.

The purity of my intentions had not mattered. The new thoughts struggling to emerge had had their say without regard for my attempts to suppress them. At some point during the day, I had left off copying and started writing original words. During the conversation between Christ and the Pharisee Nicodemus, wherein our Lord asserts the necessity of a person's being born from above in order to enter the kingdom of heaven, my book had been transformed radically, through a shocking shift in vocabulary and theology, into something else.

I could not say precisely what this new thing was, but it was certainly not the Word of God. Nowhere in the Deposit of Faith, either oral or written, could one find teachings of such a horrific and subversive cast. I read through the pages with a sense of mounting wonder and terror as I began to gain a powerful impression of imminent doom from certain words that appeared repeatedly in a patterned regularity whose scheme I could not divine. They spoke of "darkness" and "disorder," "dispersion" and "depletion," and of "the great deep, the watery waste of oblivion" that "laps hungrily at the shore of creation." The world as I knew it— the world of life, light, and order, where God, man, and nature stood in fixed and unalterable relation to each other—was framed by those words into a loathsome perspective of weariness, worthlessness, and wasted effort.

As this portrait gained clarity in my mind's eye, the room around me appeared to darken. The desk before me grew hazy. The spread pages of my book became like two windows peering out upon a midnight sky. For a timeless moment, I gazed through those windows into an impenetrable gloom. My thoughts slowed to a halt, and my fleshly heart seemed to freeze while the new heart of seething darkness beat with a sound like approaching thunder.

When I returned to myself and looked back at my brothers, I saw they had undergone a transformation. Instead of solid flesh and bone, inhabited by the quickening spirit of the living God, they now appeared to me as no more than empty frames, animate dirt held together temporarily by some precarious whim. The outline of their familiar human forms trembled liquidly as they bent over their books, like the slop in the pigsty at the rear of the monastery. I feared that if I but blinked or looked away, I might turn back to see them collapse into piles of steaming refuse.

My horror was magnified all the more when I looked down at my own hand and saw the same subtle transformation existing implicitly, hidden away within my flesh like an embryo of corruption. It was as if an inbuilt potentiality for dissolution lurked in the crevices of my physical being, and merely awaited the arrival of a clandestine signal before springing to life and overrunning my entire body.

Even as I reeled from these revelations, I heard the door scrape open behind me, and the abbot entered the room. Like a man in a dream, I remained paralyzed on my bench, unable to breathe, unable to reach out and shut the pages of my book to hide them from his gaze. I waited in agony while he passed from brother to brother with quiet words of encouragement. But when he approached me, I was astonished for the second time in as many days when he emitted no shout of horror at the vileness vibrating on my pages. For an excruciating moment he paused, and it was as if all the air fled from the room in a rushing whisper. We remained briefly in a silent vacuum, I on my bench and he standing behind me, while I awaited my judgment.

Then he did a most extraordinary thing: He leaned forward, reached over my shoulder, and ran his hand down the pages in a loving caress. He was careful to avoid the fresh ink. His fingers merely brushed the margins and traced the contours of certain words. Despite the absurdity of the thought, I had the undeniable impression that he was savoring what he saw.

The rasping of his papery skin on the parchment sent a chill scuttling down my spine. I blinked and tried to clear my head of the freezing fog that had settled over it, but my mind was like a block of ice as the abbot lowered his lips to my ear and gave me his usual blessing. Then he whispered—or, more precisely, hissed—"The mind of Christ," and left me to my frozen thoughts.

Afterward, I was more numb than horrified. My mind and spirit felt unable to take in all that had transpired, and I passed the next few hours in a sickened bewilderment. It was not until later that night, during the reading of Vespers, that the shock of what had happened finally hit me. When it did, I felt the abbot's words begin to stir within me like a living presence. His blessing felt as if it were alive, lodged in my brain, and in search of a deeper destination than my mere conscious thoughts. Almost as soon as I realized this, the words plunged downward toward the new heart within me, and when they found it, began to nourish it with their meaning. It leaped in recognition at their arrival, and on the instant my lungs let go, having remained in a state of semi-paralysis all afternoon. My first great gasping inhalation was succeeded by another involuntary groan, which, in the sanctified air of the chapel, my brothers might easily have mistaken for an expression of spiritual ardor.

3. THE DEEP AND SECRET THINGS

These events troubled me to the point of desperation, and I spent many days meditating on their possible meaning. At what point, I wondered, had I become susceptible to the attacks of demons? For that was surely what such occurrences must signify. Despite all my exalted spiritual passions, I had fallen prey to the influence of a demon that was working through me to defile the Word of God. Briefly, I tried to console myself with the thought that this attack must be an indication of my advanced spiritual status, since demonic affliction customarily came only to those souls who had attained such an advanced state of grace that the enemy of God took note and inflicted all sorts of horrible inner and outer torments in order to drag them down from their lofty height. If that were indeed the case with me, then I knew I should count it an honor to be singled out by Satan himself as worthy of special attention.

But these thoughts did not comfort me, for they did not seem to reach to the heart of the matter. The vision of the world as a kind of empty shell, congealed around a core of nothingness, continued to haunt me. The memory of the strangeness in the abbot's manner filled me with fear and loathing, even when I saw that he had returned to normal and displayed no more signs of a sinister alteration. Somehow, I could sense that the scope of my affliction extended far beyond the possibility of Satan and his demons, and I was all the more terrified by this unshakable notion that the understanding of the cosmic order I had received from the Church was pitifully inadequate.

Most of all, I was troubled by the continued alteration in my work. On the first day after the abbot's strange blessing, I arrived back at the scriptorium with the intention of ripping out the offending pages and burning them. But when I went to do it, my hand was stayed by a sudden impulse that shot out like a lightning bolt from my new heart. I trembled so violently as I fought against it that I was forced to grip my hand with the other in order to avoid alerting my brothers that something was amiss. For a time I sat collecting myself. Then I tried to begin working as if nothing had happened.

That was when it became piercingly evident that I would not so easily be able to reclaim my former life. For no sooner did I pick up the pen than I began writing without reference to the exemplar. I filled several lines before I noticed what had happened, and the new words were of the same tenor as the ones I had written on the previous day. I gasped and immediately tried to drop the pen, but it was locked in my hand as if by an invisible fist gripping my own. Shock and weariness had taken their toll, and all at once I was too tired to resist the impulse that kept gnawing at me from the inside. Hot tears scalded my cheeks as I understood the helplessness of my position, and with a silent prayer of protection I reluctantly allowed my hand to begin writing again of its own will.

The result was even more terrifying than before. The words that appeared mocked the Word of God not only with their meaning, but also with their very appearance on the page. My hand seemed to have gone mad, for it refused to follow the guidelines of the rubric, and instead seemed determined to forge a new path. I watched in horror as it created a kind of woven pattern of text, where sacred teachings of love, trust, purity, order, and holiness were coupled with, and sometimes even negated by, wildly coiling statements of madness and pandemonium.

After awhile, I began to feel as if I had stepped away from my desk, away from the room, away from the world itself, and was watching helplessly—and, I will admit, with a growing fascination—as my hand wrote things that were an absolute defilement of the truths it should have been transcribing. "Darkness" and "disease" shrieked up at me from the pages. Christ's teachings about the necessity of rebirth, the urgency of salvation, and the primacy of love were transformed into admonitions to "suckle from the breast of the unborn, which has never seen the light" and to "drink deep the nectar of oblivion."

At the end of the day, when the impulse finally let go, my hand dropped to the desk and rested there like an alien appendage. I was spiritually and physically drained, and afflicted by a sour sickness in my stomach and spirit. But when I looked again at the pages filled with their bizarre textual nightmares, I experienced an even greater shock at the flutter of exhilaration that tickled my breast, and that whispered to me that the book was now more truly mine than anything else had ever been. The blasphemous new teachings felt connected, in a way I could neither describe nor deny, to that well of spiritual ecstasy buried deep within my soul. A hot pulse of excitement, much akin to the rush of love that had overwhelmed me when I first beheld the abbot sixteen years ago, began to beat behind my eyes. For the second time that day, my eyes filled with tears, but now they were tears of gratitude, which dried quickly and left me all the more wretched and confused.

My actual conscious capitulation occurred a few days later, during the reading of Terce. In keeping with the obscure rhythms of the inner life, it was while I prayed aloud with my brothers that my decision was fully formed to embrace this new direction and see where it would take me. I glanced around at the brothers, observed them chanting the litany with supreme devotion, and knew with a thrill of deep longing that I was no longer one in spirit with them. Hints of a strange truth that had built up over a lifetime of spiritual yearning finally came together to form a clear picture, and for the first time I understood that my passion outstripped theirs not only in depth but in kind. Not only did I want something more, I wanted something different than what the monastic life had given them. My fear of being influenced by evil spirits dwindled as I opened myself fully to the possibility that there was more to the cosmic order than what I had allowed myself to believe, and certainly much more than the Church had ever suspected. I was embarked on a solitary journey, with nothing to guide me but a limitless yearning for absolute union with the original source of life and consciousness.

That day in the scriptorium, I made my customary ritual of positioning the exemplar, lifting the quill, and dipping it reverently into the inkpot. Then I paused as I knew that I was about to embark upon an unprecedented journey. Sitting there with the pen hovering above the page, I felt as if I were staring at the smooth surface of a darkened ocean. With a sense of plunging forward, downward, inward, I averted my eyes from the exemplar and began to write, not to copy but to write, to say things original and unheard of, and to regard them deliberately not with horror, but with an open spirit.

Instantly, the second heart was loosed within me, and a flood of new revelation began to shape itself into written words. My hand wrote with what seemed a supernatural speed and accuracy. Instead of cramping and requiring frequent rest, my fingers were charged with an inexhaustible energy. The new words filled lines, then paragraphs, then pages, while I sat by like a mere spectator. A rushing and a roaring, like the crashing of ocean surf on a rocky shore, filled my ears with increasing vividness throughout the day, and I felt the unseen presence of the abbot standing behind me.

Late in the afternoon, I cut off the flow of words, set down the pen, and with pounding heart scanned back over what I had written. Not a single word was copied. Everything was original. And all of it was high blasphemy, by my former way of reckoning.

The pages before me spoke of something not of God's creation, and thus not subject to the redemptive work of Christ; something existing not in the world of God but outside it, seething in a void of utter confusion. Reading these words, I began to envision dimly, as through a pane of smoked glass, a vast and ancient realm of uncreated darkness, a great gulf of eternal night where chaos churned through infinite circles of futility. It was fantastic, breathtaking, overwhelming in its immensity and grotesquery. Through a strange kind of epistemological alchemy, the mere sight of this realm began to impress upon me a sense of ancient secrets being laid bare. I saw plainly the absolute immanence, the impossible nearness, of this other realm. I saw the way it pressed in upon the world of life and light at the edges, and not only there, but also in our very midst, at the interstices where the components of the created order cohere. I saw the true nature of the ordered cosmos upon which I had based my hopes: its mutability and insubstantiality, as if it were merely a castle in the sand waiting helplessly and absurdly upon a deserted shore for the ravenous tide to flow in and devour it.

Abruptly, insights that had lain dormant in my breast for years surged to life and circulated upwards to my brain, where they revealed to me at last the truth of what I was seeing. This, I now understood, was the primal chaos, the formless raw matter of creation. This was the ultimate truth beyond God and Satan, good and evil, light and darkness, for it had existed long before the advent of these opposing forces, long before God spoke the creative words to bring forth an ordered cosmos peopled with conscious spiritual and physical beings. In fact—most shocking of all, a realization that I could scarcely accept—I saw that the God whom I had devoted my life to serving was the offspring of the abyss, and that both He and His cosmos were negated by its universality. Like a corrosive spiritual acid, the ocean of the uncreated was forever eating away at the shore of creation, and of its Creator.

As if he had been summoned by the culmination of the vision, the abbot slipped silently into the room at that very moment and began to make his way from desk to desk. I waited dumbly for him to finish with the others, and when he did, he paused behind me as he had done before. Then he reached down and once again ran his hand over the pages.

In a kind of trance, I looked down at his hand and saw that it, too, was infected with the seed of corruption, as indeed all flesh must be. But I could also see, as if with the aid of an invisible lens held before my eyes, that behind his ephemeral flesh, or below it, or prior to it, extending outward from some inconceivably concentrated well of entity, there lurked a vast, churning thunderhead of chaos. It shifted unendingly, appearing now as a massive black cloud looming heavy with rain, now as the elastic scaly skin of a serpent, now as the surface of an oily ocean. It was all these things and more, for no representation could convey the reality of the monstrous thing that dwelled within the flesh of this man whom for sixteen years I had loved and called my spiritual father.

He waited patiently with his hand before my eyes until the insight came clear and I understood that I was seeing the hand of the abyss itself, which had momentarily decided, for reasons hidden in the gloom of its bottomless depths, to adopt the form of a man.

4. WHEN HE SHALL APPEAR

What kept me from fleeing in the face of all this was my longing for transcendence. This had been the start of the matter, and now it formed the end of it. I had seen so much and felt so deeply that I simply could not leave, not when the goal of my spiritual pilgrimage finally lay within reach. Drawing strength from one of the promises of St. Paul that I hoped might still apply to me, even after everything that I had learned, I began to think my true life must be hidden elsewhere—not with Christ in God, but in the blackest reaches of the abyss. I eagerly anticipated the revelation of this true self when the time was right, and its point of contact in my soul glowed with an exquisite burning coldness every day, assuring me that I would not have long to wait.

Weeks passed as time flowed by like a black river that I regarded from a stationary point on some undefined shore. I hovered above everything, clung to nothing, and consider the world and its inhabitants as figments of a fleeting and pointless dream. The sight of the abbot and my brothers sickened me, but it was a sickness that I had now transcended, for I knew that none of my thoughts, feelings, or reactions were of any consequence, save for the exquisite responsiveness that I had developed to the hints of dark enlightenment that continuously flew up from my spirit like sparks from a fire.

Aided by this ongoing inner transformation, my work continued to undergo a mutation. Nothing that came from my pen could surprise me. I did not wonder when my hand left off with words and began to produce elaborate illustrations that were far beyond my natural capacity. Drolleries and illuminations of the most intricate craftsmanship appeared in my book, twisting and twining in serpentine chains of meaning. Fanged faces with forked tongues and porcine snouts peered out from behind words or upward and inward from the borders of pages, leering at the text and adding their own silent commentaries. From time to time, a word or phrase from the Holy Scriptures themselves would spew forth from my pen, followed closely by yet another of those faces, which would bare its fangs and grin at the quotation as if to say, "Ah, yes, but . . ." or "Come now, could you really have believed . . . ?"

As for the other aspects of my life in the abbey—my daily fulfillment of the Divine Office, my association with my brothers—I had never played the game more splendidly, and was especially helped in this by a new sense of superiority far different from the one I had formerly harbored. I had always found it easier, even before joining the order, to be kind, patient, and even loving toward those whom I considered my inferiors. Thus it was natural that I was never so tender with my brothers as during those final days when I saw them as from a great height. Even my old self, centered upon my original heart, found something to satisfy its altruistic longings when it was able to look with compassion upon walking, quivering sacks of corruption that believed themselves to be men.

The abbot and I appeared to have reached an unspoken agreement. Each time I saw him, I gained a momentary glimpse of a roaring blackness that wore his face like a mask. But I said nothing about this to the others. He, for his part, stopped speaking to me entirely, and merely fixed me with a hawkish eye every day in the scriptorium after he had finished with the others, before exiting without a word. The brethren noticed this, of course, and took it as a sign that I had advanced beyond them. Formerly, my false sense of humility would have led me to deny such speculations, but now I knew they spoke nothing but the truth, so I let them speculate as they would.

Still, time was winding down, and soon the end was upon us all. It began with a vision that plagued me one night while I lay awake in my cell, buzzing with hot excitement. I had finished the day in a rush of passion. My eyes had grown wet every time I spoke softly to a brother. I had encouraged them all, prayed for them all, loved them all, and had known from their shining eyes that they were talking with awe among themselves about the amazing progress I had shown in the spiritual life. After Vespers, I had retired to my cell and known immediately that it would be a sleepless night, for I was much too energized by a wondrous sense of well being, which surged outward from my dark heart to the farthest reaches of my extremities, deadening any lingering inclination that I might have had to place stock in that body and its desires, tantalizing me with visions of the world as it would appear when the truth began to shine through the cracks of creation like rays from a black sun.

I lay awake for hours, looking up through the window at the night sky and noticing for the first time how strikingly similar it was to the abyss that bordered creation. The stars were strewn from one end of the heavens to the other in a staggering profusion on that moonless night, and their positions appeared strangely fluid. A ripple of motion skittered across them, and I wondered whether I had unknowingly fallen asleep and begun to dream. The face of that sky might have been a vast black ocean, with the stars mere sparkles upon its ever-shifting surface, or perhaps they were the shining eyes of a billion shadowy creatures hovering just beneath the water, waiting in the womblike silence of the void, staring into the cosmos from across unfathomable distances, regarding this little sphere with a rapacious interest.

Without warning, as I gazed up in awe, a bit of darkness detached itself from the stellar tableau, coalesced into an animate form , and shot like a comet toward the earth. As it came nearer, I saw that it was vaguely man-shaped, and that its proportions were the same as my own. It took only an instant for me to realize that it was headed for the monastery, and only an instant more for all the pent up longings of a lifetime to surge upward into my eyes. My new heart began to pound out a hymn of joy, and tears began to fall like rain, as I eagerly awaited the arrival of what I recognized as my true self.

But then I found that I did not even have to wait, for suddenly, through an impossible shift of perspective, I no longer lay inside my cell but gazed down upon the huddled gray roofs of the monastery from a dizzying height. As I drew closer, I saw that everything appeared brittle and hollow. The magnificent stonework of the church, the columns and tilestones of the cloister, the roofs and archways—all appeared as flimsy as parchment. Even the towering façade of Mont-Saint-Michel itself was not exempt; I thought that I might reach out and punch through its massive face like an eggshell, dig through ancient layers of volcanic rock like dry cotton, and find only an echoing emptiness on the other side.

I shot like a spear toward the rooftops and, coming nearer, spied through a certain window a slight figure clothed in a rough brown robe and lying stiff as a rod on his pallet while he stared up at me with wide, blank eyes. It was impossible to suppress a laugh of pure joy at the sight of my old self. The sound rang out like a hiss of raindrops upon the stonework of the abbey.

Guided by an unerring instinct, I directed this new body of darkness toward a particular rooftop and then sank effortlessly through the wood and stone, coming to rest in the scriptorium, where I found my precious book lying closed upon its wooden desk beside the inkpot. My love for it raged like a black fire in my breast. Tears of darkness welled up in my new eyes. With a hand reeking of the smoky effulgence of the abyss, I reached down and opened to a random page.

There it was: the evidence of the change that had been wrought within me, the statement of the new revelation that had swallowed all my old hopes. Love and loathing vied for dominance within me, but the fire in my breast consumed them both and roared silently of its own absoluteness. Without further hesitation, I dove forward into the book.

It was like leaping through an open window. The night of uncreation rolled out before me in vast waves whose sable surfaces glowed hotly with veins of red and gold. Dimly, far off in the distant reaches of a realm where distance had no meaning, I glimpsed a coiling, pulsating nest of living shapes, like half-formed nightmares of the ancient monster of the Scriptures: "Leviathan the piercing serpent, even Leviathan that crooked serpent, the dragon that is in the sea." Their sinister, spasmodic motion, constricting and unfurling across multiply insane dimensions, beckoned me to come home.

My last thought before I closed the distance and flew into their impossibly malformed arms was that I had finally achieved my lifelong goal. At last I was reborn, as my former Lord had said that I must be. But it was a type of rebirth that neither He nor I had ever foreseen.

5. Our Grandfathers Which Art in Chaos

What followed might have lasted for eons or for an infinitesimal fraction of a second. Time warped and blurred, and I sank into a sense of dreamlike calm as I was torn apart and reconstructed again and again, enduring endless transformations into all manner of fantastic and grotesque shapes while a cacophony of screeches raged around me. Eventually the Lords of the Abyss settled on a form much like the one in which I had arrived. Then they sent me shooting back across the empty expanse toward a window that sparkled in the distance with the glow of created light.

When I awoke in my cell, in my old body of flesh, my first thought was that I had been dreaming. Then the presence of my true self, newly remade, pressed upward from the well in my soul, and the ecstasy of invulnerability washed over me.

I ignored Matins, instead making my way directly to the scriptorium, where I stared down with love at my book. For an instant I experienced a strange sensation of doubleness as I looked right through the pages as if through a clear window and locked gazes with my true self, which hovered in darkness on the other side, peering dispassionately into the world of creation. The resulting perceptual alchemy was akin to Ouroboros swallowing his own tail. For a time I lost the ability to distinguish between the end of my false self and the beginning of my true one.

The brothers came for me soon. They found me hunched over my book, scribbling furiously in its pages. They were so very concerned and sweet as they asked the reason for my strange actions. But when they caught sight of the swirling inked chaos on the pages, their loving looks melted into grimaces, and the long-awaited shrieks of horror finally resounded from the clammy stone walls.

I remained silent and dispassionate when they attacked this body like a pack of wolves, beating and tearing it until blood spattered like rain on the cold stone floor. The pain, like everything else in this fleeting world, was inconsequential. I remained equally remote when they took me before the abbot. Of course they brought the incriminating evidence with them, and when they showed him a sample page, he feigned all the appropriate expressions of outrage and horror. Then they all together, the brothers and the abbot, threw this body into its cell and dispatched a messenger to Paris, with instructions to forward a letter all the way to Rome regarding the awful thing that had happened in their midst.

The book they locked in the abbot's own quarters, so that none of them would be tempted to gaze upon its contents. Of course he and I then spent many long nights eye to eye, with him gazing through the windows of the pages into the bowels of the abyss. Elsewhere in the abbey, this body in its cell laughed heartily at the irony, to the great consternation of the brother who stood guard outside the door. He tried to speak with me, perhaps to offer comfort or instruction, but I had only to open this mouth and quote a few lines from the book to silence him and send him fleeing. They were my words, from my book, and the pleasure I found in speaking freely from my own heart, unhindered by thoughts of emptying myself for the sake of God's truth, was unutterably delicious.

Three months passed before the envoy from Rome finally arrived to hear the case—an agonizing eternity for the brothers, but the mere blink of an eye to me. Time had become meaningless, and the shadows that crawled across the floor of my cell every day with the sun's passage moved with the swiftness of an advancing storm.

During those months, I discovered that my brothers could not endure the force of my gaze upon them. The ones who brought me food would gasp and stagger backward when our eyes met. Darkness would begin to shine from their joints and pores, and they would look as if they might disintegrate into ragged pieces of rotting flesh at the merest hint of a breath. Eventually I began to suspect that my eyes had become like two lamps glowing with the dark light of the void. Perhaps when I bathed my brothers in this otherworldly radiance, it kindled within them visions of their own imminent undoing.

When the Roman envoy arrived, headed by a bishop of imposing rank and title, I eagerly anticipated the chance to test this new faculty on him. Late one night, when he entered my cell and tried to speak what he called sanity to me, I gazed coolly upon him until his eyes began to glow with darkness. His breath grew ragged, but he must have been a stout soul, for he fought off the cold shadow and sat down beside me. He had brought with him a copy of the Gospel of St. John, and without further ado he opened it to the first page and began to read to me of Christ the incarnate Word.

Thinking to humor him, I looked down at the text and experienced a final and inevitable shock as my eye caught something astonishing. After the moment I began to laugh. The sense of hilarity grew and grew until I was screaming and weeping with laughter. My visitor's composure broke, and he trembled as he looked at me with fear and consternation. Then he looked back down at the book in his hand, and a moment later he slammed it shut and fled my cell in a panic, although not before I saw the blackness begin to weep from his eyes. It was a fitting reaction from someone who had just glimpsed the impossible truth for the very first time.

For there on the pages of the Scripture itself were statements of the things I had so recently learned—not written in the text itself, but etched between the lines in darkly glowing letters that lit up for anyone who had eyes to see. From the beginning to the ends of eternity, the incarnate Word had always been matched and throttled by its negation, and it was those hidden lines that I had unknowingly copied and made explicit in my book. Irony of ironies, the Scriptures themselves, the supposed repositories and bringers of revealed spiritual light, were in fact the hidden carrier of the great darkness waiting on the other side.

It was then that I began to suspect what the dark powers were planning. Sitting in my cell, abandoned by everyone, I saw the disparate pieces of the puzzle fall together, and I knew that everything had been premeditated and foreordained.

I knew that the abbot, himself an avatar of the abyss, had been placed high in the ranks of the church in order to shepherd and guide groups of spiritually minded men toward the hidden truth, until one would appear whose passion would be of such depth and scope that it would mark him as a fit vehicle for the revelation of darkness. The abyss needed a scribe. Where better to find one than among the ranks of the church with its scattered army of copyists? There could hardly have been an environment more conducive to the nurturing of my spiritual sensibilities than the Abbey of Mont-Saint-Michel, nor a duty more favorable for the exercising of my innate endowments than the work of copying the Holy Scriptures. My sickness, my downfall, my pending judgment at the hands of the Church—all had been planned long in advance. The extent of the conspiracy staggered me, and I shivered to think how deeply the influence of the void must reach into the very heart of the Church in order for it to successfully execute such an epic scheme, all of it centered upon my recent efforts.

In a case such as mine, the presiding bishop will surely demand that the book be produced before a court of inquiry, so that he can judge the basis of the charges against me for himself. He will surely ask to have it opened in the presence of those assembled for the hearing. And that will signal the beginning of the end and the close of creation's opening act. My new masters have already used my hand of flesh as a vehicle for their written revelation. Now they plan to use the work of that hand as a bridge for their entrance into the created order. When the book is opened before the assembled monks and masters, the blackness of the abyss will shine forth in their midst, and its Lords will charge across the parchment bridge and will pierce the tender flesh of creation even as the spear pierced the side of Christ Himself. Then everyone present will see and know the truth that hides behind the veil of creation. And the work of uncreation will begin.

I have heard the others talking about me as I sit awaiting the culmination of these things. Their conversation has made reference to Satan and demons, just as my own thoughts initially did. They think an evil spirit possesses me. Such ignorance would be laughable were it not so pitiful. They have yet to understand that the truth shining from my eyes is far older than any demon, far older even than Satan himself. Our familiar spiritual universe, all its powers and principalities, demonic and divine alike—God and His angels, Satan and his demons—are swallowed whole by the abyss, which leaves in their place a roaring emptiness like the echo of a vast cataract flowing eternally into a bottomless pit.

What a pity that my brothers cannot join me in celebrating this vast emptiness, where the peace of oblivion masks the madness of chaos. But I suppose such pleasures are reserved only for the chosen few.

Last night one of them began whispering to me through the door to my cell. I recognized his words as the pater noster, and I was strangely moved to find that he was still working for what he thought of as the salvation of my soul. I felt for the first time a sense of what I have lost, and as I looked around at the cold stone walls of my cell, I began to wish desperately for them to appear solid to me again, and not as empty shells waiting for a puff of wind to knock them down. I raised my hand and wished for it to appear sound and whole again, and not as a repository for the seed of ultimate corruption. My original yearning for spiritual light began to pant and sob like an abandoned child in my breast, and I was overcome by a desire to offer some sort of comfort or reassurance to this brother who still loved me for what I had been. So I opened my mouth and, in a voice choked with tears, tried to give him a reply in kind.

What came out instead was another quotation from my book. Of course it sent him fleeing with a whimper. I had not meant to say such a thing, but it was past my lips before I recognized it. This new truth, it seems, is no longer my own. What happened with my hand is now happening to the rest of me. I could sense my new self laughing deep within my soul, even as I began to weep and mourn the loss of my old self.

I cannot allow myself to reflect on the possible depth of my wretchedness. I cannot consider how much of a pawn I have been. Instead, I must hope that the words I spoke to my brother will prove to have been enough to plant the seed of true understanding in his heart, so that he will be able to stand with the abbot and me when the black flood of reality comes to wash away everything that is unreal.

After all, what I whispered to him was none other than the new pater noster, which is the counterpoint to the old one and the invocation of all that is inescapably true:

> Our Grandfathers which art in chaos
> Fallow be thy names
> Thy kingdom scour, Thy will devour
> The earth, and hell, and heaven.

Here at the end of everything, this is all the comfort or reassurance I have left to offer anyone. May it prove to be enough for my brother, and for me.

The Basement Theater

I looked up and found myself gazing at the faded marquee of a crumbling theater, where no title was displayed. The street and sidewalks were dingy, the fronts of the buildings on either side pockmarked and weather-beaten. The once-white rows of the marquee were stained a sooty black, and the red trim was cracked. In spite of its singularly drab appearance, the marquee seemed almost to glow with a grainy saturation of color, like an overdeveloped photograph.

It jutted out from the face of the theater and overhung a set of glass doors with curiously ornate handles that appeared to have been fashioned from some coppery metal. When I employed one of these handles, I entered a cavernous lobby with an atmosphere redolent of moldy carpet and ancient concession food. The carpet, currently cluttered with chunks of plaster from the cracked ceiling, had once boasted a garish pattern of mauves and blues, but the passage of time had long since bleached both hues to a nearly uniform gray whose monotony was punctuated only by the presence of numerous water stains. Ragged tapestries hung with faded magnificence from the walls, and ancient cobwebs clotted the intricate molding of the high corners.

As I stood surveying this spiritless scene, I began to hear a muffled, intermittent humming sound drifting toward me from somewhere in the building. It took me a moment to identify this sound as a human voice. The dusky sunlight filtering through the grime on the doors disappeared into shadows as I wandered farther into the theater.

Halfway down a particularly cramped hallway, which I had assumed would lead me to the auditorium, I discovered that the sound was issuing from behind a black wooden door set inconspicuously into a wall on my right. It was a door that I might well have taken for a maintenance closet. The knob turned easily and the door opened soundlessly to reveal not a closet but a set of concrete stairs leading downward into darkness. The voice drifting up from this darkness as I began my descent was more clearly audible than before, but still unintelligible.

After thirty steps I began to notice a faint illumination shining from below. Then the stairs ended, and the wall opened out on my left, and upon turning the corner I found myself in a long, low-ceilinged basement with a burnished concrete floor and unfinished walls. A harsh light streamed from several naked, clear-glassed bulbs hanging at intervals from exposed wooden beams overhead, and the very harshness of it seemed to impart an abnormal inky blackness to the shadows at the extremities of the room. Amid these bulbs were gathered a number of thespians, standing alone or in groups of two or three. They murmured to one another in low tones and pored over stacked sheets of paper as they performed exaggerated motions with their bodies and faces.

Then I heard the voice begin to speak once again, and when I peered past the assembled actors, I immediately recognized the figure that came threading his way through them. Herbert's bald head and dark, almond-shaped eyes (so curious for an occidental) were unchanged, as were his neatly trimmed goatee and his slight frame with its small paunch. He was clad in a black turtleneck, black pants, and black shoes, and he waved his arms and shouted out blocking and performance directions to his troupe as he came to greet me.

"Thank you for coming," he said as he stopped before me with a broad and rather bland smile. "We're all so pleased to have you with us!" Then he turned abruptly and began making his way back through the crowd, barking directions the entire time, and I realized that I was supposed to follow him. Looking past his receding form, I saw a curious wood-and-cardboard flat against the far wall, like the backside of a piece of stage scenery, or like an unfinished room divider, located several feet from the wall so as to create a concealed space. Situated in front of this flat were a long-legged stool and a high, thin wooden table.

I struggled to keep pace with Herbert, but as I passed one of the glaring bulbs, the thespian standing alone beneath it, a fair-skinned man wearing a crimson sweater, suddenly sprang at me with his arm upraised and what appeared to be a dagger in his hand. My own hands shot up involuntarily, and a scream ripped from my throat as he plunged the dagger into my chest. Then he snatched it back and stood there, grinning, and I realized the weapon was merely a stage prop with a retractable blade. My breathing was ragged as the others applauded his performance. He bowed to them and returned to his private pursuit.

Herbert had seated himself on the stool behind the long wooden table, and with my heart still pounding, I hastened to join him.

"What's happening here?" I demanded when I reached the table. My voice was shaking. The fraudulent attack had generated a strong and disturbing sense of déjà vu, and I was poised emotionally between anger and dread. "That man who just attacked me—Herbert, I *dreamed* him last night. I think I dreamed all this." I waited for a reaction, but he merely picked up a blue pencil and began to make marks on a sheet of typewritten paper lying on the table. "Do you hear me, Herbert? I dreamed this! I dreamed of this rehearsal, or whatever it is, and in the dream I was a part of it. How can this be? What's going on?"

He barely paused in his editing to glance up at me. "Just theater."

After another moment of silence, I became enraged. "Look at me, goddamn it!" I grabbed his black-clad arm and jerked him violently toward me. "I have a life! I have a wife and a child and a job, and I don't have time to spend here with you, so you'd better explain yourself!"

"I told you," he said with total dispassion. "It's just theater."

"I don't work for you anymore!" I said. "I'm through with that!"

"Of course you do," he replied. "Everyone does." He looked at me until I released his arm, and then he resumed his editing.

"I used to run a spotlight for you." I said. "Then I quit. Remember?"

"You quit *that* job, yes," he replied, not stopping for a moment in his editing of the script. "But you still work for me. In fact, you've been promoted. Instead of running a spotlight, you're now *in* the spotlight. I should think you'd be pleased."

I couldn't believe what I was hearing. "This is insane. Why aren't you listening to me? I don't have anything to do with this place. I don't work for you!"

"Well—actually, you're partially correct," he admitted, lowering his voice. "You really work for *him*." He motioned behind himself toward the wood-and-cardboard flat, and my anger abruptly dwindled as dread began to gain the upper hand.

"You mean . . . there's somebody back there?"

"Of course!" Herbert's countenance brightened with a momentary and incongruous happiness. "I'm just the director. He's the playwright, and in this theater, he has the final word."

"I don't . . . I don't follow you." I was beginning to feel dizzy and sick to my stomach.

"He wrote your part," Herbert explained patiently. "First as a spotlight operator, and now as a lead performer. He's writing your part right now. Oh, he lets me make a few changes here and there, but it's really his show." He assumed a confidential attitude and leaned closer to me over the table. "And although I'm never allowed to see him or speak with him, I have reason to believe that he's taken a special interest in you. I think he likes your style. You seem so natural, so sincere. You even think you're *being* natural instead of playing a role, and I think he enjoys this. Call it artistic pride, if you will. But then"—he paused here to hold up the sheet of paper on which he had been writing—"I'm just reading between the lines." I looked at the paper, which was upside down to me as I stood across the table from him, and which displayed numerous edits, additions, excisions, and inserted lines of dialogue and description. And I knew in my sickness that I did not want to know what it said.

"I want to go home," I said. "I have a family. I have a life."

"Oh, certainly!" Herbert slid down from his stool to come around the table and clap me on the shoulder. "Yes, yes, by all means go home. You'll need your rest for the next act." He began ushering me back through the assembled thespians, who paused in their obscure motions to nod silently at me as I passed.

When we reached the foot of the stairs, Herbert shook my hand and stepped back with a smile. He seemed to be waiting for something.

"I don't even know how I got here," I said weakly. "How do I get back home?"

"Oh, I wouldn't worry about that!" he said with histrionic joviality. "You'll find your way back again in no time!"

And, as it turned out, he was right. Somehow I found my way home again without any trouble at all. My wife and my child, my job and my life, were all waiting for me when I arrived, and nobody appeared to know that I had been absent at all. In time, I tried to forget the episode.

But sometimes when my life seems to slow to a pause—when I lie awake in the dead of night staring at the white-textured ceiling of my bedroom, or when I raise my eyes to a sky blanketed by smoky clouds and glimpse pinpricks of starlight shining through, or when I hear the muffled hiss of a winter wind snaking its way through icy branches and skimming across snow-covered fields— at such times the murky depths of my soul rise to the surface, and the life I have so carefully cultivated cracks open like a hollow egg, and I realize that I have been visiting Herbert and his basement theater again. Each visit is virtually identical to the first: I find myself approaching the exterior of the crumbling theater with its ancient, empty marquee, and I step into the lobby and follow the sound of Herbert's voice down into the bowels of the building, where I find the same assembled thespians speaking the same lines to each other in hushed tones as they perform the same meaningless motions. The only thing that changes is my mood during my conversation with Herbert. He picks up his blue pencil and starts writing as we speak, and sometimes I feel panicked, sometimes angry, sometimes almost giddy. But I can never make him understand that the situation simply cannot be real, and always the thought of the playwright hard at work behind his wood-and-cardboard flat fills me with a profound dread.

My family never seems to suspect that I have been gone, and so I might have learned to accept these strange visits with a degree of equanimity were it not for the fact that I have been given a vision of their eventual culmination. Somehow I know that one day—whether soon or late is unclear—I will be walking through the throng of thespians in pursuit of Herbert, and the fair-skinned one in the crimson sweater will lunge at me again with his dagger, only this time it will not be a stage prop but a real blade. The dagger will slide between my ribs to prick my heart, and my life's blood will stain the burnished concrete floor of the basement theater while Herbert and his troupe gather around my twitching body to applaud what they will call my "final performance."

And although this last part is most obscure, I have in my mind's eye a vision of the playwright emerging at last from his concealment behind the wood-and-cardboard flat to stoop down and gaze firsthand upon my interpretation of the role he has written for me. Whether I shall get a glimpse of his face is unclear, but even if I do, this much is certain: the only thing that I will ever truly know is my own ignorance. The details of my role in this production will remain shrouded in obscurity right up until my death, and in the end my performance will have been solely for the playwright's private enjoyment. I will never even know the title of the play. And the full extent of my ignorance will be demonstrated in a final bit of irony that he must surely be anticipating with the greatest sense of artistic pride: I shall die without even knowing why he chose to damn me with this unwanted glimpse into the spaces between the lines of my life.

If It Had Eyes

Have you entered into the springs of the sea? Or have you walked in the recesses of the deep? Have the gates of death been revealed to you? Or have you seen the gates of deep darkness?
—Job 38:16, 17

The fog swirls about me as I approach the noisome tavern on Front Street. It whispers softly to me as I pull open the door and fan the surrounding cloud into graceful motion. Feathery fingers caress my face and hands with a moist, velvety softness, and I hear a chorus of sighs encouraging me to commit my soul eternally to this mournful embrace.

Closing the door and curtly surveying my dim surroundings, I smile inwardly as I walk unnoticed past the rough-clad fishermen and take a seat in a murky corner. These numinous moods of mine are so ancient, their foundations so deeply established in my soul, that I am not even frightened by them anymore. No one in the village knows the fog as I do. No one else here has cultivated such an exquisite sensitivity to its subtle tempers and messages, such a keen ear for the sibilant voice that speaks of long-forgotten mysteries and half-remembered myths. In the dank tavern where I sit with my back to the corner and my eyes to the rough wooden door, not a single person besides me cares to acknowledge the nature of the ancient presence that saturates the very air we breathe. I drink disdain to them, not from any glass but from the chalice of my own mind, as I watch them pour endless beers down their throats in a feeble attempt to drown the pain of their thoughts and feelings, the despair of their worthless lives. The contrast between us generates a warm glow of satisfaction in my breast.

The fog waits for me all the while, churning and roiling as it snakes its way through the twisting streets and alleyways of the autumn-shrouded village, catching and diffusing the light of a hundred scattered street lamps to produce wreathed halos of soft gold, enshrouding wood and brick and bodies in such a thick mantle of white vapor that one could almost envision the town founded not on solid earth but on a cloud floating somewhere miles above, with the bottomless starry vault glaring down infinite and unknowable wisdom on the rooftops.

The barmaid approaches, all curly brown locks and overabundant bosom, but I refuse to acknowledge her, for to dull my senses with drink on this night would be to commit the worst sin of a deeply sinful life.

For yesterday, I finally learned the secret of painting the fog. As the sun began to dip below the crest of Malvent Hill, setting ablaze all the panels of the great stained glass window of Saint Simon's Cathedral at the summit (a window whose eccentric and suggestively horrifying depiction of the Harrowing of Hell has led me to study it often as a model for my own paintings), and as the air began to grow cool with a bittersweet expectancy of the encroaching twilight, I positioned my easel on the rocks beneath the Eastern Point Light and flung my gaze seaward to watch the whiteness roll in from the unknown reaches of mother Ocean. God, but she was beautiful, the great black Atlantic with her secret worlds hidden away in chambers and caverns so deep and measureless as to explode the semantic and philosophical capacities of the very word "mystery." Within these nighted caverns, I knew, there lay concealed the very heart of the Ocean herself, those great wellsprings of the deep that, for a short time long ago, had reclaimed the dry land as their own. And from these chambers, I knew—I *alone* knew—the fog emanated, offspring of mother Ocean, intent on a nightly mission to mimic the primeval flood by enshrouding the island in moist wrappings. A deep love of this phenomenon, a veritable divine adoration for it, had grown on me over a span of years, and I had often labored to commit my secret passion to canvas, following the artistic impulse that had been implanted in me from birth. But the colors would never tell the tale aright. I could never achieve the correct proportion of white, cream, and pearl, and my paintings invariably emerged as agonizing failures.

Why, then, on that night, after so many years of frustration and mounting desperation, had I finally been blessed with the power to actualize my numinous longing? When the fog began to roll in once more from the black waters, claiming first the breakwater, then the harbor, and then the creaking village itself, I was shocked, overjoyed, elated beyond my wildest expectation, when fingers of moist and delicate whiteness curled lightly about my arm and hand, guiding me to the colors and strokes, the blendings and shadings, that would express at last the color of my soul. I expended no effort, but simply tilted my head back to gaze up into the hazy white void while the fog worked through me to reproduce itself on the canvas.

And when, after a time, I looked back down to examine the results, I was shocked to find . . . nothing. No painting. Not even a canvas. Just an empty easel where I had expected to find my life's masterwork. Thunderstruck and horrified, I reached out a trembling hand to the empty space and felt it strike a rough and sticky solidity. With tingling fingers I traced its square contours, brushed my fingertips over its wet surface, and although I could see nothing, the tactile sensation of the canvas was unmistakable.

I had almost begun to sob with bewilderment and despair when a sudden suspicion inserted itself into my psyche. Hesitantly, even fearfully, I reached out again for the unseen canvas—and there it was, undeniably present yet completely invisible in the surrounding sea of vapor. And all at once, comprehension bloomed.

Yes, the miracle had happened. The fog had painted itself, using me as the conduit for the expression of its ancient nature. In fact, it had painted itself with a perfection exceeding all human skill. Standing before me on that easel, produced by my own hand through the agency of an unfathomable will, was the absolute artistic embodiment of the white cloud that billowed up from the depths of mother Ocean each night, the cloud that whispered to me of wonders unseen by the crude mass of men but granted as revelations to the devoted few. The painting before me had surpassed art to remake itself as reality.

I raised my arms in ecstatic triumph—and experienced an even greater shock when my right hand presented itself as a smooth and bloodless amputation. All four fingers were cleanly and smoothly sheared off below the second knuckle. In a panic, I grabbed my right hand with my left—and experienced a greater shock still when the missing fingers announced themselves through their intact sense of touch as still present, still healthy and whole. They also bore a thick, wet, sticky coating, and after a moment of dazed contemplation, during which I continued to reassure myself of my hand's wholeness by rubbing it gently with the other, I held it up to compare it against the backdrop of the invisible, transfigured canvas. Four smooth stumps stood out against a milky field. Then I held up the other hand and saw the smears now affecting its own visibility, appearing as pale, luminous craters in its surface: the result of the stickiness transferred from its mate.

Any passerby during the next few moments must have judged me a madman who filled the night air with whooping, giddy laughter among the sharp rocks of the Eastern Point. And if it is possible to go mad with joy, with rapture, with a dark spiritual ecstasy, then their judgment would have been correct.

It was those events of last night that have given rise to my current design. They are the reason why I sit here in this smoke-filled tavern awaiting the right moment, awaiting a sign from the fog that I am indeed invited to join with it. There will be no more poverty-stricken, half-starved days and nights spent in the seclusion of my drafty room surrounded by mounting evidence of an artistic abortion, an existential failure, a life doomed to betraying its own divinely implanted craving, in the form of piled stacks of half-finished images towering all around me. There will be no more humiliation when not a single tourist will pause on wharf or the sidewalk to look at one of my paintings and offer a word of encouragement. I will endure no more coarse jokes from the fishermen who laugh at a man who fancies himself an artist and yet produces an endless succession of paintings that a quick and uncaring glance can misread as empty canvases. There will be no more misery, no more loneliness, no more disillusionment, no more suffering. There will, in fact, be *nothing*. I will merge with the great white cloud, and I will arise nightly with it from the darkest depths to creep landward and wrap the village in its burial clothes. I will whisper to its inhabitants of their fate: how they must soon return with me to those submarine chambers whose deepest recesses lie beyond the farthest reach of human comprehension. I will observe and know every hidden corner of the village, all its boats and wharfs and taverns and houses. I will be privy to every aspect of every secret life: the joys, pains, loves, sorrows, and hidden sins. And I will dissolve them all in a cloud of white nothingness. I shall be the shroud, and this town the corpse.

The tavern door opens. A lone fisherman lumbers in, ignores me, joins his fellows at a table. The fog still clings to his beard as he drinks what is surely the first of many drafts. He has failed to pull the door fully shut, and I watch intently as vaporous white fingers slither through the crack and caress the inner edges of the doorjamb.

I rise from my chair, leaving the fishermen and everyone else to their meaningless lives, and make my way to the lighthouse in whose shadow the plan of my salvation became apparent. The bucket in my hand sloshes with a sufficient amount of paint to coat the lighthouse itself. Tonight, it will surely suffice for my own transcendent purpose.

I walk a quarter-mile out onto the breakwater and strip off my clothing. The damp chill of the night air on my exposed skin fails to elicit even a shiver. Dipping my hands into the bucket and starting with my feet, I begin coating my skin with the milky white substance. My toes vanish first, right before my hungry eyes, and then my feet, leaving me standing several inches above the concrete on bloodless stumps. The laughter flutters up in my breast again, and I let it convulse and speak its voice as I continue to work upward. The waters outside the harbor stir with a strange agitation. Shadows darker than the night itself appear to coalesce and hover just beneath the surface, undulating in anticipation. I am coated from foot to neck, and a godlike excitement is welling up in my throat. I massage the paint onto my neck, my hair, my scalp, my face. And it is done.

Except for my eyes. I dread the stinging moment of pain that awaits me as I erase this final trace of my existence, and in the moment of hesitation, a deeper, more substantial fear surfaces. Something whispers of a *false bargain* and a *fool's bet*. The fear is hot and natural, a residue of my earthly life. As such, I loathe it. My two eyes hover in the all-encompassing fog, my last points of contact with the life I have regretted to live, the reddened remnants of a birth that should never have happened.

The churning waters hiss their approval and the watery shadows beneath throb in agreement as I thrust my fingers against my eyeballs and coat them completely. There is no pain, but only an utter, liberating numbness, like the bliss lying on the far side of the stabbing agony from an icy death at sea. I close my invisible, unseeing eyes, and it intensifies. A great, dark light appears from below, shining in a nonspace, an inverted sun rising from a subterranean sky to illuminate the new world of my nonlife. I open myself to infinitude, sighing without lungs and weeping without eyes.

And then, it all stops. After a moment's suspension between heaven and hell, the expected enlightenment retreats. I am still conscious, still thinking, still aware. I still *am*. But I am lost in a place that is no place, trapped in a mind that is no mind, paralyzed in a form that is not a body but a nonbody, the antithesis of flesh, something like stone or lead or hard-packed earth but diffuse, without articulation, the depths of the dense black earth in a borderless cosmic cemetery.

The deep fear that had hindered me earlier returns amid and alongside my mounting horror, and for the first time the questions that I have purposely avoided announce themselves clearly. What does the fog want? Why should it use me as its artistic conduit? What possible motive could it have for granting my prayer? The images that I have always nursed, those stupendous scenes of measureless subterranean caverns, a submarine kingdom whose secrets form the very foundation of the world, return with force.

Has the fog ever really known itself? Has it been able to pierce the wall of its own gloom, to glimpse its own hidden heart? No, it has not. The fog, I now know, is blind. The horror of my current entombment is the horror the fog has always inhabited within the space of its own awareness. It knows nothing of the people and the things, the cities and the civilizations, that it embraces, that it has always embraced, since before human memory. It is completely blind, and equally so to its own self as to the world it enwraps in ancient sheets of funereal white in a perpetual cycle of nocturnal death and sunlit rebirth.

But what if it *could* know? What if, through some hellish exchange, it could perhaps gain a pair of eyes, and thus a reflective knowledge of its own depth and nature? What would it see when it retreated back to its hiding place at the appearance of the dawn? What secrets might it learn about itself, secrets that have remained hidden since before the foundation of the world? What knowledge might it bring back on its next nightly journey? What might it show to those trapped within its newly enlightened embrace?

If the fog had eyes, might it not go mad at the sight of its own soul? And might it not bring this madness roaring back to the surface world of men and women, villages and harbors, cities and civilizations? Might it not reveal what must remain forgotten, buried, repressed, locked away within those nighted caverns of uncreation, if the consummate disaster, the unmaking of all, is to be avoided?

It might. If it had eyes.

Judas of the Infinite

I observe him sprawled like a tattered rag doll on the nearly deserted sidewalk in this unkempt quarter of the great city. The urine staining the front of his trousers might well be blood for all the occasional passersby are aware, and yet they step over and around his sodden bulk as if he were just another pile of garbage. He flinches as the first few raindrops spatter onto his face and hands from the dimly glowing sky. They catch in his grizzled beard and hang there like liquid diamonds. He groans and hauls himself painfully toward the wall of the abandoned office building, which affords scant protection.

I smile to myself at the thought of his misery, and of the joy that I am about to bring him. This is the day of his redemption, if only he knew. I have come to bring him a peace and fulfillment greater than any he might find in the grimy bottle now clutched in his fist.

I speak to him:

Remember yourself, poor child. Who are you? Where do you come from? What brings you to this state? Remember and be healed.

His brow furrows, his hand trembles, and the bottle slips from numb fingers to crack on the concrete sidewalk. Strong-smelling fluid leaks out to mingle with the rain.

"You—you are here?" he whispers. His voice carries the sound of tears, and I love him all the more.

Yes, I am with you.

The tears well up and begin to spill from his eyes, carving pale tracks in the filth lining his cheeks. "Please help me. Please save me."

But even as he speaks these words, the first glimmer of long-ago memory resurfaces in his mind, and he gasps. His eyes widen, his hands convulse, and his body shudders, as if with revulsion. "No!" he cries. "No, no, no!" He begins to claw at his scalp, attempting to rip the memories from his brain. The woman passing by on the sidewalk (Mary Beth Wilkerson, from Fair Grove, Missouri, a new resident of this great and crumbling city) shoots him a look of fear mixed with contempt. She worries for her safety, thinks of her children (Rebecca and Will, ages six and four), and clutches her purse more tightly as she hurries on to catch the subway to her neighborhood.

Peace, I say to him. *Be still! You have nothing to fear from your memories. It is only by embracing them that you will come to your senses and find healing. Open yourself to me, and be made whole.*

My words have their intended effect, and he ceases from his frantic motions and sits quietly for a time. After a moment he opens his mouth. His vocal cords have grown so rusty from disuse that his voice comes out as a dry croak, but yes, he is speaking and remembering, and our reunion is imminent. With a surge of self-congratulation, I regard the darkening evening sky, which has the appearance of a mirror smeared with black ash.

"I haven't thought back for so long," he says. "I've just lain in alleyways and prayed for oblivion. Please don't make me remember."

I leave him with my silence, and his resistance crumbles. The memories well up like his tears of a moment ago, and I watch them play across the screen of his mind's eye as he relives them.

"Yes, I remember. I remember the life I once had in your service, my life of obsession with everything *spiritual.* When I was admitted to the order, I thought my life had reached its happy conclusion. I thought I could lose myself in endless contemplation of your glory." He pauses to bury his head in his hands, and the rain increases from a sprinkle to a drizzle. A sheet of lightning cuts through the low-hanging clouds, outlining massive furrows of seemingly endless depth. A low rumble, like the tumult of a distant war, sounds ominously. So beautiful, I think with pride.

He moans and speaks through fingers tightly pressed to his

face. "Oh, God. That empty place, that hole inside of me. What was it? I wanted to know Christ inside my soul, but one day during my meditations I looked too deeply and found a truth deeper than Christ. All the light and joy I was so accustomed to feeling during my prayers was sucked into an invisible whirlpool, and in the dark night of spiritual blindness, I saw a spot like a hole in the wall of the world. It glowed without light. It blossomed like a black rose, and I realized that I was seeing a bloody wound in my own soul. It was so empty inside! So hollow! I felt as if I had swallowed Hell's abyss, but in the next moment I was horrified because I knew, somehow I *knew,* that it was the other way around, and that this hole was swallowing *me,* and that it would devour everything it encountered through me. It would devour the universe itself if I kept feeding it with my attention. I shrieked in my cell and disturbed my brothers, and when they came running, I horrified them all with my talk of a spiritual abyss that would devour God."

He pauses again, having fallen into a trance of memory. *Yes,* I coax him, *remember it all. Tread the path of memory to arrive at the present.*

He resumes his reliving of it. "They didn't believe me at first, but soon they couldn't deny what I kept telling them. The unlit candles melting into puddles of wax. The food rotting on the plates in front of us. The statues of the saints growing old and brittle overnight, with their features flaking off like skin from a corpse. My brothers couldn't deny the horror anymore. They charged me with blasphemy, and even though I was innocent of any crime, I knew they were correct. The spiritual darkness continued to radiate from my center, and I knew that my very *presence* had become a blasphemy. The thought that I might have become an unwitting host to Satan was as horrifying to me as to them, and I fled before they could shun me. I thought I could escape the horror by fleeing the order, by putting as much distance as possible between myself and my former life. When this failed, I tried to bury myself in oblivion. I tried to shut down my mind with drugs and debauchery. I wanted nothing to do with spirit, with soul, with religion. I just wanted to forget myself and the abyss I carried around inside me. But I couldn't escape from my own self. The presence was still with me, and I soon found that I could not look at anyone or anything without seeing them begin to fade and wither. Eventually even the debased friends I had made during my life of excess fled in horror or drove me away. Finally, I was left completely alone with a limitless emptiness at my core."

He struggles to get the words out, and I wait patiently for him to say what he most fears to say. A trillion worlds wait with me, although they do not know it.

"And then I knew that this emptiness was not Satan. For years I had clung to the notion that I was possessed by Satan or one of his demons, and this seemed a comforting thought in light of the other possibility. *Satan* is subject to Christ and God, *Satan* will be defeated in the end, but even God Himself cannot fill an infinite void. I finally had to admit the truth of my deepest fear: that I was the harbinger of a doom worse than Hell. This void inside me could not be Satan, because it was more ancient than even that ancient serpent. I had become host to a faceless face behind all worlds, a nothing at the center of everything, a chaos from which the cosmos has been snatched for a brief instant. I realized that I was beyond salvation or damnation. I saw beyond them both, beyond Heaven and Hell, beyond all opposites and created things into a realm of absolute negation. And this meant that even God could not save me, because the Void was older and bigger than he was."

The flow of memory subsides abruptly. His last words still hang in the air as he looks around in a daze to discover that he has remembered himself into the present. A thin, persistent rain hisses on the sidewalks and streets, winding its way in serpentine rivulets toward the gutters. I stand over him in burning splendor, my eternal light pouring down on him, illuminating not only his solitary form but also the trillion worlds of my cosmos. Behold: the sparse flow of traffic swishing past on the dampened streets, the rows of street lamps burning in halos of gold amid crystalline threads of rain, the glowering furrows of the sky spilling forth their life-giving water—these are all hallmarks of *my* genius. The sum of all created things is a diamond-edged tableau of terrible splendor, and its splendor is but a dim reflection of my own.

But he is speaking again, and I am astonished at his words:

"Leave me!" he cries. He looks up to the rainswept sky and screams as if he can see my face. "This emptiness is older than you! Even you cannot fill it! You promised to fill the soul of anyone who believes on the name of your Son, but you can't make good on this promise to me! You don't know this darkness, this emptiness beyond eternity! You can't even see it because you are blinded by your own light!"

His words trail off with a gasp, and he has spent himself. He stops raving, sinks back against the wall, looks with dazed eyes at the shimmering scene enveloping him. Then he begins to weep in loud, sobbing wails, and the old man hobbling past on the sidewalk with a cane and a brown felt hat (Walter Brogmeyer, seventy-six years old, a widower of two years, usually kind-hearted and generous, but at the moment frightened and disgusted by this raving derelict who sprawls on the sidewalk frothing and crying out to God) speeds up his pace and tries to ignore the maniac behind him.

Enough is enough.

My child, you must realize that none of what you have believed is true. I have looked deep within you to the very center of your soul, and there is no hole in you, no wound, no abyss. Recall the simple faith you held as a child when you and I had fellowship together. You knew then what you have forgotten now: that there is none other beside me. Remember my nature as I revealed it to Moses when I gave him a name by which to call Me: I AM! I cannot not be. You have been deceived by my rebellious adversary, who has appeared to you as something that cannot exist. There is no nothingness, no abyss, no negation. Such things cannot be when I AM!!!

He hears me through his sobs, and although he still doubts, I can see that I have awakened the hope that has lain dormant inside him for so long.

Open yourself to me. Allow me to keep my promise by filling your soul.

And in his moment of weakness, he yields. "My God . . . my God . . . it's been so long. Yes, my God, take this burden away. Please come into my soul and fill this emptiness!"

Ahhhh, *this* is the reason for which I created consciousness, the reason for which I created beings who have the free choice either to accept or reject me: all for the moment of coming together, the ultimate pleasure of the restored relationship between creature and creator, the return of the prodigal to his father. *Felix culpa* indeed.

Thank you, child. Thank you for allowing me inside. The rift has been healed, you have accepted my gift. Now we are one, and we shall forever rejoice in realms of eternal light, I your Creator and you my adopted child through the blood of my only begotten Son. We are one in the fullness of my light . . . one in the fullness of my light . . . in the fullness of my light . . . .

. . . . What?

No.

It is not possible.

This Darkness, this Emptiness inside you. I do not know this Emptiness.

"Oh, God! Oh, my God! I have betrayed you! I have sold you to the abyss!" He collapses forward onto the sidewalk and claws at the filthy concrete, his fingers leaving bloody streaks as the nails catch on the rough surface and break off at the roots. He frantically wipes the blood on his head, ripping out clumps of matted hair by the handful, then digs again at the sidewalk, desperate for dirt, desperate for burial, desperate for absolution from a crime of infinite magnitude.

And now I begin to see the blackly glowing void on the other side of his soul.

"Oh, God! Your light is becoming darkness! I cannot feel you! Where are you?"

This cannot happen. There is none before me or greater than

me. You are not screaming with rage and horror as I begin to spill helplessly, endlessly through the wound in your soul. I am not emerging on the other side to find myself adrift in an infinite Void, alone in a limitless Nothing where my eternal light blazes out to the farthest reaches of infinity and yet finds no end to the Darkness.

The world is not halting. The rain is not pausing in midair, the drops never to reach the earth with their life-giving touch. The clouds are not dissolving, the black furrows not parting to reveal an even more profound blackness beyond. The stars are not fading and winking out like celestial candles guttering at the end of time. I am not seeing with my all-seeing eye the deaths of a trillion worlds, not feeling the horror of a trillion trillion creatures as the created order splinters into knifelike fragments in a final moment of nightmare.

Kindly old Walter Brogmeyer is not weeping and snarling like some feral animal as he lays about himself with his cane, beating a young girl to death in sight of her mother and then slamming his head repeatedly into a lightpole until he cracks open his skull.

Pretty young Mary Beth Wilkerson is not opening the door to her children's bedroom to wish them goodnight and then screaming a scream of madness at the furious emptiness shining from their eyes like fangs of stolen starlight as they rise above their beds.

I am not dying and taking my cosmos with me as I pour unstoppably into the abyss.

I am not dying and taking my cosmos with me.

I am not dying.

I am not.

PART TWO
DARK AWAKENINGS

Were we disposed to open the [universal case history] of really insane melancholia, with its hallucinations and delusions, it would be a worse story still—desperation absolute and complete, the whole universe coagulating about the sufferer into a material of overwhelming horror, surrounding him without opening or end. Not the conception or intellectual perception of evil, but the grisly blood-freezing heart-palsying sensation of it close upon one, and no other conception or sensation able to live for a moment in its presence. How irrelevantly remote seem all our usual refined optimisms and intellectual and moral consolations in presence of a need of help like this! Here is the real core of the religious problem.
—William James, *The Varieties of Religious Experience* (1902)

Basically, all emotions are modifications of one primordial, undifferentiated emotion that has its origin in the loss of awareness of who you are beyond name and form. Because of its undifferentiated nature, it is hard to find a name that precisely describes this emotion. "Fear" comes close.

—Eckhart Tolle, *The Power of Now:*
A Guide to Spiritual Enlightenment (1997)

The oldest and strongest emotion of mankind is fear.
—H. P. Lovecraft, "Supernatural Horror in Literature" (1927)

Teeth

For in much wisdom is much grief: and he that increaseth knowledge increaseth sorrow.

—Ecclesiastes 1:18

Consciousness is a disease.

—Miguel de Unamuno

1

My first and decisive glimpse into the horror at the center of existence came unexpectedly during my second year of graduate school. I was earning a doctorate in philosophy and had stopped by the library between classes for some extracurricular research—or rather to pursue what I had long considered to be my true curriculum, regardless of whatever official degree program I might be enrolled in at the time. The object of my quest was a copy of Plotinus' *Enneads*. I had only heard of the man and his book an hour earlier while browsing the Internet in my rented house. A fortuitous combination of search terms had yielded an excerpt from his treatise on beauty, and I had experienced a flashing moment of metaphysical vertigo as I read his description of "the spirit that Beauty must ever induce, wonderment and a delicious trouble, longing and love and a trembling that is all delight." These words and their effect upon me had made it instantly clear that a printed copy of this book was definitely in order.

So there I was, winding my way silently through the second floor stacks and savoring the library's familiar aura of wondrous knowledge awaiting my discovery of it in hushed anticipation.

But instead of finding Plotinus' book, I instead turned a corner and stumbled upon my friend Marco seated at a reading kiosk in the middle of the south wall. The tall window above him spilled a shaft of dusty afternoon sunlight onto the burnished tile floor, imparting a muted glow to the kiosk and its occupant.

"Marco!" I said with genuine pleasure.

"Hello, Jason," he murmured, and went right on reading and writing without glancing up from his books. He was surrounded by piles of them, all impressive tomes of various sizes and ages and thicknesses, so numerous they were literally spilling off the table. Three were propped open on the desktop, and he appeared to be copying passages from all of them into a lined notebook. When he did not pause in his work, I lapsed back into an uncertain silence.

Marco was a visiting student from Guatemala with an exquisite command of English and an accent so slight that it left some listeners unable to discern his origin. His auburn skin, coal-black hair, and muscular physique gave him the air of a revolutionary from some Third World country. He was, without a doubt, the most brilliant and widely read person I had ever met, a genuine savant who was simultaneously pursuing separate graduate degrees in physics, philosophy, and history. We had met at the beginning of the fall semester, and I had quickly learned that his chic-terrorist look concealed a fierce intelligence. Now, at the end of the spring term, I was still amazed at his vast capabilities. He could discourse at length on almost any subject, displaying a verbal and intellectual virtuosity that put others to shame. Adding to his mystique was the fact that he was only twenty-six years old. I found it impossible to reconcile his relatively young age with his positively fearsome erudition. The books arrayed on the desktop before him now were a perfect example; I scanned their titles and found them to be of sufficiently diverse and advanced character to dizzy the average mind.

It was as I stood there watching and waiting in vain for our ongoing intellectual sparring match to resume that I felt the first prickling of unease. Our interactions had always centered on a perennial philosophical conversation that never failed to exhilarate me even as it exhausted and humbled me. But on that day, in my beloved university library, with me standing there primed for a dialogue and brimful of a craving for neoplatonic expressions of transcendent beauty, Marco apparently had nothing to say to me. I used the uncomfortable interlude to study his appearance more closely. His mouth and jaw were tight. His eyes appeared slightly sunken into dark sockets. His shoulders were tense, his motions taut and meticulous as he continued his scribal work. He fairly exuded an air of intensity mingled with exhaustion. The word "haunted" sprang involuntarily to mind as an appropriate one-word description.

Then he said, "How are your classes?" Only his mouth moved. The rest of him maintained an unbroken focus on his work.

"Um, some good, some not." I groped for a suitable entry point into this strange conversational exigency. "Teaching philosophy to uninterested freshmen is a bit like asking your cat to come to you. They really don't give a shit." I winced at my own ridiculous words.

But somehow they were enough to reach him. He paused in his writing, pen lifted above page, and appeared to reflect. "Ah, yes. Philosophy. We do love it, you and I. How was it that Will Durant once defined it? 'Total perspective, mind overspreading life and forging chaos into unity.'" His tone implied something like a rueful smile, but as I watched him speak the words, his face remained fixed in that expression of hollow intensity.

At length he set his pen down and straightened from the hunched posture he had been holding. "Do you have a few minutes before your next class?"

I was still fumbling to pick up the obscure thread of this weirdly stilted interaction. "Uh, sure, a few. What's up?"

He hesitated, then said, "I want to show you something. Something that I'm confident you will find quite interesting. Perhaps even fascinating, given what I know of your intellectual proclivities."

"How utterly mysterious," I said, attempting with a resounding thunderclap of failure to add a little levity to the scene. Marco showed no reaction other than to close and stack his books neatly, one by one, on the desktop to await collection by a library aide. Then he slid his notebook into his ever-present satchel and stood up. Without even looking at me, he headed for the stairs, and without my even hesitating, I fell in tow and forgot all about Plotinus and his promise to employ mere words to describe the impossible, delightful, delicious apotheosis of Beauty itself.

2

We stood facing each other in Marco's cramped dorm room, walled in by bland cinderblocks and beige paint. Marco held out a spiral notebook toward me. I looked at him curiously and, in light of our meeting's odd beginning, a bit cautiously.

"Take it," he said. "Look on the forty-sixth page."

I took the notebook and examined it while my mind whispered the word "anticlimax." This was nothing special, just an ordinary seventy-two-page, college-ruled spiral notebook with a red cover. It was, in fact, the same notebook that Marco had been writing in earlier at the library, and I couldn't help feeling a flash of irritation at what now seemed his rather theatrical refusal to show it to me in public.

But there was no use complaining now. I perched on the edge of one of the room's twin beds and flipped open the notebook's cover to find the first page crammed with Marco's small and scrupulous handwriting. My eyes began scanning the text while my brain registered that the notebook appeared to be a combination of commonplace book and personal journal filled with Marco's thoughts on quantum physics, history, philosophy, and a few other subjects I could not immediately identify. Instantly, my curiosity kicked in at the thought that I was being allowed a glimpse into my friend's private mind.

I began to flip slowly through the notebook in search of page forty-six, which was made easy by the fact that Marco had hand-numbered the pages in the upper right corner. Naturally, I stole as many glimpses as I could of the material on the intervening pages, and what I saw quickly sharpened my curiosity into a craving. Although the notebook's primary subject was not readily apparent, I discerned that Marco was conducting a serious inquiry into a certain matter, an inquiry that encompassed ideas from fantastically diverse fields of knowledge. He made great use of quotations from other writers, and I caught snatches of a theoretical treatise on quantum physics by Neils Bohr, a monograph by an obscure astronomer, a book of Hermetic occultism, the Hindu philosopher Sankara's commentary on the Vedanta Sutras, and the writings of Schopenhauer and Nietzsche. These last three were familiar to me; as a student of philosophy I had encountered them more than once in my own studies. The net effect of seeing all these quotations together was to generate a sense that the comforting constellation of my familiar authors, books, and philosophies opened out into a vastly wider universe of unknown properties.

I lingered for a moment on page forty-five to examine the two quotes that appeared there. One came from a book with a strange name that was vaguely reminiscent of Hindu deities. The other was from a story by H. P. Lovecraft. I had heard of the latter, but the former was completely unfamiliar to me.

My curiosity finally got the better of me, and I blurted out, "What is all this? What in the world are you getting at?"

"It will help," Marco said, "if you will turn to the next page." The tightness of his voice drew my eyes away from the notebook and up to his face. His sat opposite me on the other bed, mirroring my posture of perched attentiveness. His hands gripped the edge of the mattress. A bead of sweat slid down his temple. The expression in his dark-ringed eyes was unreadable. I stared at him for a long moment before finally looking back down and turning the page.

Of all the things I might or might not have expected to find, an elaborate sacred drawing was surely among the last. And yet that was exactly what I found. Rendered in the same blue ink that Marco had used to record his thoughts and quotes was an incredibly intricate visual pattern composed of abstract shapes, shadings, and forms. Its design was dense and complex, but what made it truly striking was its lushness and vividness, which made it seem three-dimensional. At the same time, it was reminiscent of a Zen painting with its distinct dependence on space and absence to contextualize and comment on form and presence. Most amazingly, its elements were arranged according to some alternative philosophy of design that flouted and exploded common artistic principles of harmony, emphasis, opposition, and so on. Each line led the eye to one or more angles that refracted attention like a prism dividing light. Each shape held its position and significance in relation to a hundred different elements, each of which was in turn embedded in its own peculiar nest of visual meanings and unstated implications. The overall effect was of a bold, bristling infinity.

In a word, I was dazzled. I knew the creation of mandalas to serve as objects of sacred contemplation had been developed into an exquisite art form in religious traditions both Eastern and Western, but the one I was seeing now was even more breathtaking than the ones I had encountered in my studies of Buddhism, Hinduism, and medieval Christianity. I had not known that in addition to his other prodigious gifts, Marco was an artist of genius. But there was no mistaking it. The mandala had been rendered by his pen, in his notebook.

I went to raise my head so that I could rave to him about the wonderfulness of the drawing and my awe at his secret talent. But then, with a sudden, startling sense of the impossible, I found that I could not do it. My neck was locked in place and my eyes were magnetized to the center of the picture. I blinked, or rather tried to, and found that I was likewise prevented from doing that. I was still aware of the room, still aware of the floor and bed beneath me and the walls around me, and of Marco seated across from me. But I could only attend to them with my peripheral vision. It was as if an invisible anchor had been hurled out from the page and lodged in my eyeballs, fastening them to the image and throwing me into an increasingly panicked state of immobility. I simply could not look away from the mandala, which filled my vision and began to horrify me with what I now perceived as its *obscene infinitude*.

And then it started moving. Right before my disbelieving eyes, the shapes began to stir on the page with a creeping motion like the slow boiling of liquids in an alchemist's laboratory. Every hidden implication and mini-universe of meaning in the individual elements took on countless additional connotations as the whole structure shuddered to life. The picture's three-dimensional appearance became literal as the page's center dropped away into a recess of infinite depth. I no longer sat in a room beholding a picture; the picture had become the whole of my consciousness, and *it* encompassed *me,* and I stared *through* it into a chasm of measureless meaning whose very vastness was a horror.

Then, in an instant, all motion stopped. A dark spot no bigger than a pinhead formed at the mandala's center and began to grow, as if approaching from an impossible distance. Ringed layers of shape and form fell away as this darkness accelerated its all-consuming approach. It resolved and clarified, and now wicked barbs and slivers were visible in its fabric, needled in endless rows of concentric rings like ivory spikes planted in rotten flesh. They churned and fluttered and twitched with a spasmodic motion, and in the tiny corner of my mind that I could still claim as my own I realized I was staring into a nightmare abyss of endless teeth, a fanged and insatiable cosmic gullet that endlessly devoured, devoured, devoured all things in an eternal feast of annihilation.

All had been a prelude to this. My whole life, my very conception and progress through the stages of human existence, had been preordained to lead me to this dreadful moment. I felt the attention of a massive and malevolent intelligence turned upon me, and as I began to pitch forward into the pit, and as the first of trillions of teeth began to sink into my mind, I knew with absolute, horrified certainty that this nightmare abyss was also staring into me.

3

A buzzing blackness. Darker than darkness. Corrosive and cold. That was everything.

Then it was as if a light switched on, and that light was the visual image of Marco's dorm room, and of Marco himself. He was standing on the ceiling. Either that, or the entire room had turned upside down. I watched his inverted image approach a similarly inverted medicine cabinet mounted on the wall. The slick mirrored surface flashed and waved as he opened and shut it. He approached me, still inverted, holding something out to me with his hand.

I realized I was lying on my back on one of his beds, arched up and watching him backwards over the edge of the mattress. He stepped beside me and the room righted itself as my head swiveled to watch him.

I tried to say "What?" but my lungs were paralyzed. I was suffocating. There was a momentary panic. Then my chest let go and I was sucking huge lungfuls of air.

"Take these," Marco said over the sound of my frantic gasps. Two tiny white pills rested in his outstretched palm. With the other hand he offered a bottle of water. Somehow my arms moved. I accepted the pills and washed them down while he slid back to sit at the room's single study desk.

"Those were muscle relaxers," he said. "You'll feel more composed in a moment."

To my astonishment, he was right. I could already feel the unbearable horror, the *impossible* horror, draining out of my mind and body, not completely but enough to let me live. After a minute or two I sat up and swung my legs off the bed. The feeling of my feet hitting the floor, the sensory solidity beneath the soles of my shoes, revived me even more.

I looked at Marco. He had been watching me but now he looked away and stared at the wall. Finally, he spoke.

"If the purpose of philosophy really is to overspread raw life with mind, to gain a truly totalizing perspective that forges unity from chaos, then how do you spread your mind over what just happened to you? How do you include *that* in your tidy little philosophical cosmos?"

Was he really talking this calmly? Was he really acting as if things were normal and we were back to our old conversation, when in fact nothing could ever be normal again after what I just experienced? But I could see the sweat standing out on his forehead and upper lip. He turned his gaze upon me as if awaiting my answer, and for an instant his eyes were like black holes carved in a flesh mask. The floor beneath my feet shifted ever so slightly.

Then he was Marco again, but he was still saying things I did not want to hear. "The classic philosophical project has always been held up as a *good* thing, a noble enterprise that will bring justice and order to people's lives. But what if the very attempt to gain that total perspective is tragically misguided?" He shifted in his wooden chair and leaned forward in the pose I had seen him adopt many times before when he was demolishing an opponent. "What if life and sanity depend not on finding the truth but on deliberately cultivating delusion? What if there is indeed a total perspective, but to gain and know it and identify with it is to invite your own deepest disaster?" He was still Marco but he was also something else, something more, leaning forward and splitting the air between us with the intensity of his words and vision. *"What if reality itself is finally, fundamentally evil?"*

The words hung there, and then I answered them. "What you're saying isn't new and you know it. The idea or something like it goes at least back to the ancient Greeks, and probably farther. Schopenhauer and Nietzsche gave it a classic treatment a little over a century ago." My composure shocked me. The room and my body seemed muffled and distant.

Marco straightened and slashed his hand through the air in a gesture of dismissal. "You're talking history and theory. I'm talking about reality—pure, raw, existential. You can't distance yourself from it or gain a handle on it by recalling who first thought of it or what they said about it. For proof, I refer you to your own recent experience, which you're only handling so well because I drugged you."

And indeed he was right. My calmness wasn't my own, and when I tried to see behind it I saw a raging swarm of terror and revulsion just waiting to arise. It was this subdued awfulness that now began to respond to the idea Marco was advancing, and my drug-induced surface calm suddenly seemed a positive curse. For it left me open to a nasty interplay of unwontedly dark thoughts and associations. My usual self-absorption, my narcissism, my obliviousness to my surroundings as I indulged a constant interior monologue—all these defenses had been stunned, and in the unfamiliar calm of interior silence I heard the sound of something terrible approaching.

Marco waited a beat, as if deliberately letting this chaos rage inside me. Then he picked his notebook up from the desk and tossed it onto the bed. "Read it," he said. "It will answer many of your questions. I assume I don't need to tell you to avoid looking at a certain page."

I looked at the red cover lying on the brown bedspread and felt the first real intimations of the inner upheaval that would certainly topple me once the drug had completely worn off. The entire situation had to be a dream. It could not be real, because if it were—I could not even articulate the implications. And then there was that drawing, that awesome, beautiful, horrific mandala. What had happened to me as I studied it? Flashes of unreality began to invade the edges of my vision at the mere remembrance of that mad motion, that impossible infinitude, that galactic tunnel of teeth . . .

"What is it?" My voice was small and weak, but Marco knew what I was referring to: both the drawing and the reality it revealed.

"The very question," he replied, "approximates the only suitable answer."

"But . . . you drew that picture yourself. How . . . ?" My strength to pursue the question gave out as he stood and began ushering me toward the door.

"Read the notebook," he said. "We can talk afterward. Right now you need to get home and get some rest."

I helplessly obeyed. Before I really knew what I was doing, I had left his room and was riding the elevator down to the ground floor. Then I was walking out of the dormitory and across campus to my house. Then I was unlocking the door and stepping inside.

The click of the latch as the door swung shut awoke me from my walking trance, and I saw that my hand was gripping Marco's notebook. I dropped it like a hot coal. It slapped to the floor like a snake. I left it there and walked to the bedroom, where I collapsed on the bed and fell immediately asleep. All night I wrestled with a dream that returned repeatedly and never resolved itself: Marco was standing outside my door talking with strangers. I heard their voices rumbling in response to his, but their words were indecipherable and their tones ominous. Then hands began to knock, not just one but many, rapping smartly on the door and progressing toward a thunderous pounding. The door shuddered in its frame. The knocks were somehow amiss, as if they were produced by the wrong kinds of hands beating on the wrong kind of wood. To my deep dismay, I heard my voice invite Marco and his acquaintances inside. The very invitation unlocked the door, which began to swing inward, and even before it completed its arc and revealed the visitors, I knew full well what I would see. I *knew* it; the visual confirmation would just be the culmination of a fear that had accompanied me from birth.

That was where the dream stopped, only to start again after an interlude of unconsciousness. By the time morning arrived and I awoke to the unbuffered emotions of the previous day's catastrophe, I had seen that door and known that dread half a dozen times. But that certain knowledge of the visitors' appearance, so inescapable in the dream, had not followed me into the daylight. All I recalled was the door itself, and the sound of rumbling voices, and the knowledge that I had invited my own deepest doom to come inside and make itself at home.

4

The next week of my life was devoted to reading Marco's note-book. Everything else went into hibernation, intellectually and emotionally speaking. Even though I went through the motions of my daily routine, I performed my duties without spirit. All my energy and attention was directed toward a single and singular purpose: to read and grasp the meaning of the dark philosophical testament that Marco had penned.

Grappling with it was the most grueling experience I had ever endured. This was due partly to the fact that Marco's speculations on astronomy and physics were practically incomprehensible to me, but there was another reason as well: A new sense or faculty seemed to have awakened within me, a kind of "third eye" that remained perpetually open and proved distressingly responsive to the dark suggestions unfolding on the pages before me. As I read the notebook and began to perceive the galling weight of the worldview under which Marco labored, I found that the same mingled mindstate of disgust and despair had unexpectedly taken root in my own heart, and was in fact being nourished by the reading, which, in a loathsome symbiosis, was rendered all the more clear and emotionally compelling by this new inner sense.

As I had already seen, much of the notebook consisted of long quotations carefully transcribed by Marco from a wide array of books. Schopenhauer loomed large, as did Nietzsche. It was during my undergraduate years that I had first encountered these giants of German philosophy. Back then I had exulted in the universal pessimism of the former and its extension and exhilarating trans-formation by the latter into an exploration of the meaning of hu-man subjecthood. But now I felt as if I were truly understanding them for the first time. Recorded here was Schopenhauer's famous criticism of the assertion, so common among some thinkers, that evil is merely the absence of good. "I know of no greater absurdity," he wrote, "than that propounded by most systems of philosophy in declaring evil to be negative in its character. Evil is just what is pos-itive; it makes its own existence felt." The concept was not new to me, but its import, as perceived and amplified by my new inner faculty, hit me now like a blow to the head.

Also recorded was Nietzsche's amplification of his mentor's idea:

> Nobody is very likely to consider a doctrine true merely because it makes people happy or virtuous. . . . Happiness and virtue are no arguments. But people like to forget—even sober spirits— that making unhappy and evil are no counterarguments. Something might be true while being harmful and dangerous in the highest degree. Indeed, it might be a basic characteristic of existence that those who would know it fully would perish, in which case the strength of a spirit should be measured by how much of the "truth" one could still barely endure—or to put it more clearly, to what degree one would *require* it to be thinned down, shrouded, sweetened, blunted, falsified.

The quotations spooled on and on, piling up page after page, interspersed occasionally with Marco's own notes and observations. After the Nietzsche quotation, for instance, the blue-inked letters of Marco's voice clarified, "And so the perfect lie would be the perfect sanctuary, the ultimate one-pointed perspective, and thus the ultimate weakness, while perfect strength would see reality cold, without blinking, and vast, without center, and naked, without a hint of cognitive or affective coloration."

After two days of reading, I began to despair of penetrating the notebook's secrets. On the surface it seemed to be nothing but a particularly pessimistic collection of aphorisms and observations, albeit ones whose significance I was feeling with a weight and an impact that were veritably physical. And still the searing memory of that picture on page forty-six jutted out like a broken bone in the skeleton of my psyche, leaving me frantic to find a conception and a context that would set the bone and bind the wound.

Then, on the third day, when my despairing confusion had reached its nadir, I came to a quote from the Indian philosopher Sankara that acted as the proverbial solid particle dropped into the saturated solution of my soul. Sankara wrote,

With half a stanza I will declare what has been said in thousands
of volumes:
Brahman is real, the world is false, the soul is only Brahman,
nothing else.

I had long been acquainted with the Hindu idea that the material
world is actually *maya,* illusion, a kind of mirage resting upon the
absolute reality which the Vedantic Hindus call Brahman. The
Hindu sages generally taught that *moksa,* the experience of release from this illusion and the subsequent realization of ultimate
reality, constitutes life's supreme happiness and final fulfillment.
But Marco, by contextualizing Sankara's classic one-line summa-
tion of Vedanta inside a potent exploration of Western pessimism, seemed to be positing that the uniform substratum of
being that underlies physical existence is an utter nightmare. And
if "the soul is only Brahman," meaning that the individual human
self is at root nothing but a particularized manifestation of this
pervasive primary reality—I couldn't bear to follow this perversion of the Eastern beatific vision to its conclusion. Its repercus-
sions were simply too awful to articulate.

Of the scientific line of thought interwoven with the philosophy, all I could comprehend was that Marco was struggling with
some unresolved issue in quantum physics. The mathematical
work was beyond me, but from his text notes I could gather
enough to grasp the bare essence of the matter, which had something to do with the philosophical implications of quantum me-
chanics. I read that the equations used in this science are
straightforward and uncontested in terms of their practical appli-
cations, as attested by everything from television to the hydrogen
bomb, but that no satisfactory explanation for their *meaning,*
their overall implications at the macroscopic level of existence,
had yet been established.

On the subatomic level, I read, particles flash into and out of
existence for no discernible reason, and the behavior of any single
particle is apparently arbitrary and usually unpredictable. If there
is a cause or "purpose" behind this behavior, then it is one that

the human mind is, to all appearances, structurally prevented from comprehending. In other words, for all we know, the fundamental ruling principles at the most basic level of physical reality may well be what our minds and languages must necessarily label "chaos" and "madness."

This predicament of knowledge (so I learned from Marco's commentary) had remained essentially unchanged for eighty years, and Marco possessed the audacity to believe that he had begun to solve the riddle that had haunted the keenest scientific minds for nearly a century. But he expressed his solution in a series of mathematical equations which were incomprehensible to me, and which may as well have been hieroglyphs carved on the inner wall of an Egyptian tomb.

My experience of these blossoming revelations was appalling. It was also progressively intense. The further I advanced in the notebook, the more powerful became the rising tide of revulsion inside me. At times it grew so overwhelming that I was forced to stop for several hours. On one occasion, after I had rushed to the bathroom in the grip of an actual physical sickness, I laid aside the notebook for more than a day. Late in the week I realized that what I was experiencing could only be described as *horror,* a word whose referent I had never really known. Marco's comments about the human need for illusion began to make progressively more sense, for if the ideas in his notebook really did point to reality, then I would rather be deluded. If it was strength to gaze unflinchingly into that abyss, then I would rather be weak.

It was with a veritably religious sense of fear and trembling that I turned, on the last day of the week, to the forty-fifth page of the notebook. Slowly I read through the first of the two quotations that appeared alone on the page, the one from a book whose title sounded distinctly Hindu even though I had never before encountered it and subsequently forgot it. As its significance became clear to me, I felt the words begin to sink into my mind like vicious hooks:

Foolish soul, wilt thou comprehend the All, the great Central Mystery? Man's place is the middle. Thou approachest the Gate in both the Greatest and the Least. In the face of the night sky, at the core of a dust mote—the same One. Wretched is he who hears the call, but more wretched still the one who answers it.

The final quotation was from a story by H. P. Lovecraft, and in the margin beside it Marco had written "The Capstone."

The most merciful thing in the world, I think, is the inability of the human mind to correlate all its contents. We live on a placid island of ignorance in the midst of black seas of infinity, and it was not meant that we should voyage far. The sciences, each straining in its own direction, have hitherto harmed us little; but some day the piecing together of dissociated knowledge will open up such terrifying vistas of reality, and of our frightful position therein, that we shall either go mad from the revelation or flee from the deadly light into the peace and safety of a new dark age.

5

The words on that page signaled the end of my journey through the dark corridors of Marco's obsession. Rather than trying to see what lay past page forty-six and risking another encounter with that awful picture, I closed the notebook and shoved it far back into a drawer, wishing fiercely that it could be equally easy to bury the memory of it. But try as I might, I could not stop my thoughts from returning to it and *gnawing* on it like a trapped animal might gnaw off its own leg. That was exactly the way it felt: as if I had become ensnared in some vile trap and grown so desperate to escape that I might willingly do violence to myself. But no matter how many times I examined and reexamined and struggled violently against the notebook's all-encompassing message of horror and despair, I could find no way to extricate myself from it, no loose spring or faulty trigger in its mechanism that might allow me to slip free. Its internal coherence and emotional power, as well as its universal scope, made it the perfect prison for mind and spirit.

My whole life was overturned in shockingly rapid fashion by

this festering spiritual disease. For example, my teaching and class schedules that semester were mercifully light, but even the slight strain of conducting a freshman philosophy class proved almost more than I could handle. How could I speak of epistemology and metaphysics when I had recently beheld the fanged and fleshy vortex that lies waiting to devour all knowledge? How could I teach about Socrates when I had discovered that to examine one's life is to invite a nightmarish destruction, or about Descartes when I had been shown that the thinking mind is a mere wisp of smoke blowing over a fetid ocean of entity? More than one student gave me a sidelong look as my lectures were derailed by the uncontrollable quaver that had crept into my voice. I had always basked in the knowledge of the positive impression I made on others, but now I could tell from people's reactions that my personal manner had taken a turn for the bizarre and disturbing. And yet I was helpless to rein this in. I felt a trembling all the way to my core and found myself frequently gripped by the irrational notion that people's altered reactions to me were caused by my new inner eye, which bathed everyone and everything in a beam of cold black light. This dark emanation, as I fancied it (even though I knew the idea was insane), was perceived by others as a certain indefinable aura of disturbance and dread in my personal presence.

I knew I could not go on like this, and several courses of action suggested themselves. The most obvious was to seek psychological help. A less obvious but no less compelling possibility was to seek spiritual counseling. Medical help from a neurologist was not out of the question, nor was self-medication via any number of consciousness-clouding substances. My fundamental problem seemed to be an excess of metaphysical sight. Anything that promised to blind or even temporarily blur that deadly gaze was an attractive prospect.

How, then, I ended up taking the course of action I took is still a mystery. Rather than turning to the most obvious sources of solace, I returned to the man who had done this violence to me. When all options had been considered, I could think of nothing but talking with Marco again. I had to know more about his notebook, about the impetus that had driven him to record it and the power that had led him to create that drawing. I felt that if I could not hear some answers to these and a thousand other questions, I might literally go mad with rage and confusion.

So I made up my mind to see him, and that was when it dawned on me that I had neither seen nor heard from him for ten days—not since our last conversation in his dorm room. Under normal circumstances I would have wondered why he had been so conspicuously absent, since we usually ran into each other on campus almost every day. But I had been preoccupied with his notebook and my growing distress, and now that I needed him, he was missing in action. I silently cursed his ostentatious boycott of cell phones and e-mail, which he regularly railed on as destroyers of personal solitude and public discourse. In the past I had never really felt their lack, since Marco and I had encountered each other in person as we went about our campus business. But now I found I had no way of getting in contact with him short of visiting his dorm again, which I hated to do with the memory of my awful experience there still paining me like an open wound.

But I also had no choice, and so on the eleventh day after this nightmare had begun, I returned to the site of its inception. My stomach turned cold as I rode the elevator up to Marco's floor. By the time I approached his featureless brown door, my hands were trembling. Predictably—why I should have found it predictable I don't know, but it seemed entirely appropriate in a poetic sort of way—he did not answer when I knocked. I stood there in the hallway for a long moment, staring alternately down at the faded gray carpet and then back up at the door as I debated whether to try the knob. Each time I reached for it, a thrill of panic surged through me. Finally, in a kind of daze at the depth of my own wretchedness, I gave up and admitted that I could not do it. The situation was just too symmetrical, albeit in reverse fashion, to the door scenario in my recent dream.

But I still had to find him, so next I went and inquired of his professors. They told me that he hadn't attended classes since Monday of the previous week—the last day I had seen him. One of them, Dr. Albert Kreeft of the physics department, told me, "Be sure to tell him the entire scientific community is waiting with bated breath for his theory of everything." The mockery in the white-haired man's thickly accented voice was blatant, and when I asked him what he meant, he said, "Ask him sometime to show you his preliminary work suggesting a new unified field theory. The finished thesis ought to make for an interesting novel." The physics department lay outside of my usual academic orbit, and I was unfamiliar with this thoroughly unpleasant little man. When I asked him about his relationship to Marco, he said with a sour edge, "I'm his thesis advisor," and turned back to his computer screen, refusing even to acknowledge me anymore.

And that was that. I walked out of the physics building realizing that I had already exhausted my useful options. The extent of my ignorance of Marco hit home as I recognized that the only thing left to do was to visit the places where we normally crossed paths—the library, the quad, the student commons—and hope that I would see him. So I went to those places even though I hated to be around crowds in my current condition. And of course he was nowhere to be found. I ended up on the second floor of the library at the same study kiosk where I had run into him while seeking a copy of Plotinus. Standing there beneath that tall window in that silent hall filled with row upon row of stately books, I tried to conjure a spark of my former aesthetic bliss. My unconscious mind responded by throwing up an image of chittering teeth and a mood of stark, staring barrenness.

Maybe my next move was inspired by the fact that I had come full circle to the starting point of my present unhappy state. From the library I set out for Marco's dorm again. Last time I had been following the flesh-and-blood man himself; this time I was following the thought of him. Once again, when I reached his room and knocked on the door, there was no answer. Before the memory of my dream could throw me again into that panicked paralysis, I seized the knob and wrenched it violently.

Much to my surprise, it turned easily and the door swung open on silent hinges. I stepped gingerly inside and found a room where Marco was absent and nothing at all was out of order. His bed was made, his bookshelves were full, and upon opening his closet I found a rack full of clothes. I had half expected to find evidence of some sort of disturbance—clothes flung everywhere, a shattered window, who knows what. The other half of me had expected to be overwhelmed by a nameless horror. So the sight of his empty, tidy, unmolested room threw me into a fit of unfulfilled foreboding. Everything was as silent and still as a cemetery, and in that stillness an approaching culmination trembled in the air.

I sat down on his bed with a hot lump in my throat, and realized with something like humor that I was about to break down and weep. Nothing made sense. Everything was wrecked and hopeless. How had I come to this in so short a time? Less than two weeks earlier, I had been leading a fairly contented life with a bright future in academia. I had taken pleasure in my work and my modest social life, including the occasional romance. I had possessed a shining intellectual and emotional intensity that brought praise from my professors. And yet, that had all been overturned and undermined in shockingly short order. When I tried now to consider my future, I saw nothing but an endless black tunnel lined with

(Teeth)

painful and meaningless experiences. The future was a dark, empty road winding through a blasted landscape toward the shell of a dead city. The journey was a nightmare and the destination a hell. My former goals and pleasures littered my psyche like the dry corpses of dead loved ones, and I wanted nothing more than to sink into oblivion, whether sleep or death did not matter.

Was all of this really true? Was my life, was existence itself, truly what I now perceived it to be—nothing more than a short interlude in an otherwise unbroken continuum of horror, a sometimes distracting but ultimately vain dream that was destined to end with a terrible awakening to the abiding reality of chaos, of madness, of nightmare, of . . .

(Teeth)

The floor lurched beneath my feet, and with a silent hiss like the seething of stars, that gaping hole in reality opened up again, not on any page this time but within me. My nostrils were clotted with the stench of rotting, half-digested worlds, and I felt the eternal agony of infinite rows of needle teeth sinking into my soul.

That should have been the end. I should have known nothing else for all eternity. But then, impossibly, it was over. The room blinked back into view. The floor rushed back into place. And I was sitting on a plain institutional bed in an ordinary dorm room on a bright spring day. The horror had claimed me and then spat me out.

I was still reeling in a daze as I stood and exited Marco's room. I could hardly walk, but a sudden impulse had taken hold of me: I wanted to finish reading Marco's notebook. I was, in fact, desperate to do so. Caution be damned, I was going to learn what he had written beyond the page with the picture. I was going to find out everything there was to know about the thought process, emotional pattern, and dark epiphany that had flowed out of and led up to this catastrophe that had engulfed not only me but, as I strongly suspected, him as well.

Riding the elevator down to the ground floor, I experienced repeated waves of joy at finding that I could still feel a sense of purpose.

6

The walk back to my house was a preview of hell itself. Although the afternoon sun hung bright and warm in a brilliant sky, and college students lounged everywhere in the refreshing air, chatting at tables and lolling on fresh green patches of landscaped lawn, I saw it all as if through a dark-tinted pane of glass. The light appeared shaded and muted, like night scenes in a movie that were obviously shot in broad daylight with a filter on the lens. I kept noticing movements in the periphery of my vision wherever shadows and dark spots lay: beneath a bench, at the foot of a hickory tree, under the granite lip of a merrily splashing fountain. In each shadow I saw what looked like living forms crouched and waiting, but when I looked directly at them they disappeared. It gradually became apparent to me that I was seeing shadows more clearly than the objects that cast them, and that my inner eye was revealing a lurking presence in them that I had never suspected.

Traumatized and terrified, I finally arrived at my lonely house north of campus and collapsed on the couch. After listening to my own shaking breath for a few moments, I dragged myself to my feet and went to fetch the notebook. It remained where I had left it, at the back of my desk drawer, and I felt vaguely surprised since I had half expected the thing to have disappeared like its author. Its dull red cover seemed to mock me, as if its very muteness represented its defiance of my understanding. I sat at the desk and flipped through to page forty-seven, feeling not nearly as foolish as I had expected when I actually squeezed my eyes shut as I turned past the mandala.

I opened them to see that, sure enough, there was more writing in the notebook's latter pages. Text that normally would have filled only half a page in Marco's virtually microscopic hand now sprawled across three pages. Reading it, I began to shiver even more violently as I understood the cause of this atypical sloppiness: Marco had scribbled these notes immediately after his own first experience with the mandala, which, as it turned out, he had not drawn of his own free will. His notes insinuated far more than they stated, and glanced upon several unfamiliar items, but I recognized their guiding emotion of horrified hysteria all too well. Ironically, they also underscored yet again just how greatly his awesome intellect and fearsome self-control exceeded mine, since it was a marvel that he was able to marshal any coherent thoughts and write any words at all in such a state.

This is what he wrote:

Almost sucked in. It almost pushed completely through. God, how? The perfect sequence of shapes, the perfect placement and size on the infinite continuum of distance between points. Their precise purpose in guiding my hand. Would it open the gate for anyone, render all preparation unnecessary? Chance . . . purpose . . . meaning . . . what damned idiocy! Our insane desire for "truth" when *illusion* is the need—fantasy, dreams, divine delusions. What price the true vision? What must we become? Lovecraft correct not only about our frightful position in the universe but about the vast conceit of those who babble of the *malignant* Ancient Ones. Not hostile to consciousness, indifferent to it. "Consciousness is a disease"—if only you knew, Miguel! Final horror reserved for mind, not body. Azathoth not conscious, pure Being. Consciousness, intelligence, *mind* the ultimate tragedy. To be somehow self-aware yet wholly incidental to the "purpose" of the universe: chaos and psychosis in human terms. Ultimate irony of human predicament: perfection of specifically human quality results in self-negation. Conscious only to become aware of the utter horror of consciousness.

The ideas encoded in these words flamed inside me as I read and reread them. Much of what he had written was obscure, but I understood enough. Somehow Marco had been offered a glimpse into the chaos at the center of Being. For reasons known only to Itself, some power had chosen him as a conduit for the revelation of "our frightful position in the universe," and then Marco, for reasons known only to himself, had shared his affliction with me.

Of course this only intensified my need to find him, since I now feared that he had suffered some cosmically awful fate, and that if I continued on my current course, I would join him in it.

In my anguish, I unthinkingly reached down and turned one more page of the notebook, and what I saw on the following page initiated the final phase of my descent into horror. I froze and read the item three times while its significance sank in. Then I sprang from the chair and lurched for the door, where I fumbled with the knob for a miniature eternity before finally turning it.

Then I was outside and racing across campus, not caring that my front door was still banging open and the notebook was still lying open on the living room floor where I had dropped it.

What I had seen was a brief news notice that Marco had clipped from the *Terence Sun-Gazette*, the local daily newspaper, and had pasted carefully onto the page following his feverish final notes. It stared up at my empty living room as I ran to avert an inconceivable catastrophe, its words saying far more than the journalist who wrote them had intended.

WORLD-RENOWNED SCIENTIST
TO LECTURE AT TERENCE UNIVERSITY

British physicist and astronomer Nigel Williamson will deliver a lecture entitled "Chance, Meaning, and the Hidden Variable in the Quantum Universe" at the Terence University campus. Williamson, a Cambridge professor who is visiting Terence as the first stop on a worldwide lecture tour, is known for his tendency to ruffle the feathers of his colleagues with his unorthodox theories. His claim to have arrived at an explanation for "the seemingly causeless actions of subatomic particles" has aroused worldwide interest and a great deal of skepticism in the scientific community. He is scheduled to speak on Thursday, May 2 at 7 p.m. in the lecture hall of the Stockwell Science Building on the Terence University campus. The lecture is free and open to the public.

7

I reached the Stockwell Science Building in a matter of minutes. The run of barely a single mile had exhausted my soft scholar's body, and I fell gasping and heaving against the double door entrance. Peering inside, I saw a digital clock on the far wall of the foyer that read 7:24. This encouraged me a little. The lecture would have already started by now and there was no obvious commotion going on, so perhaps my awful hunch had been mistaken.

Still gasping, I glanced up for a moment at the twilight sky and saw a yellowish half moon shining through the branches of a scraggly tree. The once familiar disc was now the dead, decaying fetal carcass of some unimaginably monstrous creature, and while I watched in awe with my dark inner light burning like a beacon, the creature began to stir and wake. Dread washed back over me like an icy wave, and I flung myself through the door of the science building as much to escape the awakening gaze of the moon as to stop the tragedy I feared might be occurring within.

I burst into the lecture hall to find a small group of middle-aged men and women checking their watches, tapping their feet, and exchanging glances filled with annoyance and unease. No lecture was in progress, and I gathered that I had entered as the impatience of the tiny crowd had reached a snapping point. Most were seated but a few had gathered around the lectern down front, where a small, nervous, balding man was blinking through thick-lensed eyeglasses and trying to placate them. Several people looked up when I entered, and I saw their faces tighten into angry-worried lines at the sight of me.

Ignoring them as best I could, I made my way down to the bespectacled man. He stammered and finally stopped in his nervous explanations when I approached, and the cluster of people turned to stare at me.

I asked, "Where is Professor Williamson?" and my voice emerged as a harsh demand. It also seemed to reach me from a distance, and I noticed that I didn't feel a part of the situation at all, but rather like a spectator watching a theatrical presentation in which I and the others were performing.

The jittery little man played his part admirably. "I was just explaining—" he began, and then tripped over his own jitteriness. His role was obviously that of the Flustered Mousy Man, whereas mine was at least partly that of The One Who Flusters. He finally gave up and gestured miserably toward a door behind him that appeared to lead into a conference room. "He's in there."

"Is he alone?"

Mousy Man was growing more unhappy with each passing second. "Well, no. There's somebody in there with him. As I've been telling these people, a very agitated young man showed up a few minutes before seven and demanded to see the professor. I told him we were busy, but then Nigel came out and chatted with him for a minute, and seemed quite interested in what the young man had to say. Fascinated, actually. They went into the conference room half an hour ago and haven't come out."

"Have you *knocked?*" By this point I was all but yelling, and the other performers' eyes were widening as they shifted visibly away and left me alone to dominate the stage and my unfortunate foil.

"Well, no," he said, and began shifting from foot to foot. "I didn't feel comfortable interrupting them. And the young man, he was quite . . . passionate. His eyes were wild, like—" He cut himself short and looked to someone, anyone, for help, but I could read the unspoken words in his anxious and forlorn expression: *like your eyes.*

I opened my mouth to speak another line, but a sudden loud *thump* from the conference room silenced us all. It sounded like a heavy chair or table falling over. Then: a wild, incoherent shouting that froze my blood. For even through the thick oaken door and the hysterical tone, I recognized the voice and accent of my friend Marco.

I bolted past the stunned group of spectators and grabbed the door handle, only to find it locked. Now another voice, panicked and British and sharp with terror, answered Marco's, and the rest of the scene played out offstage, behind the locked door.

WILLIAMSON

(Terrified)

What are you doing?

MARCO

(Frantically yelling)

You *must* not! Those who know it fully would perish! The Gate is in the great *and* the small! You cannot let the madness become sanity!

(There is a tremendous sound of shattering glass.)

WILLIAMSON

Stop it! What are you doing?

> (Shouting and pounding on the door)

Roger! Open the door! Roger!

> (Rising to a shriek)

NO! STOP!

> (There is a sound like a knife stabbing into a side of beef. WILLIAMSON's words shatter into an incoherent screech, followed by a liquid choking. A second sound emerges: a wet tearing like the shredding of damp cloth. WILLIAMSON's voice falls silent.)

MARCO

> (Screaming as if in mortal agony)

The Gate above and below! The One in the many! Oh God, the teeth! The TEEEEETH!

> (Silence, textured by the sly, slick tinkling of some heavy object being dragged through shards of glass.)

(BLACKOUT)

(END OF SCENE)

The play was over. The spectator feeling dissolved and I stepped off the stage into reality. Everything was completely, horribly present and actual. A woman in the crowd was weeping. A man had run halfway up the stairs toward the rear exit and then stopped, and now stood there blinking in befuddlement as if he had lost his way. The rest of the group stood and sat in various states of paralyzed shock.

Then the spell broke all at once and panic set in. Some sprang for the exits while others rushed toward me. Everyone screamed and shouted something different to do, until finally someone ran out to the hallway, blundered into an unlocked maintenance closet, and returned with an enormous claw hammer. I snatched it from him and set to work on the door handle while somebody else phoned the police.

The handle separated and crashed to the carpet after six stout blows. Clutching the hammer like a talisman, I pushed the door open and took a faltering step forward while the others clustered behind me in a sudden, awed silence.

The room I had entered was a standard conference room stocked with a long, narrow table and eight plastic chairs. One of these was sprawled on its back amidst the wreckage of an overturned barrister's bookcase, whose windows had exploded on impact with the edge of the table and then the face of the floor. The resulting spray of glass was soaked with what looked like gallons of blood. The net effect was a floor carpeted with crimson diamonds and jagged, bloody eggshells.

My eyes followed a distinctly differentiated blood trail through the carnage, tracing it to the point where it disappeared behind the table. As if caught in a nightmare, I crunched unhesitatingly across the crimson carpet to gaze upon what it was that I had gone there to prevent.

Nigel Williamson—physicist, astronomer, Cambridge professor, brilliant iconoclast—would never have the chance to reveal to the world his grand theory concerning the inner purpose of the universe as embodied in the chaotic irrationalities of the quantum realm. His intellectual brilliance had not been enough to save him, for now he lay on his back behind the table where Marco had dragged him, the nine-inch piece of glass Marco had used to eviscerate him still protruding from his side. His frozen expression of horror must have matched the one that slowly began to twist my own face, but if so, I was unaware of it. My eyes, my mind, my awareness, my very being, were all filled to bursting by a sight that blazed with a too-real intensity and became an instant symbol of everything I had realized and endured: the blood-spattered, empty-eyed face of my friend Marco as he crouched over the professor's body and mechanically devoured his innards.

8

That gruesome image with its oversaturated quality of ontological vividness remained with me forever, even after the passing of years had begun to blunt some of the other memories. Some of the first of those to go were the ones concerning the immediate aftermath of that final event. I remember there was quite a furor on campus and in the town, and even in the national news media. I know I was asked many questions by people acting in official capacities. But the specifics of it all, just like the specifics of the actions that I and the others took right after we found Marco in there with the professor, have been swallowed up by the image of that bloody face with its blank eyes and mechanical masticating motion.

What I do remember with clarity are my broad reactions to the uproar, since they changed the course of my life and brought me to my present circumstance. At the height of it all, when I feared I might literally go insane from everything, I quit my beloved studies and relocated to another town where nobody knew me and I could live in relative anonymity. I still live there today, and hold down the most trivial job I could find that will still provide me with enough income to afford a shoddy apartment where I hide from the world and hope for a merciful end to my existence. In general, I apply myself diligently to ignoring and forgetting the world outside the bubble of boredom that I have created. But from time to time I buy a newspaper or switch on my little television to see if the direction of world events might have changed a little. And of course it has not, nor will it ever.

For everything is still disintegrating inexorably into madness, and I, unlike most people, know precisely why. Before Marco dragged me into his living nightmare, I was worried like everyone else about the mass cultural insanity that had gripped the twentieth and early twenty-first centuries. Like everyone else, I noticed that things seemed to be roaring toward an apocalyptic climax, and I had my pet theories to explain it all. But now I see how absurd they all were.

Because what is happening is in fact a profound and far-reaching reordering of reality itself—societal, cultural, personal, and even physical. In essence, the prophecies of Lovecraft and Nietzsche are coming true right before our eyes, with effects that are not only personal and cultural but ontological. Our excess of vast scientific knowledge and technological prowess has proceeded in lockstep with a collective descent into species-level insanity. You only have to watch two minutes of television, glance at a headline, or eavesdrop on a random conversation to learn of it. Ignorance and idiocy. Riots and revolutions. These and a thousand other signposts like them are only the most pointed and obvious manifestations of the all-pervasive malaise that has come to define us. And since, as Sankara observed, we are nothing but particularized manifestations of the Ground of Being itself, we are not only witnesses to this breakdown but participants in it, enablers of the transformation of the world into a vale of horror through the metaphysical potency of our very witnessing. God looks out through each of our eyes, an abyss of insatiable hunger and infinite teeth, and the dark light of His consciousness makes each of us a lamp that illuminates a new and terrible truth.

I find it ironic that the man who cursed me with this vision of the world will not even be aware of it when everything comes to fruition. Marco spends his days and nights screaming out his madness in a prison for the criminally insane. I visited him only once, when the police were still trying to discover where he had hidden himself during his ten-day absence (a question they never answered, nor did I). I almost couldn't bear to look at him, and when I finally did meet his gaze, I knew at once that my friend was dead. His eyes had gone permanently dark in the manner I had briefly glimpsed so long ago in his dorm room, and I recognized his condition as an advanced case of the same state that would sooner or later manifest in every person on the planet. Something had compelled me to bring the notebook, which I had retrieved from my living room floor and then carefully preserved for no reason I could articulate. When I showed it to Marco, he sprang at me without warning and knocked me to the floor, snarling and shrieking in a feral frenzy. The savagery of his attack stunned me, and before I could recover, he had seized the notebook with his teeth and shaken it to shreds like a dog with a rat. Then he turned on me again, and it was only the intervention of the hospital staff that saved me from having my throat torn out. His doctors said it would be best if I stayed away after that. Later, I heard that he managed to break his restraints after I left, and that in the absence of another object he turned on himself. Before the orderlies could reach him, he chewed off and swallowed two of his own fingers.

What scares me the most is knowing that the transcendent insanity gnawing at the shell of Marco is the same insanity that waits to welcome me in death. All too well do I understand the wisdom of the ancient Greeks, which held that the best thing is never to have been born. To exist at all is to know the horror of no escape. Nietzsche said the thought of suicide can comfort a man through many a dark night, but it is no comfort to someone like me who knows all too well what awaits.

There is only one hope for my salvation. Over the years I have become an assiduous student of Lovecraft, not just his stories but his essays and letters. And I have marveled at the man's uncanny ability to see so deeply into the truth and yet remain so composed and kindhearted. Perhaps this gentle New Englander knew something that I do not, something he tried to convey when he wrote of the "vast conceit of those who had babbled of the *malignant* Ancient Ones." Perhaps the horror exists only in me, not in reality. Perhaps Marco was wrong, and there is no need to fear the truth. After all, It knows only Itself, and maybe I will not perceive It as horrific after I die. Perhaps I will be so thoroughly consumed by and identified with it that "I" will not even exist at all, and my sense of horror will prove to be as fleeting and finite as the self that sensed it. If this is true, then may it come quickly.

But this hope, however appealing, can never sustain me for long. For it is clear that I am *already* identified with that horrible truth, and yet I still find it a horror. The clear evidence of this identification manifests in my own body, in the fundamental physical drive that compels me to take nourishment and the anatomical structures that have been evolved to accomplish this purpose: lips and tongue, teeth and gums, throat and stomach. Life, as Joseph Campbell once observed, is a horrific thing that sustains itself by feeding on other life. I have gained a new and awful awareness of this fact in the form of a certain nagging sensitivity in my mouth. All day and night I am plagued by an unpleasant awareness of those protruding bits of bone whose function is to grind plant and animal flesh to a pulp in order to sustain this bodily life. Sometimes when this awareness has tortured me for hours on end, I will go to the mirror and draw back my lips to gaze at the truth. This mockery of the facial expression that conventionally expresses pleasure reminds me a bit of the bliss I once hoped to find in philosophies of ultimate beauty. But even that is gone now, swallowed down the bottomless throat of the cosmic mystery that forever feeds on all things.

Do I seem mad? Do I sound like a man who has become lost in his own private delusion of hell? Then let me remind you that you, too, exhibit the same stigmata in your own body. Show me your smile and I will show you your fate.

The Stars Shine without Me

For some reason, I worked for Viggo Brand. Several times each day as I sat at my desk or wandered around my office and went about my regular routine of boredom and unproductiveness, it occurred to me that way: *For some reason, I work for Viggo Brand.*

Of course I knew the real reasons. I could look back over the pattern of my past and survey the series of causes and effects, motivations and necessities, which had led me to this job in a cramped office on the ninetieth floor of the Brand Building. It was all too clear why I worked for him. The reason could be summed up in a single word: *fear.* Not fear of Mr. Brand, whom I had never seen, but whose guardian presence presided like an invisible eye over his organization. It was more a fear of not knowing what else to do. I was afraid to do anything but continue working there, because working there was all I had ever done, and I felt comfortable with and comforted by the boredom, even when it sometimes proved indistinguishable from desperation.

But still, although the simple, literal answer was readily available, I sometimes liked to narrow my attention to the present—to that infinitesimal, perpetually dying point of the present moment—and from that restricted viewpoint consider my employment at the Brand Corporation. When I did this, I truly did not know why I was there. Without the present awareness of my past laid out for easy viewing, I could almost imagine that I had never been anywhere else. On long afternoons when the sky scoured over with a matting of dark clouds and the hours seemed to stretch into eternity before and behind me, I could almost imagine that I had never known any place but my office, nor any existence but the routine of monotony and boredom that made up my every day.

The ennui of my situation was augmented by the fact that I did not know what I was supposed to be doing for the company. Beginning on my first day, many years past, I had shown up every morning, and nobody had ever asked me to leave, so I had stayed. The woman who acted as my secretary, and also as the secretary for the eight or nine other employees in my division, and whose name I had never learned during all my long years of employment, would peek in the door to my office each morning to verify that I was present at my desk. When she saw me, she would give a curt nod and close the door, leaving me to lean back in my chair and look out the window, or maybe take a nap, or maybe scribble meaningless shapes on the notepad that awaited me on my desk each morning.

I had become very deft at these illustrations. Often I put great care into them, but then I just left them sitting there, and each morning when I arrived they were neatly stacked with a fresh blank pad on top. Over time, I had perfected a style of doodling all my own. Sometimes I spent entire weeks blackening a single sheet of notepaper with curly lines and boxes, diamonds and stars, dots and dashes, and jagged, meshy patterns that made my eyes ache when I looked at them later. This had become just another automatic act, like everything else I did for the Brand Corporation.

The Brand Building was an imposing structure. Every morning when I climbed up from the subway and approached the sparkling row of front doors, I would raise my eyes and peer up through the mist to catch a glimpse of the sharp spire, and would think of Mr. Brand living there at the very top in unknown quarters. And I would wonder what he looked like and what he did with his days, and where he had acquired his great wealth, and why he had built this magnificent structure for a purpose that I still did not know after all those years of working for him.

The Brand Building was shaped like a needle, or like a four-cornered pyramid elongated to an absurd proportion, with an exterior surface of smooth, obsidian-colored stone. It stabbed upward two hundred stories and appeared to prick the outer edge of the sky. I remember thinking when I first glimpsed it from a distant bridge many years ago, as I was entering the city for the first time, that the great tower seemed to watch over the dull buildings below like a harsh and haughty ruler. They huddled around its base in crazy clusters, all dirty brick and concrete. I had felt like the proverbial rat in a trap as I drove through the maze of streets and slums, and looked up at the faded façades and crumbling brickwork. Worst of all were the pallid faces I saw framed in the windows. Some were lighter than others, some darker. Some were young and some were old. All wore a look of vacancy and hopelessness.

Then I had come nearer the Brand Building, and the squalor had disappeared at once and given way to a sterile open space many hundreds of yards wide, where Renaissance-style fountains stood dry and flaking, and statues of strange forms lined up in severe rows to flank visitors like me and guide us toward the row of front doors that were always revolving, always turning in perpetual circles to allow unhindered, universal access or exit. After I had been employed there for several months, someone finally told me about the subway access right there on the grounds, reserved exclusively for Brand Corporation employees. After that I never navigated the unnerving maze of the old city again.

As I sat there looking out of my window, which covered an entire wall of my office, I could gaze down upon those old structures huddled together several hundred yards from the foot of the Brand Building and feel a pleasant sense of weightlessness rising up in my breast like a cloud of feathers. This had been my primary preoccupation during all my long years in that office: simply to look down on the old city and enjoy it from this dizzying height. The atmosphere around the Brand Building was clear as crystal, like freshly washed glass, except for a white mist that clung to the black exterior in the early morning hours. This always burned away in the sunlight by mid-morning, leaving me with a totally unobstructed view of the scene below. It was truly magnificent to look down on the old buildings with their cloak of muddy gray smog, and to feel somehow purified and rarefied by the mere fact of my height and their distance.

My favorite time for this activity was during the long evenings of winter, when sunset came early and the lights of the old city shone visibly in dim haloes through the smog for a long period before the end of my workday. On such evenings, I would sometimes dance my eyes over those lights in quick darts, making them blur into streaks and tracers, and then raise my head and steady my half-closed eyes upon a horizon line stretching from east to west, located right on the precise division between the city below and the sky above. The stars would be out overhead, shining like shards of crystal in a black celestial ocean. I would watch them from the tops of my eyes while keeping the lights of the old city centered in the lower half of my vision. And sometimes for a split second that felt like a miniature eternity, I could fancy that the stars above and the lights below formed a single unbroken continuum of night sky. It would look as if a great constellation had fallen to earth, or better yet, as if there were no earth at all but only the stars shining brilliantly in their cold and cruel distance. I would gasp and feel tears start to my eyes, and would sense myself on the verge of some great revelation, some unknowable fulfillment that would justify all the long years of my blundering, inarticulate yearning for something beyond the dreary pall of everyday existence.

But then the moment would pass, and my eyes would clear, and the stars would return to their inaccessible heights, and the city below would settle once again into its unromantic guise as a dirty jumble of smog-shrouded bricks, and I would be alone in my office on the ninetieth floor of the Brand Building with no understanding—or at least no *real* one, none that would explain to me the longings and confusions of a meaningless past and present— of why I was there.

This all changed late one evening when my secretary opened the door to my office and walked in to stand before my desk.

I swiveled around in my chair and regarded her with surprise. She had never entered my office before, and I could not possibly guess what she might want. I took the opportunity to observe her more closely. She was slim and bony and dressed in a navy blue skirt. Her hair was rust-red and pulled back in a bun. Her face was white and narrow. A network of delicate dry lines textured the skin of her cheeks and forehead. She might have been thirty years old or twice that.

"Mr. Brand wants to see you," she said. When I looked at her dumbly, she said it again: "Mr. Brand wants to see you."

I did not know how to react. My eyes were still filled with after-flashes from the stars and city lights, and I must have looked as dazed as I felt. After a moment I rose from my chair and came around the desk to stand beside her.

"Gather those and take them with you," she said, pointing to the pile of papers that lay on the desk. I complied as if in a dream. These were the papers on which I had been scribbling meaningless pictures for months and years. She turned and exited, and I hurried after her with the sheaf of papers flapping under my arm as I tried to straighten my necktie.

She led me out of my office and down a hallway in a direction I had never gone before. I looked back and saw my eight or nine coworkers in that division standing singly outside their doors. They were watching me with awed expressions, exactly as I would have looked at them if the situation had been reversed and they had received the mysterious summons.

Then they were lost from sight as I was led around a corner into an ill-lit hallway. We walked halfway down it to an open elevator door, where the secretary stopped and gestured for me to enter, which I did.

"He's waiting for me right now?" I asked. In reply, she reached inside and pressed the button for the two hundredth floor. Then she backed out and walked away, leaving me alone as the doors closed.

The inside of the elevator was uncharacteristically cramped for the Brand Building, whose spacious interiors had always belied the limitation of its exterior shape. But the decoration was much more ornate than what I had grown accustomed to. I grasped a handrail of polished brass to steady myself as I felt the car shoot upward at a positively terrifying speed. The light fixture depending from the ceiling was multi-bulbed and hooded with tiny lampshades mounted on curling metal arms that looked like gold. It hung so low that it nearly brushed the top of my head. For a moment I tried to imagine the elevator car and myself as we must have appeared from the outside. I closed my eyes and caught a momentary mental glimpse of a tiny metal box rocketing upward through the core of the needle-like Brand Building toward the stars above. My lungs labored as I fancied the atmosphere grew thinner. Immediately, I cut off my imaginings and opened my eyes to dispel the vertigo. When the car eventually slowed and stopped, the light fixture vibrated and its bulbs trembled and tinkled.

I was breathing hard when the doors opened. Grasping my papers in sweaty hands, I emerged into an antechamber that was like nothing else I had ever seen in the Brand Building. It was spacious and geometrical, shaped almost like a perfect cube except for the slight inward slope of the walls that made the ceiling smaller than the floor. All the surfaces were black and gleaming. An enormous burgundy rug with a vaguely oriental pattern stretched nearly from wall to wall, and laid out on it were a number of exhibits that reminded me of pieces in a museum. Some were in clear cases while others sat uncovered. Some were made of polished wood or bone and looked like tribal idols or fetishes. Others were crystalline or metal and looked sleek and new.

From this inscrutable assemblage, I gathered an odd sense of excitement, tempered with anxiety. It was a familiar feeling, and I was on the verge of remembering where I had felt it before when a voice issued from a hidden speaker and told me to approach the doors on the opposite wall. I had not even noticed them. In order to obey the faceless command I was obliged to walk through the museum display, and for some reason I felt a strong reluctance to touch anything. I had the sense that I was navigating through a mysterious sea whose pristine beauty my very presence might defile.

Once across, I stepped gingerly off the carpet and back onto the shiny black floor. The door handles were huge and made of brass. When I touched them, the doors opened easily and silently, and I stepped into what I knew must be Mr. Brand's office.

It was long and low and all of a shiny black, just like the antechamber. Mr. Brand was seated on the far side behind a black desk, framed against a massive window that dwarfed the one down in my own office. I had never laid eyes on him before, but there could be no question of his identity. His face and throat were thick, his shoulders broad, his head high-browed and square. Indeed, he was powerfully built all over. Even seated there behind his desk, he exuded an aura of authority. From this alone I could well understand why everyone in the building, and also in the city below, walked in awe of him. His hair was white and straight and combed back from his forehead to fall in stern lines down to his shoulders. He was dressed in a black coat with a black shirt fastened tightly about his neck. I did not doubt that if he were to rise and walk around the desk, I would be greeted with the sight of black pants and black shoes, impeccably polished. Somehow I also knew that he would prove to be disturbingly tall, a veritable giant of a man, and I fervently hoped that he would remain seated. A pair of black spectacles, completely impenetrable and perfectly round, completed the ensemble.

"Please," he said, "sit down." He spoke with a faint accent that I could not place. His voice was fully as deep and commanding as his appearance would imply, but it was more cultured than I would have expected, carrying a kind of measured grace that was quite pleasing to the ear. Up until now his hands had remained folded before him in an attitude of waiting, but now he gestured for me to take a seat in the single sable-colored chair that was positioned to face him from across the desk.

I did not dare disobey. A moment later, I was seated face-to-face with him while he regarded me from behind his spectacles.

"You have done good work for me," he said at last. "That is why I've called you here: to thank you. Of all my many employees, you are the hardest working and most loyal, and you deserve to know that."

My heart sank as I heard these words. I was certain he must have gotten my file mixed up with someone else's, with the record of some other employee who actually knew his job and truly deserved a commendation. I dreaded to think what would happen when Mr. Brand discovered that he had invited the wrong person into his inner sanctum.

"No, you are the right man," he said. A little shock went off in my chest as he seemed to read my thoughts. I felt I should say something, but all my faculties were paralyzed. For a wordless moment we faced each other across the desk.

Then I noticed the vista that spread out behind him.

Gleaming from below, the lights of the city cast up an aurora that tinted the bottom half of his long, single-paned window with a milky radiance. Simultaneously, the window's upper half was populated from end to end by an assemblage of stars the likes of which I had never seen. It must have been due to the clarity of the atmosphere at that altitude. The night sky was a black velvet curtain encrusted with diamonds. It was the smooth surface of an oily ocean shining with the phosphorescent eyes of a billion unknown, underwater creatures.

The sight so overwhelmed me that I felt the breath sucked out of my lungs, as if I had stepped through those windows into the vacuum of outer space. The papers in my hand slipped from numb fingers and plopped down on the desk.

In the midst of my transport, I was aware that Mr. Brand was regarding me with what I might have taken for affection if the thought had not been so ridiculous. Then he looked at the papers and smiled, showing me two rows of tiny perfect teeth.

"Ah, yes," he said. "May I?" The unexplained request confused me, so I tore my loving gaze away from the mystical windows and saw that he was holding out his hand. I watched my own hand pick up the papers and pass them to him. His meaty fingers closed around them with a kind of greedy relish, and then he was scouring them with his hidden gaze, flipping from one page to the next, turning to look at the fronts and backs of pages whose every available inch was covered with a meaningless chaos of designs. I watched as his body bowed slightly in its seat. The lapel of his coat crinkled. A lock of white hair fell down over his forehead and bisected one of his black lenses. He seemed to be devouring the pages with his eyes. I was fascinated by this display of utter abandoned greed, and then I stopped to wonder what that word could possibly mean in this connection, and why it had arisen so immediately and naturally in my mind: *greed.*

After a few minutes, he raised his eyes from the papers and gave me that same tiny-toothed smile. "Oh, so good," he said in a voluptuous voice. "So very, very good. You are a positive treasure. I assure you that from now on, you will receive your just due from me. Please forgive the years of tedium, but I had to be certain. And now I am." He looked back down at the pages and laughed at some private joke. "Am I *ever* certain!"

My head was swimming as if I were drunk. Perhaps it was the thinness of the atmosphere. "Mr. Brand." It was the first thing I had said to him, and the sound of my own voice unnerved me. He looked at me with that same pleased expression.

"Mr. Brand," I repeated. "I don't understand. Thank you for your praise, but I just don't understand. I'm ashamed to admit it, but I don't even know what I do for you or your company. What can you possibly see in those scribbles?"

He laughed again, in a tone full of affection, and at last arose from his chair. I had been correct in my suspicion: He towered over me. The top of his head nearly touched the ceiling, and when he walked around the desk to stand beside me, his pants and shoes were black, and the shoes gleamed even more brightly than the floor.

"Oh, my child, if only you knew. If only you could understand. I wish I could explain it to you, truly. But then the Brand Corporation would be out of business, and you would be out of a job, and I would be toppled from my perch here in the eye of the needle, and the only thing left in all the world would be that dirty, crumbling city below. And neither of us could live with that result. You want it no more than I."

I was nodding and agreeing with him before I even realized it. Although I had no idea what he was talking about, I positively shuddered at the thought of the old city existing on its own without the Brand Building's redemptive presence presiding over it, with Mr. Brand securely ensconced at the top.

"You see?" he said. "We indeed understand each other."

Then he laid his heavy hand on my shoulder, and everything changed. Even through the barriers of my coat and shirt, I could feel the heat of his flesh, which penetrated those thin layers of fabric and spread over my skin like hot oil, and I knew in my soul that I was permanently altered by his touch. I knew that even if I were to remove my shirt and find no visible mark, I would still be forever changed by that contact with Mr. Brand. In the space of a second, he had taken something from me and given something else in return, something new and unimagined. As he stepped away from me and walked back around the desk to his chair, I felt a tingling vibration begin to shimmer inside me. It soothed me from neck to groin, and between my eyes, from behind my skull, a warm pressure like a finger pressed gently outward. Mr. Brand resumed his seat and looked at me.

"Thank you again," he said. "Thank you, sir, for your hard work and loyalty."

Some indeterminate amount of time later, when I stood up from my seat and returned to the black double-door, I moved as if I were walking underwater. My head spun with a flurry of new insights that came coursing through my awareness like spray from a black waterfall.

I saw dimly, as though reflected in a dirty mirror, the extent of the organization for which I worked. I saw the way its influence

extended like a network of invisible arteries into the old city below, into the hearts of its inhabitants. I saw how it sucked away
the lifeblood of their souls and fed on their dreams, using those
tender psychic morsels to fortify and amplify the black tower,
bringing its apex ever closer to the outer edge of the sky and the
inner edge of heaven.

And more: I saw this influence reaching away from the known
world, rounding strange corners and meeting at odd intersections
with the teeming edges of other worlds, worlds beyond the known
rim of light and darkness, sense and solidity, the foundations of
all that I knew and thought possible. In countless other worlds, I
saw countless other beings lined up in hovels like the sickly people in the windows of the old city below, like the ignorant employees stacked up in their slivered tiers throughout the
monstrous height of the Brand Building. They all labored somehow, these beings, even the ones who no longer moved or spoke
or thought, and their labor bore fruit in the form of grotesque and
fantastic productions that could never coalesce into any kind of
order that would make sense to sanity as I knew it.

But in some unaccountable fashion, these productions, when
they were brought together and arranged in the proper order, co-
hered like the serrated edges of a lethal jigsaw, and always proved
to be precisely what Mr. Brand needed for the furtherance of his
business. His corporation grew with the expansion of his soul, and
his soul drew its nourishment from the silent labor of a network
of unwitting worlds.

There the vision reached its limit. Having seen so far into
things that were undreamed of, my newly awakened inner sight
came up against something like a black, shimmering shield that
repelled vision as a mirror repels light. I knew that beyond this
barrier must lie the knowledge of the ultimate end, the pattern
and purpose for which this vast network of ignorant organized labor was being bled dry by a man who had somehow attained the
status of a demigod and now wanted to make his transition into
divinity complete.

The visions coiled and glimmered in the beam of my inner sight, and my knees grew weak. The black inner barrier receded and solidified, gaining form and shape until I found myself gazing at my own watery reflection in the smooth, polished wall of Mr. Brand's sanctum.

As I touched the door handle, I knew without looking back that he had again taken up the papers, my own unwitting contribution to his Promethean endeavor, and was again feasting upon their contents. I almost felt that I could see the lines and shapes twisting before my own eyes instead of his.

But something was different now. Something had been altered within me, for now when I looked with these new eyes upon the randomness of those designs that had been spawned by boredom, I glimpsed a phenomenon that transcended mere ink and paper. It seemed to be a pattern, a subtle arrangement of shape, position, and proportion that brought order out of chaos. It was, I understood, a higher kind of order, one that made perfect sense out of senselessness and imparted meaning to the meaningless. I fancied that in the depths of Mr. Brand's soul, through the agency of the things I had drawn, this patternless pattern was spreading out two black-feathered wings, or perhaps they were doors, which could open up and transport a person to the heights of an unimaginable bliss in some unimaginable realm situated far beyond the need for reasons or the lack of them. Somewhere in a cold Arcadia, in a skyward abyss of utter inaccessibility, there was a place where ennui was unknown and the stars shone forever without obstruction. This was the paradise Mr. Brand was bound for, and I recognized in its beauty the fulfillment of everything I had ever wanted for myself.

The pressure in my forehead was beautiful. The tingling warmth in my abdomen was delicious.

I shut the doors behind me and walked boldly back through the menagerie of artifacts, no longer fearing that I might defile them. With uncharacteristic courage, I stopped and caressed them one by one, feeling a new exultation well up within me at the feel of their textures.

The elevator door was open and waiting for me. I rode it back down in complete inner and outer silence without holding onto the rail. The hanging light fixture was motionless and silent as the car came to a halt and I stepped back onto my accustomed ninetieth floor. The hallways were dark. Everyone had gone home for the evening, and I walked in total solitude to my office, where I found the door still open and the lights still on.

It was not until I sat down at my desk and swiveled the chair to face the window that I discovered the true nature of the gift Mr. Brand had given me.

Outside, there were only stars. Instead of looking down upon the hopeless squalor of the old city, my window-wall now sat at the glowing hot center of a spiral galaxy. Delicate arms of silver and white fire unfurled away from me like flaming roads to paradise, like star-dusted snowbanks, and the spaces between them shimmered with a golden glow like the light of a sunrise.

Nothing stood between us now, the stars and me, no obstruction at all. Even this cold pane was utterly insubstantial. If I tipped forward I might pass through the window as through a sheet of water, and on the other side fall forever into a vast well of endless beauty. The city below had turned invisible in the cosmic light of this sacred gallery, and I wept with joy as I realized that I no longer had to wonder why I was here instead of somewhere else, or worry about whether I should be doing this instead of that. Enjoyment of the ultimate mystery might be reserved for another, but I no longer felt any sense of loss. All my questions had vanished, leaving only this dazzling cold beauty outside my window and inside my heart. Most miraculous and wonderful of all, I knew that it would all continue to shine on without me forever, and imparted meaning to the meaningless. It was shining without me even now, immediately outside my window in that inconceivably beautiful swirl of fiery night.

Mr. Brand saw it all as well, and understood the vision in its entirety from the protection of his shadowy sanctum perched high in the eye of the needle: Mr. Brand, who alone possessed the secret of joy, whose tower pierced through the heart of heaven like a spear; Mr. Brand, who banished all fear and desperation with his touch, because he alone knew what was ultimately needed.

For no reason at all, I work for Viggo Brand.

Desert Places

Men with minds sensitive to hereditary impulse will always tremble at the thought of the hidden and fathomless worlds of strange life which may pulsate in the gulfs beyond the stars.

—H. P. Lovecraft

They cannot scare me with their empty spaces
Between stars—on stars where no human race is.
I have it in me so much nearer home
To scare myself with my own desert places.

—Robert Frost

1

When Dr. Pryor told me that my friend Paul had been involved in a terrible accident, I was sitting in the heart of the Utah desert fifteen miles outside Vernal, brushing away flecks of dirt from the leg bone of an as-yet unidentified fossil. We only knew that it was some sort of dinosaur, right from the heart of the Jurassic period. Only a small portion had been exposed by our efforts. The bulk of it was still buried under the dry Utah soil. It would take many more days of painstaking effort to excavate the piece with all of its secrets still intact.

The light of the early evening sun spilled over my shoulder like a flow of warm liquid, bathing the earth before me with a ruddy glow. That moment, with my eyes fixed on the long-buried bone of an extinct reptile and my brain reeling from the news I'd just heard, burned itself instantly, irrevocably, into my soul. The sense of being deeply and painfully marked was almost physical.

"I'm sorry," Dr. Pryor said. "The woman on the phone said I should tell you exactly what was going on. She said you'd listen better that way." His unreadable little eyes were even more opaque than usual behind his thick eyeglasses. He shuffled his right foot through the heavy carpet of desert dust, and his work boot kicked up a dry brown cloud that lingered in the motionless air between us.

I didn't have to be told who had made the call. No one else would have had the astounding boldness—or tactlessness—to pass the message through a stranger, nor would anyone else have had such a bitingly accurate insight into my state of mind from across a distance of a thousand miles.

"Did she say how it happened?" I asked.

"Not exactly. Some sort of injury to the head. I guess it's quite serious." He shuffled his foot again.

I knew I should felt bad for my paleontologist employer. He was obviously discomfited by Lisa's awful judgment in giving the news directly to him instead of doing the sane thing and asking him to hand me the phone. But I couldn't feel anything besides a hollow dullness that seemed to breathe into me from the desert.

"I guess you'll be leaving." His words were both a statement and a question.

"Yes." I took a final glance at the great leg bone, as thick as the trunk of a small tree back in my home state of Missouri, and willed the moment to stay with me. Something about its pain, its vividness, seemed crucial. Something about the mystery of the buried bone seemed vital to my continued health and sanity. I wanted the pain of that mark on my soul, and the mystery of the dead monster, to stay with me forever, to remind me of the fact that I was indeed capable of feeling such a pure and profound emotion.

Then I took a breath and rose to my feet. Dr. Pryor stood looking at me doubtfully. I knew I was abandoning him right when he needed me the most. But then, I had only been working with him for a short time, whereas my roots with Paul and Lisa were old and deep.

"Sorry," I said. It was all I could manage.

He shrugged faintly. "You have to do what you have to do. I'm sorry about your friend."

I started to say thanks, but then I just nodded and walked away to where we had parked our vehicles. The cloud I kicked up as I drove back to the road swirled around my old Ford van like a rusty ghost. When some of it sucked in through the grill and coughed out of the dashboard vents, it tasted hot and coppery, like a splash of blood on my tongue.

2

The drive should have taken seventeen hours, but I made it last nearly thirty. This was due partly to the practical fact that my battered old van with its badly unbalanced wheels shook like a minor earthquake when I exceeded fifty miles per hour. But the real reason for my slow pace was my sharp reluctance to reach my destination. I was heading back into territory that I thought I had left behind, and every mile I traveled felt like fighting against a river current. I drove most of the way at a speed of around forty, stopping by the roadside several times to catch my breath and stare up at the sky—dappled with silvery stars by night, then cloudless and harsh with heat during the day—while I struggled to divine my own motives. Did I really want to do this? Did I really want to go back and face the remains of my old life again?

When I finally arrived at the hospital in Farrenton, Missouri, it was eleven-thirty at night and I felt like a walking dead man. My eyes throbbed with a pulsing ache and my back wanted to split in two.

True to form, Lisa displayed her talent for mind reading by greeting me in the lobby. There was no way she could have known when I would arrive, or even whether I would show up. But there she sat, waiting on a mahogany-colored sectional sofa with a crisp copy of the *Farrenton Beacon* spread open in her lap. When she saw me, she dropped the newspaper and ran to me as if I were a long-lost friend or lover. Which, of course, I was. Only she was obviously more at ease with our troubled past than I could ever be. The dark midnight mood of the lobby, with its sleek contemporary décor and black-tinted windows, reminded me of a movie set as she closed the distance between us.

"Oh, Stephen!" she cried, and buried her face in the breast of my tee shirt. As she heaved against me, I reflexively put my arm around her and then stood inhaling the scent of her perfume and looking down at the glossy black sweep of her hair. She watered my dusty shirt with her tears for a moment before stepping back.

"I'm sorry," she said, wiping her cheeks and attempting a smile. "It's good to see you. I've missed you."

I mumbled something in reply and tried not to notice that she looked delectable in a crimson turtleneck and auburn leather jacket. Her pants and boots were dark leather as well. Outside her sweater she wore a gold weave necklace that rose and fell with the curves of her breasts.

"I'm . . . sorry," she said again, and the falter in her voice caused me to notice for the first time how out-of-sorts she seemed. A sliver of pain was etched between her eyes, which still glowed an emerald cat's green, just as brightly as they ever had. The corners of her lovely mouth were taut with worry and her shoulders were drawn tightly inward. The social skills I had lost during three years of drifting through rain forests and deserts started to come back, and I took her by the arm and led her to the sofa, where I kept my hand on her until she was seated. Then I sat beside her and waited for her to make the next move.

"It's bad," she said. I knew immediately that she was referring to Paul. I had been gripped by a raging curiosity about his accident all during the long drive east, and more to the point, there was nothing else for us to talk about.

"He's not going to get any better," she said. "The doctor says he's brain-dead. He's just a vegetable." This brought on another bout of sobs, during which I again put my hand on her arm and noticed that I could feel the heat of her flesh all the way through the double layer of leather and cotton.

"Lisa," I said. It was the first time I had spoken her name in three years. She looked up at me with glassy eyes, and I knew that a part of me, a despised part that I would have given anything to be able to excise from my soul, still loved her. The question I then asked—"What the hell *happened?*"—referred to Paul's accident, but the vehemence with which I asked it arose from the fact that it may as well have referred to Lisa's and my sorry history.

The tale she related to me was absurd. That was the thought that lingered with me after she had explained everything and we were rising from the sofa. It lingered as she led me farther into the hospital, toward the elevators, toward the seventh floor, toward the sterile white room where my best friend and spiritual mentor, the wisest and kindest man I had ever known, lay attached to a respirator with a dent in his head from a wayward terra cotta planter that had fallen from a high metal shelf at a home supply store. He and Lisa had gone browsing there with idle thoughts of building a house together. Almost as an afterthought, they had wandered through the outdoor section, where a strong wind, a veritable mini-cyclone, had blown in from nowhere and toppled the fifty-pound planter off its perch and directly onto the back of his skull. He had never regained consciousness.

We rode the elevator in silence. Lisa's body glowed with warmth as she stood next to me in her red turtleneck. When the door opened, she led me in silence down a hallway, past a nurse's station, toward a room I dreaded to enter.

Paul lay under the sheets with a bandage wrapped around his head and various plastic tubes attached to his body like the limbs of a giant insect. The rasping of the respirator was dry and chilling. Several fresh flowers in plastic vases adorned the table next to the bed, along with a scattering of sympathy cards. I stepped closer and looked down into his face. Even as he lay there unconscious, his dark eyebrows still endowed him with a placid, mysterious demeanor, halfway between brooding and peaceful. If it had not been for the tubes distorting his features, his expression would have been identical to the one I had seen a thousand times before, when we had sat beside each other in meditation.

Lisa showed uncommon good taste by standing back and letting me absorb the reality of the moment. When I had seen enough, I turned to look at her.

"Lisa, I'm so sorry." And of course I really was. Despite the fact that she had chosen him over me, devastating me with such a desperate sense of grief and betrayal that I had been driven to the brink of madness, I could not feel anything but anguish at Paul's fate. And I could not help feeling a momentary surge of protectiveness toward her, like the phantom sensation of a lost limb.

She stepped up beside me and we both looked down at him. "Do you recognize that expression?" she said. "He could almost be meditating." A ripple of chills went down my spine at this latest display of her intuitive powers. I had never gotten used to that, not in all the years we had been lovers. She had always seemed connected to the universe in a way that I simply could not rival, no matter how hard I worked to develop my spirituality. The fact that Paul, too, had possessed his own special kind of connection to the absolute, and had been not only my best friend but also my informal guru, was more than just ironic. In light of what had followed, it was downright brutal.

"I keep hoping," she said, "that he's experiencing all kinds of things that he always wondered about. He always talked about death like it was a long-lost friend. He always expected it to tear away the last veil and bring him face to face with the great mystery." She looked at me and smiled a sad smile. "I don't have to tell you this. You knew him as well as I did." She had painted her lips red to match her blouse. They looked sweet as strawberry candy.

Suddenly, I knew I had to leave the room. There was no visible reason for it. I only knew that I had to step out for air. The memories and emotions were swirling too thickly beside Paul's bed, and something like a panic attack waited just beneath the surface to shatter me. I said something about needing to visit the restroom, and she offered to walk down the hallway with me.

"No, it's okay," I said. "I just need a minute to wash the dust off. It was a long drive."

"All the way from Utah," she said. Her eyes were impenetrable when I dared to look into them.

"How did you know where I was?"

"I called your mother. She gave me your employer's number."

Of course. She had called my mother. How difficult should that have been to figure out? I had left Dr. Pryor's cell number with my mother, who had always loved Lisa, even after the two of them, Lisa and Paul, had betrayed me. The thought of these two iconic women from my past chatting with each other like old friends behind my back sent another chill down my spine. I hid my uneasiness with a nod and made a hasty exit.

A sign directed me to a restroom at the end of the corridor. Most of the overhead lights in the main hallway were switched off for the evening, and the beige walls and floor tiles gave off a chalky glow in the dim illumination. A woman was perched at the nurse's station on my left, reading a paperback novel by the light of a desk lamp. She glanced up at me, but I kept my gaze purposefully forward and sighed with relief when I encountered no one else.

In the restroom I spent a moment relieving my distended bladder and then another washing my face in the utility sink. Then I paused to consider my reflection in the mirror. My tee shirt looked as if a child had daubed it with clay. There were muddy streaks where Lisa's tears had smudged the desert dust. My face and arms were tanned. I needed a shave. If I had not been the one living behind my own eyes, I might have done a double take, just to make sure that I was really the same clean-cut person who had set out from this town only a few years ago.

When I returned to Paul's room, I found Lisa seated beside the bed in one of the guest chairs. Her eyes were closed and her lips were moving. She held Paul's hand in her own, and I received the inescapable impression that she was uttering a prayer. Knowing something of her exotic spiritual proclivities, I didn't presume to venture a guess about to whom or what she might be praying, or what she might be saying to them. In the silence, I looked around and noticed a small crucifix mounted on the wall above the bed. For a few seconds I tried staring into Christ's tiny face in an effort to find some kind of solace, but the sculpted look of agony only increased my uneasiness.

Presently, Lisa's eyes opened, and when I glanced down at her it was like an icy fist suddenly seized my heart.

Something about her eyes was terribly wrong. It took me a moment to recognize it, but when I did there was no mistaking the source of the wrongness: her irises had darkened. From a bright emerald green they had turned a deep coal color while she had prayed, and even as I watched in shock, they appeared to be growing darker with each passing second. Her expression appeared unfocused, as if she were gazing not at the hospital room but at some other world that she discerned behind the surface veneer of plaster walls and vinyl floor tiles. The sliver of pain in her brow suddenly looked more cruel than wounded. Her entire demeanor exuded a kind of quiet menace that was somehow linked to her physical beauty, as if her loveliness were just a discrete facet of some other, wider reality whose overall character was awful.

Then the moment passed, and I realized she was looking at me. No trace of the sinister expression remained. She offered me a wan half-smile, and after wavering for a moment, I seated myself on the other side of Paul and tried to get a look at her eyes. They were bright green, like a cat's. Without changing position, I folded back into myself mentally and filed away the bizarre incident for later reflection. I had not experienced such a strong hallucinatory episode for quite some time. That it could come on so unexpectedly, without any warning, and in the midst of such an unlikely setting, disturbed me deeply.

We sat for a long time while I tried to figure out why I had come there, and why I was staying, and when I would leave. With a bit of surprise, I realized that I wanted to take Paul's other hand, the one Lisa wasn't holding, and tell him that I forgave him. I wanted that to be his final memory of me, if indeed he was aware of my presence at all.

But it would have been a lie anyway. Sitting there watching Lisa stroke his fingers with her face molded into an expression of loving concern, I didn't feel at all forgiving. The only attitude or emotion I could feel was a semblance of the old shock and desperation, now stiffened with disuse like a crusty wound, that had been my parting feeling toward the both of them three years earlier. And beneath it, that cold fist of deadness that was slowly, subtly squeezing my heart with an ever-tightening grip.

After awhile the wheezing of the respirator began to sound like the wind scudding over the low desert hills. Its dry whisper filled me with an aching desire for solitude, and I breathed a silent sigh of relief that I had not taken Paul's other hand.

3

"I want to ask where you've been." Lisa's voice, soft and smooth, woke me from a stupor. I blinked and realized I had been dozing. Paul was still unconscious, still a mere mechanism of flesh and bone. I looked around for a clock and saw that the one on the bedside table read 1:15 A.M. We had been sitting there for just over an hour, and I had spent most of it trying to stay awake. Apparently, I had failed.

"What?" My voice came out thick and sluggish. The coldness had coagulated in my chest and I was having trouble breathing.

"I want to ask where you've been and what you've done since you left town," she said. "You never called or wrote. We've been worried about you for three years. But I'm afraid you'll be angry if I ask."

I wiped a hand over my face, wincing at the sharp scrape of whiskers against palm, and inwardly agreed with her. By all rights, I should have been angry. She had no right to know how I had chosen to live my life after leaving Farrenton, especially since my departure had been based solely on the fact that I couldn't bear to stay there and see the two of them together.

But something about her presence was exerting a magnetic pull upon me. I had spent the last thousand miles and thirty hours steeling my resolve to remain aloof and distant. I had told myself that I was only returning to Farrenton because it would be cruel to refuse a summons under these circumstances. But as I sat there looking across the injured body of my comatose best friend and into the face of the only woman I had ever truly loved, I found I actually *wanted* to tell her what had happened to me. I wanted to shock her with the viciousness of it, to force her to experience a living measure of the pain I had borne in solitude for three years.

The words began slowly but soon gathered momentum. With growing amazement at my own willingness to open up to her like this, I began to tell her of my life without her: of how only a few weeks after I had fled from her and Paul, I had become involved with an activist group devoted to fighting the destruction of the Brazilian rain forest. The story sounded alien and ridiculous to me as I related it, almost as if I were talking about another person. Prior to encountering that activist group I had been the farthest thing from a "joiner." Despite the lip service that my self-conscious spiritual hipness had led me to pay to ecological issues, I had never done a single thing to back that up in concrete action. Nor had I imagined how frighteningly simple such hypocrisy would be to change. A chance encounter in a new city with a man handing out pamphlets on a street corner, an impulsive trip to the address listed on the cover, and one short screening session later, and I found myself seated on a Boeing 757—I, who had never left the continental United States—headed for Brazil to join the protest. Even at the time, I knew that my impulsiveness was mostly driven by my escapist fantasy. I just wanted to flee my past and forget that my two best friends, who were also the two most spiritual people I had ever known, had betrayed me for each other.

The memory of this part enhanced the pain of telling the story to Lisa. It also made it all the more delicious. I began to revel in recalling minute details of sight and sound, taste and smell, image and emotion. I told her of my first impressions of South America when I got off the plane in São Paulo: of the stifling heat and humidity, the moist ripe smell of earth and jungle, and the way the horrendous humidity acted like a lens to focus the sunlight and roast one's flesh. I told her of the protest that fizzled after just a few days, the tiny band of friends I made, and the eventual disillusionment I felt when I realized that nothing we did made a difference for the rain forest, nor for my personal pain.

Lisa asked no questions while I talked. She appeared mesmerized by my account, and maybe it was her enraptured expression that lulled me so much that when I arrived at the part of my story I had never meant to tell—the part about the revelation or vision I received one night while sleeping in the open air under a mosquito net—I just kept going, as if my words had cast a spell over both of us.

The fact was, after living for several weeks with the constant assault of the jungle noises droning in my ears—all the unidentified swishings and scrapings and screechings—I stopped noticing them. The pungent smells of earth and bark likewise faded from my awareness, until I became as oblivious to them as I was to the stink of my own body in the tropical heat.

But on that single special night, three months into my stay, with no warning or prelude, the jungle suddenly became vivid again. I awoke from a deep sleep into a state of extreme disorientation. With a tinge of panic, I realized that I had utterly lost my bearings. Where was I? Why was I lying in a tent under a net with a cacophony of tropical night buzzing all around me? I lay there in mounting terror with the jungle saturating my senses until my ears actually began to tingle with all the secretive murmurings. My nose stung with the sweat of tree bark and jungle beasts. My tongue stiffened with the tang of mold and grass. My skin inhaled the moist rotten heat of hidden decay.

And I was sickened by the florid life all around me. For no cause that I could discern—and I tried long and hard afterward to divine a reason for it—I was suddenly *horrified* by the organic eruption that was the rain forest. The sole idea that I recalled from reading Sartre in college came to mind at once: *de trop*, "too much." The jungle was *too much*. It was too ripe, too juicy, too pungent, too sharp, too *alive*. That was the crux of the matter: it was the principle of life itself, bursting and blooming all around me, that was a horror.

After that, nothing could be the same. My acquaintances in the activist group, who liked to call themselves my friends but who in truth knew nothing about me, were shocked when I quit them without explanation and left the jungle to return to São Paulo. I flew back to the States and tried to reboot my life again, but this proved impossible when I discovered that the midnight vision from Brazil had accompanied me. Leaving the original scene of its onset merely brought the new perception home to inhere in the things that were more familiar to me, as I quickly understood when the oaks, elms, cedars, and walnut trees bristling from the Ozark hills began to inspire the same reaction as the rain forest. I couldn't stop thinking about the root systems of those trees, all twined and knotted like diseased fingers digging into the loamy earth. Nor could I stop thinking about the rodents and birds nesting in those trees, and the snakes and insects toiling in secrecy beneath the matted forest floors, and below even that, the worms and grubs tilling the soil, consigning the whole pungent mass of it back to a primal black organic mash.

After awhile I uprooted again and drifted westward into Oklahoma, then northward and westward into Kansas and Colorado, following no plan. Eventually I found myself in Utah and in the presence of Dr. Malcolm Pryor, professor of vertebrate paleontology at Utah State, who hired me on the spot, on a pure whim, to serve as his informal assistant. I had no training in paleontology or archaeology or any other relevant field. I brought no necessary skills. My only job was to help with the grunt work in his ongoing excavation in the desert land outside Vernal. But he asked very few questions, apparently seeing in me a suitably solitary temperament for the lonely dry work ahead.

It turned out he was right. The arid land of the Utah desert proved a perfect environment for me, since its primary resident life was of the scaly, scrubby kind: junipers and sagebrush, lizards and vultures, the occasional mule deer and coyote. I could forget about the grubs and worms there, where the earth was a baked desert crust. My ontological panic attacks gradually faded as I spent my days helping to uncover carcasses long dead and buried, the remains of lives long desiccated and sealed off from the danger of rot and decay. I often felt a great yearning, so sweet it was painful, when I gazed at the rough desert floor and thought of the dead husks that slept comfortably beneath it.

And the memory of these husks brought me to the present. I stopped talking abruptly. The respirator pumped dryly next to the bed. Paul's face appeared darker than it had before, as if he had somehow heard me speaking from the blackness inside his head. As the spell of my words dissipated, I realized that I didn't know how much of my story had actually passed my lips. I had grown so absorbed in my personal recollections that I might have revealed far more than I had intended.

When I looked at Lisa, she was watching me with a mixed expression of pain and something else, something that might have been wonder or terror. I feared she might be doing her mind-reading thing again, and this sparked my anger.

"So what do you think of me?" I said. "What do you think of your long-lost Stephen, who always wanted to be as spiritual as you and Paul?"

The idea that I might have misjudged her—that I might have *always* misjudged her—did not occur to me until she began to cry again. This time her tears were for me. And they were beautiful to behold.

"Oh, Stephen. Oh, my God. I'm so sorry." She sat with her hands in her lap and her head bowed. When she finally looked up, her cheeks glistened and her eyes flashed with a crystal film. "We both loved you. We both wanted you to stay. I know you only left because we betrayed you. I feel like everything you've suffered is our fault."

These astonishing words hung unchallenged in the air for maybe five seconds before the night nurse entered the room to check on Paul's vitals. She was an unpleasant-looking woman with a pear-shaped body and a face full of acne, and she gave me a look of muted disgust, as if she couldn't fully accept that someone with my ragged appearance would be sitting up late with an injured friend. I kept my face blank as she told Lisa that Paul was still stable, while Lisa, for her part, struggled to compose herself and show proper politeness.

When the nurse had departed and we were alone again, the moment of intimacy had passed, and whatever Lisa had been going to say next was lost. I tried not to care, but even when I had retreated back behind the mask of my habitual apathy, I couldn't shake the feeling that I would have wanted to hear her words, even though I knew they could have done nothing but increase my suffering.

4

By three A.M. my hallucinations had returned. We had sat in total silence for over an hour, and my strung out state finally brought me to the point of full-blown delirium. With horror I realized that I was slipping into that awful state of warped perception again.

In one of the visions, I saw glowing bands of light connecting Lisa's heart to mine. The same golden strands also connected me to Paul, and Paul to her. We formed, I saw, three corners of a web of spiritual energy, but instead of peace or joy, the vision brought only shock and revulsion. The last thing I wanted was to be connected to these two people in this intimate fashion, and I fought violently against the image.

My struggles only increased the force of the vision, which was soon joined by a second one in which Paul and Lisa appeared more plantlike than human. The transition was not subtle. I simply looked away from her once, and when I looked back at her again, her face had disappeared and been replaced by a beautiful multicolored blossom. When I looked down at Paul, the same change had occurred. Instead of looking into his face I was looking into a thick nest of lush, satiny petals. Their bodies, too, had transformed, and were now delicate stalks of deep green, encased in a translucent covering of cellulose skin that revealed a clear liquid circulating through a network of veins. When I looked down at my own body, I saw only a blackened trunk, like the remains of a twisted tree after a forest fire. The blips and beeps of the medical monitors morphed into screeches and caws, and soon I couldn't tell whether I was still seated in a hospital room or lying in a tent in the rain forest.

After an hour of feeling immobilized by these impressions—which, despite their surface beauty, were no less nightmarish than my earlier vision of Lisa's darkening eyes—I awoke as if from a dream and arose on shaky legs to see if the night nurse was still at her desk. A moment later, after bidding Lisa goodnight (and noticing with relief that her face had returned to normal), I followed the nurse down the hallway to a hospitality room, feeling Lisa's gaze caress my back the entire time as she stepped into the hallway to watch me depart.

The hospitality room had a bed and bathroom, but I had left my bag of clean clothes out in the van, so I didn't shower. I just stretched out on the bed fully clothed and tried to sleep. But the mattress was hard and the pillow stale, and I soon arose and went to the bathroom for a drink of water. It tasted bitter and musty out of the paper cup, and I poured most of it down the drain. When I returned to bed, all I could think to do was to get in my van and leave, or else go back and sit with Lisa again. Both options were intolerable.

Finally, I did something I had not done for years: I laid the pillow on the floor in front of the bed and seated myself on it. Then I crossed my legs in a rather stiff half-lotus, having lost most of my former limberness from lack of practice, and focused on my breathing.

Everything slowed down after only a few minutes. All night I had been feeling like an out-of-control river rafter being swept along by a dangerous current. Now I started to feel safely aloof from the situation, and a familiar inner image resurfaced from my former meditative days: that I was safely distanced from my troubles, tucked away in a protected cave from whence I could survey my inner and outer landscape with a semblance of objectivity.

I spent maybe half an hour savoring the sweet sense of distance. Then the ache in my legs became too much to bear, and I had to stop. When I arose and stretched, the feeling of restlessness returned instantly.

I did not consciously choose to avoid Lisa when I ventured out into the hallway. I merely happened to notice a sign on the wall announcing the presence of a chapel at the end of the next wing, and before I knew what was happening, my feet were carrying me in that direction.

The irony of my intended destination was not lost on me. From informal Zen meditation to Roman Catholic hospital chapel in less than five minutes. It truly was a night for mysterious conflicts and connections.

5

I spent nearly half an hour alone in the chapel before Lisa found me. My first impression upon entering it was a sense of awe. I had known the hospital was a Catholic institution, but that hadn't prepared me for the elaborateness of what revealed itself before me. The very word "chapel" was inadequate, for the place was more like an entire church built seven stories above ground level. I stared up at the chiseled arches and saints, traced the lines of the sacred figures with their frozen gestures of holiness, and experienced a palpable sense of the numinous spilling out from the gray stonework like a physical wave.

After basking for a while in the glow of the rich ornamentation, I began to skirt the perimeter of the church and study the depictions of the Stations of the Cross mounted high on the walls. This was an element of Catholic spirituality that had always fascinated me. I studied Jesus' face in each scene, observed his expression of intense suffering, and tried to imagine the awesome depth of his sensations, both spiritual and physical, during the experience of his passion.

At last I paused before the altar, turned my face upward toward the giant crucifix where Christ hung in agony on the front wall, and then backed away and sat down on the third pew, where at last the enormity of recent events came home to me. My abrupt transition from the Utah desert to this hushed place of holy reflection seemed positively unreal, as did the fact of Lisa's waiting for me in a hospital room nearby where Paul lay dead for all practical purposes, having been reduced to a mindless engine running only by means of external aid.

In the silence, a memory spontaneously resurfaced: of Paul sitting before me on a cushion in the spare bedroom of our shared rental home, which we had decked out as a Zendo. He was smiling at me with that good-natured expression of peace and wisdom that I had come to cherish. And he was saying, "It's so easy. This is all there is to it. *Now,* outside of your head and right here with the in-your-face reality of the present moment, is the whole point. There's nothing secret about it. Enlightenment is like a big, friendly joke." When I balked and said it was still beyond my ability to grasp, he laughed, squeezed my shoulder, and said "That's nothing but enlightenment, too." And amazingly, he actually made me feel better about my spiritual dullness. I felt lighter in his presence, more alive and aware, more capable of understanding the things I had always longed to understand. He really seemed to regard his advanced state as something not to be coveted, but to be shared freely with dullards like me, and more than anything else this marked him in my eyes as the icon of everything I hoped to become.

The memory dissipated when I sensed the presence of someone else in the chapel with me. Her perfume rode the breeze ahead of her and reached me before she did. Then she was sitting beside me and I was raising my head from my hands. I hadn't been crying, but it had been something like that. My face felt twisted into knots by the forces struggling behind it.

"I thought I'd find you here," she said. "I could see it in your face. You needed to get away and reflect."

It was really too much, the way she read me as if we had been together only yesterday. Somehow she looked even prettier when I was angry with her.

"*What* could you see in my face, Lisa? How the hell do you always do that?"

"I wish I could tell you. I really do." Her voice trembled and her eyes begin to glitter with tears again. "It's like seeing another level to things. Do you remember learning to read when you were young? First there were just black marks and shapes scattered on a page. Then, like magic, they started to mean something. It's kind of like that."

"Well, it scares me. It *always* scared me." I turned my face away, searching for neutral space, and found I was now staring at Christ's nail-pierced feet on the large crucifix hanging above us.

"And you don't think it scares *me?*" she said. "Do you want to guess how much more of what's going on with Paul right now I can see than you can? Do you think I *want* to be able to see where he's going? Do you think I like seeing him drifting away?" She was crying for real now, and I had nothing to say in return.

"Please," she said at last, struggling for control, "I have to ask you something. It sounds insane. I know it will sound insane, especially since I know how much you must hate me. But I have to ask." She moved closer to me on the pew, and I tried not to smell her perfume or look at her breasts.

"First," she said, "I have to tell you something. Please just listen. Please don't make up your mind until I'm finished. Can you promise me that?" I avoided her eyes but said yes. Her breath was still labored from crying, and I could feel it on my face and hands, hot and moist, like a wet feather.

"Paul and I have been growing in new directions since you left. Our spiritual lives have taken a new turn. We've been exploring some things you may have heard of, certain pagan traditions with ancient roots. They're all about loving the earth and learning to feel at home with her. We've been learning to experience nature as a kind of enchanted garden that's powered by spirit and permeated with love." She eyed me then, and for once, in a moment of insight so intense it caused my breath to catch, I knew what she was going to say before she said it: "I think what we've been cultivating is the exact opposite of the vision you had in the rain forest."

My revulsion was immediate. She had no right to speak of my experience. It was mine, my own special revelation and cross to bear. Every instinct I possessed told me that I didn't want to hear where she was going with this, especially not if she was going to try and demonstrate some connection between what I had experienced in South America and my spiritual past with her and Paul. But in the face of her fresh-wept beauty, and amid the holy hush of the chapel, I felt strangely helpless to protest.

"I really am afraid that what you've experienced is our fault," she continued. "I'm only just now learning about it, but there's a web of invisible interconnections between us all. It's so intricate and beautiful. It's like a spiritual network that joins everything on the planet. Sometimes these connections are especially strong, like the ones between you and Paul and me." I thought of my hallucination of glowing cords earlier, but said nothing.

"I think," she said, "that when you left, we may have accidentally sent a terrible energy rushing in your direction. I think when Paul and I started trying to fall in love with the earth so soon after we hurt you the way we did, you received the opposite end of it. I'm not really sure how these things work. I may not even be sure what I'm trying to say right now. But I think you ended up seeing the opposite of everything we were trying to understand. When you described your vision in the jungle, it sounded exactly like the dark side of the beauty we're seeking."

And there it was again, that cold fist squeezing the breath out of my chest. I barely had time to register it before she did an extraordinary thing: without breaking the rhythm of her words, she reached out a hand and laid it on my thigh. It was a simple gesture, but it sent shockwaves rolling through my entire being. More specifically, it sent tingles crawling up into my groin, and a long-buried part of me suddenly lit up, glowing like a spark, at the thought that maybe, just maybe, Lisa's reasons for searching me out and asking me to come home had been more complex than I had suspected.

"I'm not asking you to believe all this," she was saying. "I'm not trying to convince you. I just want you to know how we've thought of these things over the past few years, and how we've regretted doing what we did. Earlier tonight, when you told me what you went through, I realized the extent of the damage we've done." After a pause, she scooted even closer, and my slight spark of arousal ignited into a small flame. It was fascinating, really, to watch it all happening from a vantage point of objectivity. For I still felt that the greater part of me was tucked away back in that safe meditative cave hidden high up on a riverbank. My flame of arousal, now growing into a bona fide blaze of lust, was something happening at a distance, something I was observing as a spectator. So was Lisa's beautiful face moving ever closer to mine, and also the feel of her delicate red-nailed fingers gripping my thigh with growing urgency. I knew the feeling of remoteness and safety had to be an illusion. But this didn't take away from the heady reality of its seeming, nor from the pleasure I derived from it.

She was speaking to me in a seductive whisper now: "But I do want to ask you something. Just listen to me before you decide. There's a way for us to get Paul back. The three of us share a special energy. I know you've felt it. Maybe you've even seen it. The thing is, we can *use* that energy. You and I can call out to Paul, wherever he is. We can send him a message. We can light a beacon to show him the way home, and we can give him the strength to make the journey." When she batted her eyes and assumed a kind of coy expression, her meaning was instantly clear, and the nature of her request would have been obvious even without her next words: "All we have to do is reconnect, you and I, on the most intimate level." When her red lips curled in what might have been the faintest of wicked smiles, I felt waves of warmth crash through me.

"Please," she said. "It will heal you, too. It will take away the vision of *too much*. We'll balance in the middle, and Paul and I

will take back the energy we aimed at you. You can have your life back." If she did not send the next words directly into my brain as a telepathic transmission, then she must have spoken them without moving her lips: *You can have me back, too.*

By that point she had no need to say anything else, for I was hopelessly hers. She had worked her magic with consummate skill, and I was consumed with lust. And what I lusted after was as much my former self and my own redemption as it was Lisa and her body. I wanted to possess her and regain my soul in a single stroke. And if we could help Paul in the process, in some obscure way that made no sense to me, then so much the better.

These thoughts and desires whirled within me as she took me by the hand and led me from the chapel. The giddy feeling helped to augment the sensation of spectatorship, and so it seemed almost like a cinematic special effect when I experienced—I actually *experienced,* as a physical perception—the hallowed atmosphere of the chapel folding back in on itself like a flower, preparing to lie in wait for the next soul-hungry supplicant. I seemed to glide above the floor when she pulled me down the hallway and toward the room I had entered as a stranger only a few short hours ago.

The floating feeling continued until she turned to face me beside Paul's bed, where I thought suddenly of the prehistoric bone lying partially uncovered back in the desert. The memory brought back a sweet stab of pain, and there was a moment of confusion as my resolve threatened to come unraveled. What in God's name was I doing? What did I think it would accomplish? How could it end any way but badly? I realized everything was happening too fast, it was all rushing ahead with a seemingly inbuilt logic that was in fact completely irrational.

But then her hands were on me, pulling me down to the floor, and they banished all other concerns. Her flesh-and-blood warmth and softness were irresistibly real. The memory of the dry-desert bone with its accompanying dry-desert sadness couldn't compete with this vivid reality. "Stepping out of your head and into the reality of the present is the whole point," I heard Paul's remembered voice saying. Common sense was out the window, too. I couldn't think about the fact that the hospital staff might walk in on us. I couldn't think about Paul lying comatose beside us on the bed. I could think only of the heat of her body, and the pressure of her touch, and the wetness of her lips, like the petals of a flower in the rain forest, kissing first my eyes and then my mouth, drawing me out of myself and into a fleshy reality that was far more ecstatic than any experience of isolated spectatorship could ever be.

6

The flow of time became a river of burning gold as everything went all liquid and surreal. The sound of my breath filled the whole universe like salt water sizzling on a cosmic ocean shore. I had never been so sexually inflamed. All my repressed rage and horror flowed through my limbs like a torrent, and focused itself on the burning point of contact between us. She was on top of me, and I grappled violently with her back and buttocks, pulling her so tightly against me that I worried I might snap her in two like a doll. She received it all without complaint. In fact, her passion, if anything, surpassed mine. She swiped her tongue over my lips and eyelids. Her nails scored parallel lines down my neck and chest. Her hair whipped my face like the wings of a frenzied bird.

When she had her orgasm, she arched so violently that I thought my hipbones would break. A moment later my own climax sent my head spasming backwards, and the crack of the floor tile against my skull exploded stars into my vision. I lost consciousness briefly.

When I returned to myself, she had risen and was bending naked over Paul's unconscious form. The air was chilly against my cooling flesh, and my eyes felt hot and gritty. I watched her caress Paul's face and speak tender words to him. Her nudity, which only moments before had been a veritable feast for my starving eyes, now looked slick and rubbery. She cooed to him as if he were a baby, imploring him to come back from whatever dark dimension had swallowed him. Left to myself and my thoughts, there was no way to feel that I was somehow outside or above the situation. It was all too real, and I was sickened at the thought of what I had just done.

But when I moved to sit up and cover myself, I found to my astonishment that my limbs were stiff as a corpse's. My arms felt as if they were shackled with lead weights. It took all my effort just to raise my head an inch. An invisible weight rested on my chest like an anvil, constricting my ribcage and forcing me to struggle for breath. Even as I began to worry that the crack to my head might have really injured me, the physical constriction gave way to a deeper one, and with astonished horror I felt something dragging my spirit down into a bottomless well.

Sex had never been an ultimately pleasurable experience for me. The feeling of lassitude afterward, as if I had been attacked by some kind of parasite and drained to the point of death, had invariably spoiled it. I had always felt like a walking dead man for days afterward. It had taken me years to connect my occasional feelings of an almost lethal sluggishness with my rare sexual encounters, and once I had made the connection, I had determined to try and forget that side of life altogether.

Now, it was as if all those former spiritual sappings had been mere preludes to this one great stealing of energy. I was falling backwards down a mine shaft. The ceiling receded. Lisa's naked form grew taller above me. The wheezing of the respirator reverberated like whispers in a cathedral. The heaviness in my limbs began to dissipate, not because I was coming to life but because I was plummeting inward and leaving my body behind.

Above me, beside me, Lisa looked more and more like an elongated figure in a surrealist painting. Still leaning over Paul's body, she reached down a rubbery stick-arm and probed between her thighs, gathering some of our fluids onto her fingers. Then she raised them to his lips and continued to whisper things that no longer sounded like language, but like a wordless chant, harsh and melodic.

A moment later his hand twitched. The rhythm of the respirator grew more insistent as it struggled with a competing rhythm. And Lisa uttered a sharp cry of joy.

The room continued to recede. I continued to fall backwards into a well of infinite seclusion. And yet I saw and heard everything around me. There was no end to the receding, no far edge of exile where I would find myself cut off from all contact with the external world. It was as if a hole had been punched in the back of my private cave to reveal an infinite, sucking void on the other side. The thought arose that in the hell of black emptiness opening out below me, I would not be allowed even the small comfort of forgetfulness. I would not be allowed to reside alone in a dank spiritual dungeon where I could forget that I had once tasted the air of a rain forest and smelled the dust of a desert. There would be nothing but distance—distance between the world and me, distance between everything I had ever loved and the possibility of grasping it, distance between my innate longing for spiritual wholeness and my ability to pursue it.

The restraint on my limbs let go abruptly. I blinked and rose to my elbows. Lisa was rushing to put on her clothes and throwing mine at me. In his bed, Paul was stirring with ever more vigorous motions. I knew I had just participated in some sort of rite, but I was totally ignorant of its nature. I only knew that my life force had been transferred to Paul, and that he had gladly accepted it. For this was, after all, nothing but the logical extension of the theft he had committed three years ago. The little moment of happiness unfolding beside me, where he had opened his eyes, and where he and Lisa were touching each other's faces with shared tears of reunion, was not meant for me. I was excluded by a gulf that now separated me not only from them but from everyone and everything, from all of the ten thousand things that made up this vast and dismal universe.

I rose on legs that belonged to a dead man and finished putting on my clothes. With the eyes of a dead man, I surveyed for a final time the sight of a shared love that should have been mine. And with these new eyes, I *annihilated* it all. I brought the sight within me and felt it slip away instantly, back through that hole in the cave wall, where it sparked out into ambient nothingness and disappeared forever. No memory was left, no feeling, no emotion or reaction to the things before me. The sight of Paul and Lisa was being born anew in my consciousness with each passing instant, and with each new instant I was devouring it and watching it be reborn again. It was like swallowing an ocean and finding that I was still thirsty. It was like eating the world and finding that I was still ravenous. I watched the two of them press down under the weight of my gaze, trembling with an unknown terror that confused them both, clinging to each other for warmth and comfort. Then I turned and left the room without looking back.

The hallway was still dim with nighttime illumination. The nurse still sat reading her paperback novel in a pale aureole of lamplight. When I looked at her, she shifted in her seat and glanced about her with a look of confusion and fear. She did not appear to see me when I passed right by her. I shared the elevator to the ground floor with an old black man pushing a janitor's cart. He appeared not to notice my presence, not even when I looked directly at him and saw his face blanch with dread as the visual impression of him passed through me on its way to everlasting oblivion. When I exited through the lobby and passed several people bound on early morning errands, none of them noticed me, but they gasped and nearly stumbled when I took the sight of them into myself.

A light rain was falling in the parking lot. I paused just outside the sliding glass doors to lift my face to the murky sky, where a delicate flash of lightning outlined a mountain of dark clouds. A moment later, a rumble of thunder rattled the windows behind me. I stood there with the rain spattering my face and hands like tappings on a distant roof. And from my fixed position there in the midst of it all, rooted at the center of my perceptual universe like the eye of a cyclone, I *annihilated* everything: the clouds and thunder, windows and pavement, even the slick yellow reflections of the street lamps in the myriad puddles dotting the asphalt. The depth inside me was bottomless, and the life around me to be devoured, infinite.

The rain kept falling for hours while the eastern sky behind me grew gray with the approaching dawn, and while I stood looking at everything with a new pair of eyes that would never grow old, and that would accompany me to deserts or rain forests or wherever I might go next, devouring and renewing all things in my path, and forever finding them insufficient.

The dawn, when it came, was cold.

Blackbrain Dwarf

But of *course* everything was all wrong. Derek knew it the minute he opened his eyes and perceived the vileness resounding from every angle and object in the room. Indeed, how could it be otherwise in a red-glowing world where *the stench of blacksouls mounts to a deadening sky?*

Then he awoke fully and realized he was dream-thinking again. It took even longer than usual for the waking world to slide into focus while his psyche struggled to flush away the dregs of the putrescent dreamland that had lately been casting an ever-lengthening shadow across his days. And even after the mental purification was otherwise accomplished, when he could think, feel, look, and smell without the black-red reality of the other-world interposing itself between his awareness and the prosy solidity of the white-walled master bedroom of his two-thousand-square-foot suburban house—even then, he still caught a glimpse of wrongness pressing in at every conceivable crack, hitching a ride on the fiery beams of sunlight that bled through the drapes, peering with beady black eyes through the dark spots in the mottled wooden texture of the bureau next to the bed.

It radiated with an especial intensity from his left side. He turned his head and regarded Linda as she lay next to him, still encased in sleep, wrapped in a bedsheet cocoon with her pale lips parted and a half-snore dragging in the back of her throat. He felt his testicles draw up as if in anticipation of a blow. Surely, he reasoned with himself, his recent inability to tolerate his wife's presence had nothing to do with her, and everything to do with his own secret disorder, whose most dramatic manifestation occurred in those regular oneiric journeys through a land of rotten wrongness.

When he stood, the familiar creak of the loose floorboard beside the bed rippled up through his leg and into his groin like a snake seeking a warm cave. He shivered and shuffled to the bathroom to urinate and shower.

Standing in front of the toilet with his boxer briefs pulled down, he considered calling the office to tell Candace, his secretary, that he was ill and would be staying home that day. The idea of temporary seclusion was exceptionally attractive in light of the fact that Wilfred J. Tyson was his first appointment of the morning, scheduled for nine A.M. sharp "or I'm gonna stab and gutfuck somebody"—as Tyson himself had phrased it in his charming mid-Texas manner—and that the meeting would almost certainly spell the death of Derek's legal career. But then he thought of the maddening wrongness that still flitted like a cloud of black wings about the edges of everything, and found to his surprise and semi-relief that his dreadful unpreparedness for the meeting seemed, well, not so very important. Why not just go ahead and see the thing through to its limping conclusion? "Why not?" he said aloud, and then blinked at the cavelike reverberation of his voice off the slick porcelain surfaces.

In the shower his eyesight went momentarily gray, as if someone had switched off the light. He came to himself crouched in the tub with the hot water beating against his back and clouds of steam billowing up around him like fog from a midnight lake. Afterward, when he stood before the sink and shaved, his hand was trembling. The blade nicked his throat and drew a bead of blood, which transfixed him with its crimson-on-snow vibrancy. A black-winged shadow fluttered in the corner of his eye. He caught a microflash vision of something he had seen recently, perhaps while crouched in the shower—crouched low and happy in the swirling mist with the hot water beading on his back, *the happy dark heat, pulsating feather of foulness*—

The faucet sang a tinkling little tune. Water spiraled merrily down the drain of the pedestal sink. Lather and whiskers littered the porcelain. As if in a trance, he wiped it all off and used the same towel on his face, hardly feeling the scrape of soft cotton against his skin.

He sat at the kitchen table while Linda poured some sort of whole-grain, prepackaged breakfast substance into a plastic bowl. "What's wrong, honey?" she asked, setting the bowl before him and taking a seat at the opposite chair.

"Nothing," he said. A single spoonful told him the cereal was stale and the milk had tipped over into the pungent no-man's-land between liquid and solid. But he sucked on the mushy mass anyway, savoring it with a grimace, and found he couldn't tell whether the staleness and sourness resided in the food or on his tongue. And still the tingling buffer from the bathroom, like a buzzing wall of bees, remained interposed between him and the external world.

"You're not still worried about your meeting, are you?" Linda reached out and tousled his dark hair. "You've worked on it all week. If anything, you're overprepared. Don't worry. You'll do fine."

"Sure," he said. "Right. Like I said, nothing's wrong." She went to rinse the dishes while saying something about getting together with Steve for dinner that night. He ignored her chatter and watched her body closely from behind. She was wrapped in a blue terrycloth bathrobe, the fuzzy fabric pulled tight against her rump. The memory of her naked body arose unbidden from some black well of the past, from the mental ruins of another lifetime when he had actually craved the sight of her white skin and soft-rounded curves. Hot shadows rustled at the edges of his eyes and brain. His stomach lurched and squirted a jet of sourness up into his throat.

His face was a carven mask when she kissed him at the door. She remained close for a moment afterwards, her ghastly ape's face thrust forward into his own, gazing quizzically into his eyes. "Don't forget," she said. When he said nothing, she helpfully clarified. "Steve. Dinner. With us. Tonight. Remember?"

He managed something like a nod, and then he turned away and walked slowly out to his car, probing the fresh cut on his throat with a trembling hand, feeling her planted there behind him and watching him from the open doorway, remembering the dream-thoughts whispering in the steam while he crouched low like some glowering little creature of fable.

The commute to work was a breathtaking kaleidoscope of wrongness. In just five years' time the small town had exploded into a thriving suburbanesque city, complete with a raging glut of unwonted traffic, resulting in a permanent nightmare of highway construction that seemed to Derek like the engineering equivalent of emergency angioplasty—a metaphor that he saw completed in the arterial pulsing of vehicles, start-stop, start-stop, through the various detours and halts of the whole bloody-tangled mess. He often reflected that maybe it would have been better just to let the old town die quietly of heart failure instead of reviving and reinventing it for the flashier fate of death by nervous seizure.

Halfway to his office he switched on the radio. The tuner scanned the stations like—and the simile seemed natural—a schizophrenic mind surveying the spectrum of its inner anarchy. Pink Floyd and Erik Satie serenaded him in five-second bursts, followed by Kansas and Count Basie. A preacher with a northern accent spoke up momentarily, asking, "Who knows what is truly human except the human spirit within a man?" and then answering, "So also no one comprehends what is truly God's except the Spirit of God." A southern-sounding preacher shouted from the next station, pounding an unseen pulpit and obviously relishing his words: "Their slain shall be cast out, and the stench of their corpses shall rise! The mountains shall flow with their blood! All the host of heaven shall rot away, and the skies roll up like a scroll!"

The tuner tripped ahead yet again, cutting the preacher off in mid-jeremiad. Derek punched the button to stop it at the next station; the changes were hurting his head. For the remainder of the commute he listened to a man speaking in measured, cultured tones about an esoteric topic whose import must have been explained earlier, at the top of the hour, and whose overall gist was thus obscure. "These and many words and names," the man said, "do not tell us *what* it is, but they do confirm *that* it is. They also point to its mysteriousness. We cannot know what exactly we are referring to because its nature remains shadowy, revealing itself mainly in hints, intuitions, whispers, and the sudden urges and oddities that disturb your life that we might continue to call symptoms. That the daimon has your interest at heart may be the part of the theory particularly hard to accept."

Derek's office was a nondescript architectural approximation composed of beige stonework and dark-tinted windows, squatting in semi-privacy on the outskirts of a street somewhere near the business district. It looked like wrongness personified as he drove up and parked. The fluorescent lights and cardboard ceiling panels were an ache to his eyeballs when he walked through the front door, and the electronic chime drilled into his molars with a nauseating pain.

Candace, she of the overpainted eyes and gargantuan breasts, looked up and wished him a cheery good morning from her spot behind the reception counter. As always, he found it hard to remember that she was only twenty-two years old when her appearance and demeanor rendered her overtly ageless in the exotic manner he had come to associate with raw female sexuality. She asked, "Would you like some coffee, Mr. Warner?"

He said no and then offered, "Thanks." She smiled and continued looking at him. She was wearing the green bodice dress again, the one that encased her breasts like a second skin and gapped dramatically at the neck whenever she reached for pens or paperclips or even moved to brush back a lock of her cherry-auburn hair. He paused for a long moment, and then he was *crouched in the shower with blacksmear eyes, scalding in steam, beating blackwater*—and then he blinked, turned, and walked down the hallway.

Thirty seconds later he ran to the speakerphone in the conference room, punched the call button with a trembling finger, and demanded, "Where are the case files?" He waited. "Candace? Hello?"

The speakerphone blipped and then her voice said, "—don't know, Mr. Warner. I haven't been back there yet today. Maybe the cleaning service moved them?"

"I thought they worked Fridays, not Thursdays."

Blip. "—just changed their schedule this week. I'm sorry, I meant to tell you." She had never learned to wait for the intercom function to engage fully before she spoke, even though he had explained it to her a dozen times. He felt like throttling her.

He turned from the phone without replying, waited to hear the *click* of the connection's closing, and uttered a firm, quiet "Fuck." Then he went into a low-grade panic. A crashing, banging search of every closet, drawer, and box in the conference and storage rooms, and also a frantic dig through the dumpster out back, turned up nothing

He returned to the conference room gasping and shaking and wondering how it was possible for fifteen manila folders, all bearing the name "Tyson" printed in prominent black marker, simply to disappear. No one on the cleaning crew could possibly have wanted them. A thief would have taken something else. Candace was afraid even to look at them, so severely had he threatened her about their importance. His thoughts accelerated to whirlwind speed while he cringed under the smug gaze of the leatherbound law books lining the dark wooden shelves in regal rows.

He bowed his head and reached up to massage his eyeballs. Splotchy colored lights blossomed in the darkness behind his lids, shimmering like luminescent fog above the surface of a vast reedy lake—

—and then it was night in the conference room, dark and deserted, and a misshapen Dwarf was entering through a strange angle at the intersection of two walls, waddling over to the table, seizing the files, and spiriting them away to a misshapen kingdom on the other side of that otherworldly access point where dark winds howled over a black corroded plain and Derek *crushed in the shower, inkydark eyes beading blood upon his throat*—

An explosion of glass brought him back to himself. He saw

crystalline shards littering the carpet next to a mangled lampshade. Then he realized a table lamp had been flung against one of the bookcases. Moreover, the culprit was his own out-stretched hand.

The speakerphone blipped. "—you there? Mr. Warner? Are you all right?"

His throat erupted and his mouth worked without his con-scious volition. "For Christ's sake, of course I'm here!"

A pause. And then of course, naturally, he should have known, her voice came back after another *blip* to say "—is here for his ap-pointment. He says he knows he's early but he has several other things waiting for him."

So. Tyson was standing right there at the counter with Can-dace, probably eyeing her epic cleavage and smirking at the fact that he had heard Derek's outburst. There was no remedy for it, nothing to do but go ahead and see this thing through. The very helplessness of the thought rekindled a spark of the comforting resignation he had embraced earlier at the house. As he walked up the hallway to face his fate, he felt his brain being gnawed from behind by the hallucinatory memory of the distorted Dwarf and its barren wasteland of a world.

"Morning, Derek!" Tyson drawled at the sight of him. "I hope I'm not too early. Sounds like you're having one hell of a day." He grinned and stuck out a ring-encrusted hand, which Derek grasped automatically. Tyson's bushy brown eyebrows and mil-lion-dollar tan, his hand-tailored suit and bolo tie, his chic os-trich-leather boots and cowboy hat with its gaudy Texas star embroidered on the front, were all unchanged. So was his manner, as Derek observed when the man refused to make eye contact with him while they shook hands, choosing instead to glance to the side and give Candace a rakish wink. It was altogether typical behavior for the sixties-ish oil tycoon.

Derek also realized for the first time that the man could un-doubtedly take Candace right then and there if he wanted to, right on the reception counter, despite his craggy, unhandsome face with which he somehow managed to radiate charm through sheer force of attitude. Derek imagined them coupling like sweaty animals under the fluorescent lights, in front of the plate-glass windows, gasping and growling while he himself crouched in the conference room *a greedy-eyed Dwarf crunching bones in the blackdark—*

"Fine, everything's fine," he heard his voice say in a smooth professional tone. "Come on back, Mr. Tyson." He led the obscenely rich oil man back to the cramped little office with the "D. Warner" nameplate on the door, wondering for the thousandth time why somebody like Wilfred J. Tyson would pick a small-time lawyer like himself for legal representation—and one who lived three states away, no less, more than five hundred miles from the city where Tyson Oil was based. He had long thought the answer must lie in those magically vanished files, which detailed with marvelous clarity Tyson's shady business dealings and financial misrepresentations. A small-time lawyer located so very far outside the circles that Tyson normally inhabited was so much less conspicuous than his big-time, big-city counterparts.

Or maybe the man just got off on dealing with lesser beings that he could manipulate and humiliate. Derek had never been able to decide which of the two explanations seemed more likely.

He seated himself in his leather executive chair and motioned for Tyson to pick one of the fabric-upholstered client versions. They faced each other over the desk, both of them waiting for Derek to say something. The question didn't need to be asked, of course. He knew Tyson was there for an account, delivered in person, of how Derek had engineered a legal miracle to rescue his client from the consequences of his latest dishonest dealings. And indeed, Derek had worked for weeks and managed to come up with an absolute ringer of a plan. That was the other possible angle to explain Tyson's retaining of him, since in his own milieu, on his own level, Derek was a young hotshot-on-the-rise.

But hotshot or not, the whole issue had become, in one fell swoop, utterly moot and meaningless. The full understanding of this fact came only now, as he sat staring helplessly into Tyson's hawkish eyes. The files were gone—whether to Dwarf World or a more prosaic locale didn't matter—and with them had gone all chance of success, and now Derek, too, was waiting for his own words, waiting for some sort of brilliant verbal song and dance to erupt spontaneously from his mouth. It *had* to come, or else he was finished, and not just career-wise. The consequences of disappointing this man would surely be severe. Tyson was famous not only for his refusal to tolerate failure but for his swiftness in punishing the responsible parties.

But of course, naturally, the saving words didn't come. How *could* such words emerge into a world where absolutely everything, from Derek's framed law diploma hanging on the wall behind him like a grinning accusation, to his pathetic desire to please this unpleasant man, to his lust for an air-headed, nubile secretary, to the walking corpse of a wife who waited for him at home like an undead symbol of all the wrong choices he had made in life—where everything, all of it, every last item and element, reeked to the skies of *wrongness?*

Abruptly, like the arrival of a perfumed breeze, the buzzing, tingling barrier that had encased him earlier in the morning reappeared and began to isolate him from the room. He gasped and felt suddenly weightless. His mouth opened, and it was just as if he needed to cough, to expel an odd blockage from his throat, but instead what came were words—words he had not chosen, words he could hardly believe he was hearing, and they were being spoken by *a blackbrain Dwarf crouched low in a bloody tub.*

The Dwarf said, "You fucking monster."

Tyson blinked. His expert smile faltered. He had been right in the middle of lighting a cigar, and now the flame sprouted uselessly from the shiny gold lighter he held in his right hand. He removed the cigar from his mouth and said, "Excuse me?"

"I said I lost the files. I said you're going to prison. I said your life is over." Derek smiled with the Dwarf. "You fucking monster."

Tyson's smile faded completely. His thumb released the lighter button, snuffing the bright flame. And before the man's predictable disbelief and rage set in, before he began to sputter and curse and rant, Derek and the Dwarf were both pleased to note that their performance had elicited a real shock. Terror and bewilderment were still evident even now behind the blustering façade of Tyson's fury.

It was really astonishingly easy, this act of career suicide. Derek let the scene play out, listening passively to threats aimed at himself and his family, destruction called down upon everyone and everything he held dear, and finally violence sworn against his person. He said nothing through it all, allowing the Dwarf to witness and absorb the energy of the moment.

And finally it was over, and Tyson was rising from his chair red-faced and quivering. "You—you—" He actually sputtered as he searched for an epithet that would convey the depth of his outrage. Derek stood up. Tyson backed away. "You're gonna regret . . . You small-time son-of-a—"

"Have you ever carved wood?" Derek's voice chopped off Tyson's sputtering invective like a knife lopping off a limb, shocking them both into momentary silence. Derek hadn't known he was going to say such a thing, and now he listened with fascination to the speech that began to emerge from his mouth.

"When I was a boy," he said, "I used to pick up sticks in the forest around my house and carve them into all kinds of shapes. I especially liked to peel back the bark of a branch and see the white woodflesh. I liked the way it looked, the way it smelled, the way it felt." He reached up unthinkingly and began to massage the cut on his throat. "I haven't thought of that in years."

Tyson took a step backward toward the door. Derek looked down and saw that his own hand had picked up a sharp silver letter opener. He twirled it with his fingers, and it seemed just like a feather, a strange, silvery feather with a razor-edged quill. He looked back up at Tyson with the feather growing heavier in his hand. "What do you think it does to a person," he said, "when you squeeze what's inside him into the wrong shape?"

He moved as if to come around the desk. Tyson fled. A moment later Derek heard the sound of the front door bursting open and the electronic chime singing its meaningless song.

The phone blipped. "—Warner?" Candace's voice trembled so near and yet so very far away, all the way on the other side of the black electronic box that still linked him to the world he had inhabited only moments ago. "What—what happened?"

Before he could answer, the Dwarf told him that dangerous men would surely show up before long to vent the Texan's rage upon anybody they could find. So he said, "Listen, I'm taking the rest of the day off. Why don't you take off, too? Just make a sign and stick it in the window. Tell everybody we'll be back on Monday. Go shopping or something."

There was no reply for a moment. Then: *Blip.* "Is—is everything all right?" *My God,* he thought, *she actually used the phone correctly.* A surge of warmth flooded through him.

Then she said, "Derek?" It was the first time she had ever addressed him by his first name. Visions of huge-nippled breasts bursting through bodice and buttons spilled through his brain like candy. But his new inner sense told him unequivocally that he simply couldn't pursue them, he couldn't answer the invitation contained in her use of his name, because there was something else he had to do, a task whose fulfillment would exert a positively talismanic effect upon the shape of the remainder of his life.

He did not answer her query, instead leaving their final contact deliciously unresolved. He slipped out the back entrance, past the Dumpster and around the building to his car. As he drove away he watched the office building reflected in the rearview mirror. It appeared crusty and dilapidated, like an ancient, abandoned prison, and it stood in stark relief against a lurid sky full of weirdly churning clouds, all red and black and ashy like a charcoal drawing.

The commute home was a voyage through a transformed world. He sailed through the highway construction without a hitch, as if pulled along by an invisible current. Road crews paused in their labors to look up with startled expressions as he passed. Fellow motorists veered away and stared wide-eyed through their windows. The radio spoke from the same station he had left it on earlier, the same cultured male voice talking in the same quiet, smooth tones: ". . . a *diabolical* mysticism, a sort of religious mysticism turned upside down. The same sense of ineffable importance in the smallest events, the same texts and words coming with new meanings, the same voices and visions and leadings and missions, the same controlling extraneous powers; only this time the emotion is pessimistic: instead of consolations we have desolations; the meanings are dreadful; and the powers are enemies to life. The classic mysticism and these lower mysticisms spring from the same mental level, from that great subliminal or transmarginal region. That region contains every kind of matter: 'seraph and snake' abide there side by side."

By the time he reached his suburban subdivision, the chaotic sky was darkening toward early night. The clock on the dashboard read barely eleven in the morning, but it was as if a vast bowl of ash had been dumped on the heavens, and the world was gray and glaring with the strange intensity of a solar eclipse. All down the street, the trees lining the lawns of the neighboring houses were tossing their branches in the growing darkness like rows of monstrous lions shaking their manes.

The radio said, "Each of us is in reality an abiding psychical entity far more extensive than he knows—an individuality which can never express itself completely through any corporal manifestation. The Self manifests itself through the organism; but there is always some part of the Self unmanifested; and always, as it seems, some power of organic expression in abeyance or reserve."

He pulled into his driveway behind a familiar vehicle, an expensive sports car that belonged to someone he had once known, someone he had formerly called his friend. (*Steve,* the Dwarf whispered into the back of his brain.) When he stepped out of his own car, the stirrings of a mysterious hot breeze grazed his face and ruffled his hair. A muted roar began to creep across the sky from west to east, rolling and crackling like the aftershock of a thunderclap.

The current carried him across the lawn, around to the back of the house, where he approached the bedroom window and peered through it into the gloom. Two pale bodies were pressed together and pulsating with pleasure on the bed. (*Linda and Steve,* the Dwarf hissed.) He followed the current back around to the front of the house and entered through the door, making no effort to be quiet.

The television was turned on in the living room. The picture showed a white field of shivery static. A cultured male voice lectured through the speakers: "So long as we deal with the cosmic and the general, we deal only with the symbols of reality, but *as soon as we deal with private and personal phenomena as such, we deal with realities in the completest sense of the term.*"

"Linda!" he called. He plinked his keys loudly into the dish beside the door. "Linda! Come here!" He listened for a response. There was a stillness louder than a shout, and then from down the hallway: a whisper of bedsheets being pulled back, followed by the familiar creak of the floorboard beside his bed.

He crept down the hallway soundlessly, flowing like liquid night. At the doorway he paused for an instant, giving everyone time to prepare. Then he stepped inside and noticed simultaneously that the bathroom door was shut and the bedroom window open. The bedcovers were an obvious hasty job of pulling up and smoothing down. The blue drapes flapped and fluttered in the hot breeze.

The breeze was a whisper of sea spray. The room was a barren windswept plain located on the far side of an odd angular intersection; it was a misshapen cluster of towers tottering under a cold blood moon. He felt the letter opener in his hand twirling faster and faster. Had he indeed brought it with him and only now noticed it? The sound of the shower starting abruptly on the far side of the bathroom door mingled with the ocean-spray breeze and melded with the watery waves of blue light radiating from the drapes and cascading down the white walls in liquid ripples to give life to this cracked desert.

A delicate, tinny sound, like the scraping of an insect, began to tickle his ears, and he realized it was the bedside radio, switched on and dialed to a by-now familiar station. "The apprehension," it said in tiny insect tones, "of a coming dissolution, the grim conviction that this state was the last state of the conscious Self, the sense that I had followed the last thread of being to the verge of an abyss . . ."

Another sound intruded upon the voice, layering itself gently over the tiers of speech and oceanic flowing, wafting through the open window on the back of the swelling wind: the starting roar of an expensive automobile engine. But there was nowhere the driver could go. For Derek had parked behind him, and Derek was *a bloodhungry Dwarf crouched low in the dark,* and he carried in his huge hand *the pulsing feather of vengeance, plucked from a bloodangel's wing.*

The current lulled him to sleep even as it swept him down the hallway and out the front door onto the lawn, where a wide-eyed man in a foreign car was backing over the grass to get around the car blocking his exit. Derek saw, as if in a blissful vision, this man's mouth open to jabber and scream as the Dwarf reached out with that *blackplucked feather* and jabbed it through the Jaguar's open window again and again, plunging it repeatedly into a pulpy softness that felt like paradise as the black sky roared and the lions shook their manes in regal rows, lifting their heads to bellow and join voices with the storm.

Despite the sudden thunderstorm raging outside, Linda stayed in the shower until the water ran cold. She jumped with each flash of lightning and peal of thunder, remembering the urban myths about people being electrocuted in such situations. Finally, when she could stand it no longer, she stepped out and toweled off, shivering violently and struggling to catch her breath.

She considered jeans and a tee shirt but then changed her mind and wrapped her torso with the white towel. She also tousled her wet hair to give it the sexy leonine look that had always turned Derek on. Or at least it had done so for the first six years of their marriage, up until a few months ago when he had begun acting like a stranger and looking at her as if she were some ugly creature that had washed up on the shore of his life.

Surely he couldn't know about her and Steve. Of that she was confident. And it was easy enough to explain Steve's car in the driveway, since he was friends with their neighbors and could claim he had just walked over there to say hello (which was exactly what he had fled to do only moments ago). But today's brush with disaster was the closest yet. Before leaving the bathroom she adjusted the towel again, making sure it rode low enough to expose generous portions of both breasts, which were still stiffened with gooseflesh from the icy water. Especially in the present circumstance, she thought a little misdirection couldn't hurt at all.

She saw no one when she peered into the bedroom. The hallway was likewise deserted, so she walked confidently down to the living room, holding the towel up with one hand, and then stopped short beside the living room recliner, arrested in mid-step by the sight of her husband crouched low in the open front doorway with his back to her. The storm still raged outside, buffeting the house with heavy winds, blowing the sharp-sweet smell of ozone and ravaged maple trees in through the door. He appeared to be surveying the spectacle, heedless of the rain slapping him in the face. His head rotated back and forth in regular, slow sweeps, and the odd motion, combined with his incomprehensible squatting pose and hunched shoulders, made him look almost comical. She barely suppressed a burst of nervous laughter, raising a hand to her mouth and nearly dropping the towel in the process. When she spoke, her voice still trembled with the inner pressure of giddy humor.

"Oh, hi, honey. I was in the shower. I didn't hear you come in. Why are you home so early? Shouldn't you shut the door?"

She was about to ask, "What's wrong?" when he turned to face her. He remained low in the doorway, crouched like a caveman. Her words stuck in her throat, trapped there by the sudden paralysis in her chest. Derek looked like some primitive tribal chief drenched in red war paint. His eyes were wide and flashing. The corners of his mouth were drawn down in an unearthly grimace. In one hand he gripped a sharp blade that glistened with the same red paint.

Before she could speak or move, he exploded from his crouch and came at her like lightning. She saw a bright burst and felt a concussive blow like a thundercrack. Then she was falling in slow motion, floating down, down to the floor and landing hard with a broken jaw. The storm hit her wrist next, and then two ribs, and then her nose. Strong, sticky hands were tangled in her wet hair, dragging her across rough shag carpet that burned her legs and back as the towel pulled away. Then it was cold ceramic tile sliding beneath her naked body, and the cabinets and refrigerator loomed overhead.

Soured milk was produced and poured over her face. The splash of the cold liquid brought her partly back, and she screeched through a mangled mouth as she awoke for the first time to the horror of what was happening.

But when she tried to scream for help, the only words that came out were, "What's wrong?" She screamed again and still the same words erupted: "What's wrong? What's wrong?" Over and over she repeated it, unable to stop, asking desperately for the answer to a question whose implications, as she was only just beginning to understand, extended far beyond anything she had ever imagined.

For bending over her was not her bland, lost husband but *the Dwarf with blacksmear eyes*. Reaching out to her were not his soft office-worker's hands but *the horny hands of the rottenblood host*. And clutched in those hands was not a thin, blood-drenched blade but *the piercing vengeance of the greedy-eyed God* which would *carve the secret shape that swims in the deep*. The words and phrases arose like a whirling chant in her head, and she could not tell if they entered through her ears or spoke from a deeper source.

The Dwarf stood above her and raised a misshapen hand, and gripped in that hand was the light of a four-pointed star, which gathered and swelled until it was a blazing beacon of truth in the dimness, scorching her eyes and burning her face, casting shimmering dark shadows across the suddenly real angles and planes of a barren landscape that had enveloped them.

The Dwarf seized her throat and pricked the tender flesh with *the star of destiny,* which was *the black feather of vengeance,* drawing out a mesmerizing bead of crimson-on-white, and the fiery pain of it, and the smell of sizzling flesh, refused to let her slip into shock and believe it was a nightmare.

The Dwarf spoke, opening its misshapen mouth for the first time, and its voice was the roar of hot winds and the hissing of blood rains. It said:

"*The seraph is a snake. The Self is an abyss. Who knows the stench of God? The blood shall rot away!*"

Then it reached down into the naked mystery quivering before it and patiently, joyfully began to make everything right.

Nightmares, Imported and Domestic

With Mark McLaughlin

His name was Lafcadio, and he was an artist, a creator of lavish and colorful landscapes. Or at least, this accounted for part of his life: the part lived by the conscious, waking, sensing self that opened eyes on the external world and breathed in the scents and sights of sun-filled skies and rain-wet streets. Lafcadio the artist spent endless hours reading Zen literature and attempting to incorporate esoteric ideas into his paintings. Lafcadio the artist thrived on the sensuous impressions of the outer world and the intricate thoughts to which they inspired his overheated imagination.

But he was a man divided, and the other part of his life was not nearly so vibrant. For approximately eight hours out of every twenty-four, he assumed the identity of Brian, an accountant, a creator of neatly filled-out forms, who spent his days locked within the taupe walls of an aging suburban office. Lafcadio's life as Brian was uncommonly realistic for a nocturnal vision. As Brian, he felt pain, hunger, all the usual sensations, and knew them in all their day-to-day, five-sensory vividity. But he did not see his Brian-self through the twin windows of his own eyes. Rather, he watched himself from a distance, as one might watch a character in a television show. Appropriately, this dream-life, Brian's life, took place in a world of black-and-white, like an old episode of *The Andy Griffith Show* or *I Love Lucy*. And the tenor of this dream-existence was entirely in keeping with its grayscaled hues.

The tension between the two selves—the glorious sensuality of the artist and the drab conventionality of the accountant—expressed itself in all the habits and mores of Lafcadio's life. One of his most oft-indulged amusements was to sample exotic coffees with his eyes closed and try to guess the precise blend and origin of the beans. By contrast, one of Brian's favorite drinks was instant coffee, mixed with one package of artificial sweetener and one teaspoon of nondairy creamer. He preferred Folgers, but he usually couldn't detect it when somebody substituted Maxwell House or Sanka.

The only person who had ever slept more than once in Lafcadio's bed was Lafcadio himself. The right half of Brian's bed had never held anyone but Susan, his wife for as many years as he could remember.

Lafcadio was high-strung and temperamental. Brian was even-tempered and meek.

The line of contrasts ran right down to physical appearance. Lafcadio was tall and thin, with a vaguely catlike appearance to his bony, bald head. Brian was of average height and weight, with a blandly amiable, slightly rounded face, and a ten-dollar haircut.

Some mornings Lafcadio awoke to a momentary disorientation, brought about by trying to decide whose bed he was lying in. The feeling lasted until after his shower, when the first sip of coffee hit his tongue and he discovered with relief that it was not Folgers but Jamaica Blue Mountain. The bitter hot tang of the black liquid always confirmed that he was indeed the effervescent artist and not the dreary accountant. But as time went by—months running into years, years into more than a decade, and all the while the nocturnal life of Brian playing like a classic TV show on the screen of his eyelids at night—he found that he slowly came to look forward to his nightly ramblings in a world of white-bread banality.

True, the morning disorientation sometimes left him with a lingering fear that one day he might wake up to find himself in a two-tone world with Susan beside him in bed and his life as Lafcadio the Magnificent receding like foam from the shore of a dream ocean. But in the end he discovered that it was really quite easy to convince himself that a life as Brian the Maudlin wouldn't be all that bad. Not if Brian were able to spend at least eight hours of every twenty-four dreaming that he was Lafcadio the Magnificent.

"So this Brian," said Cornelia, Lafcadio's best friend, over steaming mugs one day at their favorite coffee house, Mondo Mocha. "Your dream buddy. What's he up to these days? You haven't mentioned him in a while."

Lafcadio reflected for a moment before answering. "He's not really my buddy," he said at last. "He's me. And Susan has been talking about flowers."

"Flowers?" Cornelia looked at him blankly over a Café Corretto.

"She thinks the house looks too plain on the outside. All the other houses on the block have tons of flowers. We have to keep up with the Joneses, you know." He smiled privately to himself and turned his attention to the steam rising from his Espresso Macchiato. The swirling vapor hinted at a snow-covered landscape, mottled by bizarre seismic convulsions. He allowed the image to take its course in his imagination, hoping it might lead him to his next artistic project.

Cornelia gave him a hard little smile. But then, practically everything about her was hard, though admirably so. She was into boxing and weightlifting, and it showed on her arms and shoulders. Her abs were like a rippled brick wall (as he had discovered once, long ago, on the sole occasion when they had become physically intimate and he had been able to indulge his long-held desire of placing the flat of his palm upon her stomach). Years ago she had served on the police force, before she decided to open a beauty and exercise spa for women only. "This Susan sounds like a perfectly hideous frau," she was saying, as his snow-swept reverie became transmogrified by her chiseled physique into a Dali-esque scene of powder-and-ice piled into abdominal ripples on an arctic tundra. "Brian has to play gardener now? Tell me everything!"

"Oh, but I like it. I mean, *he* likes it." He could tell she didn't believe him, so he tapped his manicured nails on the tile tabletop in syncopation with his words to emphasize his sincerity. "No, really! All that housey-spousey stuff is actually kind of fun in Brian-world."

Cornelia tapped her chin with a long maroon-lacquered fingernail. "So, do they ever *do* it? Or is life all just chores and church socials?"

"Oh sure, they have sex. But I never get to see"—He twirled his forefingers in the direction of his crotch—"the works in action. It's like watching a soft-core porn channel in a hotel room. No close-ups allowed, in case a kid enters the room. The camera moves toward them, then it veers off toward a fireplace or an open window with a pretty sky outside."

Cornelia's smile dipped down into a smirk. "How dreary. Must be terribly boring for you."

"Nooo. . . ." Lafcadio thought for a moment. "In a way, it's rather sweet. And the lack of visuals isn't a total loss. I mean, I do still feel every sensation that Brian is feeling." He looked into Cornelia's eyes. "I think sometimes Susan is supposed to be you."

Her eyes hardened into a stare that clearly said, *Don't go there.* "You will recall," she said, "that we only slept together once. Before I'd figured myself out. I'm Susan? That hardly seems likely."

"Is it likely that I should be Brian?" he countered. To lighten the mood, he cocked his head and widened his eyes in a mock posture of exaggerated artsy-fartsy pretension, and she laughed. Her teeth were whiter than the foam on his Macchiato, whiter than arctic ice, and they transfixed him in a momentary flash of near-revelation.

"It's so like you," she said, "to have such complicated relationship issues even in your dreams." She was still laughing when she glanced at the clock on the wall. "Whoops, I'd better get going. I've got a class coming up. Keep me posted on all the exciting developments in Brian-land." She leaned over and pecked him on the cheek, then gathered her purse (more like a suitcase, he thought) and headed for the door.

He watched as her long, lanky strides carried her away from him. The rippled muscles of the arctic waste were still taking shape in his imagination, and for the millionth time in his high-strung life he silently thanked the gods—any gods, whatever gods there might be, he didn't care who they were—for gifting him with a dreary dream life of almost archetypal normality, since it freed him from the fetters of psyche-bound inspiration and allowed him to take in, as if by osmosis, every subtle sensation of the world around him. Without anything of equal vibrancy buzzing in his subconscious to compete with the splendor of the outside world, he could work in complete inner freedom, allowing the obscure mechanism of his own creative faculty to transform scattered sense perceptions into magnificent paintings that made him the awe of the arthouse community.

The gods bless you, Brian, he said to his alter ego. Through the plate glass storefront, he could see Cornelia standing on the sidewalk, squinting up at the sun. After a moment she pulled out her flaming-orange sunglasses and slipped them on. As she loped down the sidewalk and out of sight, he found that he still couldn't decide whether or not he loved her.

But then he reasoned, if he couldn't decide, that probably meant he didn't.

The dream, as always, was in black-and-white, except for the part with the startling new addition of blood, which fountained and sprayed in gouts like bright red finger-paint. The color shocked him, but not into full consciousness. He soon discovered another fact about this remarkable dream: it could get amazingly tactile, almost more so than real life. Brian's world had always been pinch-yourself-and-wake-up solid, but never like this. The blood was warm and sticky as maple syrup, and the pain was a white-hot pocket of concentrated agony searing into the socket of his right eye.

What had happened was that Susan had asked Brian to unload a pickup bed full of potted flowers. He had backed the vehicle up to the front porch like the dutiful dream-husband he was, and had lowered the tailgate and climbed into the bed to unstack the dull plastic pots with their colorless floral occupants.

(Lafcadio, watching from a nonlocalized point some distance away while simultaneously identifying with his dream-self, had thought the grayish blooms most distasteful.)

It happened on the first jump. Brian realized it would be much easier to hop down than to squat and climb, so he steadied the pot in his hands and stepped off the edge of the tailgate, intending to drop lightly onto the balls of his feet. Susan's scream burst out with an impossible loudness and hung in the air with a ringing reverberation that could only happen in a dream. He hadn't noticed the hook projecting from the porch ceiling, right near the edge under which he had opened the tailgate. It was meant for hanging a plant on, obviously. Susan must have mounted it there without telling him. The gray-silver point extended an absurd length past the overhang, maybe three inches or more, and was located precisely at eye-level from his standing position in the pickup bed.

The curved end was vicious-looking, almost medieval. It caught him in the top rim of his right eye socket, and his weight did the rest. He fell forward, the point gouged into the bone of his skull, his legs left the tailgate, and then he was lodged there, hooked like a great flailing fish. The plastic pot hit the lawn without breaking, although potting soil sprayed everywhere, and the colorless bloom was crushed. His body went out of control then, legs kicking and spasming as if he were trying to pedal up Mount Everest, hands and fingers slapping and clawing at the smooth vinyl siding of the eave in a vain attempt to lift himself up. While all this went on, his throat opened up and spouted a veritably Pentecostal string of gibberish that seemed to have something to do with screaming for help.

Then Susan was grabbing his legs. She was grunting and lifting him up, heaving, thrusting, while her impossibly loud and long scream still hung in the air. At last she succeeded. The hook ripped free, dragging a few bone splinters with it, and he dropped to the truck, slammed into the open tailgate with the small of his back, and hit the lawn still writhing.

That was when the blood began to spurt from his eye in can-
dy-red finger-paint gouts. The pain was a knot of acid searing its
way inward from his eye to his brain. Susan was pawing at him in
panic, weeping, asking him what to do. And in the midst of it all,
rather absurdly, he vomited.

"He puked? So what happened then? Did he die? Tell me everything!" Cornelia's eyes shone with eager interest. Lafcadio drew in
a sharp, tobacco-laden breath and let it out slowly, trying to buy
time to fathom the reason for her eagerness. This time they had
met at their favorite bar, the Twilight Lounge. The decor was an
edgy mix of Goth and camp imagery: ABBA posters and black
candles arranged into arcane geometric patterns, G.I. Joe dolls
tangled in faux spiderwebs. Cornelia was dressed for the occasion
in a black velvet catsuit with a denim jacket.

"No, he didn't die." Lafcadio floated the words out on the tail-
end of a smoky exhalation. Cornelia interrupted him before he
could say more.

"What?" She blinked and leaned closer, bringing with her a
mingled scent of sweet perfume and sour gin. "Did you say 'Oh, he
sits and cries'? Lafcadio, my darling, you're incomprehensible
when you mumble, especially amidst all the lovely musical ac-
companiment." A bassy club beat throbbed in the atmosphere
around them, overlaid with a glassy texture of synthesized strings.

"I said he *didn't die.*" He repeated the words with a hint of annoyance. "People usually don't die in their own dreams, right?
And after all, he is me." He held up his cigarette before him in an
attitude of detachment and regarded the cherry-red ember glowing on the tip. "Things seemed like they were getting better before
I woke up. Susan took care of him. She dialed 911, and an ambu-
lance came and rushed him off to the hospital. I opened my eyes
just as they started to wheel him into the ER."

"Interesting. . . ." Cornelia took a sip from her gin and tonic.
"So Susan saved his life. But then, she's the one who installed the
hook in the first place. And you say it hurt his *eye?*" She mused for

a moment while the smoky air continued to throb around them like the interior of an artery, and while Lafcadio remained deliberately absorbed in his cigarette meditation. In his mind, a fiery orange sinkhole had opened up in the abdominal arctic waste. Volcanic flames were beginning to lick out from the edges and melt the snow to slush. The water first dripped, then drizzled into the hole, and its touch only seemed to fuel the flames.

"Hey." Cornelia's ruminations seemed to reach a point of sudden synthesis. "Do you think that's symbolic—'eye' equals capital 'I'? Maybe the hook in your eye represents a buried feeling of hostility toward your deathly-dull dream life." She smiled with an almost childish glee, and he thought she seemed just a little too pleased with herself.

"It's a fundamental tenet of my belief system," he said in a far frostier voice than he had intended, "that there is ultimately no such thing as a fixed center of identity." He saw her eyes roll in a familiar expression of boredom, but he went on. "These chairs underneath our asses right now are just as much a part of who we are as anything rattling around inside these juicy little heads." He raised his right hand, the one holding the cigarette, and tapped his index finger against a veiny temple. A tendril of smoke found its way from the tip of the cigarette to the corner of his eye, where it brushed a stinging tail against the tender pink tissues. He waved it away and tried to ignore Cornelia's look of amusement.

"The injured *eye* once again," she said. "Do you think someone is trying to tell you something?"

He refused to acknowledge her comment. "I have no reason to be hostile toward Brian or his life," he continued, "because he may as well be me, and his life mine. My life may as well be his. Just as yours may as well be mine, and mine yours. Our souls are both located in this cigarette I'm smoking here. They're also in that gin and tonic you're sucking down." She was in the midst of downing the rest of her drink, and she made a face at him, holding the liquid in her cheeks for a moment before swallowing it.

"Really, darling," she said with a sigh, "sometimes your attempts at Zen-like wisdom are too much. What the hell are you talking about?"

"I'm saying there's no boundary between identities, so what's to be afraid of?"

She shrugged. "Who said anything about being afraid?"

"It's the same thing with my art," he went on, ignoring her question. "I deliberately make the perspective undiscoverable. The viewer might be looking at any one point from any other. Have you heard of Indra's net?"

She shook her head, clearly having lost interest in his monologue. But that did not prevent him from continuing.

"It's a metaphor in Hinduism for the infinity of perspectives in the universe. Indra's net is an endless web that has a jewel located at the intersection of every strand. Each jewel reflects all the others, so you have infinity contained in every finite point on the net. A long time ago I decided to use this idea as the philosophical basis for my paintings. When you view any one of my pieces, you don't know where you're supposed to be seeing it from. What's more, this means the frame itself isn't the boundary of the scene. My landscapes fold in on themselves and create a self-contained infinity. In this way, my work mirrors the reality of subjective personal existence, just like the metaphor of Indra's net. Because ultimately, there's nothing outside the frame for any of us. There's just an endless hall of mirrors with no boundary." He started to say more, but then he abruptly shut his mouth and sucked on his cigarette as he realized that the words he had never spoken, and never wanted to speak, were rising to his lips. These words expressed a fear that had dawned on him one day in a quiet moment when he was reiterating his credo to himself for the thousandth time: *No boundary means no escape.*

"Is there anything else?" Cornelia asked. She was watching him with her ruby red lips screwed up into a wry grin.

"Just the fact that your eye/I theory doesn't hold water," he said. "The injury wasn't a threat at all. In fact, it might turn out to have been a liberation. Brian and Susan's marital relationship has been at kind of a low ebb lately. Then he ran into trouble and she saved him. Maybe this will revitalize things between them."

"Yes," Cornelia said, "but Susan put up the hook, remember?" She smiled at him with eyes that were as pretty and hard as the rest of her. "If I remember correctly, you also told me that I'm Susan. Is that how you see me—a disturbing mix of destroyer and savior?"

Lafcadio barked out a small, sharp laugh. "Hardly, my sweet. Listen, we could spend all night on this. This autopsy of my dreams. But do you know what? Sometimes a cigar is just a cigar, a rose is a rose is a rose, and diamonds are forever. Let's just say it's all really interesting, and leave it at that. Will you indulge me?"

"Oh, darling!" she cried. "This is too much, coming from the enlightened Zen-master of the avant garde art world!" She laughed and laughed until he feared she would hurt herself. When she had recovered, she said, "Certainly, my sweet. But one question first: Doesn't it bother you to know that Brian-world is now a painful place to be? You've talked so much about how realistic it is. Well, I'm not so sure the marriage or anything else will be better now. Brian may be disfigured, and he'll definitely be blind in one eye. He'll probably suffer brain damage. I'm surprised you haven't acted more concerned about this. What will your dreams be like now, my wise Lafcadio?" She looked deeply into his eyes, and even in the midst of his consternation, he wondered again whether he loved her.

"Don't know." The artist slumped back in his seat, his meditative mood broken. The arctic landscape remained unaltered in his mind's eye, although the drizzle of water pouring through the hole in the ice had grown to become a steadily flowing waterfall. The flames were hidden now, but they were still there, still burning below the frozen crust, as evidenced by the flickering orange sheen they imparted to the ice around the hole. He had a momentary flash of something new: a human figure curled into a fetal position, located deep within that fiery pit. Its eyes and mouth were open wide. He couldn't tell whether it was laughing, crying, or screaming. Perhaps it was doing all three.

He frowned at Cornelia as he ground out his cigarette in the glossy black ashtray on the table. "You're just a sweet little ray of sunshine, aren't you?"

Of course the dream was monochrome. How could it be otherwise? And yet Brian sensed that something was different. Something was missing from the room around him, some indefinable aspect of solidity whose absence made everything seem vaguely flat and unreal, like cardboard stage props and scenery.

(Lafcadio, hovering in extra-dimensional space somewhere near the ceiling, shared his alter ego's confusion.)

Brian was parked in a wheelchair in the center of his black-and-white living room, slumped in front of a black-and-white television set, watching a black-and-white program unfold on the screen. He couldn't budge an inch. The insipid TV world was inescapable, and he was positioned to face it for a full frontal assault. Susan had engaged the wheel locks on the chair to prevent the incessant squeaking of the spokes he had been causing by rocking back and forth, back and forth. She was in the kitchen behind him right now, making his lunch, from the sound of it. She must be chopping celery—*crunch crunch crunch, crunch crunch crunch*. To his right and left, adorning coffee tables, walls, and windowsills, a tangled profusion of potted flowers bristled with muddy gray blooms that emitted an incongruously sweet perfume. It saturated the atmosphere of the room like a syrupy fog. He almost thought he could see it shifting and shimmering in the cold light of the television.

Drool was gathered in a heavy glistening lobe on his lower lip, but he lacked the energy to care about it. He felt nauseous and dizzy, and had no idea what was happening on the program before him. Something about a perky family stranded on some planet with a prissy bad guy and a robot with floppy arms. A black rotary telephone perched atop the set with a ridiculously long cord dangling down in front of the screen. It slithered across the concave surface, unevenly dividing the flickering image, and ended up as a bunched pile of gleaming black coils on the gray-carpeted floor.

His injured right eye was smothered in bandages, as were most of his cheek and forehead. His exposed left eye kept blinking, rolling, and refocusing as he tried to fathom what the characters on the television screen were so concerned about. The prissy bad-guy was bitching at the robot while the robot waved its accordion-pleated tube-arms.

His poor wounded head pulsed with an odd liquid surging sound. In his grogginess and sickness, he imagined that he must be hearing the primal sound of the ocean deeps, where colorless fluorescent fish glided with rippling fan-fins through an eternal night, and where the currents murmured of secrets too ancient to be spoken aloud. Such thoughts were new and strange, and they scared him. He longed for his accounting forms and the familiar taupe walls of his office. But the ocean sound seemed to be a permanent addition, and he feared he would never see the comforting interior of his office again. Now, one week after the accident, he still rocked to the sound of the tidal rhythm, but the wheel locks kept him from creating the soothing back-and-forth motion that had been the only comfort he could find in this new half-conscious existence.

Susan entered the room holding a plate with a sandwich on it. She was smiling and talking to him, but her words sounded like gibberish. When he tried to raise his hands to accept the plate, his arms felt as if someone had tied them down with lead weights. Her voice came to him as if through water, all muffled and murky, and the words sounded like *blah, blah, blah,* spoken in relentlessly perky tones, so upbeat they rang utterly false.

She held the sandwich to his mouth, and his nostrils were suddenly filled with the clean yet musty smell of whole-wheat bread. With the cloying perfume of the flowers now mercifully muted, he found that his nausea had concealed a fierce hunger. He was positively ravenous. His lips parted of their own accord, and the spongy bread sopped up the bead of spit on his lower lip as Susan fed him the sandwich bite by bite. While he ate, he couldn't help noticing that she wore low-riding pants with a high-cut shirt, and that her navel stared at him from the smooth white expanse of her stomach like an unblinking eye that mirrored and mocked his own newly monocular face. It fascinated him for some reason. He felt he should be reminded of something.

He still had four bites left when the phone rang. Susan set the plate on his lap and took two steps over to the television while he stared down at the unfinished sandwich with a mute cry of frustration sealed off in his throat. His hands clenched and unclenched, but his wrists were pinned to the arms of the wheelchair by invisible straps.

"Blah, blah, blah?" Susan chimed into the black mouthpiece. She listened a moment, then "Blah, blah, blah!" she replied. A look of pleasure crossed her face as she brushed past him to the coffee table, where she consulted a phone book for the caller. Her smile faded as her finger stopped on the page before a name and number.

"Oh, blah, blah, blah," she continued in a more serious tone, moving behind him toward the kitchen on some errand, dragging the long black cord in her wake so that it pulled up against his arm. He flinched at its stiff spiral touch and continued to look with longing at his sandwich.

After a moment, she returned on some other errand. "Blah, blah, blah!" she enthused, racing in front of him toward the phone book again, still chatting away to that all-important caller, still pulling that super-long springy cord so that it worked its way up and encircled his neck. The coils were as smooth and cool as snakeskin against his throat.

From some point buried deep inside his brain, out of some black well of selfhood where the ocean currents murmured in soothing tones, a thought emerged. The whispering voices coalesced into an intelligible sentence, and the sentence began to flow toward his throat. He opened his mouth and grunted, but the cord was slowly strangling him. He coughed as if he were trying to expel some bit of sandwich lodged in his windpipe. The words were almost there, they would almost form. His mouth worked and his lips gathered more spit, but his voice would not come, it could not break free of the constriction around his throat. In desperation he mouthed the words silently with his crumb-covered lips, wondering as he did so what the thought might mean, and where it might have come from: *No boundary means no escape.*

(Lafcadio, who had been watching these events unfold with growing agitation, felt his disembodied heart skip a beat.)

Susan was now out of sight in the dining room, or perhaps even beyond that, and the cord was growing tighter and tighter. The television world continued to blather with incomprehensible characters and concerns while the cold spiral coils dug deeper and deeper into his Adam's apple like a garrote. Straining, trembling, he jerked his arms against the invisible straps, but try as he might, he was immobilized.

As the dull throb of medicated pain in his bandaged eye blossomed into a bright burning agony, and as the robot continued to wave its arms and the prissy bad guy went on with his outrageous accusations, Brian finally realized the nature of what was wrong with the room: *There was no difference between the world around him and the world on the television.* The gibberish spouting from the mouths of the TV characters was no more comprehensible than the gibberish his wife was still spouting in the other room—or, come to think of it, from the gibberish he had spouted himself when he was hanging by his eye socket from the porch ceiling. None of it made sense. All of it was insipid and pointless. There was a tangible lack of *realness* to his surroundings, an absence of something that would have given everything more weight and caused it all to make sense again. But what exactly was this indefinable quality whose absence made life nothing more than a TV show where people spoke nonsense, and where there could be no escape?

It wasn't until rivulets of shocking-bright red began to seep out from beneath his bandages and spatter onto the colorless sleeves of his pajamas that he found his answer.

No boundary means no escape.

When the change came, it came quickly. The room receded suddenly and sharply, as if he were backing down a tunnel at incredible speed. The pain in his face and constriction in his throat faded like someone had turned down the volume on the television. For a time, he knew only an insensate bliss.

When he opened his eyes—his *eyes,* both of them intact and functional—he found himself lying in a bed that was not his own, located in a room he had never seen, where the walls displayed a dazzling array of surreal painted landscapes, and where he somehow knew that nobody had ever slept beside him more than once, not even Susan.

His throat finally opened and released an impressive array of shrieks when he realized that his name was supposed to be Lafcadio, and that he had awakened into the wrong life.

"So is he dead?' Cornelia asked. "You haven't talked about him for—what is it, two weeks now? I can only assume that he died from his injuries. What's Susan doing with the life insurance money? Installing a greenhouse?" She smiled and laughed, but he refused to look at her.

This time they were sharing a pizza in their favorite trendy restaurant, Mad for Pie, which served every sort of pizza one could imagine—except the traditional sausage, cheese and tomato sauce kind. The entrée steaming on the table before them now was the specialty of the house, an exotic mélange called The Swordfish, Artichoke, and White Sauce (with Just a Touch of Cilantro) Dream Pie. Lafcadio's stomach was out of sorts. He sat back in his tall wicker-backed chair and tried to avoid the overpowering scent of seafood and cilantro that rose to his nostrils in heady waves.

"To be honest," he said in his best nonchalant voice, "I'm not sure what's going on with Brian right now."

"What do you mean?" She shoveled another lump of swordfish-laden crust into her mouth, and he watched the motion of her jaw with sickened fascination: its determined scissoring and champing as it ground the fishy flesh to a pulp, then the spasm in her throat as she swallowed the pungent lump and it began to stretch its way downward through her esophagus toward her waiting stomach. His own stomach lurched ominously, and he looked down at his cigarette.

"I, uh—how do I say this?" He picked up a heavy burgundy-colored napkin and mopped his sweating brow. "I haven't dreamed about Brian for sixteen days now."

She stopped her chewing and regarded him from across the pie with an expression of disbelief.

"Yes," he said, "I'm serious."

"Lafcadio," she said. The swordfish suddenly stuck in her throat, and she groped for her glass of water. When she had taken a drink, she licked her lips and continued to look at him. "What's happened? Hasn't Brian been with you for years now?"

"Yes," he said.

"Aren't you concerned about this?"

"Yes."

"So why haven't you said anything?" Her wounded pout dismayed him, and for a moment he considered telling her the tale he had been concealing for over two weeks: of how he had awakened in his silk-sheeted bed thinking that he was Brian; of the profound panic that had gripped him for hours as he struggled to remember how he had awakened into someone else's life; of how the delusion had hung on until mid-morning, when for no apparent reason his own name had seemed to attach to him with a new assertiveness, and the dream-identity had evaporated from his consciousness like a moist fog; of how he had found himself standing in his kitchen, holding a cup of Jamaica Blue Mountain and wondering where somebody had hidden the Folgers.

For the rest of that horrible day he had been unable to stop the trembling in his chest. He had canceled a dinner date with Cornelia (she had gracefully declined to ask the reason) and spent the night in his studio looking at his easel and allowing the arctic vision to gain further clarity and intensity in his mind's eye. He had known the time would soon arrive for him to begin committing the vision to canvas, but on that night some inner impulse had told him to wait, and he had heeded its restraint. Later, when he slept, he had found that his classic TV dreams were gone for the first time in over a decade.

Instead of watching Brian's soothingly banal ramblings, he had found himself floating high over an arctic tundra, watching a volcanic sinkhole widen into a veritable crater amidst the icy furrows, wondering whether the abdominal ripples stretching away toward the horizon might ever meet with the rest of the torso, with breasts and a neck, and with a face. It was the first time he had ever dreamt himself into one of his own artistic visions, and he hadn't known how to feel about it the following morning. The next night the dream had been the same. And the next, and the next.

He considered telling Cornelia this. But how could he, when he knew that it was her face he half feared to see past the icy horizon?

"I just needed time to adjust," he finally said with a weak smile. "You know you're my most beloved confidante, Cornelia. Please don't be upset with me."

"I'm not upset, dearest. I'm just surprised." She shoved away her plate and began looking around for a server to take away the remains of the pie. Once their table was cleared and wiped down and they were alone again, she leaned forward with her forearms resting on the glossy brown surface and looked into his eyes.

"Do you know I talked to my therapist last week about you and Brian?"

For a moment he thought she was joking. He kept expecting her serious expression to break into a smile, but her mouth was a determined line, and her eyes were as hard as sapphires.

"You told Dr. Breckenridge about this? About my *dreams?*"

Her severity broke easily in the face of his indignation. Immediately she was pouting again, but now in a rather hard way. "I was missing you, Lafcadio. I really wanted to hear about the latest episodes of the Brian and Susan Show. I always look forward to our conversations. I just called Dr. Breckenridge to change my appointment, but we ended up talking about you. How could I not mention you, when you were the main thing on my mind?"

Lafcadio could not sit still. He twisted in his seat and tried unsuccessfully to find a comfortable position. He picked up his drink, but his hand shook so badly that he had to set it back down. He looked around at the waiters and waitresses servicing tables, at the upscale married couples and college students, all of them wearing trendy clothes and devouring various nonstandard delights. The sight only angered him. As a last resort, he turned to examine his cigarette, but its usual soothing influence was nowhere to be found. Then he gave up and looked at Cornelia's face.

"So what did you tell him?"

"I only told him what you've told me. I described your dream life, all black-and-white and cozy. He found it quite fascinating. I could tell he wanted to ask me to introduce you to him, but he was too afraid of crossing a professional line."

Lafcadio considered this for a moment and then began to nod, slowly at first, then with increasing vigor. "Of course." He recalled the sensation of a curling phone cord pressed cold against Brian's throat, and he snickered a little, then laughed. "Of *course*." Once again he gazed into Cornelia's eyes, considered her toned and taut physique, now tastefully attired in a green sparkling jacket with black satin shirt and pants. He drank in the sight of her masculine femininity, and found in it an impression of dawning realization. The full knowledge waited just beyond the horizon, like an arctic mountain range chiseled by the elements into the shape of a familiar face.

She was speaking to him. Her words came to him all murky and muffled, as if through water. "After all, Lafcadio, you were the one who said . . . what was it? Sometimes a dream is just a cigar? Something like that. You were quoting somebody. But the more I think about it, the more I believe you had the right idea. Don't take any of this seriously. Dr. Breckenridge didn't know what he was saying when he told me your dreams are unlike anything in the history of psychology." She shut her mouth when she realized she had said too much, but he found it funny. It was all funny now. She was a million miles away, and her confusion and misery were of no consequence.

It also just so happened that her face and clothing were losing their color. He blinked rapidly as the color drained away from her like dye being leached from a canvas. Her blue eyes became a stony gray. Her ruddy expression became a murky white. Her sparkling green jacket became a sickly weak shade of gray, like library paste flecked with glitter. In just a few seconds she was flushed of all color. He was so startled that it was a moment before he realized the same effect had overtaken the restaurant around him. Mad for Pie had taken on the appearance of *Father Knows Best*. The pies and pizzas were gray cardboard, and the patrons and scenery were colorless stage props and cutouts.

(Somewhere close by, in some nonlocalized portion of extra-dimensional space, another center of identity began to make itself known: a buzzing unit of self-consciousness that felt somehow like a vane protruding from the back of his head; an unknown self whose reality ran much deeper and held more solidity than the Magnificent Artist identity he had cultivated for most of his life. This new self was sharing his vision and consciousness, watching his life unfold like a fiction. And it was judging everything about him and his life, considering it all impassively, and finding it all to be quaint and comforting in a banal, white-bread sort of way.)

He felt his hand rise to his mouth to suck in a lungful of nicotine smoke. His lips curled into a smile, and for a moment he almost felt like his old self. "Cornelia, my sweet, don't worry about it." His voice carried through the stale air with a vibrancy that was almost visible, as if its very timbre might bring back a hint of color to the room. He felt a strange power surging in his breast, a kind of exhilaration beyond anything he had ever known. The landscape in his mind's eye pulsed with an intensity that almost obscured the sight of the restaurant. For once, his inner vision was stronger than the world around him, and in this fact he found his release.

If life was unbounded, he thought, just like his landscapes, and if no boundary meant no escape, then the only way out, the only way to achieve the ultimate transcendence, was to turn inward toward the source and center of consciousness itself, and find his longed-for infinity *inside* the world. Just like the self-contained infinity of Indra's net, which he had never truly understood until now.

(The newly awakened higher self nodded behind him in approval of his insight. He could sense its benevolent attention upon him.)

Cornelia's face loomed in front of him, and also beyond the icy horizon in his mind's eye. In the restaurant she appeared gray and flat. In the arctic waste her features were chiseled from crackling blue ice, and the light of a slivered moon overhead glinted in silver sparkles on her face like flashes on the facets of a diamond.

"You're not mad?" the Cornelia of the outer world was asking. "Are you sure, Lafcadio? Because I don't think I could bear it."

"No," he heard himself say. "Far from it. In fact, I think you may have liberated me. I'm thinking that maybe Brian is gone now because he woke up. I'm thinking that maybe he and I have finally come together."

She looked at him somewhat suspiciously. "Should I congratulate you?"

"Perhaps. What say we find out for sure?" He rapped on the table with the knuckles of his free hand and sat forward abruptly in his chair. He felt positively giddy with good will. "Will you come over to my place tonight, my dear? I have something prepared to show you. I haven't told you anything about my latest project, you know I always keep them private until they're finished, but it's about time you saw it, even if it is only a work in progress. Because you're directly involved in it."

Her smile returned then, and he saw that her teeth were still icy white, a flashing beacon in the grayness surrounding her. "Lafcadio! Do you mean that I'm featured in it somehow?"

"Oh, yes!" He laughed and allowed her to grab his hand. "Yes, you are! I think you'll be positively amazed at the role you've played."

After that, he found he could simply allow himself to act the part of Lafcadio for the remainder of their time together at Mad for Pie. He chatted and laughed, and she laughed and chatted back, and they made plans for her to arrive at his flat at eight o'clock, at which time he promised to reveal to her a facet of herself that she had never suspected. He even managed to keep up the old appearance of the Magnificent Artist when her chattering words lost all meaning and began to sound like "Blah, blah, blah."

When they parted, each was riding on a wave of giddiness, although he knew that hers did not match his. She thought she was going to be immortalized in one of his paintings. He, on the other hand, knew they were both going to be immortalized in a scheme much bigger than any she could ever imagine.

He labored all afternoon in his studio. The painting seemed to shape itself.

He had to take extra care to blend the colors for the fiery crater, since his colorblindness precluded his assessing it with a simple glance, but he felt his hand being guided by a higher power, and he knew, even without being able to judge the quality of the work with his eyes, that it was the best thing he had ever painted. And after all, he would soon awaken to the actual scene of the vision, and the pathetic oil-based facsimile would no longer have a significance.

As he continued to work toward completion, he began to feel as if a key had been fitted into a lock. The door that opened allowed a flood of insights to spill through his brain. Brian's world had been less real than Lafcadio's, and its unreality had been reflected in its monochromity. That much Lafcadio had always known. But he had never suspected that perhaps his own reality was being watched from a still wider perspective by another layer of himself, a layer that was even more awake, more vibrant, more *real.* The thought of the sensuous delights, the manifold impressions, that might be available to that wider identity, sent him into paroxysms of aesthetic delight.

Brian had awakened to the insubstantiality of his position. It had seemed impossible—in fact, neither of them had ever so much as considered the possibility—but it had happened nonetheless, through the agency of an unexpected injury, brought about by Susan's unwitting help. Now Brian was gone—or, more accurately, he was more fully *here* with Lafcadio than he had ever been before—and it was Lafcadio's turn to wake up.

Dull-brained Brian would never have thought of the possibility of intentionally inducing an awakening, even if somebody had described it to him. He had even proved incapable of realizing that the half-consciousness of his newly mutilated existence was a blessing in disguise, since it limited his external options and forcibly opened him to the enhanced consciousness of the inner world. Lafcadio was not so dull. He knew what had happened, and he was able to recognize its value and purposefully work to take himself to the next level.

The only question that remained was how to accomplish it. What means would he use to rouse himself from the relative dream of his life and rise to a greater reality? And again, it was not really a question in need of an answer, for Brian had already provided the solution. His awakening had been accomplished through involuntary suffering. Having reflected on the situation, Lafcadio came to realize that he could engineer his own circumstances and awaken himself through a voluntary act.

It had to be the right eye, of course, the one most directly wired to the left side of the brain. Once the channel of vision leading to the logical, rational, intellectual hemisphere had been destroyed, all that would remain would be the channel leading to the intuitive, emotional, mystical half. Then all the visual impressions of the sensuous world around him would be funneled exclusively to the wider mystical self that even now was hovering behind him in extra-dimensional space. And he would see himself left behind and transformed.

The gods bless you, Brian, he whispered to himself over and over during that long afternoon of creation, as he shaped the world on the canvas and contemplated the stainless steel hook he had hidden in his pocket. He would have gone ahead and mounted it on one of the exposed ceiling beams in the studio of his loft apartment, if it weren't for the fact that this would have disrupted the correct sequence of events.

There was a protocol to follow.

The mounting of the hook, of course, was Cornelia's job.

She arrived at eight, right on time. She wore the same satin black shirt and pants, but had exchanged the sparkling green jacket for a sparkling blue one. In her right hand she clutched a bottle of red wine. In her left she carried a rose, which she intended to present to her beloved artist in gratitude for including her in one of his magnificent creations.

She remembered the walk up the narrow dark steps to his loft all too well, even though it was three years since her last visit. The one-time exception to their formerly platonic relationship had been disastrous. They had both known immediately that it wasn't working, even though the physical pleasure had been exquisite. It had seemed too much like incest, and she could tell from his pained expression afterward that he was experiencing his own private regrets. When he had moved down to bring his face level with her stomach, and when he had placed the palm of his hand across her belly in a lovingly gentle way, she had fought back tears that threatened to squeeze from beneath her lids and sear not only him but her. After a moment he had climbed from the bed and thrown on his clothes. She had done the same, and they had never spoken of the incident again.

The staircase had not changed. The off-white walls were still too narrow, and the brown wooden steps still creaked and popped even under the modest weight of her lean, toned body. At the top of the stairs, on the right, stood the brown wooden door to the artist's lair. She smiled and felt a rush of happiness, thinking that this visit would surely turn out better than the last.

She rapped on the door with the hand holding the rose. The

delicate bloom, so deeply red that it seemed almost to ache with the saturation of its own hue, bobbed on the end of the thorned stem like a human head. She watched it for a moment and then knocked again.

"Lafcadio?" Her voice rang out with a hollow resonance in the cramped stairway. Tentatively, she reached out with her left hand and tried the brassy knob. It turned smoothly, and the door whispered open to reveal Lafcadio's living room.

She shut the door behind her and took the wine to the kitchen. The rose she laid on the dining room table. Then she went in search of the artist.

His studio was still located in the same room he had used three years ago. The walls and floor were dark and immaculate. The ceiling was high and crossed by wooden beams that gave the studio a rustic ambiance. A sheet of tarpaulin was spread beneath the easel, and upon the easel rested the artist's newest creation. She stopped before it and took in the scene it displayed. After a moment, her heart began to pound.

The icy waste stretched away from her in barren rolls like lumps of fat. She could tell they were meant to mimic the human form by their arrangement into abdominal ripples, and by the snowy hillocks that sprouted like breasts in the upper half of the scene, and by the visage that gazed upward from the diamond-like mountains at the far upper edge. Overhead, a waning crescent moon cast a sickly light onto the surreal landscape.

When she looked back down to the ice itself, she saw that where the navel should have been, there was a gaping hole, like a wound ripped open from the inside. Streaks and splashes of crimson and orange jetted out from the hole like liquid fire, like hot blood and pus, and she thought she could see, buried somewhere deep within the chaos of ripe colors, the shape of a body curled into a fetal position. Its head was bony and bald, with an almost catlike aspect. When she leaned closer, she saw that its mouth was opened in a scream, and that one of its eyes—the right one—had been gouged out.

She knew who it was, of course, just as she recognized the chiseled face at the top of the picture. She almost had time to gasp before Lafcadio pounced on her from behind.

"My sweet!" he cried as he grabbed her shoulders and spun her around. She shrieked, then tried to laugh with relief when she saw his wild-eyed expression.

"Dear God, Lafcadio! You scared the living hell out of me!" Her hands trembled violently, and she rubbed them against her upper arms while still laughing in a shaky voice. "You look like you've seen a ghost. Not Brian's, I hope?"

He stared at her for a moment. Then he laughed with her. "Ah, yes. You always see more than I give you credit for, my dear Cornelia. Let me thank you right now, since it may be the last chance I have, for your many years of friendship."

"Well, of course, darling," she said. Her weak laughter died down to silence. "And why should this be your last chance?"

He laughed again and said, "No, I don't think so." While she puzzled over this non sequitur of an answer, he reached into his pocket and pulled out something silver and shiny. He then took her hand and placed the hook gently on her palm. She saw that it was long and vicious looking, with a sharply curved point. The other end was threaded for screwing into a wall or ceiling.

"Up there," he said, pointing to a ceiling beam high above his painting. "I've already set up a ladder, as you can see. Now, if I know you at all, you've probably brought some wine. Why don't I open the bottle and let it breathe while you mount that hook?"

"Lafcadio, what is this for?"

"No, I don't think so," he said again with a laugh. "Believe me, we understand each other very well. It'll be fun! No matter how unpleasant it might seem for a time, it will be fun, believe you me." He patted her shoulder lovingly and then departed for the kitchen, where she heard him pop the cork on the bottle. The hook was cold against her palm, and she looked at it almost in wonder.

As she climbed the ladder and labored to screw the hook into the tough oaken beam, she felt as if she had stepped into a dream.

It was not her own, but somebody else's. Yes, she was a character in somebody else's dream. Below her, the painting was visible on its easel, and she stared down at her own icy face with mixed feelings of dread and awe. From her vantage point near the ceiling, the painting was inverted. Her icy reflection stared up at her with an expression of supernatural peace and wisdom. In the arctic waste of Lafcadio's vision, she had become an avatar of spiritual insight. She could discern this without his giving her a word of explanation.

From the bottom of the painting, the fiery-bloody hole gaped with a fierce determination, its hot and juicy depths standing in stark contrast to the supernal peace above. The counterbalance left her feeling sick for some reason. When she looked up and saw that she had finished screwing the hook into the beam, she descended the ladder quickly and turned her back on the canvas.

Lafcadio returned and saw that she had accomplished her mission. "Excellent!" he said. "Would you please go and pour two glasses for us, darling? I've set them out for you already. Everything is waiting." He stepped closer, and she forced herself not to flinch. "Thank you, too, for the rose. A wonderfully symbolic gesture, and all too appropriate in light of recent developments." He leaned down and kissed her cheek. When he stood back up, his smile was warm and his eyes were calm. She felt herself relax, and allowed herself to hope once more for a pleasant evening.

"Will you explain this to me when I get back?" She gestured toward the canvas. He glanced at it, reflected for a moment, and nodded.

"Whatever you say, Cornelia. It's our night."

She smiled then; it felt good to break through the icy numbness that had overtaken her face without her even noticing it. At some point between her arrival at his flat and his return from the kitchen, her face had grown stiff and cold. Smiling was an effort, but it brought life back to her cheeks and eyes. Still smiling, she went to the kitchen and poured the wine into two stemmed glasses that were waiting on the countertop.

"Lafcadio," she called. "I think you should tell me about Brian again. I've been thinking about it, and I have a theory. Maybe the incident with the hook was a dream of emasculation. Maybe it represents some sort of archetypal male fear of living in a matriarchy. A lot of intelligent people have been saying in recent years that we're turning into a matriarchal society. Or I guess I should say, *back* into one, just like it was in prehistory. Do you think maybe you've tapped into a hidden fear in the male subconscious? Maybe you dreamed Brian into a situation where his fear of women had to come out." She set the bottle down and lifted a wine-filled glass in each hand. The bouquet rose to her nostrils with a delicate aroma of vanilla and cloves.

"What do you think?" She turned the corner and stopped inside the doorway to the studio. "Lafcadio?"

The wine spilled, of course, when the glasses hit the floor, but the area of the stain was relatively small. Some droplets hit the cream-colored carpet of the hallway, marking it forever with a permanent speckling of purplish-crimson. The rest of it pooled on the hardwood floor like blood. It was a long time before Cornelia or anybody else thought to wipe it up, and by that time most of it had seeped through the cracks and into the pores, leaving an equally permanent stain on the wood.

Cleaning up spilled wine was the least of Cornelia's concerns at the moment. She was transfixed by the sight of Lafcadio dangling high above her from the rafter, the silver hook buried deep in the socket of his right eye, his legs and arms twitching in spastic birdlike motions, his mouth working silently to shape a whispered stream of veritably Pentecostal gibberish. The gore spattering onto the hardwood floor touched everything around the painting. Some of it splashed onto the canvas itself, adding its own crimson hue to the reds and oranges of the fiery crater. Below the flailing artist, above the deep-gouging sinkhole in the belly of the frozen wasteland, the supernally peaceful face of Cornelia the Ice Goddess brooded silently in eternal bliss.

When the flesh-and-blood Cornelia had recovered from her

horrified paralysis, she raced up the ladder and began tugging madly at the legs of the artist, whose spastic motions were growing less vigorous as his strength expired. She grunted and lifted him up, heaving, thrusting. At last she succeeded. The hook ripped free, dragging a few bone splinters with it, and he dropped ten feet to the floor and landed with a meaty thud.

Of course the blood began to spurt from his eye then, in red gouts like finger-paint. It looked red even to him, even with his colorblind field of vision rapidly fading and growing distant, as if he were backing down a tunnel at incredible speed. The pain was even more vicious than he had anticipated: a white-hot ball of electric agony, searing its way inward from his eye to his brain. Cornelia was crouching beside him, pawing at him in a panic, weeping, asking him what to do.

In the midst of it all, rather wonderfully, he found himself floating in an airy sea of transcendent bliss, gazing down from a dizzying height at the outline of an arctic tundra below. The furrows stretched away toward the horizon like lumps of shiny vanilla ice cream, until they met with the mountains of two icy breasts, and even farther north, with the glittering-diamond surface of a gargantuan icon that presented its face eternally to the gaze of vast, moonlit sky.

I am home, he thought, even as the borders of his consciousness began to crumble and allow the pure seed of awareness to expand outward to the next level of selfhood.

The next thought was unexpected. It was different in tenor from any he had ever thought before, and yet it seemed familiar. Coming from his higher self, it was more intense and profound than what he was used to; the sheer truth of it seemed to touch the landscape below, to fill the frigid atmosphere between them, and to saturate the glaze of moonlight cascading down onto the icy hillocks like iridescent milk. The sound of it was the sound of the primal ocean depths, like a million voices whispering into his ear from every direction at once. For a moment, just a final moment of private desire, Lafcadio held onto the perspective of his small self and translated the thought into the language he was accustomed to thinking and speaking. The million voices coalesced into one, and it was the familiar voice of his own private self. He stared in stark horror at the words that seemed almost to float before him in visible waves upon the snow: *No boundary means no escape.*

For an instant he refused to believe them. He refused to believe that even in this new, blissful existence of ultimate transcendence and freedom, he was still unable to escape the clutches of his deepest-held fear. It simply could not be true, not with the unbounded horizon of a mystical frozen landscape stretching away from him on all sides like the receding outer edge of an ecstatic dream.

Then the grip on his old perspective proved too difficult to maintain. Even as he contemplated these mysteries, he lost his hold on Lafcadio and expanded fully, finally, into the wider perspective of the ancient Self that had always been floating and lurking behind the façade of his consciousness like the ghost of a future incarnation. At last the transition was complete, and he could leave behind all his fears, the old and the new, and glory forever in the exuberance of an unbounded aesthetic delight.

It wasn't until he fully used his new eyes for the first time that he recognized the flaw in his plans.

Lafcadio was long-gone, left far behind in that dull, flat other realm where the senses could never get their fill because there was simply not enough to fill them up. But the *memory* of Lafcadio was not gone, and in this new existence, where consciousness had no boundaries, he discovered there could be no distinction between memory and present reality. The incarnate ghost of Lafcadio the Magnificent was still a presence, still a truth, and Lafcadio's subjectivity was still inextricably intertwined with that of the higher Self who was even now dreaming him back into existence.

The dream placed him in the belly of the beast, deep within the womblike innards of the arctic landscape, where molten fire burned in scalding jets of orange and red, and where self-inflicted wounds assumed all the permanence and significance of religious stigmata. The old Lafcadio screamed in this fiery, freezing hell, and the new-ancient Self screamed with him. They were locked together in twin perspectives of mutual suffering.

There could be no escape, for there was no boundary.

(And somewhere in a black-and-white world of cardboard lives and flimsy stage-prop dreams, Cornelia crouched over the body of her beloved artist and wept as she saw his dying features twist into an expression of horror. He gave one final, mighty convulsion, and then flopped onto his side and curled inward upon himself like a slug. She could not force herself to raise her eyes to the painting that presided over them like an icon of everything they had ever hoped to gain from each other. She dared not gaze at the image and see, within the glowing depths of her own icy belly, a transformed image of the bloody artist stretched out before her. As she fell backward onto the rough wooden floor and felt its warm, sticky wetness stain her hands and clothes, a momentary desire flashed through her mind, a habit ingrained from years of brash conversations. Absurdly, she wanted to demand, "Tell me everything." But she knew that even if he could answer, she would not want to hear what he had to say.)

The Devil and One Lump

I woke up that morning and stepped right into a story that I might have written myself—back when I could still write, that is. And even then I only would have written such a story if I were a hack who dealt in shameless clichés instead of a serious student of the dark self.

For the Devil himself sat waiting for me in my living room on that beautiful, sunny morning. And he looked like he had been dispatched to my house right from central casting.

Here's how it happened: I crawled out of bed all fuzzy-eyed and disappointed that the daylight had come so quickly, since I had spent the night sitting up late by myself and imbibing vast quantities of wine in the very same chair where you-know-who would greet me a few hours later. My television had sat silent and my bookcases unmolested. And the damned computer had stayed locked in the closet. No entertainment for me. The plan had been to devote the entire evening to indulging deliberately in my private misery, exploring each shading of its symptoms and every cranny of its causes. It had ended up a magnificent success, all things considered.

And of course I paid for it the morning after, as I had known full well I would. Catharsis wasn't something I sought; I had given up on that long ago. The emotional hangover from the night's excess of self-pity was actually worse than the alcohol-induced one, a truth that glared at me in the wretched light of a despicable sun as it squeezed its violating rays through loathsomely disloyal window blinds. (See what I mean?) So as soon as my feet hit the berber, I raced straightway for the kitchen—or rather stumbled on legs made of some miraculous hybrid substance, part gelatin, part rubber—to get the coffee started. The holy liquid blast of caffeine was set to be my savior that day, and I was eager to begin the worship service.

As I stood filling the carafe with tap water and earnestly striving to achieve total cognitive annihilation through sheer force of will, I heard somebody clear his throat. If ever I heard a dignified realignment of mucus, it was in the cultured sound of that musical *ahem*. Later, after the incident was over, I thought back and realized that everything that came afterward had already been previewed in that single, phlegm-filled sound.

Not that I knew this consciously at the time, what with the outer world coming to me through a perceptual filter of extreme ugliness while my craving for coffee ramped upward toward junkie level. At the time, I was simply startled to hear that I was not alone. So I whirled around to see who was there, and when my head stopped spinning a few seconds after my body, what should I see but a man in a dark business suit, exquisitely tailored, sitting in the sun room off the kitchen. That room faces east, so at 7 A.M. it was flooded with golden light from the overeager sun. This meant the guy was silhouetted against a row of window panes awash in liquid gold. Naturally, I blinked, and the afterimage of the fiery silhouette that was seared onto my retinas showed somebody bigger and bulkier than this normal-sized person, somebody with what appeared to be wing joints jutting up above his shoulders and goat's horns protruding from his temples.

So I blinked again, several times, rapidly. All this did was to strobe both images, the regular guy and the mountainous devil, against each other in rapid alternation. When I stopped blinking and stared, he was just a regular guy, albeit a very scrubbed and handsome-looking one. And he was sitting in my vintage La-Z-Boy recliner with his legs crossed and his hands templed. He said to me, "Having fun with the blinking thing? I can't say I blame you. It's an interesting effect, isn't it? Sometimes I wish my eyes worked like yours." He spoke in a rich baritone, melodious and smooth.

To say I was dazed is an understatement. To say I was pissed off at the man's desecration of my sacred sulking chair is entirely accurate. A cold splash of liquid on my hand made me jump, and I realized I was letting the water overflow the carafe. I quickly shut off the tap and set down the carafe. My coffee rhythm was broken. My mental and physical misery morphed into outrage. Okay, so *pissed off* was going to trump freaked out, at least for now.

The guy just looked at me as I hobbled into the sun room and tried to muster a poisonous glare. Before I could summon an appropriate verbal challenge to his presence, he said, "Please, Evan, have a seat," and indicated I should join him by settling on the nearby sofa. His voice and mannerism were pure silk. How could you hate a guy with a set of vocal cords like that and a personal style to match? I was amazed at the way I instantly began to melt. I obeyed him and sat on the sofa—but on the end farthest from him.

"I know," he continued, "this is all very sudden. You didn't wake up expecting to see me here. That's all right. I've grown very accustomed to poor receptions. So please don't trouble yourself with feelings of remorse about your poor reaction to me, even though as your guest I do deserve better treatment, at least under a set of older cultural codes whose loss I lament."

It sounds insane, but the casualness of his manner and soothingness of his voice, combined with his oddly complex and formal speech pattern, set me back on my regular schedule. I stared at him open-mouthed for a moment, then rose and returned to the kitchen to finish with the coffee. The comforting nature of the ritual began to pacify me: fill the carafe, then fill the reservoir. Set the paper filter, then scoop in some Folgers. Press the "brew" button, then wait for the miracle. As the trickle of hot dark liquid began tinkling into the carafe, I realized I really needed to visit the toilet.

"Evan?" That wondrous baritone again, like a pipe organ speaking through a human vocal apparatus. "This will take only a moment. I'd appreciate your full attention. We really need to talk."

"Why would I talk with someone who's not even there?" These words, tossed over my shoulder with arch impertinence, were a

blatantly manufactured attempt to appear nonchalant. "I'm reminded of the sage words of Ebenezer Scrooge concerning the
sometimes dramatic hallucinatory effects of digestion upon perception. You're probably just a bit of undigested beef, or a blot of
mustard, or a crumb of cheese. Or, as the case may be, a gallon or
two of cheap wine. So go away. I'm about to drink the elixir of life,
so I have precious little time to chat."

"Evan." His voicing of my name this time landed like a boulder. The very walls shook, and his tone cracked slightly but ominously, not on the high end the low one, his baritone betraying a
hint of impossibly deep bass like the foghorn roar of a primeval
monster. The thick vibrations actually rumbled in my chest, momentarily seizing my lungs and squeezing the breath out of them.
In the ensuing silence, I listened to the delicate tinkling of the coffee while silently willing my visitor to be nothing more than
Scrooge's digestive hallucination. But when I turned to look, he
was not only still there but still seated in my La-Z Boy.

He said, "Are we on the same page now?" and his voice was
back to normal. I suppose we must indeed have been reading the
same text by then, for I meekly returned to the sun room and re-
settled on the sofa, this time on the end nearest him. From this
closer angle I verified that he really was ruggedly handsome, in a
corporate-man sort of way: hair slicked back, perfect teeth, square
jaw, nice tan, flawless complexion. He wore expensive cologne,
too, and I savored the spicy tang of it even as I noticed that it
failed to completely mask another, less pleasant smell that hung
about him like an invisible cloud: the stink of smoke and sulfur,
like rotten eggs in a burnt-out house.

He gave me a pointed look. "I'm here about your books." Then
he waited for my response.

In my brilliance, I came up with, "What?"

"Let's not mince words, Evan." He assumed a shrewd expression. "Horror novels are one thing, but *religious* horror novels—or
horrific religious novels, if you prefer—are quite another. The
books you write have produced the unfortunate result of crossing

certain wires, as it were, and thereby producing certain, shall we say, *problematic* effects amongst a wide swath of readers. The purpose of my visit this morning is to set you on a different course."

"You . . . I . . ." My eloquence continued to astound.

"The problem," he said, "is that you have taken the entire Christian cosmology and, more importantly, the characteristic emotional tenor of those who consider themselves Christians, and you have turned these on their head. You have created protagonists whose very search for salvation produces a backfire effect that damns them to a worse hell than they had ever imagined. You have speculated that the Bible contains a hidden subtext that runs between the actual printed lines and undermines the surface message at every turn. You have written of a narcissistic demiurge who is so enraptured by the beauty of his own creation that he represses the memory of his birth from a monstrous prior reality, so that when he is forcibly reawakened to this memory, he suffers a psychological breakdown that generates cataclysmic consequences both for himself and for the cosmos he created. In these ways and many others, you've launched a subversive assault on the deepest philosophical and theological foundations of the enemy camp."

He actually said "the enemy camp." Was he referring to *God?* To *Christians?* Did this fact, and also the smell and the voice and the Dante-esque shape that still sizzled on my retinas, indicate the man's true identity? Was this truly the type of story that I had stepped into? A "Devil in the morning" rehash?

As I wondered these things with my jaw hanging down, he concluded: "You might reasonably think that I would approve of your efforts. But you would be mistaken. God, to put it bluntly, does not need depth therapy. He can't handle it—precisely as you have intuited in your books. And I'm here to make sure that your future creative efforts are focused in a different and, shall we say, more fruitful direction."

Despite or because of my astonishment, my blood began to boil again. The guy was talking about my books. My *books,* those hated relics from the former life I had lost. And he was speaking as if I were somehow still responsible for them. The heat of my rising fury began to clear away some of the remaining fog in my brain, and I let this irate clarity shape my words.

"Even though this is all a dream, I'm still not going to sit here and listen to such accusations. Let's get this straight right now: I do not *write* those goddamned books, I *wrote* those goddamned books. And now it's hands off, once and for all. So don't you dare come here to my house and interrupt my coffee and sit in my chair and accuse me of . . . of whatever it is you're accusing me of. Because you're talking to an *ex*-author who doesn't give a *damn* about those books."

"Of all the delicious sins in this sinfully delicious universe," he said, "there's none more delicious or endearing than self-deception. Especially of the willful kind, which you're demonstrating with aplomb at the moment. Bravo, Evan!" He sized me up, smiled with that handsome mouth, and nodded. "Go ahead. Tell me what you want to tell me. Share the whole sad story of your private woe, which, as I strangely regret to inform you, really hasn't been all that private."

I felt as if I were coming unglued. Literally. My brain reeled and my heart wanted to hammer a hole in my sternum. "The . . . the books . . ." He nodded again with obvious approval, encouraging me to share and tell.

And just like that, the logjam in my mouth and heart and brain broke wide. "My books almost killed me! Do you think I *wanted* to become the king of mid-list horror? Hell, no! All I ever wanted was to spend my life writing about religion and beauty and truth and spirit and mystical awakening. That's what I loved since I was a kid! When those novels about God's psychosis and all that crap came flooding out instead, I was more horrified than any of my readers. I was absolutely mortified at the metaphysical sewage spewing from my pen."

"But," he pointed out helpfully, "not so mortified that you refused to cash the checks."

"What else could I do?" My fury was erupting to volcanic heights. "My whole life imploded! My wife said she couldn't live with somebody who put 'hell on paper.' She called me a monster to my face and then left me, after which her family cleaned me out in a lawsuit over 'emotional damages.'"

"And oh, irony of ironies, what happened next?"

Next? "There was no next. That was the end of it. Just as soon as my life had completely imploded, the curse went away. I couldn't write those things anymore. I couldn't write *anything* anymore. I went from being a working writer to being a blocked writer overnight. And the well wasn't just empty, it was concreted over and laced with trip wires. I got pounding headaches every time I tried to think about writing. My thoughts scrambled when I even sat down in front of the typewriter, let alone tried to put words together. It got so bad I wondered if I might have a brain tumor. I returned all the publishers' advances, broke my contracts, and live now on a few royalty checks that get smaller every time."

"And so," he said with an air of finality, "here we sit, I in your chair and you on that sofa, which I'm noticing could stand to be reupholstered."

I was drained. My eyes felt feverish and my gut cold. "Here we sit," I repeated.

"Evan," he said, "somebody—I forget who—once said, 'You shall know the truth, and the truth shall set you free.' I come to you now bearing that truth and offering that freedom."

I was too numb even to summon another "What?"

He continued: "Would you like to write again? Would you like to return to your first love? Don't tell me you haven't thought about it these past several years while you've been drinking alone."

"You can help me write again." It was a question that plopped out as a lifeless statement, like I had somehow spat a dead cat out on the floor.

"Yes, I can help you write *again*." He gave a special emphasis to the final word and smiled faintly. "After all, I did it once before."

He cut off my look of blank confusion with more words. "It's time to come clean, I suppose. You noticed, naturally, that your authorial aspirations took a decidedly different turn than what you had originally intended. Please don't pretend to be shocked when I inform you of what you long suspected: that the unexpected change was of course my doing. I gave you a little, shall we say, *push* in a new direction, and then nature—*your* nature, to be exact—simply took its course."

"A push?"

"Yes, Evan. More fully, I assigned you a muse, and she whispered things into your inner mind, certain dark and hidden truths which most people never manage to intuit, and you then processed these promptings through that magnificent literary sensibility of yours to produce some of the finest horrific writings this side of the Abyss. As I said, there's no use pretending that you didn't speculate a few times in your darkest moments that you were the victim of a demonic curse. The fact is, you *were*. And the fact is, it's not fair. There's no justice in it. So don't bother searching for any. Just ask a man I once knew by the name of Job."

"You . . . cursed me?" That dreamy feeling again, really rippling and powerful this time. Not real. None of it. Not happening.

"All part of a master plan that I was and still am working," he said. "And oh, how it did work! Watching you run with those ineffable evil truths was so very refreshing. You were truly a fine vehicle, and don't think I didn't appreciate it.

"But then the backfire effect I alluded to earlier began to set in. You went too deep and started breaking out of the proper boundaries that my opponent and I had set. I guess I didn't take proper account of your keen philosophical bent, because your exposés and deconstructions of the Almighty—as he obtusely insists on referring to himself—started exposing and undermining the very foundations of the game that he and I have set for ourselves. In a nutshell, it doesn't benefit me at all when people start thinking 'off the grid' in matters of good and evil. I'm in this war to win it, not to see myself rendered irrelevant by people who see through it. And so I find myself in the unenviable position of paying you a visit today in order to shore up my opponent's ego." His smile now was rueful and none too pleasant. "Who would have thought?"

Despite my rising astonishment, incredulity, and horror, it was all quite fascinating, really, this revelation from the Devil, and in a deep and thrilling way that I hadn't experienced for years. Damn, but those were ideas that I sure could have run with, back in the days when I could write.

But the greater part of my attention at the moment was occupied by memories of all those years when I had been writing horror fiction and feeling as if I were either possessed by a demon or suffering from a progressive form of nightmarish schizophrenia. The shadows in my closet and under the bed had begun to inspire a profound sense of dread. I had been plagued by nightmares of suffocating darkness and demonic presences, from which I would awaken with keening shrieks that terrified my wife. The only outlet I had found for my growing horror had been my typewriter and the blank pages I rolled into it, which I had blackened with fictional visions more awful than anything I had ever heard of, let alone wanted to midwife into the world.

And now I was hearing the reason for my life's ruin explained in plain language, spoken by the Devil in a Gucci suit.

"You did this to me," I said in a quiet voice. And then, "*You* did *this* to *me!*"

"Evan," he said, and that volcanic rumbling tremored again through the floor and up through the sofa and into my soft, fleshy body. "Shut up. Just shut up and listen. 'Here's the deal,' as people in your increasingly illiterate and verbally barbaric culture and historical period are wont to say. I can't have you exposing God's and my cosmic game of Spy Versus Spy, and you can't stand living with yourself in your current state any longer. So this is what's going to happen."

Why was the room beginning to heat up and the air shimmer with a hellish red glare even as my consciousness of the crystalline chirping of the birds in the backyard beyond the windows grew more delicate and precise? Why did I catch a whiff of rotting flesh and acrid, ashy waste even as the morning sunlight appeared more golden and pure than I had known it for many years?

"I am assigning you another muse." This was the Devil speaking to me, I reminded myself, and he nodded, reading my thought and never wavering in his declaration. "She has been instructed to fill your soul with the inspiration you have always desired. You will find that everything you ever wanted will now come to you. And from your pen—sorry, typewriter—from the very same channel that brought into the world those subversive revelations which have so imperiled my operations, there shall flow revelations that will once again shore up the dam, patch the damaged parts, make the straight places crooked again, and shove those damned exalted valleys back down to their proper place."

He lifted a hand and made a strange sign in the air, almost as if he were making the sign of the cross, but it was a different symbol he traced, one that shot a bolt of sickness through my gut. My face and eyes burned with the hot red glow that had overtaken the sun room. My body trembled with the volcanic-oceanic roar that had infiltrated the bass frequencies built into the acoustics of those sheetrocked, texture-splattered, white-painted walls.

And then *poof!* all was cool and silent. Except for the warm golden sunbeams and gaily chirping birds. Cool air kissed my cheeks. It was a beautiful morning.

And I was alone. No Corporate-Miltonic Satan confronted me from the hallowed folds of my La-Z Boy, which was now blessedly empty, although its seat and back cushions bore a phantom discoloration akin to smoke damage in the shape of a man.

I managed to stand up, and after testing my balance, hopped into the recliner and snuggled down into it for a moment, just to assure myself that I still fit. Which I did, although the trace warmth of another very warm body still clinging to the cushions was distinctly less than pleasant.

And then I did the only thing there was to do. I got up and went to the kitchen, where the coffee waited for me to brew it. In sixty seconds flat the splashy little burblings of the coffee maker were soothing my spirit while the sharp-musky scent cleared my head. Everything seemed so crisp and fresh. Even the texture of my bathrobe against my skin felt remarkably new and delightful.

"Is this for real?" I asked aloud of no one in particular. "Is this the leading edge of new inspiration?" Enough coffee had already trickled into the pot for me to pour a mug, so I did and then returned the pot to its cradle. "Because," I said aloud again, "I can tell you right now that it's *no deal.* I'm not writing for you or anybody else. That's all over. This is *my* life, as crappy as it may be, and I'm going to suck all the misery out of it while I can, gods and devils be damned."

Still facing the counter and the kitchen cabinets, holding the white china mug with the black steaming liquid in my utterly steady hand, I raised my face to the ceiling and shouted. "Do you hear me? *No deal!*"

I added one lump of sugar and stirred lightly. Then I took a sip and sighed in ecstasy. No more devils for me that day.

The room went red before I could swallow. The roaring of a titanic cataract set me to shaking like a victim of Saint Vitus' Dance. A furnace blast of heat seared my flesh.

A voice boomed from behind me: *"This is not a negotiation."* No melodious baritone there. This was a lion roaring in a hurricane.

I whirled around, hot coffee drooling from my lips and down my chin and chest, to find a shriekingly hideous Dantean Devil towering over me in full gothic-reptilian splendor. Black wings and talons. Ram's horns sprouting from a misshapen head. Gray-skinned, rotten-textured, with yellow moonsliver feline eyes and a porcine snout surmounting an impossibly wide mouth whose lips were drawn back in a smile that revealed far too many silvery teeth, each one as long as a dagger. The creature must have stood nearly eight feet tall, and would have been obliged to hunch its head if the ceiling had still been there, but that cozy lid had been ripped off the top of my world, and the bare tops of my kitchen walls now outlined a blackish-crimson skyscape of roiling clouds where bolt lightning carved out jagged trails and leering wolf's faces formed and reformed endlessly in the furrows.

The blackstretched lips of the mountainous Devil before me moved and formed words. *"You* will *accept your gift and set things aright again. You* will *repair the damage you have wrought. And the pleasure you derive from fulfilling your deepest desire* will *be your damnation. That's the deal."*

Then he reached out a taloned hand, plucked the little white cup from my fingers, and dumped the drop of dark liquid down his throat. *"Mmmmmm,"* he sighed. *"The best part of waking up."*

And that's what I found myself doing next: waking up. In my bed. At my normal time. With a hangover and a fading memory of some dreamworld encounter that could not possibly be real. No way. Not a chance.

But when I crawled out of bed all fuzzy-eyed and disappointed that the daylight had come so quickly, I was arrested in mid-shuffle by a curious phenomenon: the sunlight squeezing through the slats of the window blinds didn't seem despicable, but delightful. I felt that if I were given to bouts of synesthesia, I might hear those delicate golden rays humming a hushed hymn to the beauties of creation.

I stayed rooted to the carpeted floor while the outlandishness of this development worked its way through me. Then I cautiously approached the blinds and raised my hand to pull the cord. It was a veritable Lux Aeterna moment, with the choral voices keening while the subhuman creature crept toward the ominous monolith with trembling outstretched hand. At last I seized the cord and pulled it.

A Hallelujah Chorus of celestial sunlight nearly knocked me back onto the bed. It flooded the room with divine joy and penetrated all the way to the heart of my dark misery.

No way. No *way.*

Next stop, the kitchen, where I peered anxiously into the adjoining sun room and saw nothing but sunlight singing like the

Mormon Tabernacle Choir while dust motes swirled in the blaze like heavenly fireflies.

The only part of my usual schedule that this explosion of mind-blowing joy could not disrupt was the Ritual of the Coffee. I prepped the pot and pressed the button while the chorus continued to sing.

Without warning, before the brew cycle had finished, I was gripped by the knowledge that there was something I simply had to do, even though the thought of it elicited a stab of cold dread.

I crept to the spare bedroom and dug through the closet until I located my typewriter buried beneath mounds of deliberately piled junk. I dusted off the card table where my best work had always taken place, and gently laid the typewriter on its surface. Another quick dig, this one through my old file cabinet, produced a stack of fresh white 16 pound bond paper, which I hadn't remembered still owning.

I sat down softly and rolled in a sheet. I caressed a key. Then I punched it. The letter appeared on the pristine paper with a satisfying *thwack*. I punched another, and then another. I raised my other hand to the qwerty keyboard and was soon typing words. And then sentences. And then paragraphs.

The tripwires had been removed and the concrete blasted away. The well of inspiration was wide open and brimming with cool waters of redemption.

I wrote, and wrote, and then wrote some more while the coffeemaker burbled and whispered in the next room and my long-pent-up craving for spiritual peace and enlightenment poured itself onto the pages. I already saw the full outline of the essay I was composing and, beyond that, the structure of the book of which it would be the opening piece. And there was another book after that, and then yet another, all perfectly formed in my head. Impossibly, after years of wretched emptiness, I had exploded in the course of a single morning into full-blown, super-genius Mozart mode, with fully finished works crowding in my head and just waiting for me to release them.

After awhile, when the stack of finished pages had grown thick and still the flow of words showed no signs of letting up, I found I was weeping as I wrote. Perfectly natural, I told myself. A function of joy, an excess of cleansing emotion at the lifting of my sterile curse. I already saw how the very fact of my sobs could be worked gracefully into the very paragraph I was then crafting about redemptive changes of mind and heart, by referring to the "gift of tears" the early Christian fathers wrote so much about.

Pointedly, purposefully, I kept typing and ignored the transition that came when the clacking of the keys began to sound like dry little laughs.

The God of Foulness

And what, Ananda, is contemplation of foulness? Herein, Ananda, a monk contemplates this body upwards from the soles of the feet, downwards from the top of the hair, enclosed in skin, as being full of many impurities. In this body there are head-hairs, body-hairs, nails, teeth, skin, flesh, sinews, bones, marrow, kidneys, heart, liver, pleura, spleen, lungs, intestines, intestinal tract, stomach, faeces, bile, phlegm, pus, blood, sweat, fat, tears, grease, saliva, nasal mucous, synovium (oil lubricating the joints), and urine. Thus he dwells contemplating foulness in this body. This, Ananda, is called contemplation of foulness.

—From *Pirit Potha* ("The Book of Protection"), a Pali Buddhist text

Disgust at what things are made of: liquid, dust, bones, filth. . . . Turn the body inside out, and see what kind of thing it is, and when it has grown old, what kind of thing it becomes, and when it is diseased. . . . Stop letting yourself be distracted. That is not allowed. Instead, as if you were dying right now, despise your flesh. A mess of blood, pieces of bone, a woven tangle of nerves, veins, arteries. . . . The stench of decay. Rotting meat in a bag. Look at it clearly. If you can.

—Marcus Aurelius, *Meditations*

Am now acutely ill with intestinal trouble following grippe. No strength—constant pain. Bloated with gas and have to sit and sleep constantly in chair with pillows. Doctor is going to call in a stomach specialist Tuesday. So I fear I shan't be able to do much for a long time to come.

—H. P. Lovecraft, from a letter dated fifteen days before his death

As a foulness shall ye know Them.

—*Necronomicon*

1

At first I thought it was just a perverse reaction to several decades' worth of bombardment by conflicting pronouncements from the medical establishment about what constitutes a "healthy lifestyle." That was my working hypothesis, held with tongue firmly in cheek, when my editor at the *Terence Sun-Gazette* assigned me to cover the grassroots phenomenon known as the Sick and Saved movement. The movement had garnered an insane amount of publicity in recent months because of its shocking—some would say *appalling*—claim. Its members worshiped sickness and disease. The media had dubbed them the "Sick Seekers" and given them enough coverage to lead some commentators to call them the story of the century. The Sick Seekers came from all walks of life and boasted all manner of physical and mental disorders, and their defining characteristic was that they viewed any kind of sickness as evidence of a special spiritual grace. At least, this was the best guess the commentators could come up with, since the Sick Seekers were notoriously close-mouthed to outsiders about the particulars of their beliefs and practices.

The only thing anybody knew for certain about them was that they prominently refused all medical treatments. This of course threw the official government bodies charged with safeguarding the public health into a collective panic. In the United States, the American Medical Association, the Centers for Disease Control, and National Institutes of Mental Health all wrung their hands with great public display. "What if people start actively *trying* to become sick?" they asked with clockwork regularity on all the nightly news programs. Obviously, the media themselves thought this was happening already, hence their popularization of the term "Sick Seekers."

The insurance and pharmaceutical industries were none too happy about the situation, either. The pharmaceutical companies in particular were scrambling for a solution, since their business was dealt a near death blow by the sheer numbers of the new movement, which was composed largely of elderly people who would otherwise have been their biggest customers. By the most recent estimate, which had been performed by a sociologist at Harvard and publicized in *Time* magazine, the Sick Seekers numbered around the million mark in the United States alone. This meant there were more of them than there were Unitarians.

As I said, my immediate reaction was to view all this with a rather cynical eye. To begin with, I decided to regard the term "Sick Seekers" with wry amusement, since it contained a semantic ambiguity, probably unnoticed by whoever had coined it, that didn't specify whether "sick" referred to what the people were seeking to become or how they ought to be morally perceived. Next, I turned to speculating about the origins of the movement, and arrived at my above-mentioned theory about a collective disgust at the inability of the medical community to arrive at a consensus regarding how one ought to eat, exercise, and so on. (My theory didn't explain why the same movement had cropped up in undeveloped nations where this information overload wasn't a problem, but I put that item on a back burner.) I myself had grown annoyed at the way the morning news programs always seemed to present at least one new doctor per day, who advanced at least one new theory about which foods to avoid, which medicines to take, which tests to have run, and which exercises to do. I amused myself by speculating that the Sick Seekers were people who had just decided to throw in the towel and forget about trying to wade through the mass of conflicting information. This allowed me to applaud their audacity from the sidelines.

When I first came to understand that they were engendering real concern not only among government authorities but the populace at large, I realized I should take them a bit more seriously. Their arrival on the world scene had created a truly apocalyptic mood in countries around the globe, one that harmonized beautifully with the mass premonition of approaching doom that had already begun to grip the globe during the early twenty-first century. But even so, after reading and reflecting on the matter I still found it easy just to write the whole thing off as a mass hysteria, admittedly a repugnant one, but in essence no different from the millennial madness that had gripped the Western nations at the end of the twentieth century or the rise of the charismatic Christian movement and its bastard child, the "signs and wonders" movement or "Third Wave" of Pentecostalism that was still providing so much research fodder for sociologists and scholars of religion who were caught up in the perennial quest for tenure.

I had once thought that I would number myself among those professional academicians. My interest in the Sick and Saved movement was more than just an idle amusement. Early in life, I had found that I was possessed of a seemingly inborn fascination with religion and spirituality. I was raised in no formal religious tradition, but when I discovered the literature of Zen Buddhism at the age of thirteen, it was as if a door were suddenly unlocked inside me, one that I hadn't even known existed. Suddenly, I was gripped by an intense yearning for spiritual knowledge, and by the time I graduated from high school, I was already planning to major in religious studies at the university and then go on to earn my doctorate. The thought of spending all my days walled up inside the comfortable ivory tower of academia, surrounded by books that fed my thirst for spiritual ideas, filled me with delicious feelings of security and comfort.

All had gone well for the first few years of my enrollment in the religious studies program at Terence University. But then, for reasons that still eluded me ten years later, everything had grown stale just two months before I was scheduled to earn my master's degree. I had been shocked as I experienced the pent-up excitement of my imminent academic career leaking like air from a punctured tire. Somehow, without my knowing it, a sense of hollowness and staleness had crept into everything I held dear, everything I thought my life was about, and I suddenly realized that I didn't know where to go or what to do. My sense of being on track with a life mission was gone, and had been replaced by a feeling of bleak hopelessness and confusion. Briefly, I fell into a personal and professional tailspin.

Then one of my professors, Dr. Daniel Baumann, advised me to consider another career. Since my awakening at the age of thirteen, I had never even thought of doing anything else, but when I turned my mind to it everything happened quickly. Within a matter of days, practically on a whim, I somehow fell into the journalism master's degree program. All thoughts of a career in academia fled down the same invisible drain that had siphoned away my passion for religion. I set my sights on becoming a Pulitzer Prize-winning journalist, and for years I didn't look back.

Eight years after obtaining the master's degree, I was still seeking the Pulitzer. More than anything else, those years had taught me that the confusion I had felt upon the death of my former sense of identity with a life mission was merely the front end of a long initiation into the arbitrary caprices of the inner life. I tried not to dwell too much on it, since I could tell that to do so would send me into a paralyzing depression, but eight years into my post-college career the foreground of my steady, normal outer life was paralleled precisely by an inner life of virulent nihilism, punctuated by periods of manic emotional abandon. The term "bipolar" played on my mind often, but I never sought a medical diagnosis. My spiritual and philosophical side wasn't totally gone; it had merely undergone a mutation. My love of ideas had somehow evolved into a kind of philosophical schizophrenia that expressed itself in terms of a kaleidoscopic shifting of worldviews, many of them mutually exclusive or even actively antagonistic toward one another. In this condition, I thought it would be useless to receive an official diagnosis of a chemical imbalance, since I would probably find myself arguing the very next day against the logical axioms upon which the diagnosis was founded. To add insult to injury, my cognizance of my condition only exacerbated its severity. By the time the Sick Seekers arrived on the scene, I had reached a point of near-burnout where all my emotional reserves were depleted and I had trouble believing anything, even my own thoughts. At times I diverted myself with a kind of gallows humor by speculating that my philosophical schizophrenia might qualify me for membership in the new movement.

But when I was assigned to cover them for the newspaper, I saw no humor in it, for I recognized an immediate problem: so many things had already been said about the Sick Seekers that there was surely nothing left for me to write.

I raised this point to Bobby, my managing editor, but he countered by letting me know his reasons for wanting the story.

"There's a local group of them," he told me on a Tuesday afternoon, after having given me the assignment the day before via an e-mail. He was drinking coffee to perk himself up for the final few hours of his workday, and he stared at me over the steaming cup as he took a sip. I was seated across the desk from him with notepad in hand, prepared to take what I had expected to be meaningless notes.

"Are you sure?" I said after a long pause. I habitually measured my words and actions carefully around other people, but it was difficult to conceal the fact that this unexpected information had ignited a spark of interest in me. I carefully distanced myself from the feeling and kept my eyes steadily upon Bobby.

"Not entirely," he said. "That's part of what I want you to find out. Believe me, I know how hard it will be to think of anything new to say. But if there really is a local group, then we've got the chance to do something special. You know how private these people are supposed to be."

And indeed, I did know of their notorious reticence. Even their closest family members didn't know what they really believed. Everything in the news was just second-hand testimony from friends, family, neighbors, and supposed "experts" whose theories were pure conjecture.

As I considered this, a strange feeling began to creep over me. It was as if a wheel had started to turn in the back of my head. I introspected for a moment and gained the impression of an old waterwheel, slick and wooden, revolving slowly on an unseen axle. The feeling it produced in me was strangely soothing. I was taken aback by this unexpected psychic event, and when I returned my attention to the outside world, I found that my skepticism about the proposed project had completely vanished, leaving me eager to jump on the story.

"So how do you know about this?" I asked.

"Peg told me," he said. Peg was his wife. She was a registered nurse who worked in the emergency room at the university hospital. The three of us had gone out to dinner a couple of times. "She's been saying for months now that she suspects something, but she wasn't sure until just a few days ago. Saturday night some lady brought an old man into the emergency room and said she had nearly run over him when she found him just lying in the middle of the road. He was still unconscious, so Peg checked his I.D. and looked to see if they had any records on him. Turns out he's been there before. He has cancer of the larynx. Thirteen months ago he started refusing treatment. Nobody ever saw him there again until the other night. When he woke up, he looked around and flew into a rage. He refused to let anybody see about him. His file says he lives alone at a private residence and isn't under anybody's supervised care, so they just had to let him go. Peg said he stormed outside and hailed a cab.

"The reason she thinks this means something," he continued, setting his styrofoam cup down on the desk, "is because more and more people have started refusing medical treatment at the hospital over the past year. Especially in the past two months. It's only a very small number, just a dozen or so, but these are people with some very serious medical conditions." He caught me with his eye as he paused. "Plus, the old guy said something as he was leaving."

"Wait, let me guess," I said. "He told them, 'As a foulness shall ye know them.' Am I right?"

Bobby seemed to stumble. After a moment he said, "Yeah, exactly." He was looking at me strangely.

I was as surprised as he was. A number of news stories had linked this cryptic saying to the cult, and I had just been spouting off when I said it. I told him this and he relaxed.

"Well, I guess you're the right guy for the job. You're almost psychic about it." He resumed his former easy manner of speaking. "Yeah, he said that weird Sick Seekers thing. Peg said his voice was awful to hear. She didn't even want to think about how far along his cancer must have advanced by now. From the way she was so spooked, I'm guessing it must be pretty bad." He glanced at his watch and then back up at me. "Well, I can put two and two together as well as she can, and when she told me what she was thinking, I knew she was right. There's got to be a cult group right here in Terence." He rose from his chair and started shuffling things around on his desk in the afternoon ritual I had come to know so well, the one that indicated he was about to be done with work for the day, regardless of how much time might be left on the clock. "What I want you to do," he said, "is find this group and get a story. With your background in religion, you should be able to talk to these people in a way that other people can't. Maybe you can make them feel comfortable, express some sort of understanding, get their sympathy. I don't care how you do it. Just find out something that nobody else has written about them yet."

"But Bobby," I said, "I *don't* understand them. Yes, I've studied up on them, but for the life of me I can't figure out why anybody would choose to live with terminal intestinal cancer, let alone *celebrate* it." I was thinking of a story I had watched just the night before on a weekly television news magazine. A man in Montana had refused to submit to having a large part of his colon removed, and had said things that indicated a link to the Sick and Saved movement. His wife had gone crying to the newspapers. "What am I supposed to do? How do I even *find* any of these people?"

"I told you," he said, "they have a file on this old man down at the hospital. Peg got his name: Mitchell Billings." He spelled it while I wrote it down.

"What else did she get?" I asked with pen poised to write.

"Nothing," he said. I blinked in surprise. "She's not going to risk her job over this, Lawrence. She already had her mind made up when she came to me, and I agree with her. It's not only against the rules, but it's a crime for her to divulge what's in those records. You're going to have to dig for yourself. I'm sure you can think of some way to use your pretty face to get access." He smiled wickedly, but at the moment I didn't think it was funny, especially since he was asking me to risk *my* neck. "By the way," he continued, "if you're thinking of going the easy way and looking in the phone book, don't bother. I checked already. Then I called information and checked the Internet. It's not that he's unlisted, he just doesn't have a phone number."

"What about the lady who brought him in? What did she have to say? Where did she find him?"

"Odd thing," Bobby said. "She must have stepped out during the ruckus. Peg couldn't find her anywhere."

I was still absorbing this when he reached for his tie, which he always hung on the coat rack in the corner after lunch. "Gonna call it an early day, *compadre*. Peg and I are going out to dinner and a concert tonight at the performing arts hall."

"Who's playing?" I asked without really caring. That wheel was still turning slowly in the back of my head, like an old waterwheel bearing buckets of fresh, cool water out of a silent spring. For the first time in many years, I felt the desire to sit in meditation for an extended period.

"The university symphony orchestra," he was saying. "Some Mozart piece. Or Bach or Beethoven. I really don't care. It's Peg's idea." He waved goodbye and walked out still carrying his tie, leaving me sitting there alone in his office, evidence of the trust he had built up for me after eight years of my devoted service.

I sat there for quite awhile watching the cool water being carried up from a spring in the back of my mind. When I got up to leave, I was feeling more alive than I had felt in years. But I was all too experienced at this sort of mood-revolution, and was far too jaded to allow myself to relax into any sort of good feeling, no matter how sweet and refreshing it seemed on the surface. Painful experience had taught me there was always a bottomless chasm of despair waiting on the other side.

2

After such thorough contemplation [of foulness], actual realization will unfailingly follow. If he now sees women, he is no longer dominated by the animal urge of carnal desire, but he sees *through* it; he sees them as skeletons. Looking ahead he, already now, perceives the flesh, how after death, it will be devoured by worms.

—*Going Forth*

I decided to go ahead and visit the hospital that very night. No time like the present for breaking the law, I thought. But first I stopped by my apartment to change clothes and freshen up. Bobby hadn't been kidding about my "pretty face." I was a strikingly handsome man. I had always been that way, even as a child. For years my mother had harbored fantasies about my being a professional model. She had taught me all about color coding, how to dress for best effect and fix my hair to look just right for my eyes, skin tone, facial shape, and all that. She was a failed model herself. Sometimes, I think she would have been happier with a daughter.

When I was in college, I found my looks to be a useful tool for getting into bed with just about any girl I liked, but that was as far as I took it. After I started working for the newspaper, I occasionally found that I could exploit my appearance by endearing myself to people who might not otherwise be inclined to talk to me. It even worked with men, for some reason. It wasn't that I ever engaged in any really tough investigative journalism. Far from it; my assignments were all cushy and soft. As the paper's religion reporter I got to sit through services at dozens of churches, interview rabbis and priests and preachers, go to funerals and bar mitzvahs, and so on. I even got to talk occasionally with my old professors in the religious studies department at the university, whenever I needed one of their sagacious comments to pad out some minor piece of journalistic fluff with an air of intellectual respectability. But even in those non-threatening situations, I sometimes liked to go for the throat, so to speak. Whenever I found people who were reticent or distracted and wouldn't give me their full attention, all I had to do was turn on the old charm and let my looks draw them to me like a magnet.

For my trip to the hospital, I chose a solid forest green shirt, black jeans, and black shoes. My hair was exceedingly dark, not quite black but just barely shy of it, and my eyes were a piercing green. I had learned years ago that when I wanted to look my most striking, I should wear dark, solid colors. When I looked in the mirror for a final inspection, my hair was still wet from a quick shower. The curls were soft and gleamed like sable. The shirt drew out the color of my eyes and gave me an appearance of intensity and wisdom. I knew I looked damned good.

Down at the hospital, I searched out the first female employee I could find. Fortunately, she was the one behind the reception-ist's counter. Her name was Lindy, and she was blonde and slight-ly overweight. We talked for a few minutes about nothing in particular before I explained to her that I was a reporter and needed to see a patient's file. Of course she told me this would be impossible, but then I turned on the charm and let her know that she was somebody I could really learn to like spending more time with. I had never been so blatantly manipulative with my looks, and I was mildly sickened at myself. But that was easily overcome by an exercise of mental transcendence (a leftover from my spir-itual days) wherein I stood back and suspended judgment on eve-rything I was feeling or doing. This never failed to put me in a comfortable place where nothing could touch me, either from the inside or the outside, and I could just watch things happen like a spectator. I padded my lie by telling her that I knew the patient personally, and that I was looking up his information as a favor to him. It was a muddled story, one that didn't hold together (which wasn't surprising, considering that I had made it up right there on the spot), but she bought it. She glanced around to make sure no-body was watching, and then she let me behind the counter and took me back to the office where the files were kept.

It was a long room, tall and narrow, filled with rows of gray metal shelves like a library. I thanked her profusely as she searched out Mitchell Billings's medical file. I thanked her again when she allowed me to stay there alone while she minded the front desk. As she was walking away, I watched the backs of her thighs. The cotton legs of her pants (standard nurse-issue) were stretched tight against her skin, and I found myself thinking that maybe I hadn't been kidding when I said I would like to get to know her better.

I flipped through the file quickly, standing there in the cramped aisleway between the shelves. The evidence of Mr. Billings's laryngeal cancer was there, along with his refusal on July 13th of the previous year to be treated. The doctors had wanted to perform a tracheostomy or laryngectomy more than a year ago, but he had declined. The record then skipped ahead to just four nights past, when someone had recorded in blue ink the tale of Billings's unexpected return to, and belligerent departure from, the university hospital. There was also a scribbled note about the unnamed Good Samaritan who had brought him in.

Before closing the file, I turned back to the cover page and copied down Billings's address: Route 3, Box 147, Terence, Missouri. I was vaguely familiar with Route 3, more commonly known as Highway M. It ran east out of Terence toward Mountain Glen and was populated mostly by farmer types. As Bobby had already previewed for me, there was no phone number listed, so I knew that my day was planned out for me tomorrow. Apparently, I would have to drive out Highway M and physically track the man down.

Having achieved my goal, I closed the manila-colored file and slid it back into its place on the shelf. Then I slipped out to the reception area (checking first to make sure nobody was around; I truly didn't want to get Lindy into trouble) and scooted out from behind the counter. On the way past I paused to thank Lindy yet again. She looked a little troubled, as if she were conflicted over her violation of the rules, so I reiterated that I wouldn't tell a single soul. I also assured her that she had helped Mr. Billings immensely. Her complexion was pale and milky, a nice match for her blond hair, and her cheeks were now colored with a slight flush from the heat of her troubled feelings. She was positively lovely. I found myself wondering as I exited through the automatic doors and emerged back into the humid August night whether I might not find myself back at the hospital soon, this time not under a ruse, but with the honest intention of getting closer to her. I supposed it might not be totally impossible.

The wheel was still turning.

3

What, Ananda, is contemplation of disadvantage? Herein, Ananda, a monk having gone to the forest, or to the foot of a tree, or to a lonely place, contemplates thus: 'Many are the sufferings, many are the disadvantages of this body since diverse diseases are engendered in this body, such as the following: Eye-disease, ear-disease, nose-disease, tongue-disease, body-disease, headache, mumps, mouth-disease, tooth-ache, cough, asthma, catarrh, heart-burn, fever, stomach ailment, fainting, dysentery, swelling, gripes, leprosy, boils, scrofula, consumption, epilepsy, ringworm, itch, eruption, tetter, pustule, plethora, diabetes, piles, cancer, fistula, and diseases originating from bile, from phlegm, from wind, from conflict of the humors, from changes of weather, from adverse conditions . . . and cold, heat, hunger, thirst, excrement, and urine.' Thus he dwells contemplating disadvantage in this body. This Ananda, is called contemplation of disadvantage.

—*Pirit Potha*

The next day I waited until mid-morning to begin my search. It was a hot day, the hottest by far in what had already been a sweltering summer. The old saying about the humidity being worse than the heat was amply realized on that day. I couldn't seem to get dried off after my shower, and by the time I made it to the ground floor of my apartment building and then out to my car, where I turned on the air conditioner at full blast, I was already dripping with sweat. I was glad I had picked a dark color that would hide the sweat rings already starting to appear under my arms, but I also realized it was quite foolish to be wearing such a heat-absorbing shirt on such a scorching day. My mother's old adage of "appearance over comfort" played on my mind annoyingly as I pulled out of the parking lot. To help silence it, I dialed the office on my cell phone and asked Susie, the receptionist, to tell Bobby that I had secured the information he mentioned and was headed out to speak with the guy today.

On the east edge of Terence, after the old downtown buildings gave way to densely populated residential subdivisions composed of new houses, which in turn gave way to more sparsely populated neighborhoods with older houses, Highway M turned south off Broadway Avenue, crossed the train tracks, jogged sharply to the left, and rapidly became something that looked more like a country lane than a conventional highway. I knew the road only by name. I had never driven it before, and found it rather odd, and oddly refreshing, to find such a completely rural-looking farm road branching off like an aging artery from the edge of a mid-sized university town like Terence. I took great pleasure in the sight of the oaks and hickory trees that flanked the road and created a latticed canopy of leafy branches overhead. The sun still hung in the eastern sky as I sped across the pavement, and its light rippled through the trees like a burning waterfall, shooting dazzling flashes of golden spray into the corners of my eyes.

I had to drive nearly ten miles to get to Billings's house. Highway M proved to be one of those typical Missouri country roads that wind and twist and seem to be taking you farther into the heart of nowhere even when you know where you're going. When you're bound for parts unknown, the effect is even more pronounced. Time stretches into an endless asphalt carpet ahead of you, and you start thinking you may never reach your destination. By the time I came across the house, I was imagining that I must have crossed some invisible dimensional barrier separating the normal universe with its known laws of physics from a strange realm where distance multiplied and space elongated the farther and faster you traveled.

The house appeared suddenly as I was rounding a sharp curve. It sat off the left side of the road about thirty yards, an old two-story structure built farmhouse style, with a brown slate rock exterior and a rust-colored front porch surmounted by two dormers. Mitchell Billings was sitting in the porch swing. I knew it had to be him as I braked sharply to avoid missing the driveway, which was an unpaved riot of gravel and dirt. My momentum was a bit more than I had expected, and I hit the edge of the dirtline at thirty miles per hour and kicked up a cloud of brown dust. Cursing aloud, I pulled up to the house and sat with my door shut while the cloud settled. Through my closed window and above the roar of the air conditioner, I could hear the screeching and buzzing of tree frogs and cicadas spilling out of the woods to my left. The tree line bordered the driveway, coming to within just a few yards of the house.

Mr. Billings sat there and looked at me from his porch swing without a hint of surprise on his wizened face. He looked ancient in a way that only old farmers can look, with sun-browned skin and a face so full of wrinkles it appeared his bones were clothed in aged cowhide. He had a full head of snowy white hair and was dressed in blue denim overalls, a red-checkered shirt, and brown work boots. His feet rested on the porch and swung him back forth an inch or two at a time as he looked at me through my windshield.

I saw all this from my car with the clarity of a close-up photograph. His overall appearance seemed almost archetypal, as if he were the model for the ubiquitous farmer character I had seen portrayed in various picture books as a child. When I climbed out of the car and felt the sun's rays strike my dark Polo shirt with the force of a blowtorch, I determined not to show any weakness before this man.

"Excuse me," I said as I approached the porch steps. "Are you Mitchell Billings?" He looked at me for a moment and then nodded. His hands never left his chest, where they were tucked under the straps of his overalls. I noticed an odd noise, a kind of dry, rhythmic rasping sound, but I couldn't locate it, so I put it out of mind while I made my introduction.

"My name is Lawrence Palmer." I stepped closer to the porch and took the direct approach I had decided upon ahead of time. "I'm a reporter with the *Terence Sun-Gazette*. Would it be all right if I stayed awhile to talk with you? Maybe sit down and ask you some questions?"

The chains holding the porch swing squealed against the support hooks as he swayed back and forth. The sound raised the hackles on the back of my neck.

Then he nodded again and rose to his feet. He detached one of his hands from beneath its overall strap and motioned for me to follow him into the house. The front door was open and the screen door shut, and he pulled open the screen and walked inside without saying a word, obviously expecting me to follow him. I hurried up the steps and caught the door. Inside, I could see a dimly lit living room reaching away toward what looked like a kitchen. There was an old cloth-covered sofa and a ratty recliner. The carpet was dirt-colored and worn thin from age and traffic. Mr. Billings had disappeared into the kitchen, where I heard him rattling around, running water, opening a cabinet. With a self-directed nod of affirmation, I stepped across the threshold and let the screen door hiss shut behind me.

Instantly, the noise of the insects outside grew muted in a way that didn't seem possible from just that thin door. Then I noticed the two electric box fans purring in the living room windowsills. The house was not air-conditioned, and the atmosphere inside felt unbearably stuffy. It was also hushed and filled with a sense of expectancy that I attributed to the light value. The window shades were drawn down to the tops of the fans, allowing a dusky sheen of sunlight to filter throughout the room. I stood watching a couple of flies buzz angrily around each other in crazy circles above the sofa until he returned.

He was carrying a glass of iced tea, which he offered to me. I noticed he hadn't brought a glass for himself. In his other hand he carried a notepad. He motioned for me to sit on the sofa, which I did, while he took a seat in the chair. He unclipped an ink pen from a pocket on the front of his overalls and scribbled something on the pad while I raised my glass and waved away the flies. The tea was instant, not brewed, but he had added a lot of sugar and a lemon slice as well, and it was sweet and refreshing in the oppressive atmosphere.

I noticed the odd rasping sound again while I was in the middle of a swallow, and again I couldn't locate it. The mystery was banished from my attention when he turned the notebook around and showed it to me. I had to lean forward to read the spidery black letters.

"I'm Mitchell Billings. You can call me Mitch. I have throat cancer so I can't talk. Ask me your questions and I'll write down my answers."

This was stranger than anything I had expected. It was also more fortuitous, since it gave me an easy lead-in to the questions I wanted to ask. I noticed that his eyes were as bright as silver dollars as I brought out my tape recorder and then realized the absurdity of what I was doing. With a sheepish grin, I returned it to my briefcase and took out a pencil and pad.

"I know about your cancer," I said, stepping into the story I had prepared. "I've been researching a story about patients in the Terence area who have refused medical treatment in the last year. When I spoke with someone at the university hospital, your name came up, and I couldn't find a phone number so I decided to drop in on you." I was banking on the fact that he wouldn't be offended by this admission of my forwardness, nor by the news that somebody had been talking about him. He merely continued to smile at me, so I went on. "But before we get to that, may I ask you some general questions? You look like you're about my grandfather's age. I'm guessing you're in your early eighties?" It was a standard ploy: start out strong and direct, then veer off into neutral territory to put the subject at ease.

He smiled and began to write, and that began our conversation. He was obviously quite accustomed to speaking with his pen and notebook, for he wrote exceptionally rapidly and legibly. He was also very forthcoming, as I soon discovered as we began passing the notebook back and forth, and I realized early in our conversation that he was far more intelligent than I had expected from his Farmer Brown appearance. His answers were coherent, even eloquent, which raised my opinion of him considerably.

He said he was ninety-one years old, which shocked me. The lightness of his movements and gleam in his eye had made him seem much younger despite his leathery appearance. I began to make my usual banter about wanting to know about his past, his upbringing, his family, his interests. When I asked my questions, he looked at me with those bright eyes and seemed to be riding upon some bubbling fountain of mild inner mirth. While he wrote his replies, I listened to the hum of the fans and the faint scrapings of insect noises from outside.

About his upbringing and education he wrote, "I grew up right here on Highway M, about three miles back toward Terence. We called it Beecher Road back then. Terence wasn't much to speak of in those days, but when the university came in, the town grew up in a hurry. I never went to college myself. I was educated in a one-room school house that's still standing. When you drive back toward town, a mile from here start looking for an old abandoned rock building off the right side of the road, down in a valley. I'm kind of sentimental about it."

In answer to my question about whether he had ever traveled away from southwest Missouri, he told me that he had served as a navigator on a B17 bomber in World War II. He had flown thirteen combat missions over Germany and had been awarded the Purple Heart and sent home when he was wounded through the throat by a piece of flak. "Kind of ironic," he wrote, "that after surviving that wound sixty years ago I would get cancer in the same spot."

When I asked about his family, whether he had a wife or children, he grew somber for the first time. The light dimmed in his eyes, and he paused to brush back a lock of white hair from his forehead with a callused hand. But he quickly went back to writing, and I soon had my reply: "I was married to a woman named Stella for fifty-four years. She died last year in the spring. We never had any children." This seemed an uncharacteristically reticent response given his extended answers to my previous questions, but I didn't push the matter. I did make a mental note of the fact that the timing of his wife's death would have coincided roughly with his own refusal to receive medical treatment.

That led me to the series of questions I had wanted to ask from the beginning.

"Mitch," I began. My tea glass was long since empty, and I looked around for a place to put it. He took it from me and set it on the floor beside his chair. The flies returned from somewhere and began buzzing around my face, apparently trying to settle on my left cheek. I waved them away with an irritated swipe of my hand.

"I don't want you to think I'm prying," I said, "but I have an important question to ask you. Of course you don't have to answer it if you don't want to." He just gave me that same bright-eyed stare. It was almost as if he knew where I was going with this.

I asked, "Have you heard of the Sick Seekers?" In response, he laughed. It was the first sound to come out of his throat since I had met him an hour ago, and it was horrible, a kind of wet rattling noise, like a drain coming unclogged and sucking down a sink full of dirty gray water. I masked my revulsion with a blank expression.

He was already writing on his pad. When he handed it to me, I flipped it over and read, "I wondered whether you were ever going to get around to that."

My astonishment was considerable. The rest of our conversation, which lasted until well after sunset, formed a transcript that nearly overwhelmed me with its fantastic implications. I quickly abandoned my list of prepared questions in favor of pursuing the various tangents Mitch presented to me. We sat there in the muggy atmosphere of his living room, me asking questions and him writing answers as the sun made its way west, and I felt as if I were seeing the outlines of a surreal puzzle or painting take shape in my mind. Sometimes he wrote for five minutes or more, during which time I would sit there trying unsuccessfully to digest his previous replies. It was also while he wrote that I managed to identify the rasping sound I had heard earlier. It was his breath. The air had to squeeze past the malignant growth in his neck to reach his lungs. I shivered slightly at the thought. I also pitied him a little, even though I knew it was a virtual miracle that he was sitting there at all, given that he shouldn't have been able to breathe or swallow for over a year.

He let me take his written replies home with me, and that night I reconstructed my own questions and comments as accurately as I could from memory and from the cues contained in his answers. What I couldn't capture on paper was my mounting sense of incredulity as I discovered that his beliefs were far more bizarre and grotesque than I had suspected from the nature of our interaction up to that point.

Me: I assume you guessed why I'm here when I mentioned the story I'm writing?

Mitch: Yes. I figured it would only be a matter of time before somebody like you came around wanting to talk to me.

Me: Why were you at the hospital the other night? What happened?

Mitch: I have these spells sometimes.

Me: What kind of spells?

Mitch: I pass out. Later on I don't remember anything.

Me: Who took you to the hospital?

Mitch: A friend.

Me: Are you one of the Sick Seekers? Is there a local group?

Mitch: Yes. We've been together for a little over a year now. There are twelve members. We call ourselves a "body." I'm sure you know from keeping up with the news that there are other bodies all over the world.

Me: Are you willing to answer some detailed questions? From what I've read, most members of your movement don't want to talk to reporters.

Mitch: It's about time we stopped that nonsense. People need to hear what we have to say.

Me: Is it true that you worship your diseases?

Mitch: We don't worship our diseases. We worship the One they point to.

Me: What do they point to?

Mitch: Our God.

Me: Who is your god?

Mitch: Let me tell you something else first. People have the wrong idea about disease and health. Everybody gets sick and dies. That's just the way of things. Most of us fight against it. To hear all the doctors talk, you'd think nobody was *supposed* to get sick or die. When the God started talking to people around the world, He told us that sickness doesn't have to be something bad. He told us that sickness can set you free. Some people think life is hopeless and meaningless because everybody is headed for certain sickness and death, but our God gives us hope and meaning by showing us that our diseases are taking us somewhere.

Me: Where are they taking you?

Mitch: They're taking us all the way to Him. The normal view of health is wrong-headed. A healthy body is like a dirty pair of eyeglasses. It gets in the way of seeing the truth for what it really is. When your body has what everybody calls a "disease," it's like the lenses are cleaned off, and you have the chance to see things differently.

Me: How do you see things differently?

Mitch: You see that having a body is what keeps you separate from everything else and makes you miserable. A healthy body is the truest and worst form of disease.

Stella and I fought against our cancers for three years. We tried chemotherapy, radiation, everything. She had a double mastectomy. I was about to let them take out my larynx, and then Stella died and the God started talking to me right afterward. I saw then how we'd been chasing after the wind. What did we think we were trying to save? Every minute you're alive, you're dying. We just made it worse by fighting it. Now I won't ever make that mistake again. I had reached a point where I was completely fed up with being sick. I couldn't stand it for another minute. Then the God showed me the way out. Until you've experienced it yourself, you can't know how peaceful it is to accept what the God tells you and just relax into your sickness.

Me: How does your god talk to you? What is he like?

Mitch: He's a God the regular churches don't know. They have to just "believe" in their god, but we know ours for real. We know Him through our diseases. He *is* our diseases. That's what they are. They're His presence in our bodies. He talks to us through them. I don't mean the old preacher's claim that "the Lord told me so." I'm talking about real speaking. He tells us what He wants and how He's going to give us peace after we die. And He takes away our pain.

Me: What do you mean by that?

Mitch: We just give our pain to Him and He takes it away. None of us feels pain at all anymore. I'm supposed to be in total agony right now, but I'm just fine. It's better than any drug the doctors could give you. My friends in the local body have arthritis, cancer, all kinds of things, and they don't feel anything either.

Me: Were you a religious man before you got involved with the Sick Seekers?

Mitch: I was a member of Mount Tabor General Baptist Church for fifty-four years, the whole time I was married to Stella. Right after she died, the God started talking to me through my throat cancer. I wouldn't let Pastor James give her a funeral in the church after that. Of course that ran off all my old friends, but I found better ones when I met the other members of the body.

Me: Can you explain more about what you expect to happen after you die, and what your god says to you?

Mitch: We will be taken into the God after we die. That's what He tells us. He takes our pain away from us, and it builds Him up, and when we are gone there will only be Him.

Me: Do you think you will survive after death? If there's only him, where will you be?

Mitch: The part of us that seems like a disease now is the most important part. It will become a part of Him. Whatever's left will just rot away, and good riddance to it.

Me: What's the meaning of the saying "As a foulness shall ye know them"?

Mitch: That's taken from our holy book. We have a Bible too. [At this I was filled with eager hopes of seeing a copy of this book, but he merely smiled at me in a secretive sort of way, so I didn't push it.]

Me: But what does the saying mean?

Mitch: "As a foulness shall ye know Them" talks about how our God and the others like Him always appear to people on the outside. He shows up as a horrible disease in people's bodies, and that scares everybody who's not one of us. They think it's awful. You've heard what they say about us on TV. Outsiders know Him as a "foulness." But there's a double meaning to it, because even though you start out knowing Him as a foulness, when you listen to Him, and you decide to give up your right to yourself and really let Him work in your body, you learn that He has the most special kind of peace in the world hidden away inside Him. The god of the regular churches is just the opposite. He talks about peace and love, but when

you get on the inside and study the Bible you find out
he's full of anger and hatred. He does all kinds of horrible things. He's a deceiver, but our God is exactly what
He says He is.

Me: How is the God of the regular churches a deceiver?

Mitch: Remember, I was a Baptist for fifty-four years. I took it
seriously. I went to Sunday School and studied my Bible.
In Philippians 4:9 Paul says, "The God of peace will be
with you." For years I tried to believe that he really is a
god of peace. But I never knew what to do with things
like Deuteronomy 28:22: "The LORD will strike you with
wasting disease, with fever and inflammation, with
scorching heat and drought, with blight and mildew,
which will plague you until you perish." Those kinds of
things are all through the Bible. God is one way, then
he's another. It wouldn't be so bad if all those punish-
ments were meant to set you free from the body, but
that's not what they're about. They're just cruel things
being done to you by a cruel god for no good reason. I
made myself miserable trying to figure it all out. When
Stella died after all those years of suffering, I understood
how things really are. She grew up as a good Baptist. The
whole time she was sick, she never stopped praying and
believing her God would heal her. I prayed and tried to
believe, too, but all those contradictions wouldn't let me
alone. "The proof is in the pudding," they say. The god
she worshipped never took an ounce of pain away from
her. My new God, the one the outsiders think is a foulness, takes away my pain all the time. I'll take a God who
looks foul on the outside but has bliss for you on the inside over the opposite kind any day. Plus, my God really
talks to me. I don't have to pray and whine to try to convince myself that I'm hearing His voice.

Me: You said your god is not alone, that there are others like
him. What are their names? What do you call your god?

[Mitch laughed again at this point, and the wet sucking sound revolted me even more than it had before. He was still suppressing more laughter as he wrote on his pad.]

Mitch: I could tell you their names, but they wouldn't mean anything to you. Don't worry. You'll understand it all soon enough.

When I read this last line, I looked up and saw him smiling at me. It was not a pleasant expression. Up until then, I had liked him a great deal for his intelligence and good humor, even though his description of his beliefs had struck me as positively nuts. It was sounding like the theology of the Sick and Saved movement bordered on insanity, but I had still found myself liking the old guy. He possessed a palpable and undeniable charisma.

But now this had suddenly gone underground and been replaced by a sinister look that I hadn't seen before. Being a professional writer, I thought of it as more a *leer* than a smile. Its menacing character was made all the more apparent by the yellow light of the lamp he had switched on when the sun went down. The dim rays slanted across his face from the left, casting his features into high relief, calling out every nuance of the webwork of lines on his skin and showing me clearly that he thought he knew something I didn't, something that made him feel smug with superiority. It was so blatant, and it gave his last comment such a threatening quality, that I almost crossed a journalistic line and demanded to know what he was holding back. But then I caught myself and purposely returned his smile. His breathing was like the scraping of the nocturnal forest noises outside the windows as he continued to look at me.

I was about to say something, I didn't know what, when he handed me his notepad again. He had written a new message while I wasn't looking. "The God gives you a choice," he said. "First He gives you a taste of the bliss He's offering you. Then He shows you what it's going to cost you to accept it." When I looked at him, the smug smile was still planted on his lips. What I had taken to be evidence of an inner mirth glinting in his eyes now looked like cold calculation. I could think of nothing to say in response. Suddenly I felt hot, tired, and worn out by the conversation. My vision flickered with dark spots, and I realized with a shock that it would take only a slight relaxation of vigilance for me to pass out. This had never happened before. My stomach quivered as I wiped a hand over my face.

To hide what was happening, I ended our meeting. "Mitch," I said, "it's getting late, and I should get out of here and stop bothering you. I've enjoyed the hospitality. You've been very generous with your time." My hands were shaking as I gathered my things and shut my briefcase. When I rose to my feet, the backs of my thighs had sweated through my slacks, and the fabric of the sofa cushion peeled away from my legs like the skin of a soggy fruit.

He stayed seated and wrote something. "We're having a meeting this Saturday night," the words said. "I'd like you to come."

I didn't know what to say. This was far more than I had hoped for. Sixty seconds earlier, I would have jumped at the chance without hesitating. No reporter had ever attended one of the worship services—or whatever they were—of the Sick Seekers. With the inside information I would gain from such a meeting, I might be looking at a substantial journalistic project that I could expand and sell to a national publication after I had turned in a perfunctory piece to Bobby.

But Mitch's change of expression had filled me with doubt and distaste, and I hesitated. In the silence, the flies came back and started trying to settle on my left cheek again. Thinking they were probably attracted to a spot of sweet tea that I must have unknowingly splashed on myself, I rubbed my face and used the gesture to look as if I were mulling over his invitation. Which, in fact, I was.

"I'm very interested," I finally said. "Where do you meet?"

"Right here at my house," was his written reply. "You already know the way. The meeting is at seven o'clock. Why don't you come on out and meet the rest of us? There's lots more for you to learn."

Despite my suspicion, I knew it was unlikely that I could turn down such an invitation, and I think he knew it, too. All afternoon as he and I had talked, I had felt that wheel in my head turning slowly and steadily. My spirit was energized by a vitality that seemed totally out of step with the tenor of the conversation and the dizziness that still threatened to overturn me. Even as I stood there struggling to understand all that I had learned, a warm pulse of well being throbbed in my chest.

But I still couldn't bring myself to accept his invitation at the moment. I thanked him and said I'd think about it. He seemed satisfied with this, for he rose from his chair and extended his hand. His skin was rough and dry as sandpaper, and his grip felt like a vise. My own hand was soft and smooth from years of desk work, and was practically swallowed whole by his enormous grasp. I tried not to look him in the eye, but I couldn't help noticing that he was still watching me closely, as if he were waiting for something. When he released my hand, I headed immediately for the door.

Outside, darkness had taken complete hold of the house and the highway. The daytime buzzing of insects had given way to the nighttime screeching and whirring of crickets and tree frogs. It had been a long time since I spent an evening in the country, and the sounds and smells of summer night conjured up nostalgic memories of long-ago childhood evenings filled with creek swimming and backyard barbecuing and chasing after lightning bugs.

At the bottom of the porch steps I turned and gave him a wave. Crunching through the gravel toward my car, I still had a thousand questions to ask him. I had failed to follow up on all kinds of details that needed filling in. On first impression his beliefs struck me as nothing so much as a perverted mysticism, not far from the spiritual attitude I had embraced while in college, but in a horribly twisted form. His determination to give himself up to his cancer paralleled my own erstwhile attitude of detached transcendence. But he didn't just give himself up to his disease, he conceived of it as some kind of deity, and he *identified* himself with it, just as a Christian mystic might identify his soul with God or a Vedantic Hindu might identify himself with Brahman.

My head boiled with these thoughts as I settled into the driver's seat and inserted the key in the ignition. I looked up briefly and saw Mitch seated once again in the porch swing. He hadn't turned the outside light on. The pale light of the lamp in his living room shone feebly through the screen door, illuminating him again with a chiaroscuro effect. I found myself searching reflexively for that inner wheel, and there it was, turning in the shadows of my psyche, drawing up fresh water from a well in my soul. I felt a pressing need to write about it in my journal, for it had been years since I was so spontaneously aware of my inner spiritual state.

As I started the engine, I saw Mitch reach up for the first time since my arrival and probe gently at his throat. It was a gesture I would have expected from a man whose medical charts said he should have already been dead from cancer of the larynx. But from those same charts, I never would have expected him to touch that diseased area of his body with such an apparent attitude of affection.

4

... those sorrows which are sent to wean us from the earth.

—Mary Shelley, *Frankenstein*

The next day, the first person I thought of turning to for my post-interview research was Dr. Baumann from the religious studies department at Terence University. The last time I had spoken with him, I had been writing a profile about the local Baha'i group, whose worship center was located on the university grounds. He was the natural choice to call for a scholarly comment on such matters, since his specialty area was comparative religion. As the son of Methodist missionaries who had raised him while living and ministering in India, he was the perfect source of information and opinions on such matters.

But beyond his professional qualifications, currently I just wanted to talk with him as a friend. He was more than a former teacher, he was a mentor, a status he had assumed when I lost my mother to cancer during my second year of grad school. He had noticed how distraught I was, and had offered me some free pastoral counseling. Although his orthodox Christian outlook hadn't coincided with my mystic-cum-agnostic one, I had deeply appreciated his moral support and words of wisdom. After I graduated, he was always the first one I approached when I needed a quotation for a story. Now I found myself seeking his advice once again for personal reasons. I didn't know how to understand what was happening inside me, and I hoped to get a grip on it by having him explain to me the obscurities of all that I had learned from Mitch. Somehow the two were connected, the Sick Seekers story and the wheel of peace that was turning in my head. I needed input from an objective source to make sense of it.

Wanting to surprise him, I went directly to his office on the second floor of Markham Hall without phoning ahead. Then, standing there in the hallway before his locked door, I called myself an idiot—out loud, and then looked around to see whether any passerby had heard me—for not having called to check on his summer office hours.

My next stop was the religious studies departmental office, where I found a new secretary seated behind the reception desk. She was a dull, flat-eyed woman who seemed to be totally devoid of personality. This was in marked contrast to Josie, the vivacious middle-aged neo-pagan who had been the department's secretary for the entire length of my involvement there. But oddly enough, the new woman looked a little bit like Josie, with the same stringy gray hair, pale skin, and thin nose. She might have been Josie's slightly older and significantly duller sister. She told me in a monotone that Dr. Baumann was on sabbatical and that I could e-mail him or leave a message on his voice mail if I wanted. When I asked where he was, she mumbled, "He's checking out those Sick Seekers down in Nevada."

My astonishment was profound. When I pressed her for more, she told me that Dr. Baumann's brother had become involved with the Sick Seekers after discovering that he was suffering from end stage liver disease, the result of a longtime undiagnosed infection with both hepatitis A and B. He had refused to seek a liver transplant, and Dr. Baumann was in Las Vegas to see if he could rescue his brother from the cult. He was also using the opportunity to do some research into the theology of the group, which he said deserved more attention than the mass media had given it.

By the way she ticked this information off, I could tell the new woman was probably just repeating information that she had gained by eavesdropping on conversations with Dr. Allee, the department head, whose office door was right behind her. In the past Josie had always enjoyed passing on this same kind of gossip, but she had done it with far more flair, interspersing the gossipy information with lots of smiling and flirting. I had always come away feeling pepped up and kind of turned on. The new lady, by contrast, made me feel weary and vaguely disgusted.

My thoughts were racing every which way as I left her and headed for the stairwell. Mitch and his maniacal beliefs. Dr. Baumann and his sick brother. Josie's replacement by a pod person. The story I was supposed to be writing for Bobby. It was all a giant puzzle, or perhaps a "magic eye" picture, one of those computer generated images that revealed three-dimensional depths when you relaxed your eyes and let the hidden image coalesce like magic.

But walking down the sterile institutional length of Markham Hall's second floor with my head buzzing with competing claims to attention, I found a new and unexpected thought jostling its way to the forefront. It was more of an emotion, really: for no good reason I was pining for the innocent passion of my college years. For a long time those years had seemed frozen in eternity, like a snapshot of an idyllic childhood. This new evidence of elements from my miserable present invading the pristine happiness of my past—Dr. Baumann, my mentor, getting mixed up with the damned Sick Seekers—felt like the most profound kind of invasion. It was like somebody had started to rewrite my past to make it conform more to the way I saw the world currently when I was in one of my darker moods: full of suffering, devoid of meaning, going nowhere.

I caught myself scratching the left side of my face as I took the stairs down to the first floor and walked outside to visitor parking. As always, the campus was dotted with lovely instances of female flesh. The fall semester would be starting on Monday, and thousands of students were in town a few days early to get settled into their dorms and fraternities and sorority houses. Always when I came to campus, I basked in the appreciative looks I got from all the girls. It was especially fun at this time of year, when the new crop of freshmen were in town. But suddenly, out of nowhere, my face was itching so badly that I couldn't enjoy the attention.

It rapidly burgeoned into some sort of attack. By the time I got to my car, the itching had become a burning. When I looked in the rearview mirror, I saw my left cheek mottled with angry red splotches from all the rubbing and scratching I had already done. I couldn't imagine where I might have come in contact with poison oak or ivy, but they seemed the likely culprits. I had been susceptible to their influence since I was a boy, when I had caught a rash from one or both at least once per summer.

On the way home I stopped by a drugstore to get some allergy cream. A poster prominently displayed above the prescription counseling window shouted three words in tall, white letters on a black background: "TAKE YOUR MEDICINE!" A roundabout reference to the Sick Seekers, I assumed.

The lady behind the counter was attractive in a more mature way than the girls on campus. Her hair was red and her eyes green like mine. She wore a lot of mascara, which contrasted nicely with her white lab coat. I smiled at her as she took my money and handed me my purchase in a white paper bag, but her eyes were drawn to the left side of my face, and the smile she gave me was only the perfunctory kind that she would have given any other customer.

5

The purpose of the world is for you to suffer, to create the suffering that seems to be what is necessary for the awakening to happen.

—Eckhart Tolle

When I awoke on Friday morning, a black spot had developed on my face overnight.

I had arrived back at my apartment on Thursday afternoon in a virtual frenzy of itching and burning, and had raced upstairs, torn open the box containing the cream, and slathered nearly a quarter of the tube onto my inflamed skin. It had helped briefly with its cooling and softening effect, but an hour later the pain returned. By eight o'clock the cream was gone. Then I started with the moisturizing lotion. It turned out the antihistamine effect of the allergy cream hadn't been doing anything, because the lotion worked just as well.

Or just as poorly. I lay awake on the couch in front of the television until one o'clock in the morning, unable to relax or think about anything except the maddening pain in my face. Right before drifting off to sleep at last, I got up for a final look at my cheek in the bathroom mirror. By that time the red splotches had swelled into burning welts from my constant scratching. On closer inspection, I thought my face looked a little distorted and rather out-of-proportion, as if the left side were bigger and heavier than the right. The thought of visiting the emergency room flickered through my mind, but only briefly. Of course I was scared and wanted to know just what the hell was going on, but those concerns were outweighed by the fact that in my current condition I didn't want to go anyplace where I might run the risk of being recognized. I couldn't imagine going to the hospital and running into Bobby's wife Peg, or even worse, the virginal Lindy, and having them see me like this. Especially not Lindy. Not when I still had half-formed plans for the two of us.

So I just returned to the couch and rubbed on another layer of lotion. Then I closed my eyes and concentrated on breathing slowly and steadily while the voice of the announcer on the television news network droned on and on, saying something about the Sick Seekers.

My first stop when I awoke in the morning was the bathroom again, where I discovered the black spot on my cheek. It arrested my attention as soon as I flipped the light switch, and I examined it in the harsh glare of the vanity bulbs with my face so close to the mirror that my breath steamed the glass. The red welts had disappeared and been replaced by an uneven circle about the size of a pea. It rode high on my left cheekbone, a blobby mole with a ragged border, colored with an irregular hue. Its center was black as tar, but toward the edges it thinned out and half blended with the normal peachy color of my skin to form a sickly dark brew like weak coffee.

With growing panic, I realized it was a familiar shape that had lodged on my face. The coloration touched a chord of memory. An awful thought occurred to me, one that I tried to shove down and forget, but it wouldn't be denied.

Years earlier, when I was nineteen years old and a sophomore in college, I had undergone surgery to have cancerous cells removed from that same cheek. For several weeks I had watched with curiosity as the new moles had appeared. They had been small and faint, and I had thought they were just the aftereffects of the severe sunburn I had suffered while celebrating Spring Break on Padre Island. But when I arrived back home in May after the semester ended, my mother flew into a panic at the sight of them. We hadn't seen each other since Christmas, so I had hoped she would greet me warmly. Instead, she pounced on the spots and drilled me over their history—when and where they had first appeared, whether they were painful, and so on—almost before she saw fit to say hello. Her behavior was typical, but I still felt disappointed.

I did what she wanted and made an appointment with a local

dermatologist, who surprised me by suggesting a biopsy, which then astounded me by showing a malignancy. It surprised the doctor, too, because, as he told me, sudden onset usually indicates a benign growth. As things stood, he told me the spots had to be removed immediately.

I submitted to the operation in a kind of daze. He burned the cells off with a surgical laser and I wore a bandage on my face for a week. When the time arrived to take it off, there were only a few minor marks on my skin to show that anything had ever happened, and these faded within a few days. The moment when I stood before my mother and proudly showed her my virgin cheek glowing with new health was forever seared into my memory. She looked at it with a faintly crazed expression. Then she burst into tears and fled to her bedroom, where she refused to open the door for two days. After that we never spoke about the matter again, not even when she developed the breast cancer that would eventually kill her.

It was impossible, of course, for the new overnight growth on my face to be what I feared it was. Even the term "sudden onset" couldn't cover the appearance of a cancerous mole in something like seven hours. But that was the fear that gripped me as I stood there looking at my marred face in the bathroom mirror. It literally caused me to shiver as I slowly showered and got dressed and ate a breakfast of cold cereal and hot toast. I had planned to put in some time at the office that day, but any activity that involved leaving my apartment was now out of the question. I couldn't go and confront Susie at the receptionist's counter and see the shock in her eyes when she saw my face. I couldn't deal with the other women in the newsroom—Ginny with her big-toothed smile, Elaine with her plaid skirts, Larissa with her long brown hair and seemingly endless supply of bows—and know they were watching me not with desire but in horrified fascination at the obscenity on my cheek. In the end I resolved to stay home and phone in a report about my progress to Bobby.

Susie put me through to his extension, and when I told him

that I had confirmed the existence of a Sick Seekers group in Terence, I heard him pound his desk as he fairly shouted, "I knew it!"
His excitement made it all the easier for me to gloss over my
meeting with Mitch. I said I had spoken with him briefly, and that
I planned to ask some follow-up questions soon. I promised I
would tell Bobby everything just as soon as I had gathered enough
information for a story. He bought the whole thing, and we hung
up with him expressing pleasure and excitement while I felt like a
loser for lying to him.

I spent the day alternating between lying on the couch and poring over Mitch's written words. A little before noon, I caved in to
my lonely feelings and called Dr. Baumann's voice mail, hoping that
he might check it remotely and knowing that he probably wouldn't
receive an e-mail, so legendary was his disdain for "that impersonal,
ephemeral excuse for a letter." In my message, I apologized for not
having been in contact for so long and explained that I was doing a
story about the Sick Seekers and wanted his input, since I had
heard he was researching the same subject. In contrast to my in-
complete disclosure to Bobby, I told Dr. Baumann everything about
my meeting with Mitch. I took particular pains in describing the
Sick Seekers' theology exactly as Mitch had explained it to me, and
I asked if Dr. Baumann knew of any historical antecedents to it. I
mentioned that Mitch had claimed to have an actual scripture in
his possession, and I asked whether Dr. Baumann knew of this text.
Before I hung up, I wished him well with his brother and asked him
to call me at his earliest opportunity.

It seemed the sun took twice as long as normal to complete its
circuit across the sky that day. The shadows crept across my carpeted living room floor like black molasses, and the long hours of
solitude allowed a number of dark thoughts to steal into my consciousness. While studying the transcript of the interview, I kept
returning to the last thing Mitch had told me about his beliefs:
"The God gives you a choice. First He gives you a taste of the bliss
He's offering you. Then He shows you what it's going to cost you
to accept it." I knew it was dangerous for me to think what I was

thinking. I could hardly believe I was entertaining the idea, especially in light of my already precarious psychological life. But try
as I might to warn myself away, I couldn't help identifying my situation with Mitch's words. My involuntary tendency to try on new
worldviews like suits of clothes led me to think that maybe my recent sense of spiritual lightness was the gift of the God, whatever
His name was, and that the growth on my face was a sign of the
price I would have to pay for accepting it. I knew it was madness,
but in the silence of my apartment, cut off from the rest of the
world, with Dr. Baumann thousands of miles away, the transcript
of a surreal spiritual puzzle in my hand, and an impossible mark
riding on my cheek, I didn't know how to convince myself otherwise. My philosophical schizophrenia was working overtime to
undermine all my attempts at reasoning with myself. Nor was I
helped by the fact that I was increasingly plagued by the mental
image of these thoughts as deformed crabs that had been clinging
to the underside of my consciousness for a very long time, awaiting
a quiet moment in which to scuttle to the top and sink their claws
into the soft gray folds where my sense of self resided.

By five o'clock I was utterly wretched. I felt dizzy, hot, and
sick with worry, but at least my wooziness helped me for awhile as
I tried to deny a phenomenon that I had noticed several times
during the day but refused to acknowledge. At last it was undeniable, and that was when my world definitively began to tilt.

For even though it was impossible, the black spot was visibly
growing. When I had first examined it around seven in the morning, it was the size of a pea. By noon, when I had fixed myself a
half-hearted lunch of canned tomato soup and a grilled cheese
sandwich, it was big as a dime. I was just overwrought, I told myself as I chewed the cheesy bread. I was just letting my vivid mental and imaginative powers get away from me. Of course the spot
couldn't be growing. Not like that. Not so quickly that by the next
morning it would surely cover the whole of my face like a putrid
black mask.

But at five in the afternoon it was the size of a large marble, and its growth was impossible to deny. I stared at it in the mirror while the evening news blared from the TV set in the other room. My supernatural gift from the God (stop thinking that, don't even flirt with that) had doubled its size in eight hours. I probed the area around it with trembling fingers and became aware of another astonishing fact: the pain had disappeared. There was no more itch, no more burning, no more anything. In fact, it wasn't just my face that felt fine. *All* of me felt fine.

No, more than fine, I felt *great,* even in my semi-feverish condition, which I now recognized as a very shallow phenomenon beneath which I was positively charged, invigorated, vitalized with an abundant swell of energy and well being. The image of the waterwheel suddenly reappeared to join those deformed crabs. I could almost see it turning slowly, dipping into a placid black spring, drawing up buckets of cool water and dumping them into a cistern in my soul where they refreshed me, soothed me, and buoyed me up, making even the mere possibility of unhappiness or anxiety seem absurd. In the coolness and quietness of that secret place, there was nothing but pure bliss.

It was the first time I had ever felt wonderful and awful at the same time. By all rights I should have felt nothing but panic, but there I was, enjoying a calm center of seemingly supernatural peace while my face rotted off from an impossible disease.

The very recognition of my divided state initiated a dreadful synergy between my peaceful inner feelings and my rapidly deteriorating outer situation. A nightmarish sense of unreality whispered up like a shivering black cloud from the base of my brain. The chills from my pseudo-fever edged subtly into a deeper chill, a veritable *frisson* that was so pervasive it seemed to reach all the way to the tips of my fingers and toes. My eyes looked back at me from the mirror. Their green hue was muted with fever, giving them the appearance of two cloudy emeralds. Behind them I saw a spark glowing in the darkness. Or maybe it was a wheel turning. Or maybe it was an army of crabs, crouched on the edge of consciousness, pulsing and waiting.

Again the thought of the hospital arose. Again, I stuffed it down. Sleep beckoned. It was late. The day had lasted an eternity. The sluggish shadows had finally reached the couch, and I dragged myself to the living room and sank into the cushions with a sense of unknown activities and strange transformations still taking place behind the facade of my soul. Sleep rose like the waters of a cool dark spring, and I gratefully let it claim me.

6

> Only when we are sick of our sickness
> Shall we cease to be sick.
> The Sage is not sick, being sick of sickness;
> This is the secret of health.
>
> —*Tao Te Ching,* chapter 71

I overslept the next day by nearly eight hours. Instead of my usual wake-up time of seven-thirty, my eyes stayed shut and then opened of their own accord just before three-thirty in the afternoon. All night long I had inhabited a dream that seemed to last for a timeless moment. I had been frozen in perpetual motion, suspended in a formless darkness that folded and separated into well-defined shapes, while I listened to a voice speaking silently into my inner ear. It whispered and slobbered things I never should have been able to understand, but in the murky clarity of the dream I *did* understand. The words spoke to me on a level of selfhood that resided in a timeless dimension prior to language, a primal plane where identity was nothing but the formless, structured chaos of the darkness that seethed and breathed around me.

I heard a name spoken. It was the name of a god. The voice was the god's very voice, the words were its very words, and the sound of it was the sound of all foulness, like the liquid lapping of a bottomless whirlpool sucking down the stinking dregs of a stagnant, polluted ocean.

When I awoke to the half-light of my white-walled bedroom,

the dim, dreamy color of the atmosphere reminded me of Mitch's house. I shot upright in bed with the sheets still wrapped around my chest and arms, terrified for a moment that I would find myself lying on his tattered old couch while he sat beside me in his ratty recliner and murmured strange things into my ear.

My relief at finding myself in my bedroom was short-lived, for when I looked at the clock and read its red-trembling digital numbers, a cold adrenaline jolt of panic shot through my gut. I had slept away nearly the entire day. Yesterday seemed impossibly distant. What was I supposed to be doing? I couldn't remember. Was I pursuing a doctorate in religious studies? Was my mother alive? Was I working for a newspaper and writing a story about the Sick Seekers? All seemed possible. None would fall into place as the real present.

Then I remembered the meeting at Mitch's house scheduled for that very night. Simultaneously, as I was still rubbing my stubbly growth of beard, I remembered the mark on my face, and the coldness in my gut surged like an electric current.

I reached up with shaking fingers to rub my left cheekbone. My fingers found an irregular bump, and a groan escaped my mouth. I ran to the bathroom and flipped on the switch, expecting with the certainty of nightmarish foresight to see my entire face ravaged by a tar-black, pestilent growth.

But the mark hadn't grown at all. It was still the size of a large marble, still black in the middle and fading toward the edges. It might have flattened out a little during the night, but otherwise there was no change.

A cinematic flash of memory eclipsed the present moment. I was nineteen years old and standing before my mother as I revealed my newly healed face to her. I showed her proudly that everything was fine, that my beauty was unmarred. Her face froze like a porcelain doll for the briefest of moments. Then it shattered, releasing a flood of tears and sobs that shocked me with their violence. When she turned and ran, I stayed rooted to the spot, listening to her footfalls retreat up the stairs and across the plush-carpeted hallway to her bedroom, where the door slammed shut with the finality of a coffin lid.

Too many emotions washed over me, far more and far deeper than I knew how to cope with. I knew that if I accepted them they would overwhelm me and destroy all my cherished plans for a comfortable future far away from home, locked safely away in a high ivory tower. I did not possess the inner resources to handle such an ocean of negativity. So I did what I had to do. I took hold of something like a mental key, inserted it into something like a lock, and shut all my bleak feelings into something like a dark storehouse in my soul, where they would never be able to reach me. Afterwards, I felt numbed, but cleansed.

The memory ended and there I was, standing in the bathroom of my apartment with a horrible spot on my face and a surreal puzzle about a god of foulness taking shape in my mind. And I realized the door to that secret storehouse, which I had forgotten for all those years, was not as secure as I had imagined when I first discovered it. For years it had been leaking into my soul, polluting my life with an icy undercurrent of misery. Now, in the face of my rising tide of confusion and fear, it was threatening to burst wide open and destroy me with a deluge of despair.

One thing at a time, I told myself. Calm down and focus. Make everything ordinary. Make every act a mindful one. First, step away from the mirror and refuse to think about what it shows. Next, stop before the toilet to urinate. Then put one foot in front of the other to march into the living room and soak in the normality of the furniture arranged in its ordinary pattern, with the reassuring glow of the afternoon sunlight spilling through the front windows. Inhale, then exhale. Find that sweet center of mental and emotional transcendence, from where you can live as the witness of your life.

My cell phone had three voicemails on it when I reached the living room. I had missed three phone calls while I overslept. I dialed my account and pressed the button to hear my messages. Dr. Baumann's voice began to speak into my ear.

"Lawrence! I'm stunned you're researching the Sick Seekers too. Please forgive me, I don't have time for small talk. I've learned more about the Sick Seekers in one week of visiting my brother than I learned from a year of reading the research literature. Listen to me: don't have anything to do with that old man again. You asked if there's a historical antecedent to the Sick Seekers' theology. I can tell you that their insistence on the foulness of the body sounds a bit like an obscure Buddhist practice of meditating on corpses. It's hardly practiced at all today. But there's more to what's happening than just the recurrence of an outdated contemplative practice. Lawrence, I mean it, listen to me: *stay away* from these people. There's something unprecedented going on. While I've been down here in Las Vegas, my brother has mentioned some of the same things you've been saying, and I have a hunch—this is going to sound crazy, I know—that the Sick Seekers are worshipping deities that haven't been worshipped for nearly six thousand years. There was a cult in the ancient Middle East centered around them. You remember the seminar I taught on the dark side of religion. Well, this cult could have filled up the entire semester, but I never mentioned it because I didn't know anybody even remembered those gods, let alone worshipped them. Only a handful of scholars know the cult ever existed, but now the Sick Seekers have come along and shaken us all up. This is absolutely amazing stuff. It looks like the spontaneous resurrection of a cult that—" At this point the available space for his message ran out. I pressed the key to play the next one.

"Sorry," he said, "I'm getting long-winded here, but you have to hear this. Something's not right, Lawrence. This ancient cult posited more than one god in their cosmology. The first was a god of primal chaos. The second was a kind of mystical bridge between this chaos and the created world. The worship of these gods was about undoing everything, uncreating creation, destroying the cosmos. The rituals devoted to them were positively nightmarish. They involved human sacrifice and something more: the attempted sacrifice of a worshipper's very soul. But the cultists didn't conceive of the body as a separate thing. Lawrence, in a way these people were proto-Gnostics! They believed the body was a cesspool of corruption. But the really unique thing that distinguished them from all the other sects and cults around them was that they believed the same thing about the individual soul. They regarded body and soul as dual facets of a single, horrible aberration. Salvation was conceived in terms of escaping the nightmare of created existence and returning to the bliss of uncreated chaos. The god of primal chaos was the goal. The second god was the bridge and the key. Then there was a third god. Do you understand what I'm telling you? A *third* god, Lawrence. He was never named in the ancient literature. His worshippers were zealous about guarding his identity. But we do know that this god was thought to be the manifest presence of the other two gods in the worshiper's body. From what I've learned recently, I'm thinking there may be some correspondences with the trinitarian theology of orthodox Christianity, with its doctrine of the hypostatic union and mutual interpenetration of the three members of the godhead. I'm just speechless, Lawrence. This is all so exciting, I can barely contain myself. All these things I'm telling you are like playing connect the dots with a six-thousand-year-old puzzle. My brother has told me things that have allowed me to connect scattered bits of information I haven't known what to do with for decades. If I can just—" End of message two. I pressed the button to play the final one.

"We have to talk about this in person. I'm sure we have many hours' worth of things to share with each other. But please, please listen to me, Lawrence. Don't let my professional excitement throw you off track. These people were the spiritual pariahs of the ancient world. Everybody else was utterly horrified by them. If the Sick Seekers really are the continuation of this ancient religion, then they're the apocalyptic cult to end all apocalyptic cults. And if they've really got hold of the scripture you say they have, they're the most dangerous thing the modern world has ever seen. I don't pretend to know how it's possible for them to be what I'm thinking they must be. I mean, it's completely *impossible* by any normal standard of logic. It flies in the face of common sense and every other measure of sanity. It may take decades to unravel it all. But just *stay away*, no matter how curious you are. My brother has told me things that have stood my hair on end. I'll tell you, I'm actually getting a bit nervous around him. I would have already taken him away from here by force, but he seems so enraptured by his new religion that I'm afraid the psychological damage of a sudden uprooting might be severe. I'm at a loss for what to do right now. Wish me luck. I promise to call you just as soon as I get back to Terence. Be safe, Lawrence."

That was the end. An electronic voice asked me whether I wanted to save or delete the messages, but I just stood there. My eyes were open and my mind awake, but the mental sight of the picture taking shape in my soul had begun to obscure the hard physical reality of the room around me. The outline was becoming clear. The pieces were malformed. Thousands of sickly, pulsating shapes with serrated edges and pale pincers had locked together to form a long figure with a handle to grasp and sharp teeth for fitting into a lock.

There had never been any real question about whether I would attend the meeting at Mitch's house. I had known when he first invited me that I couldn't refuse, and he had known it, too. To run from this unfolding reality would be to run from the possibility of ever reestablishing a connection with all those unnamed spiritual treasures that I had always regarded, even in the midst of my nihilism, as making life worth living. Or at least they made it bearable enough to get out of bed each morning. Through a kind of lateral logic that made no sense to my rational brain, I realized that my psychic survival was bound up with the Sick Seekers and their crazy, dangerous theology. I would go to Mitch's house, I told myself, and would discover what they did at their worship services, and I would return safely to share my knowledge with Dr. Baumann and expose the cult for what it was. Along the way, maybe I would become a whole person again.

Despite my newfound resolve, I did place a bandage over my

left cheek after I dressed, and I did wonder as I walked out the front door just how deeply the mark reached inward into my body, and whether its fingers might touch the latches of any other doors that I had locked and then forgotten.

7

And now you know what is holding him back, so that he may be revealed at the proper time.

—2 Thessalonians 2:6

Mitch's house was different in the darkness. Gray clouds choked the sky as I pulled into his driveway at five minutes till seven, with only a ragged gap here and there allowing a flicker of starlight to shine through. Dusk had come early, and the house looked vaguely humanlike with its red-lipped porch for a mouth and yellow glowing dormer windows for eyes. The windows drew my attention as I parked behind several other cars that were already lined up. From the look of it, those upper rooms would be used for something tonight, for I saw moving shadows through the glass.

I walked up the porch steps without hesitation, carrying my briefcase even though it felt useless, and rapped on the metal frame of the screen door. Through the screen I saw several people standing or sitting in Mitch's living room. They were all elderly. One of them, an old man dressed in a gray sweat suit and brown slippers, was seated on the couch with an aluminum walker parked beside him. He looked at me through the wire mesh barrier and smiled broadly with a closed mouth.

Then Mitch approached from somewhere and opened the door for me. His smile was rather sardonic, as if to say that he had known all along I would show up. I refused to meet his eyes but nodded my head in greeting. He seemed satisfied with this and stepped aside to let me enter.

He introduced me to everyone right away. Of course he didn't speak. He merely pointed to them one by one as they told me their names and the nature of their diseases, in what felt like a customary ritual. There was Maggie, an old woman whose eyes were completely obscured by milky white cataracts. There was Alice, another old woman with hands shriveled and twisted into eagle-like claws from rheumatoid arthritis. There was Sherman, an old man with a brain tumor. There was Doyle, the old man seated on the couch beside the walker. He suffered from testicular cancer, and he smiled that broad-lipped smile the whole time I looked at him. The others, all elderly and liver-spotted, crowded forward to tell me of their various ailments. Together they chanted a litany of sickness and suffering, but their voices were happy and their eyes bright. Their faces were all shining with eager anticipation of something to come, and I silently renewed my resolve to keep my guard up.

I counted ten people, including Mitch, and then I began to wonder where the other two were. He had said there were twelve, hadn't he?

"There's the last one," said Maggie. I don't know how she knew where to point in her blindness, but she directed a bony finger through the wall of aged bodies gathered before me, and my jaw dropped nearly to my chest as the people parted to reveal Lindy standing near the doorway to the kitchen with a shy grin on her fair-skinned face. She said she was suffering from uterine cancer and had only been a member of the body for two weeks.

No, I thought, this isn't right. This can't be right. My eyes felt hot, and the bandage on my cheek was suffocating me. My knees were turning to water. Nobody had asked about the bandage yet, but they had all been looking at it with a piercing interest in their eyes. Now Lindy was there, one of the last people in the world I had expected or wanted to see, and she was staring at the bandage as if she saw through it and wanted to kiss what was on the other side.

Not Lindy. She couldn't be a part of this. She was too pure. And it would mean that I had been manipulated from the beginning. Mitch wouldn't have had to suffer any kind of "spell." He and Lindy might have planned his trip to the hospital together, so that he would arrive when Peg was on duty, and she would tell

Bobby about the incident, and he would tell me. One of the other members of the body might have driven Mitch there and then slipped out on cue. Then all they would have had to do was wait for me to show up on Mitch's doorstep thinking that I was paying him an unexpected visit.

But why? What possible reason could they have for tricking me into coming out there and meeting him?

A blurry wave rippled across my field of vision. Suddenly, I was unsure whether I was standing there in Mitch's living room or still hanging in the timeless darkness of my recent dream. My briefcase slipped from my fingers and dropped to the worn carpet with a thump. I felt a tingling start up in my face again. It swelled rapidly to an itching but then held off, refusing to surge into the agony I had known once in a distant past that was separated from me by less than forty-eight hours. The feeling rippled like an electric centipede down to my chest, and further, into my groin, where it became a ball of prickling energy that was somehow wrapped up in the cool embrace of a deep cistern that even now was continuing to receive bucket after bucket of fresh, dark water from a steadily turning wheel.

When the diseased old people gathered around me and touched me with their vile hands, I tried to resist but found that I was mute and helpless. Even the voice of my own thoughts was unable to articulate a clear refusal. I was dumb as an infant.

They led me to the staircase, which was old and wooden, and then up the stairs to a trapdoor, which I saw was suspended open by a rope and two iron counterweights shaped like the weights of a grandfather clock. Brittle hands clothed with papery skin pawed and caressed me, carried me forward, lifted me. I was not walking, I was being borne along by a tidal swell of aging flesh.

The upper floor had no partitions or dividing walls. It was a single large room that reached to the outer walls of the house. Everything was of brown wood like the staircase, and the ceiling was low. Two bare bulbs with pull cords were suspended from the ceiling and doing a poor job of illuminating the corners. Two four-paned windows on the far wall peered out over the front yard, which may as well have been a million miles and a lifetime away.

The worshippers whispered around me and sat me down near a corner. My awareness was the blank surface of a black sea as they peeled off me one by one, moving in a hushed silence toward other positions, lining the outer walls until everyone was seated in a rough circle. Maggie was positioned across from me. Even in the blankness of my thoughts, I could not escape the impression that her blind eyes with their milky growths were regarding me with compassion. Lindy was seated several feet away on my left, swaying and humming to herself.

Then Mitch began to speak. He was to my right, and his voice was the voice of the God.

"The body is a blocked wish. The body is not different from the soul." It was the sound of all foulness and corruption, a voice too horrible to be real, and yet it kept speaking as I swayed like a drunken man and looked around for a way to escape.

"The body is meant to rot. The soul is meant to rot. Sickness of the body and soul is the doorway to your bliss. You have tried and failed to make peace with the body. You have tried and failed to find the truth of your soul. Peace with the body and truth in the soul are illusions. You are good for nothing but to rot."

They were all swaying now, moving like serpents in a circle. I would not have thought their wasted old bodies capable of such supple motion. Doyle looked as if he were about to twist the upper half of his body away from the lower. His walker rested beside him, forgotten in the fray.

The God's voice continued to issue from Mitch's throat. "Give up your disease. Give it to me, and I will take it from you and leave you with blissful nothing."

Maggie was still staring at me. Her eyes were too bright to be blind. Even from across the room, I saw what might have been an army of misshapen crabs chittering behind them. Something connected within me, some nascent circuit of realization, and suddenly I knew with undeniable certainty that it was the God looking out at me from behind that milky stare. She had become the vessel for His sight, and her eyes were now His.

Alice sat next to her with clawed arthritic hands moving in serpentine patterns. They slithered in the air and then came to point at me with eight fingers and two thumbs. Their motion mimicked something. It looked as if she were caressing my face from across the room. The same blossoming realization continued to expand: her hands were the hands of the God. She had become a vessel for the God of foulness. I looked up and saw her eyes closed and her head thrown back in ecstasy.

The others were all beginning to manifest the God in various ways. They twisted and flopped and beat the floor. They hummed and moaned and wailed while Mitch continued to speak of the body as a disease, and disease as a new kind of health. Sherman, the old man with the brain tumor, sat stiff-backed with his arms spread out like a music conductor. The motions of his hands caused waves of activity across the room. It was almost as if he were a puppeteer, and I knew that he was the brain of the God, manifesting itself through a tumor implanted in his own brain like a rotten plum.

Then Lindy and Doyle began to crawl across the floor toward each other. They were tearing their clothes off. *Oh, God.* The thought struck me with a desperate absurdity, for the God I was referring to had no place in that room. Within a moment's time, an old man with testicular cancer had begun to copulate with a young woman suffering from cancer of the uterus. I could not bear to watch, and yet I could not rip my eyes away from them.

My face was burning and itching and swelling and suffocating beneath its bandage. Sherman waved his hand at me, and against my conscious will my own hand shot up and ripped away the gauze and tape, baring my secret horror to the assembled appendages of the God while a flabby old man and a soft young woman coupled on the floor in the midst of us.

It was as if scales fell from my eyes. With my mark exposed, I could see what I had been unable to see before: a presence like oily smoke floating near the ceiling. It churned softly with a strangely organic motion, dropping down flickering tendrils to caress the assembled worshipers.

No, it did not caress them, it *entered* them through the various means of access they had brought with them in the form of their diseases. It drove black spikes into Maggie's eyes. It wound like a leprous fog around Alice's shriveled hands and sank in through her pores to animate her fingers with that caressing motion that was still directed at me. It formed a seething funnel like a miniature cyclone above Sherman's head and poured into his skull in an ever-shifting plume. When I looked to my right, I saw it entering Mitch's mouth with every inhalation and exiting as grotesquely shaped puffs that trembled in sympathetic vibration to the words he spoke.

Lindy and Doyle were still locked in a coital embrace. He was on his back and she sat astride him, and I felt my gorge rise. The cloud swirled above them and formed a vortex like an open mouth. A single tongue of greasy blackness lolled out and fell down to brush over their writhing bodies. Then it snaked between them to caress the point of their union.

The thought came in a flash: what would be the issue of a woman with a diseased womb, impregnated by a man with diseased testes, formed by the power of a God of foulness, nurtured by the collective worship of a group of ailing fanatics? What exactly would be the shape of a God whose nature was foulness and corruption? What would be the appearance of the God of rottenness made incarnate?

These thoughts were cut off by the phenomenon that had been steadily growing in my face. In the midst of the nightmare that was taking shape around me, I had been feeling a growing pressure in my cheek. Now it swelled suddenly to bursting. My head was tugged violently to one side as if gravity itself were pulling me toward the center of the circle, or as if a hook were lodged in my cheek and someone were reeling me in. I looked up to see the tendril of the God reaching down toward me, sinking into the diseased skin of my face, then reaching even further down inside, searching out the whole branching network of a cancer that had metastasized throughout my body with impossible rapidity. The God already possessed eyes and hands. He had a brain and a body. He was organizing the separate parts and forming Himself through the union of the two who were even now finishing up before me. What more was wanting?

The God needed a face.

At the moment I realized it, Mitch began to speak again next to me.

"Our Father in chaos. And His brother, the all-in-one, the gate and the key. Hear Me, and give Me form so that I may reclaim this world of putrid flesh for Our own, that I may sweep away its illusions to reveal Our reality burning bright behind the veil of matter." As the God spoke, the worshippers wailed, and their sound became a component of the Voice.

"I am the procession of your union in separateness," the God proclaimed to His counterparts in infinity. "Now give me a name and a form to be Our presence in this world. It is I who ask You this—I, Our selves manifested in flesh!"

Then the God spoke His own name. It was not true speech, not the production of any type of vocal equipment, human or otherwise. It was not even a sound, in the normal meaning of the word. It was an actual animate thing, the aural embodiment of the essence of the God Himself, the living Word of Corruption. And it was a palpable horror.

At the sound of it, my face ripped loose from my skull. It flew off like a ragged rubber mask, flapped upward toward the seething purplish abyss of the ceiling like a blood-drenched bird, and disappeared into the maw of the God. Something in me died as it disappeared. And then an avalanche of disease begin to rumble up and pour forth from every orifice of my body. Blood and bone spewed from my eyes. My organs dissolved into jellied lumps and erupted from my mouth. And yet somehow I was still conscious through it all. Somehow, I still saw.

The others around me were coming unbound as well. The tendrils trailing from the ceiling were tearing them apart, wrenching themselves out of pale fat bodies and taking lumps of disease with them. Leathery black coils like the length of a whip were withdrawing from the tender point of contact between Lindy and Sherman, and it was as if a nest of fishhooks were drawing up a monster catch from the depths of a putrid ocean. The things squirming on the ends of those hooks were rotten and full of teeth, dripping with a blackish ichor, and mewling like kittens. They smelled like a sewer. I saw them drawn into the greedy black cloud, and it seemed that its edges expanded slightly, as if it were growing from the nourishment it received. It pushed against the shuddering walls, bulging out between attic boards, swelling the house like a human head with its cranium about to burst.

And then I returned to myself and found that I was lying on the floor in a rubbery pile like an empty body suit. The others around me were wilting, too, like peach-colored balloons. Nothing remained of them but the cast-off shells of their human flesh. The God had taken back what belonged to Him and left the remnant to rot.

Sherman and Lindy had pulled away from each other. She lay on her back before me in a totally immodest pose with her empty flesh collapsing in on itself, exposing in a horrid display those parts of her that I had once thought (was it only a few short days ago?) that I would enjoy coaxing her into exposing under different circumstances.

Next to me, Mitch was the only one still standing. He had stopped speaking but his breath still emitted a steady scrape like the sound of a saw rasping in the distance. He turned his eyes to the ceiling, where the swirling black mass was already receding into the impossible abyss whence it had come, and I saw him reach up to probe his throat gently in an attitude of affection. Then he turned his gaze down upon me and opened his mouth to speak.

What came out were not sounds, but written words. They issued from his lips like trails of black butterflies and stayed suspended against a smooth white background that shimmered up from somewhere to become a paper surface. I recognized them.

"The God gives you a choice," they said. "First He gives you a taste of the bliss He's offering you. Then He shows you what it's going to cost you to accept it." Mitch's eyes looked deeply into mine. Then he bent at the knees and sat down in a ratty old recliner that appeared behind him from out of nowhere.

8

They're here already! You're next!
—Miles Bennell

I was sitting on Mitch's sofa with a notebook in my hands. He sat in the recliner before me, waiting. Two box fans purred in the living room windows with the shades pulled down to the tops of them. The atmosphere was stuffy, and the backs of my legs had sweated through to the sofa.

I blinked and looked around. An empty glass rested on the floor beside Mitch's chair. The faint scrapings of insect noises filtered through the walls from outside and mingled with the sound of his breathing. When I looked back up at him, he was staring at me with shiny-bright silver dollar eyes.

I don't have the heart to describe what came next: all the gasping and panting as my pulse began to pound and my face began to throb like a beating drum; the collapse into quivering panic that laid me out on the sofa; the hateful care he gave me like some sort of surrogate mother; the long night of hallucinatory dread in which I saw smoky black tendrils drooping from the ceiling, reaching down into the living room from the attic above, waiting to sink whiplike fingers into my skull. All night long I kept reaching up to touch my face and registering surprise when my fingers found only the smooth, unblemished surface of my skin. But the flood of relief I kept expecting to wash over me never came.

I left at dawn, when I found I was strong enough to walk. The early-morning air whispered against my skin like a mantle of damp silk. As I emerged from the house and stumbled down the porch steps, I heard the forest sounds blended together into a smooth chirring like the electrified whine of a telephone. I thought I had risen early enough that Mitch would not see me, but as I backed out of his driveway I saw him framed inside the black border of the screen door. His hand was probing his throat, and I could feel his eyes seeking out mine. I tried to tell myself that the voice I heard speaking faintly in my brain over the roar of the engine was merely the sound of a morning bird chirping in the forest. But it didn't go away as I picked up speed and shot down the highway toward Terence.

I had no idea what day it was. The enormity of my disorientation only made itself known gradually as I tried to figure out what had happened to me. I kept fearing that I might blink at any minute and find myself seated once again on Mitch's sofa, or worse, in his attic, with the other members of the body manifesting the God all around me.

Terence had not properly awakened when I reached the city limits. The residential areas were still cloaked with a gray blanket of pre-dawn stillness, and the downtown streets were deserted except for a police cruiser that paused at the corner of Grand and Broadway to let me pass. The sight of the fresh-faced young officer seated behind the steering wheel pricked an unexpected bubble of hysteria in my chest. Here was a man devoted to keeping peace and order in human society, but now I knew that those two principles could never coexist. Peace could only be bought by sacrificing oneself to the God of chaos, by identifying oneself with the disease at the center of infinity, where there could be no unpeace, no pain, no dis-ease, because there was no longer a conscious self to feel pain or anxiety. The thoughts felt alien to me, as if they had been implanted in my head through the agency of some external will. But there was no way to escape them, as they seemed to form the foundation of my perspective now.

I'm confident the young policeman must have thought seriously about stopping me as I swerved and braked to avoid wrecking my car in a fit of laughter. But in the end he just let me pass. Maybe he had his own concerns to attend to, and harbored no wish to face the possible difficulties of dealing in the early morning hours with a hysterical man cackling like an idiot behind the wheel of his car. Or maybe the God was making my crooked paths straight and my rough ways smooth.

When I got home, I locked the door behind me and wandered from room to room in a dreamlike daze. My apartment was untouched, but everything had changed. It was as if somebody had taken away everything I knew, all my familiar possessions and surroundings, and replaced them with exact facsimiles composed of smoke. I felt they might dissipate at any moment to reveal some unthinkable vista of infinity lying behind their façade of solidity.

But the real revelation did not come until I looked down at my own body and saw the same insubstantiality built into my flesh. My vision pierced like an X-ray through skin and muscle, blood and bone, and found a seed of corruption implanted in the very workings of what I had always considered to be health. This body was a vapor that would be consumed by a principle of decay built into its innermost workings. All that would remain was the God.

I could not be certain whether I was laughing or crying as I congratulated myself on having attained the enlightenment that I had been seeking for as long as I could remember.

This new perspective has proved to be a permanent conversion. As those first days and weeks passed, I found that I was operating from an unknown center. Some new framework had been successfully erected like a psychic scaffolding behind the façade of my self, and my thoughts and sense of identity were now built upon and around its distorted shape. I saw infinity in everything and found comfort in nothing.

It was impossible to continue working at the newspaper. I could not bear to face anyone from my former life. Bobby asked me what was wrong when I phoned him to tender my resignation. At first he didn't think I was serious, but then he became concerned and angry, and said I couldn't just quit on him like that without giving him a reason or a warning. But that was exactly what I did. I made my resignation effective that day, and we never saw or spoke to each other again.

Dr. Baumann never returned from his sabbatical, which didn't really surprise me. I followed the stories in the newspaper about the search for him, and I laughed or cried when I saw them sometimes situated next to AP wire pieces about the Sick Seekers. Even though nobody knows what happened to him, I feel certain that I *do* know, if only I could articulate it. But I have no particular desire to envision him being torn apart by the whiplike fingers of the God.

Physically, externally, I have remained whole. I check the mirror each morning to see whether a black spot has erupted on my face, but every morning I find that I am still clothed with the same meaningless, beautiful mask that once sat at the center of my world. Now I am amazed and disgusted when I think of how much stock I placed in such a worthless layer of muscle and fat. Sometimes I fancy that I am engaging in the corpse meditation that Dr. Baumann mentioned, and that the object of my meditation is my own body.

On my own I have continued to speculate about the Sick Seekers. It is an idle amusement, as I now know life itself to be, but it passes the time. I indulge my vestigial passion for the study of religion by looking for similarities between the Sick Seekers' theology and the doctrines of various world religions. On some days I seem to find echoes of the ancient chaos religion resonating in the trinitarian theology of orthodox Christianity, the mystical identification of the individual soul with Brahman in Vedantic Hinduism, and the "meditation on foulness" recommended by the Buddha in the Girimananda Sutta. I speculate that there are sinister hints of something ancient and monstrous peering through the seemingly innocent and life-affirming ideas of non-resistance and *wu wei*, effortless action, in Chinese Taoism. I fancy that I can see the words of the God of Foulness shining through some of the more outlandish pronouncements of Yahweh in the Hebrew Scriptures, despite Mitch's belief that the god of the ancient Jews is not his own God. On other days I realize that these speculations are worthless, and that I am just using them to while away the hours on the way to my certain annihilation.

The media coverage of the Sick Seekers continues to proliferate, and the size of the cult continues to grow. In Haiti there is a body that claims to have an AIDS sufferer among their ranks. The stories say they view him as a kind of avatar, since his flesh is an open channel for every pathogen in the environment around him. When I first read this, I realized that other Sick Seekers around the world must have started talking openly to the press, just as Mitch talked to me. They are spreading their gospel of disease, and I cannot doubt but that their ranks will grow even faster as people discover the freedom from suffering that awaits them in the embrace of the God. In the midst of an increasingly insane global society, they will surely find many miserable people who welcome such relief.

Locally, I have no desire to seek out Mitch and the others. They have remained silent toward me, probably—or so I presume—because they expect me to join them eventually of my own free will. On some days I am tempted to visit the hospital and seek out Lindy to see whether she really is a part of all this, or whether I am just the victim of terrible delusion. It might be comforting to know that I am insane, and that none of what I think has happened to me has really happened. But the thought of looking into her soft white face and maybe seeing a hunger in her blue eyes to kiss my cheek keeps me away.

As my state and situation continue to degenerate, and as I wait for the numbers of the Sick Seekers to reach some sort of critical mass that will signal the moment for the God to set in motion His master plan, two things have come to dominate my newly enlightened thoughts. The first involves my mother. Mitch told me that his wife never stopped believing her god would heal her, right up until she died. One of the last doors to be unlocked inside me brought forth a memory of my own mother experiencing a deathbed conversion to the Christianity of her parents. She had always been so brittle and empty, like a porcelain doll, that to see her wasting her dying moments on a futile attempt to atone for a life lived in self-absorption and empty vanity made me hate her. But I also knew that she had passed the same traits on to me, and even though I locked away the knowledge of it in the same psychic storehouse where I hid all my other unpleasant feelings, it followed me through graduate school and eventually became the pinprick that deflated my spiritual passion. I could never escape the subconscious thought that I was just as false as she was, and that my pose of spirituality was just a clumsy compensation for the emptiness and pettiness of my true nature. But now my awakening had purged me of all that. How much easier, I now understood, simply to drop the whole sad charade and be *nothing*.

It was the remembrance of that sorry chapter in my life that brought forth the second factor that has come to dominate my attention. During my college years, while I was under the sway of all those buried motivations, I became fascinated by the novel *Invasion of the Body Snatchers* and its cinematic adaptations. This became bound up with my ersatz Zen perspective, and I sometimes found myself thinking that the arguments of the pod people in Finney's novel were correct. What does it matter whether the body, or even the mind or soul, is replaced by a facsimile? There is only one ultimate consciousness looking out from behind every set of eyes, and to insist upon the absolute value of any given individual form is to buy into the very illusion of separateness that constitutes the unenlightened state. An enlightened master faced with the threat of replacement by an alien replica would not view it as a threat at all, for he would know that in the end there would be no real difference, and thus no loss to mourn.

I have found myself returning to these thoughts more and more. With increasing frequency and intensity, I find myself doubting whether there really is such a thing as authenticity, since there is no real "me" to which I should feel honor-bound. At the deepest level, the level of absolute, unconditioned truth, there is only the one Self churning in infinite chaos, and It does not know or care whether I am real. I feel sickened when I dwell upon the fact that I am backed into a corner where the only authentic act I can perform—the most authentic act of my life, the one that will redeem a lifetime spent in pretension and falsehood—will be to give myself up to the God of Foulness, the manifest presence of the infinite corruption that constitutes the heart of reality. This God speaks to me constantly through the disease of my individuated selfhood—the last and truest disease—and shows me that the only way out, the only way to reconnect with what I once thought I had, is to choose the inner over the outer, peace over beauty. It is a soul-searing choice, for I know that when I eventually give in, a virulent cancer will erupt on my face, and the God will reclaim what is rightfully His.

I can put it off as long as I want. He says He gives me a choice. But then, how can it be a true choice when nothing else is real? Everything is empty and good for nothing but to rot, except for this chaos, this madness, this sickness, this filth. In the end, there is no real choice for me to make, for I have nothing else from which to choose. Nor do any of us.

PART THREE
APOCRYPHON

I have had much trouble getting along with my ideas. There was a daimon in me, and in the end its presence proved decisive.
—Carl Jung, *Memories, Dreams, Reflections* (1961)

There is something at work in my soul which I do not understand.
—Mary Shelley, *Frankenstein* (1818)

The lunatic's visions of horror are all drawn from the material of daily fact. Our civilization is founded on the shambles, and every individual existence goes out in a lonely spasm of helpless agony. If you protest, my friend, wait till you arrive there yourself!
—William James, *The Varieties of Religious Experience* (1902)

Chimeras & Grotesqueries

UNSIGNED PREFACE TO THE UNPUBLISHED AND
UNFINISHED MANUSCRIPT
"CHIMERAS & GROTESQUERIES" BY PHILIP LASINE

I realized early on that it would be necessary for me to introduce the following manuscript with a brief preface explaining my involvement in bringing it to light. I can only hope that the unorthodox nature of this involvement will not cast doubt on the manuscript's authenticity or, worse, detract from its impact by distracting the reader from its profound implications.

For years I tried to explain to myself the unearthly influence that Philip Lasine exerted over me with his writings. My fascination with his bizarre, horrific, outlandish, and thoroughly transformative stories revolved largely around the fates of his protagonists, who, speaking in the first person, encountered things they could not explain—nightmarish things, awful eruptions of unearthly monstrousness in circumstance, event, person, and entity—and were invariably destroyed in the end. But they were also, somehow, transformed and preserved in a permanently shattered state from which they could meditate eternally on the impenetrable mystery of their own doom.

Lasine's success in depicting such things and conveying their full, devastating emotional and philosophical impact was an authorial feat of sheer, shocking genius that I tried to emulate in my own stumbling way by writing stories that aped his signature style of marrying narrative prose fiction to Montaigne-like essayistic explorations. Eventually, and fortunately, I recognized my singular lack of literary talent in this vein, and decided to aim my desire for spiritual depth in another direction. A philosophy degree, training at a respected Protestant seminary, and an ordination to a ministerial career as a Methodist pastor were swiftly forthcoming.

But still, Philip Lasine had assumed for me the status of a distant master, and even when I grew up and out of my childhood attitude that imparted a permanent mystique to the authors of books, and finally came to understand that real people with real lives and bodies and voices and histories really do stand behind all those printed and bound volumes—as witnessed by the fact that I myself wrote and saw published a number of modestly successful books of Christian theology—Philip Lasine still seemed an iconic presence, a beacon of impossible literary perfection shining like a star from the peak of some intra-psychic Sinai. I could not keep from regarding him as an embodied archetype, and found myself thinking of him from time to time and feeling, even though I knew it was childish, that the author of *those* books could not possibly be a real, living, breathing man with a real physical appearance and a concrete geographical location. He had to be a myth, a nexus of daimonic-divine power that had somehow focused into the form of a man for long enough to produce that perfect and powerful body of work, after which the body dissolved and the power withdrew back to the astral plane. This was my private fantasy, which I never actually articulated to myself, holding it as a kind of half-belief that surfaced occasionally into conscious awareness, at which times I observed it with an attempt at ironic amusement and made certain that I did not breathe a word of it to my parishioners.

Here my preface ends, for the spiritual and artistic relationship between Philip and me is more important than the later, more literal one that arose. There is also the fact that this literal relationship resulted from such an outlandish set of coincidental circumstances, and was of such a bizarre nature (especially considering my longstanding literary worship of the man), that I would not blame the reader for disbelieving it and therefore doubting the authenticity of what follows. When a man finds himself standing beside the deathbed of his idol, having been

summoned there in an official capacity because he is a professional clergyman, he may begin to mistrust even his own perceptions
and memories, and would not want to impart these doubts to his
readers by giving too detailed an account of things that may or
may not have happened exactly as he recalls them.

Here, then, is Philip Lasine's last story, which is especially
striking for being both like and unlike his other writings. I do not
know whether it was meant to be self-contained or part of a longer work. I do know that it is clearly unfinished in its current state.
I will admit to indulging in the thought that I might try to finish it
myself, so close was I to its author when he died and bequeathed
it to me, and so intimately do its ideas resonate not only with my
thoughts but with my very being. But in the end I have decided to
present it exactly as he left it, on the suspicion that some sort of
hidden conclusion resides within the work as it stands. I have limited my editorial involvement to the minor expansion of a few key
passages that were embryonic in their received form. The reader
may well recognize these passages by their heavy-handedness and
overly expository tone; I did not seek to emulate Philip's style but
to clarify the vision he was incompletely expressing as he wrote by
hand while lying on his deathbed.

The story as a whole may be intended as an allegory of sorts,
although the grounds of its metaphors are obscure. Then again,
they may not be as obscure as they appear; they may only seem so
because of their extreme spiritual intimacy to us all, the repercus-
sions of which I have not yet begun to work out for my ministerial
vocation.

This last suspicion is at least partly verified by the experience
that I have just had between writing the preceding paragraph and
the present one. I paused in my work to step outside and rest my
eyes. It is a frigid December night, and I stood perfectly still in the icy
air, gazing up at the panorama of the night sky, which bristled with
stars. As I watched, they seemed to take on the imprint of a vast human face—not looking down at me, but pressing outward, as if the
entire glittering expanse were the inner surface of a cosmic mask.

The experience was invested with a clear visionary character, as opposed to a merely hallucinatory one, and I am not nearly as ashamed as I would have expected when I admit that after the celestial monstrosity had receded and the stars had returned to their normal configuration, I reached up to feel my own face with a sense of quickening dread.

CHIMERAS & GROTESQUERIES [unfinished]
by Philip Lasine

Just when it had first occurred to me to start assembling monstrous human effigies from the garbage that littered the alley floor outside my grotto, I could not say. I only knew that this was how I spent most of my waking hours, the ones not otherwise devoted to scrounging for food and drink in the wasteland of alleyways and trash bins that made up my world.

Occasionally there were other activities to distract me. I was obliged at times to fend off, flee from, or otherwise respond to the vicious attacks of the animalistic young men who in recent years had found a new form of entertainment in beating and sometimes killing street dwellers like me. But I was more fortunate than many of my fellows, since my appearance and demeanor effectively deterred would-be assailants. Perhaps it was my size, for I was tall and hulking, and made for a singularly imposing figure as I stalked the streets in the frayed tweed overcoat that I had fished from a dumpster one icy-wet New Year's Day.

Or perhaps it was my face with its striking disfiguration, like the soft pink remains of a melted rubber mark. The feral youths who ventured downtown to the back alleys in search of their brutal amusements maintained a respectful distance from me, and I suspected it was as much their horror at my appearance as their caution at my size that kept them at bay. On the two occasions when a group of them had approached me with clubs and broken bottles in hand, I had simply stood to my full height and raised my face to greet them, freezing them in their tracks and then turning to re-enter my solitude.

The heart of that solitary existence was the pointless rigidity of my daily routine. Each morning I awoke in my grotto and lay motionless beneath my covering of newspapers until hunger or thirst impelled me to move. Then I crawled into the alleyway, climbed to my feet, and went in search of food. After that I wandered the streets for a few hours, following a circuitous path dictated by impulses that I could not fathom. People gave me a wide berth whenever I emerged, as I sometimes did, from the labyrinth of side streets and alleyways into the brightness and broadness of a sidewalk bordering a well-traveled boulevard or avenue.

After each day's travels I returned to my alley, where I scraped together heaps of trash, seated myself against the wall, and began to assemble doll-like, human-shaped figures. These were always grotesque in one way or another. A mass of grimy, shredded newspaper, impaled on the neck of a broken beer bottle, became a head whose fluttering fringe recalled the monstrous Medusa of ancient mythology. Oily flaps from the peel of a rotten banana, when attached to holes punched in the sides of an old cracker box or tobacco can, suggested arms like octopoid tentacles. The effect was especially vivid when the box or can was topped with a moldy, withered orange to serve as a head whose distorted face formed a miniature parody of my own. Sometimes I secured the pieces together with bits of string or wire. Other times I simply propped the assembled figures against the wall or laid them gently on the concrete floor of the alley in concentric half circles around the entrance to my grotto, where they often remained intact for hours or days before a stray breeze began to scatter them back into their original, unpersonified parts.

I spent endless hours assembling these shapes, which I began to think of as my "little ones." The activity seemed strange even to me, for whom it was so very familiar, and I could only imagine what it must look like to my fellow derelicts, who, on the rare occasions when our paths crossed, regarded me with expressions of fear and awe.

It was only the unfamiliar ones, the ones who were either new to this part of the city or new to street life itself, who ever dared to venture near the entrance to my alley. And there were also the ones the others referred to as "the crazies," the mentally muddled and addled, who muttered or ranted at the empty air, who soiled themselves and twitched with various tics and convulsions. I sometimes wondered what the other street-dwellers were thinking during our occasional brief encounters, which invariably ended with their flight and my resumption of my perpetual solitude and miniature demiurgic activities, and I was especially curious about the crazies with their fractured perceptions and diseased mental processes. For I thought it would be fascinating, and in fact grand, to see myself through their eyes, and to discover what their faulty faculties made of me and the domain I had created for myself.

When I tried to calculate the span of my rootless existence, I could not remember whether my memory encompassed a month, a year, or longer. At the far point of my recollection there was only a blankness, a gray and featureless barrier like a plaster wall. Or sometimes instead of a wall it carried the imaginal appearance of an inner absence or emptiness, as if I were missing a psychic organ or limb, or as if an anterior network of branching corridors in my soul had been demolished and buried beneath a mountain of dead earth. Occasionally I had the impression, so intense it bordered on a physical sensation, that behind my eyes and brain there existed a gaping hole. At such times I would reach around and probe the back of my head to verify the intactness of my skull. Then I would touch my face, brush my fingers over its smooth, pink rawness, and contemplate with wonder—never with despair—at the source and meaning of this strange disfiguration.

Other psychological dislocations occurred as well. I would start occasionally from a light doze or reverie to find myself confused and disoriented. If it were night and I had crawled into my grotto to sleep, I would emerge and gaze at my surroundings: the alleyway with its bleakness and grit, my little ones scattered sleeping all around, the strip of dark sky shining down from between the high brick walls. And although I knew this was the shape and these were the circumstances of my life, besides which I had never known any other, I would intuit deeply and sharply, with a burst of unaccountable longing, that somewhere there existed another, truer mode of existence for me.

Then the feeling would fade, and I would know there was only this life on the streets, this bulky body with its grotesque glyph of a visage, and this dark alleyway that I called home, where an incomprehensible inner compulsion drove me to assemble an ever-widening congregation of miniature monsters to worship at my feet.

At the far point of memory, I had first awakened while staggering through the streets of the city, dressed in the same rags that I later continued to wear, and filled with a fluttering sensation in my breast, a strange electrical exhilaration of joy and terror, while my face burned with an agony like acid and flame.

After what might have been hours or days of this half-blind odyssey through the city streets, I had blundered into an alleyway formed by the rough outer walls of two brick buildings, where the shadowy coolness felt like a balm. A battered gray garbage dumpster squatted next to me at the entrance. All manner of refuse— scraps of paper, shards of glass, strips of metal, the rotted remains of rats and insects and what had once been foodstuffs for humans—carpeted the alley floor. At the far end a wall of pitted wooden planks formed a barrier past which I could see nothing but distance and dimness, crossed by coils of mist.

I felt the contours of my soul expand instantly to claim and conform to this blissful haven, and my sense of belonging received further confirmation when I crept forward into the alley and sighted a promising feature ahead: a hole punched through the base of the right-hand wall. It proved to be three feet high and wide, with chalk-jagged edges where the bricks had shattered.

Without a moment's thought, I dropped to my hands and knees and crawled inside.

My gropings revealed a cramped, square-cornered cave formed by three rough concrete walls. I brushed away the chunks of brick and mortar on the floor and then lay down, finding the cave just large enough for me to stretch to my full length.

I lay there for hours, listening to the faint murmurings of the city and reaching up from time to time to touch my face and wonder at its rapidly vanishing pain. This was my home, my grotto, as I instantly thought of it in a burst of inspiration that was as incontrovertible as it was unaccountable.

The uncanny metaphysical breakdown in the world at large, which took over the life of the city soon after I awoke to my strange existence there, was heralded by a brief outburst of what the newspapers, quoting the solemn verdicts of psychiatric professionals and government offices, dubbed "mass hysteria." It took the form of what one prominent mental health authority described as a "hallucinatory disfiguration" of the city's religious architecture.

For a period of two minutes on a weekday afternoon, the city's human inhabitants saw the façades of churches, temples, synagogues, mosques, and meditation halls transmogrified into humanoid faces frozen in expressions of horror. The event made itself known in a ripple of panic that radiated outward from those buildings and through the crowds like waves on a lake. Every person who laid eyes on such a structure at that moment saw the alteration occur, and all were overcome by a frenzied psychosis in which they witnessed the world turning to nightmare.

Some blanched and stared in mute shock. Others groaned and screamed and covered their heads. Still others fell to their knees or fainted. Some vomited and went into convulsions. Later, the story that emerged from these tens of thousands of witnesses was uniform in its assertion of the unearthly influence those impossible visions had exerted. The sheer spectacle of the grotesquely twisted visages had, as one man phrased it, "flooded my eyes" and "rotted my gut." Countless people told the same story of experiencing an overpowering sense of mingled terror and revulsion that seemed to bloat their visual sense and then "spill" or "burst" or "flood" into other parts of their bodies—stomach, bowels, genitals, limbs—and bring with it an excruciating illness.

The vision vanished as suddenly as it had appeared, and in the ensuing days and weeks more than one artist attempted to paint or draw a semblance of those spectral faces. Invariably, the attempts fell short, at least according to the people who had seen the originals. I examined several of these drawings and paintings myself, as I leafed through the scattered pages from newspapers that came fluttering down the street and creeping on stray breezes into my alley, and they were indeed hideous in the extreme, with mouths, eyes, brows, nasal ridges, and underlying skeletal structures displaying a strange perversion of proportion that rendered them utterly noxious. The exact qualities that achieved such a striking effect proved impossible to isolate. In some of the pictures the eyes were blank and white, staring blindly without irises or pupils. In others they were rendered demonic by pupils in the shape of serpentine slits or goat-like wedges. Still others featured the bulbous black eyes of an insect or the berry-cluster eyes of a spider. In all the pictures, the mouths gaped wide in screams of torment, but again the details varied. Some revealed reptilian rows of fangs, others a foul nest of mucus tissues lined with rotten sores like leprosy. In others, the throat behind the tongue was replaced by a strange stone tunnel with an arched entrance, suggesting a coiling journey downward, inward, toward a pit of inconceivable darkness.

Of all those who stood within sight of a religious structure when the visions struck, I alone failed to see the faces. It happened while I was out on one of my daily tours of the city, following the unfathomable but undeniable dictates of that inner leading, which seemed designed to send me shuffling on a different route each day for the purpose of taking in the city sights in a different spatial and temporal configuration, and which on that day had brought me out of the back streets and into the open, on a sidewalk populated by many pedestrians and bordering a great, black-paved avenue. It ran past a great, gray, stone cathedral, and I was standing directly before and beneath the façade of the sacred structure, watching the crowd part around me with averted eyes, when they all began to scream and clutch their neighbors. Curious but strangely unmoved, I looked to their faces to learn the source of their panic and found them all staring wild-eyed at the church. A glance at it myself showed only the same spires and arches rearing toward the pale blue sky, and the same massive mazework of stained glass glinting in the afternoon sunlight. But it was evident that the individuals around me were seeing something much more, something far other, something that was even then causing them to fall and thrash, to gasp and retch, writhing in fits of supernatural sickness. And still I saw nothing. Within seconds I was the only one left standing, a rag-wrapped figure surrounded by shuddering, supine forms that struck me as wormlike and obscene.

For many nights afterward, when the newspapers had begun to report on what had happened and offer their useless interpretations and assessments, I pondered this event as I lay inside my grotto and felt the darkness breathe. I could not divine whether my failure to see the faces indicated a deficit or a surplus of spiritual sight. Many times I reached up to feel my forehead, cheeks, eyes, and mouth, and each time I was seized by the mental image of that great cathedral shuddering and twisting and transforming itself into a polished mirror upon whose silvery surface I saw my own reflection screaming in unbounded horror.

Not long after the appearance of the faces, the breakdown in things was signaled in more personal fashion by the incident of the man who bled to death through his eyes. It occurred during my daily journey, when I was at one of the farthest points away from my alley and tracing an unwonted path through a part of town where people wore newer clothing and drove shinier vehicles, and where the tall buildings gleamed with the freshness of new-cut stone and polished glass.

It was the screams that drew my attention and initiated the event. They came in a male voice, ragged and piercing, and were so very sincere in their expression of frantic horror that I thought they would surely shred the throat of whoever was voicing them. Like everyone else within earshot, I turned to look, and quickly located a man in a gray business suit standing at the open door of a taxicab and clutching his face with both hands. Blood spurted from between his fingers, which were capped over his eyes.

The sight exerted a preternatural power over the crowd, mesmerizing them into frozen silence. They stared as he shrieked in agony and horror. They gaped as he doubled over and vomited on his black leather shoes. They remained motionless as he fell into the crook of the cab door and began clawing at his eyes while his legs kicked spastically.

Then they heard the sound, the one that had been obscured by the initial commotion and the man's screams. It was a whispery hiss, like the melting of ice on a bed of hot coals, and it suffused the atmosphere of the avenue with an unnatural volume and vividness. After a moment, its source became evident.

The blood from the man's eyes was sizzling and burning like acid. It was eating at the flesh of his hands and face, the fabric of his suit, the leather of his shoes, even the yellow paint on the door of the taxi. Where it had spattered on the street, it bubbled like oil in a hot skillet, emitting a curling white plume of smoke and carving bowl-like indentations for itself in the pavement.

Pandemonium ensued. The explosion of panic that had been temporarily held in abeyance by horrified awe now detonated with all the more force. People fled with shrieks and shouts. I alone stayed near to watch what happened as the man's body began to collapse in on itself.

Later, when I arrived back at my alley, I crawled inside my grotto and lay there motionless for the rest of that afternoon and deep into the night, letting the events of the day replay again and again in the theater of my mind's eye. While the stars were still out and visible in the strip of sky above, I crawled out and gathered materials to make a new congregant in my church of little ones. A discarded length of rubber tubing, strapped to a body made from a rusty old gasoline can, produced the appearance of entrails protruding from a metallic abdomen. Holes punctured in the top of the can with a nail formed black, empty eyes gazing ever upward in agonized awe and a mouth screaming eternally and soundlessly in perpetual torment. I arranged the ugly figure with his fellows and settled back against the opposite wall to let them return my gaze while my mind wandered where it would, tracing the contours of a bottomless mystery that invaded the conditioned human self and corruptible human form with an absolute reality that it could not contain or abide.

More such events began to multiply throughout the city in the ensuing weeks. Even I, in my seclusion, caught wind of the horror that had begun to spill into the world through every crack and seam.

On a bitterly cold morning, when a crust of ice coated every exposed surface, an unknown variety of flower sprang up and bloomed in the city's largest public park. A policeman watched it erupt from the frozen sod, staring in astonishment as the strange shoot broke through the icy crust and rose to a height of two feet before unfolding velvety black petals clustered around a lemon-yellow core. He approached in wonder, removed a black glove, extended his hand, and brushed the petals with trembling fingers. He died later that day of a raging fever, but not before telling a doctor that the flower disintegrated into ash upon contact with his skin.

A few blocks north, a car ran over a blind man's dog, injuring it grievously. The man fell to his knees and cradled the dog's head in his lap, weeping wretchedly as his canine guide shrieked in agony. But then the bestial shrieks underwent a shocking alteration and became a human voice issuing from the inhuman mouth, begging the man not to let the dog die there in the street, howling an obscenity of mangled speech formed by lips, tongue, and throat that were never intended for such a purpose. The man strangled his dog in a burst of horrified fury, and then sobbed over and over to the shocked onlookers, "It couldn't live. It couldn't live."

These and other such events began to play on everyone's lips, even those of the street-dwellers whose life I shared. They began congregating outside the entrance to my alley, first in twos and threes and then in a growing throng, and as I eavesdropped on them, I could hear that many of the saner among them had begun to sound like the crazies as they anxiously discussed the crisis that was unfolding, while the crazies themselves came to seem positively magisterial in the intensity and sincerity of their expressed delusions. Meanwhile, I continued to read the scraps of newspaper that came my way, and I found they had come to sound unhinged in a manner formerly reserved for the tabloids, as their pages were now filled with tales of impossible occurrences. In a hastily published pamphlet that circulated by hand and word of mouth throughout the city's populace, and that was roundly denounced by religious and civil authorities, a putative and anonymous scholar who specialized in what he or she described as "an occult branch of philosophical theology" suggested that all these disruptions confirmed his or her thesis that "the godhead is insane, and the supernatural is its insanity."

Over time, the scale of the events grew greater, surpassing their former status as mere news of the bizarre to reach heights of grotesquery and hallucinatory horror that led otherwise sober commentators to speculate in all seriousness that something had come unraveled at the heart of things.

A woman entering a clothing shop on a busy avenue was killed when the plate glass window above the door suddenly came loose from its frame and fell upon her with unnatural force like a guillotine, hitting the crown of her skull broadwise and cleaving her head cleanly in half before exploding on the floor in a cascade of crystalline fragments. Her face thus remained untouched, and

when she fell to the floor, her eyes remained open, rolling wildly
in their sockets with an expression of panic while her lips worked
silently. Compounding the astonishment and horror of onlookers
were the half-dozen clumps of pulsating feathers that came spilling out of the woman's split cranium. These landed on the polished tile floor and whipped instantly into motion, unfurling to
reveal themselves as enormous black birds that someone described as misshapen crows. They took flight and dashed madly
about the interior of the store in a squawking hurricane of oily
wings, crashing into light fixtures, knocking over clothing racks,
and wounding a number of the store's patrons with slashes and
gouges from jagged beaks and black talons, and then, as if possessed by a single, demonic mind, they shot through the open
front door and out into the street. A dozen witnesses saw the
screeching black shapes flap high into the air and then out of
sight past the edge of a skyscraper.

   In another part of the city, a young woman was attacked in
her apartment by her four-year-old daughter. Two college students who lived in the adjacent unit came running in response to
the screams and found the girl buried neck-deep inside her mother's torso, which was split open like a fish. She told the police later
that she had been trying to "get back inside mama's belly." One of
the students told a journalist that when he and his roommate arrived, the girl pulled her head out of the bloody vertical wound
and turned to gaze at them with "black, burning eyes."

   As I walked silently through the city streets and byways in my
ever-widening and constantly evolving circuit, and as I sat
propped against the wall of my alley in pursuit of my demiurgic
work of monstrous creation, my thoughts kept circling round to
the inner state of those who had witnessed and participated in
such prodigies. Again and again, I returned to meditate on the
sense of *unreality* that must have overtaken them. Dwelling upon
this for endless hours, I would frequently experience an inner
upwelling of giddiness, like the onset of cosmic vertigo, which
would, if I happened to be standing at the time, oblige me to

reach out to steady myself against a wall or lamppost. My eyesight would flicker and grow dim, as if my surroundings were lit only by the glow of a guttering candle, and I would hear the faint sound of a muted, hollow roar, like the shrieking of some vast metallic gate swinging open. If this came over me while I sat in my alley pursuing my calling, I would stare curiously at the little unfinished creature in my hands, and at the others strewn about the alley floor. And all the repressed knowledge of my nature, of my origin and reason for being, would tremble at the far edge of consciousness.

I awoke in the dead of night with the buzzing awareness of some unknown visitation lying heavily upon me. The presence was receding even as I came to wakefulness and crawled out of my grotto. Something about my alley was different, and I stood blinking in the starlight for half a moment before realizing the nature of the change.

My little ones were gone. I had ended my day by setting out what was by far the largest array of them that I had ever assembled. The concentric curved rows had radiated outward from the entrance of my grotto like a veritable rainbow of deformity, reaching all the way to the facing wall. But now, several hours later, the alley floor was bare, swept clean even of its usual carpet of garbage, all of which I had used as the raw material for my creative act. Nothing remained but a thin coating of dirt.

Peering more closely, I saw a multitude of miniature indentations flowing in a path toward the alley's entrance, which, I realized, had now become an exit. Even now the receding whisper of a collective scuttling tickled my ears.

The screams began to arrive a little later, as I sat against the wall in my usual spot. First were the voices of my fellow street people, barking out in terrified surprise. Then came the sounds of panic and horror riding the frigid night air from all over the city. Hundreds of thousands of voices shrieked in a collective nightmare, and continued to shriek even after their owners had met their doom.

I rose to my feet and peered intently upward at the strip of night sky between the abandoned buildings whose outer walls defined my world. It bristled with stars. As I watched, they seemed to take on the imprint of a vast and deformed human face—not looking down at me, but pressing outward, as if the entire glittering expanse were the inner surface of a cosmic mask. I reached up to touch my own face with a sense of quickening elation and dread.

[EDITOR'S NOTE: Here the manuscript ends. It was discovered along with its anonymous preface, lying on the front porch of an abandoned Methodist rectory in the American Midwest.]

Prometheus Possessed

The scene opens on a vast city of spires and turrets. It gleams and sparkles metallic silver in the pale blaze of a high-noon sun, and its enveloping atmosphere, suffused with a dusky golden glow, winks with the lights of countless aerial vehicles carrying a similarly sunlit populace to and fro on myriad missions of recreation and consumption. Below, an epic and efficient grid of roads and walkways serves to channel foot-bound traffic through an endless round of work and play, and then back to wholesome homes each night for rest and rejuvenation, before commencing the whole round once again. In all, ninety million nominally happy, sane, and sanitized citizens inhabit this capital city of the New Society.

Gazing down silently from high above, arriving as an invisible visitor from some unknown origin, you might look upon this panorama of cold brightness and sharp beauty, and see in it the apotheosis of enlightened order and satisfied desire.

But then the presence of one particular building would cast doubt on this assessment. It calls attention to itself, out of all that immense assemblage of shining wonder, by its very lack of luster. Although it, like all the rest, sits illuminated in the light streaming down from the fathomless sky, its surface fails to reflect as fully as the others. Its hue is duller, tending downward on the spectrum toward thunderhead gray. It is squat, square, and plain, a mere dwarf compared to its towering neighbors.

If you descended from the sky for a closer look, you would see the words "Ministry of Psychic Sanitation" announced in glowing gold letters on a holographic sign above the entrance. Descending still further and passing through the roof, you would discover a maze of hallways and offices with gray metallic walls and black burnished floors, and below that, stacked in strata descending far into the earth, more than three hundred similar situations. This square building participating dully in the life of the otherwise resplendent city on the surface is the ten-percent tip of an architectural iceberg. Its dark depths mock (as you might be inclined to think of it) the upper city's majestic height.

On the lowest level, where even the hot white light of ubiquitous illuminated strips set into floors and ceilings cannot dispel the impression of encroaching shadows, which seem to press inward from the outer walls like a luminous darkness, you would come upon the person of Brother Frank, one of the Ministry's top-level Curers, a man of singular drive and brilliance, whose rise through the organization's labyrinthine bureaucracy has recently been characterized as "meteoric" by his supervising Mentor, the legendary Brother Nam'd-Law, gray and grizzled of beard, white of hair, and possessed of a high, square, thoughtful forehead.

"Our dear Brother Frank," the old man had said recently to an envoy of six members from the Ruling Council, "will one day be our Supreme Curate. Mark my words." The envoy had come to observe and judge the latest enhancements and upgrades to the Ministry's treatment techniques, which had been necessitated by the ferocious and seemingly unstoppable spread of a persistent psychic sickness throughout the Citizenry. Brother Frank had achieved more success in treating it than any other Curer, and he beamed at his Mentor's praise. "I'm not alone in this opinion," the old man said to the Council members. "Brother Frank is the very incarnation of enlightened rationality and psychic purity." Then he fixed his Mentee with a cold, weary gaze that startled and confused the younger man, who had no time to think or reflect on it, for he was obligated to entertain the Council members and then return immediately to his never-ending battle against an ever-mounting caseload of psychic infectees. "The sickness," he said to the envoy in parting, "never rests, and so neither will I." The last thing he heard from them was their murmur of approval.

That was recently. Presently, Brother Frank is rushing down

the long hallway of Ward 823 toward Treatment Room 23-Z in a profoundly agitated state. It is equal parts fury and panic, bound together by some unnamable emotion that he refuses to call *terror*. He has had no time to read the case file for Patient #231-7 in advance of the interview and evaluation, because his previous session with another Patient—#172-3, whose personal name, printed below the PsychID at the top of his file, is Milton Adamah—ran long and made him late when the man erupted into a sustained fit of frothing and shrieking in which he raved about a "burning man" who was haunting his dreams and speaking unintelligible words that "rape my mind."

"He screams in a whisper!" Adamah had insisted, fairly screaming himself and thus drawing the presence of two green-clad Restrainers, who entered the treatment room and positioned themselves on either side of him. Brother Frank remained motionless in his chair, gazing at Adamah with a carefully maintained lack of facial expression and waiting to see which way the situation would tilt. If Adamah failed to calm down, if his fit escalated from a verbal to a physical outburst, the Restrainers would apply the minimum necessary force to subdue him. Brother Frank had seen situations tilt that way many times before, especially in recent weeks as the sickness has metastasized throughout the populace with exponentially increasing swiftness, and he was always strangely thrilled to witness the exquisitely precise calibration of the Restrainers' responses to the Patients' particular needs. Only once had he seen one of them actually use lethal force, when the Patient had tried to leap across the table and attack the Curer, and had then kept flailing and fighting with almost superhuman strength after they seized him, until he almost—an impossible thought—broke free of their grasp. The Restrainer on his left had moved with lightning swiftness, wrapping the man's neck in the crook of a brawny arm and giving a quick, sharp, professional tug. The fracturing of the vertebrae had sounded strangely delicate, like a toothpick snapping underwater, and the Patient had instantly gone slack, hanging like a rag doll from the Restrainer's arm and staring at Brother Frank with dead doll's eyes to match.

Even though that had been over a month ago, the memory of it was still fresh when Milton Adamah started ranting about a burning man who screamed at him in his sleep. But mercifully, Adamah's outburst remained a purely verbal manifestation of his pathology. But it also proved uncommonly long-lived, and the Restrainers stood in silence on both sides of him as he babbled about his nocturnal visitor, who, he said, was a "shadow man" who arrived at the same time each night to stand in silence at the foot of the bed and then burst into flames, after which "He eats me with his burning eyes!" Brother Frank was obligated by the treatment protocol to stay and witness the episode until it resolved one way or the other. But beyond that, Adamah's words threw the Brother into an awful state of petrified panic that he was barely able to conceal from both the Patient and the restrainers. When Adamah finally exhausted himself and collapsed forward onto the gray tabletop, the time was irretrievably late, and the Brother bolted from the room and fled down the hallway toward 23-Z, neglecting in his haste to write down his closing notes on Adamah's behavior and condition, and leaving the man to be removed and returned to his cell by the Retrievers.

And now, at this very moment, you observe Brother Frank approaching 23-Z's bare metal door and allowing, for a moment only, his true emotions to erupt onto his face. His features twist into a grimace of unbearable conflict and horror. *This cannot be happening,* his thoughts tell him. *None of it. Not possible. Not real.* Before touching the ID-Reader to gain entrance, he calls up #231-7's Patient file on his palmscreen and has just enough time to reflect before going in to meet and treat the Patient that this lack of preparedness, this unprofessional act of entering an initial diagnostic treatment session without proper advance preparation, is the way disasters are sown. "The sickness is contagious," Brother Nam'd-Law had warned him only yesterday. "Don't think that because of its mental nature it is not communicable. What is in and of the mind is all the more potent." Brother Frank had sat up sharply at this whiff of heretical ideology from his mentor, who knew the nature of, and penalties for, this kind of disallowed thinking better than any other senior Mentor in the entire Ministry. And now Nam'd-Law's words are haunting him

(screaming in a whisper? eating me with their burning eyes?)

[Purge the unreal thought. Employ standard principles of psychic hygiene.]

(no haunting, no screaming, just contact contamination, I am Brother Frank, PsychID OZ-29991)

as Brother Frank prepares to enter a proverbial lion's den of possible psychic infectivity abetted by his own lack of preparation. He takes a breath, opens the door, and thrusts himself into the Treatment Room.

The hum of the hallway, its irregularly patterned chorus of visual and aural alerts and alarms, and the bustling background presence of his fellow Curers and other Ministry personnel—all of it clips off into utter silence with the slide-shut of the door, and now he is alone with Patient #231-7. Usually, this is his favorite part of the ritual: the moment when all extraneous vectors of contact and communication are eliminated, and it is just the three of them: the Curer, the Patient, and the Sickness. Brother Frank has never told anyone, not even Nam'd-Law, the true secret of his success as a Curer, but this, in fact, is it: he personifies the psychic sickness into Sickness, a singular, sentient entity that speaks with a consistent voice and lurks with a consistent nature inside a vast multitude of human hosts. Outwardly he follows the Ministry's protocols to the letter, but the spirit of them he illuminates with greater depth, power, and effectiveness than any other Curer, precisely because of this unspoken attitude. "An eminently useful fiction," he often describes it to himself with smugness and glee.

Milton Adamah's outburst of a moment ago, however, has called the advisability of his master tactic into question. Or rather, it has done so by falling directly in line with the syndrome that Brother Frank himself has been suffering with increasing frequency over a span of months. "A burning man," Adamah said. "He eats

(me with his burning eyes a shadow man screaming in a whisper)

[Purge the unreal thought.]

(*I am Brother Frank, PsychID OZ-29991*)

Patient #231-7 sits unmoving on the far side of the table and appears, upon first glance, to be an alarmingly deformed-looking man. He is positioned with his back to the door, facing one of the corners. This places him directly in the dark glow of a new phenomenon that Brother Frank has observed in recent weeks: the black shadow no longer presses in from the exterior walls alone, but from each angular intersection throughout the ministry's layered subworld of Cells, Wards, and Treatment Rooms. The gloom of it is starkly evident in the room's far corner, and thus the Patient's face is plunged into total darkness. Even when Brother Frank approaches the table and leans sideways to peer around the man's head, he can see nothing. Only the back of him is visible. The Patient's stringy hair is oil-black and greasy, and his head is grossly misshapen. His shoulders are massive and somehow misaligned, and his clothing, instead of the usual pale blue Patient garb, is a shapeless, ratty, charcoal-colored cloak with an oddly textured weave.

Reestablishing his mask of apathy with some effort, Brother Frank notes down his initial subjective impressions. "Patient sits facing the corner upon my arrival," he taps into the palmscreen. "Face not visible. Odd deformation of skull shape, neck, and shoulder structure, as if . . ." He pauses and struggles to find the right words. ". . . as if not fully formed. Patient is wearing non-standard, non-Ministry-issue clothing." His eyes narrow as another fact becomes evident. He inhales through his nostrils, then types, "Odd scent pervades the Treatment Room. Unpleasant. Sour. Acrid. Stench of decay."

A word for the collective impression created by these facts *in toto* steps forward from the back of his mind and announces itself, autonomously and unanswerably, as the appropriate name for them. It nearly makes its way through his fingers and onto the palmscreen, and thus into the Network's permanent database, before he realizes its madness and stops it in time. He jerks his hand away from the screen as if it were a hot rock, his fingers curved into claws. Clearing his head, he saves his notes to the Network, shoves the word to the back of his thoughts, and searches for the Patient's personal name below the listed PsychID.

To his astonishment, the name field is blank. To his greater astonishment, the PsychID field itself is simply a string of nils: "oo-oooo-o-ooo." He blinks, looks again. He taps the Update icon to refresh the screen with the latest information from the Network database, but the blank spaces remain unchanged.

This is unprecedented. More than that, it is impossible. In Brother Frank's twelve years with the Ministry, no Patient has ever arrived without a PsychID and assigned name listed on the case file. And this in turn is due to the more fundamental and all-encompassing fact that no person on the entire planet is without this vital locus of personal identification. The pairing of a personal name with a birth-assigned PsychID is tantamount to what a former age, with its imperfect and destructively naïve categories of emotional terminology (stemming from its imperfect and destructively naïve understanding of the human bio-psychic mechanism), would have categorized as "sacred." The instituting of this planet-wide system by the Ruling Council antedates the memory of any living person and embodies the shrewd insight and compassionate humanism of the Founders, who, in one of the defining acts of the Global Reformation, recognized the necessity of accomplishing human individuation along dual lines: one for the Commonwealth itself, requiring a unique identifier for each Citizen that anchors his or her bio-psychic profile, and one for each Citizen to organize and define his or her localized perspective. The PsychID fulfills the top-down need for surveillance and predictability; the personal name fulfills the human need, revealed by extensive experimentation as ineradicable, for a sense of individual identity. Their pairing for each and every member of the pared-down planetary population in the wake of the great ecological and cultural cataclysms that marked the transition from one civilization to another is the undergirding socio-organizational principle of the New Era. Without this comprehensive identifier, a person would effectively be nobody, a nonentity, utterly non-existent in the eyes and mind of the New Society.

Such an utterly non-existent nonentity now sits in the metal chair of Room 23-Z with its back to Brother Frank and its face plunged into shadow.

The Brother searches for his voice and, after a struggle, finds it. There is nothing to do but proceed. He tries to take comfort in the ritual of the opening lines.

"My name is Brother Frank. I'm here to help you." He pauses to allow a reaction that will determine the next step. The Patient remains still and silent, and Brother Frank's heart pounds as he continues with the next line of the introduction protocol. "Do you know why you are here?"

At this the Patient emits a low noise. It may be a laugh, but it is humorless and vile, with a texture like the crushing of dry leaves. The Brother has to use a portion of his frayed but still considerable powers of self-control to suppress a shudder, which would draw the disapproval of the Supervisors observing the session through their multiple screens and listening to it through their multiple monitors.

"The question before us," the Patient says, "is whether *you* know why I am here." He speaks slowly, in a voice hovering between a whisper and a murmur, and with arch-precision, his words forming with a delicate grace that belies his ragged, filthy appearance.

Brother Frank recognizes both the tone and the content of this response as a matter of standard pathological gamesmanship, a combination of deflection and projection designed to throw a Curer off balance and involve him instantly in the Patient's delusional subjective world. He has encountered it hundreds of times before, although never played in so thoroughly unnerving a manner, and he finds its familiarity blissfully reassuring. "I am not the Patient, sir," he says, his voice gaining confidence. "*I* am here to help *you*. So let us figure out together how we can accomplish that."

"You mean, good Brother, that you intend to help me in the way you helped Milton Adamah? Did he appear at all *helped* when last you saw him?" The Patient's posture appears to shift in his metal chair even though he does not exactly move, and Brother Frank's astonishment is as much at this evidence of a deformity endemic in the man's entire physical frame—a deformity that enables him to bend and flow in ways unnatural for a human body—as it is at the man's knowledge of the treatment session that has just occurred far down the hallway in another wing of the Ministry's lowest level, past multiple insulated metal walls inset with a multitude of monitors, sensors, and security measures. The treatment protocol offers no response for a statement like this one, a response that flies in the face of possibility and reason, and Brother Frank's momentary sense of comfort shatters as he feels the situation tilt suddenly, sharply, and horribly in a new and nightmarish direction.

"I . . . don't know what you're talking about." His stammer is unstoppable. The unsteadiness of his own voice makes it sound alien, and sickens him. "The issue, sir, is you."

"Then," says the Patient in that same corrupted half-whisper, "let us talk about me. Yes, let me be the object of your attention. What can you tell me about myself? What does your holy electronic icon tell you?"

Brother Frank is sweating through the fabric of his rough brown robe, staining its stylized and streamlined representation of ancient monastic garb with the stench of his own body. He passes a hand over his face and looks to the palmscreen, discovering as he does so that it is bizarrely difficult to wrench his gaze away from this foul, shifting mass of a man who sits with his face plunged into the encroaching shadow. It is as if Patient #231-7 emits a gravitational aura that repels the Brother's sensibility but attracts his sight and

(eats my eyes and rapes my mind)

[*Purge the unreal—*]

(steals my voice and swallows my name)

[*Employ standard principles of—*]

(consumes my heart and crushes my SOUL)

A sudden trembling seizes him deep within his core, spanning from heart to gut and feeling like a frigid absence, as if his torso has disappeared and he is a nothing but bare feet on the cold floor and a floating head full of encroaching insanity. This disembodied head tilts down to see the palmscreen. Below the awful lacunae where the name and PsychID should be, the bio-narrative field contains the following text:

> Subject discovered inside the Temple by a Peace Enforcer making final sector sweep to verify full evacuation before building demolition. PE transmitted a request for assistance but was cut off from further communication by unknown interference. Additional PEs arrived to find subject emerging from Temple, walking backward. All reported cognitive, emotional, and multisensory perceptual anomalies accompanying subject's presence and movements.
>
> Apprehension of subject successfully accomplished, but arresting PEs suffered unspecified injuries. Cleanup Team dispatched for assistance. Sector sweep located original PE inside Temple suffering severe multiphase trauma. PE later expired at hospital. (See attached coroner's report.) Enforcers transported subject through gathering crowd of Citizens for delivery to Peace Authority but were rerouted for delivery to Psychic Sanitation on special order relayed directly from Ruling Council. (See attached order.) Severe injuries and traumas sustained by multiple Enforcers and Citizens while en route. (See attached photos and commentary.) All require Ministry intervention by Curers with minimum certification level 5. (See attached documentation.)
>
> Ruling Council requests full evaluation of subject and recommendation regarding treatment, detainment, and disciplinary action, including possible eradication. Also requests deep-interpretive analysis of subject's pathology: its etiology, manifestations, virulence, progress, and prognosis, with special attention to means of transmission.

Brother Frank's feet and hands have gone numb as well. While reading the account of how the stranger arrived here, in this

room, to confront him with diseased unrealities, his extremities
have lost all feeling except for a heavy, anesthetized deadness. He
taps the screen with a trembling, frozen finger to call up the associated documents, and immediately photos and words begin to
scroll past his vision, feeding into his eyes like a sentient virus,
showing him human bodies littering the antiseptic streets of the
Capitol, mangled beyond all sanity by monstrous transformations,
with the remains of their faces frozen in a rictus of horrified agony
and, in some cases, elation and ecstasy. Many of their eye sockets
appear bruised and black, as do their mouths and joints, as if they
have been sprayed with coal dust, or—a thought more true to the
photos—as if this dark substance has leaked or erupted from their
joints and orifices. The coroner's report tells of an autopsy that revealed liquefied bones and calcified flesh, with accompanying
clinical photos to substantiate the outlandish claim.

Along with these and other materials are several unexplained
photos of the Temple, taken from various angles and attached
without accompanying comment. There it rests in the city's central plaza, a monolith of arcane architecture and ancient spiritual-
psychological folly, serving its function as a museum of outmoded
artifacts and beliefs about the world from before the great Transition, a nexus of ancient, irrational fears, cravings, and notions that
had all but destroyed human life. "It's a good thing the Ruling
Council has decided to destroy it," Brother Frank had said to
Brother Nam'd-Law during yesterday's mentoring session. "Its function is fulfilled. In the past it may have helped to promote the
health of the populace by providing a psychic repository for atavistic attitudes and impulses. But we have passed the point of dimin-
ishing returns. Now its presence only exacerbates all these things.
We're ready to move on, especially since the Ministry has perfected
its art. Religion and psychic hygiene are united in our work, and
the Temple undoes this. How many Patients have we sent out of
here fully purged, only to find them returning with the roots of
their sickness reestablished from a tour through the Temple, or
from the very act of walking past it or standing in its shadow?"

Nam'd-Law had not answered with the immediate agreement Brother Frank had expected, but had remained gazing silently downward in thought. Then he had said, "The ancient teachers of this science promised impossibilities and performed nothing. But we, with our *great wisdom* and *compassionate expertise,* penetrate into the recesses of nature." Far from sounding confident or comforting as he recited the heart of the Ministry's creed, his tone was weary, defeated, and ironic. Brother Frank stared at him in astonishment. The Mentor's eyes rose to greet those of his Mentee, and the elder man intoned with a strange sadness, "We even mock the invisible world with its own shadows."

Back in Treatment Room 23-Z, in the present, the stranger hisses in his dry husk of a voice, "Did you truly believe you could finish your great project of purgation? For every sickness you cast out, did you not see two more take hold?"

"The size of a shadow," Nam'd-Law had said yesterday, "is proportionate to the size of the object that casts it. Remember that, Brother. It is not in our book of doctrine and treatment, but it ought to be."

"For every one we cast out," he had also said, "two more appear. Haven't you noticed this? And haven't you noticed how the shadow in your dreams has grown larger with each new cure? Hasn't it led you to question the viability of our very mission? The validity of our psychic purity? Hasn't it led you to wonder whose motives, whose promptings, whose ends, we are really enacting?"

The shadow in Brother Frank's dreams. The shadow that has come to visit him each night for nine months, to stand at the foot of his bed, paralyze him with fear, crush him with unbearable weight, convulse him with a horrible energy, and burst into flame. The shadow that he has only spoken about in confidence to Brother Nam'd-Law.

The shadow Milton Adamah screamed about.

The shadow now elongating and rising toward the ceiling in a room buried a mile beneath the surface of the earth, where all extraneous vectors of contact and communication are cut off, and only two remain: the Curer and the Sickness.

"With each one you cast out," the Sickness says, shuddering and flowing, rippling and expanding, "you increased your stature. And mine."

The palmscreen emits a soft tone to indicate the arrival of a new communication from the remote Supervisors tucked safely away in electronic omniscience on some unspecified upper level. From his lower peripheral vision, Brother Frank sees the screen turn red, indicating that they have initiated emergency protocol. But no Restrainers arrive. No alarms sound. No one comes to rescue him from this budding, blasphemous nightmare. He tries to scream for assistance, but his mouth is gone, and he can only croak out a thoroughly atavistic sound, something not suited to a Curer of his level and reputation, nor to any civilized member of the New Society. He cannot tear his eyes away from the sinuous column of organically undulating smoke that has now begun to advance from the corner. Its surface flexes like feathers and scales, gleaming dully in the hot white light of the ceiling and floor strips.

His mind shrieks

(. . . *Sickness screaming eating raping fire Sickness Temple* . . .) and no amount of training, no amount of intricately accomplished imprinting and programming with the psychic-hygienic defenses of the Ministry, can stand up to the truth of the ancient, rejected word:

(*DAEMON*)

"Yours," the voice says. "Always."

Brother Frank falls to the frigid metal floor. His breath exhales in a misty plume. The Sickness arches over him, cascades upward, crests like a wave, then turns downward and bursts into flames. His mind continues to shriek as the wave of blackness slams into him, crushes him, sears him—and enters him.

(. . . *eats my mind in darkness screaming* . . .)

If, at this moment, you were to pull away from the spectacle of the writhing Brother in the brown robe with his blackening eyes, mouth, and joints, and if you were to rise back through the three hundred buried levels of the Ministry of Psychic Sanitation, and were to emerge into the surface city and continue your ascent back into the fathomless sky, back toward your transcendent origin, you might look down upon the city's panorama of cold brightness and sharp beauty, and see in it the apotheosis of alienated order and bottomless, infinite, tormenting desire. And in the seismic shudder now beginning to ripple through it, causing at first a mere blurring of edges, but now a breaking of windows and cracking of seams, and soon a catastrophic toppling and shattering of titanic buildings; and in the aerial crafts falling from the sunlit sky as their pilots and passengers erupt with darkness and twist into monstrous forms; and in the screams of the terrestrial multitude as they fall in the streets, crush their hands to their eyes, and thrash in tandem with the agony of their protector Brother Frank, whose doom is still unfolding a mile beneath them; in the sight and sound and smell of all this, you might intuit, however incongruous the thought with the sickening appearance of the scene, a full and final Cure, albeit a tormented one, being accomplished at long last.

The New Pauline Corpus

Seated at a small wooden desk, a humble piece of cypress wood furniture elevated to veritably mythic status by a heaping of fabulously ornate decorative flourishes, he spreads out the papers on the smooth surface before him. A rushing murmur, like the sound of ten thousand voices melding into an oceanic hush, flows through the doorway that stands open and waiting on the far side of the equally ornate room.

The papers are crammed to capacity with a chaotic jumble of handwritten markings. Rows of text run from left to right and then, often, meet the edge of the page and instead of breaking to the next line simply continue on, rebounding from the barrier in curling coils and tracing the paper's edge in circles that effectively form a written frame around the rest. Some lines appear in ink, others in pencil. Some words are miniscule to the point of near-indecipherability. Others shout hugely in hysterical looping letters.

None make sense. Not on their own, at least. Fragments. That is what he has in his possession. Pieces of a puzzle. Scraps of a portrait. Shards of a mirror, each reflecting and refracting the image of all the others to create a dazzling maze of meanings whose infinity encompasses enormous blank spaces.

The more I dwell on it, Francis, the more I am convinced that the single most fruitful result of the frightful transition which has overtaken us is the resurrection of our collective passion for *story*, for the specifically *narrative* understanding of our lives on this planet. I now view the trajectory of my former theological writings toward an almost exclusive emphasis on ontological matters as an egregious error. More than any other religious tradition in human history, our own Christian faith, along with its Jewish forebear, has always been centrally rooted in a cosmic-narrative understanding of human life and the cosmos itself. A reverence for story—as we have now been forcibly reminded—is not symptomatic of a regressive intellectual and theological naïveté but of an unblinking realism. It may simply be the case that the story in which we find ourselves existentially involved as living characters lacks any obvious correspondences with the charming drama we were told from childhood about the Eden-to-Fall-to-New Eden arc of our race. Or perhaps these elements are indeed discernible in our new tale, but in a jumbled order or—more likely—as inversions of themselves. I hope to say more about this in a future letter.

In any event, happy for me, since it means that I do not have to jettison the entirety of my former theological corpus, is the fact that theology-as-story does not *preclude* ontology but *incorporates* it. In fact, what has now been revealed to us in our dreadful recent disruptions is the express unity of these two categories of thought. That is, we are *living the story of a war between levels of reality*. Our metanarrative is the tale of how space-time, the cosmos, the created order, was usurped by a reality that is more fundamental, primary, and ancient.

This story, our story, is a tale of the deeply *inner* and *primordial* turning with hostility upon the objectively *outer* and *evolved,* and reshaping it according to a set of principles which are incomprehensible and, as we can see all around us in the fact of our wrecked cities with their new and growing populations of squamous, octopodan, and quasi-batrachian inhabitants, thoroughly revolting to the latter.

Under red-glowing smoke-filled skies I thread my way through a boulder field of shattered buildings. Fires blaze and smolder in places where no fuel ought to burn. Twisted chunks of steel and concrete burn like dryrotten wood. Sparkling shards of shattered windows and doors and street lamps catch the flickering orange glow and ignite from the pressure of the images on their glassy sur-

faces. A sea of flaming rubble, fifty miles wide. This is what remains of my city, and of all the others like it dotting the surface of the round earth like piles of autumn leaves raked together for burning.

Here is the heart of the matter, Francis, in a rush of analogies intended to distill the essence of the insights I lost when I shredded my manuscript on that terrible day:

ITS OMNIPRESENCE: My theological namesake quoted approvingly to his Greek audience a common bit of philosophical wisdom from their own cultural milieu when he spoke of God the Father as "the one in whom we live and move and have our being." Does not such a formulation recall Yog-Sothoth, who walks with the other Old Ones between the dimensions, and in whom past, present, and future are one? Does it not recall Azathoth, the primal chaos that resides not only at the center of infinity but at the center of each atom, each particle, perhaps serving as the unaccountable subatomic bond that has categorically escaped scientific explanation? But here I overstep the limits of my formal authority, so effectively does this daemonic pantheon inspire a plethora of transgressive and exhilarating speculations.

ITS ANNIHILATING HOLINESS: In the Hebrew Scriptures, in the desert, under the merciless sun, the Israelites witness repeated outbreaks of Yahweh, Who "is a consuming fire," an untamable force, a burning pestilence, a plague of serpents. And so is He revealed not just as the Holy Other but as Wholly Other, possessed of a cosmically singular *sui generis* nature that cannot and will not abide contradiction. In the words of Luther himself, if you sin "then He will *devour thee up,* for God is a fire that consumeth, devoureth, rageth; verily He is your undoing, as fire consumeth a house and maketh it dust and ashes." As Otto wrote with such frightening clarity of apprehension, there is something baffling in the way His wrath is kindled and manifested, for it is "like a hidden force of nature, like stored-up electricity, discharging itself upon anyone who comes too near. It is incalculable and arbitrary."

To see His luminance shining from the face of Moses is a horror. To see His face is to die.

This incomprehensible, inconceivable, incalculable, arbitrary horror serves as the font, finish, and focal point of our entire tradition. I trust my attempts at commentary would only weaken the blow of the brute fact itself.

"My son." The voice speaks behind him, and he looks sideways in acknowledgment of its presence without actually turning to face it. "Have you read them again?" The voice is thin as a reed, like a sick child, and also thick and murky, like a chorus chanting together in imperfect unison. But even now, with the world having passed beyond its own farthest extremity, the voice exudes a supernal calmness and control that still, astonishingly, serve to comfort and soothe.

"Some of them, yes," he replies. "But something is eluding me. They seem to contain two different strands or stories. One of them is like a dream narrative that follows an alternative plot and—perhaps—posits a world in which the efforts of the other narrative have failed, or were never made. But I'm not at all certain of any of this. I need to read the pages once more."

"Then read," the voice says. "But remember that we are waited upon." As if in confirmation, the ocean roar of voices swells momentarily to a peak, washing up from below the balcony outside and telling of a tensely waiting throng before settling back into an undulating trough.

He nods and returns to the pages.

ITS TRANSCENDENCE: In the Book of Isaiah we encounter a Yahweh who protects the cosmic order from destructive incursions by the ancient chaos serpents but also launches His own cosmos-shaking assaults against that order, all leading up to a concluding note of horror in the book's worm-infested final verse that has resounded down through the ages and brought no end of trouble for biblical exegetes, since its literary and theological effect is to stamp the book with the impossible message that *Yahweh is the ultimate chaos monster* who only saves His creation from the others so that He can destroy it Himself. (Surely you remember this subversive reading of the Isaian text from my last book, which sold relatively well but drew such scathing condemnation from my fellow theologians.)

Is it possible, can we conclude, that these and a thousand other aspects of our tradition were always both more and less than they seemed—that they were, in a word, *other* than they seemed; that instead of pointing directly toward spiritual and metaphysical truths, the great concepts, words, and icons of our tradition were in fact mere signals, hints, clues, which gestured awkwardly toward a reality whose true character was and is far different from and perhaps even *opposite to* the surface meanings?

Consider: Humanity's dual nature—conscious and unconscious, deliberate and autonomic, free and determined, physical and spiritual, cerebral and reptilian—has always singled us out as the earth's only true amphibians. We have always acted from two centers and stood with feet planted in two separate worlds. Now we have seen this duality ripped apart or brought to fruition—how to regard it is unclear—as those elements of reality represented by our reptilian brainbase, and by the darkest archetypes of our collective unconscious, and by the corresponding monstrous elements in our mythological traditions, have fulfilled a nexus of ancient race-level fears.

Does this perhaps indicate something of our role in what is transpiring? Do we perhaps serve a necessary function as bridges between the realms, *simply by the fact of our fundamental duality?*

I turn my eyes skyward and see the gargoylish figures still commanding the open air between the coiling columns of smoke. Rubbery black demonoid shapes with smooth blank faces and leathery wings swoop and careen like flakes of ash on a hot wind.

A moment later I stumble on a fragment of granite, and the in-

voluntary ducking of my head proves perfectly timed for avoiding a surely fatal encounter with a squid-like shape twenty feet long that bloats and shimmers through the air in a rhythmic pulsating pattern like a sea creature propelling itself through deep water. I stare at its underside, sick with terror, as it slides past and over me, but then note with relief that the fat torpedo-shaped body is turned so that its great blank eye looks laterally instead of downward. Had the thing been looking down, it would have done what these sentinels always do when they detect their prey: It would have paused directly over me and regarded me through that alien eye with an equally alien intelligence. Then it would have bunched itself into a knotted mass of claw-tipped tentacles ringed around a dilating sphincter-mouth set with concentric rows of needled teeth, and dropped upon me with inconceivable speed and ferocity. I have already seen those serpentine tentacles enmesh many a man in their deadly loops. I have heard the human flesh sizzle and scorch on contact with that corrosive extra-dimensional matter. I have watched shrieking people disappear into that churning meat grinder of a mouth.

As incongruous as it may sound, I now express *thanks*, not just passive resignation but a positive gratitude, for the waking nightmare that has overtaken us. For those things that otherwise seem so horrific in their surface appearances can actually serve to awaken us from our dogmatic slumbers and lead us to a more vital and viable faith, a faith that is unshakable, unassailable, impervious to doubt: a true theological exemplar of Luther's *Ein Feste Burg*, although this mighty fortress, if rendered in literal brick and stone, would embody a warped architectural schema of a pointedly non-human and non-rational nature.

It would be so easy to rearrange some of these fragments, to clarify their individual and collective meanings by connecting some of their philosophical edges where they obviously cohere. But despite his pleading for permission to do so, the rule is firm: The pages and their contents must remain in their received order, and

must be met and dealt with in that order and no other. Any interpretation must emerge from and pointedly account for that ca-
nonically unalterable jumble in its precise given form. *A new
revelation,* so many members of the hierarchy have said to him
and to each other on so many different occasions since the papers
first came into their possession at a time when the global nightmare was just beginning to invade from the shadows. *A new scripture. A third testament.* They have said such things in tones of
awe, and exultation, and confusion, and horror, and, increasingly,
with a dogmatic air of fanatical certitude.

We were both weaned, Francis, you in your Roman tradition and I
in my Protestant one, on the winsome belief that "All things work
together for good for those who love the LORD, those who are
called according to his purpose." I am writing to you now simply
to say this: Our global eruption of nightmares, which would otherwise seem to disprove this canonical statement from my theological namesake, actually serves to confirm it—not directly but
by demolishing the presumptuous prison of axioms in which it lay
incarcerated for two millennia. "All things work together for good
for those who love the LORD"—ah, but *what* good? and *which*
LORD? "Those who are called according to his purpose"—ah, but
what call, and *which* purpose?

The quotations and their implied questions point to our pressing
need. What confronts us as an awful necessity, if we and our faith
intend to survive, is a reconciliation of what we have always believed with what now presents itself as a contrary but incontrovertible truth. The classic theological antitheses—Jerusalem and
Athens, the City of God and the City of Man, Christ and Belial—no
longer apply. The only one that still retains any potency is that
which refers to the enmity between the "seed of the woman" and
the "seed of the serpent." But it requires a substantive modification.
    Our antithesis, our dilemma in the form of a sacred riddle, is
simply this: *What has Christ to do with Cthulhu?*

It comes with a corollary: *What has Jerusalem to do with R'lyeh?*

In these letters I intend to present you with the rudiments of a viable theological recalibration that will explore the avenues opened up by these shocking juxtapositions, and that, in doing so, will safeguard the possibility of our salvation, albeit in a much modified and, as I fear we shall be unable to keep from feeling it, far less agreeable form.

As I navigate the burning wasteland, another environment flickers intermittently into view around me: a crazy-tilted maze of stone columns and temples vying with the reality of the blasted city and attempting to supplant it all at once in a cinematic superimposition. The ocean, hundreds of miles from here, laps momentarily at my feet, while a monolithic mass of ancient stone towers glimmers darkly offshore. I blink, shake my head and refuse to accept the vision. After a furtive hesitation, the inland wasteland regains its foothold.

ITS AWEFULNESS: Especially in Mark's gospel, but also throughout the New Testament and also the Hebrew scriptures, manifestations of divine reality are portrayed consistently as occasions for sheer terror. Jesus calms the storm; his disciples are filled not with sweet sentiments of divine love and comfort but with terror and awe. The women find his tomb empty; they do not exit the garden singing hosannas but stumble away in soul-blasted fright, unable to speak. When angels appear in bursts of light and song, shepherds and Roman soldiers alike faint, tremble, avert their eyes, raise their hands to ward off the sight of those awful messengers of a reality from beyond this world—a reality that is *inherently* awful *because* it is from beyond this world.

He pulls his attention out of the pages like a swimmer hauling himself naked and shivering out of icy black waters. He makes to inhale deeply, to suck in cleansing air, but finds that his breath remains frozen at mid-breast, just as it has been for months now, ever since reality first went mad with the collapsing of the distinction between divine and demonic, leaving him internally paralyzed, gripped as if by a fist in his diaphragm while grotesque supernatural impossibilities erupt all around.

The voice behind him remains silent, but its presence is palpable and its command unmistakable. With fixed stare and only slightly trembling hand, he resigns himself again to the task and begins reading from the first page, scanning not only for the meanings contained in the words themselves but for evidence of the interstitial semiotic glue that binds the whole insane edifice together. As always, his attention is soon swallowed whole by the dark and deranged philosophical cathedral it has entered.

Perhaps a recounting of how our new "Great Awakening" (a term whose traditional, historical use seems gallingly blinkered now) first made itself known to me will serve to purify and clarify our mutual apprehension of these matters.

As you know, I was hard at work on my third book of theology, a substantial and career-defining exercise in theological trailblazing to be titled *The Fear of God,* in which I took on the same theme treated by John Bunyan in his classic treatise with the same title, and agreed with him that "by this word *fear* we are to understand even God himself, who is the object of our fear." I took for my orienting point Luther's subversive declaration—which exerted a veritably talismanic power over me—that God "is more terrible and frightful than the Devil. . . . For therefrom no man can refrain: if he thinketh on God aright, his heart and his body is struck with terror. . . . Yea, as soon as he heareth God named, he is filled with trepidation and fear."

One day—I distinctly remember the sun was shining sweetly through my living room window while a few birds twittered in the yard, so it must have been during the spring or summer, although my sense of time has lately become as confused and chaotic as the natural elements, which, as you know, have now taken on a schiz-

ophrenic kind of existence—one day I sat poring over a stack of
pages that I had recently written, and was struck without warning
by a thoroughly hideous vision. As I looked at my pages, I saw
peering through the typewritten words, as if from *behind* the lines
of text, a face more awful than any I had ever conceived. I need
not describe it to you: the bloated octopoid visage with its obscenity of a fanged and tentacled maw, and with saurian and humanoid characteristics all mixed together in a surreal jumble. Its
conjured involuntary thoughts of the great Dragon of John's
Apocalypse, and of the watery waste of Genesis, and of the waters
beyond the sky and below the earth, and of the chaos serpent Leviathan. But there was far more than that. Staring into the redblack effulgence of its awful eyes, I saw the skin of those biblical
images peeled back to reveal great Mother Tiamat, the ancient archetype of all dragons and serpents and extra-cosmic chaos, wearing the more familiar imagery like a cheap rubber mask.

It was more than just a visual image, it was a veritable convulsion in my total being, and its ripples spread through the very air
of the room. You well remember your own experience as you knelt
praying before a statue of St. Jude and raised your eyes to his benevolent face, only to be greeted by the same sight I am describing. So you know, too, the violent illness that overtook me. I was
gripped by a kind of mania even as my stomach and bowels twisted into searing knots, and I began turning frantically from page to
page in an effort to escape the vision, but still the words of my
magnum opus appeared as the bars of a cage holding back that
impossible face, that locus of all nightmares, that source of all ancient, evil imaginings. I dimly remember ripping the book to
shreds and even—I cannot remember why—eating portions of it,
and then vomiting them back up, only the half-digested paper had
been transformed into tiny scrolls which I then ate again, and
they tasted like honey, but then they turned so bitter in my
mouth that I vomited yet again.

These events are all peculiar to me, but the rest I think you
know. For my personal story is a microcosm of that greater story

in which we are all now trapped. Each of us has his own story of how he personally experienced that terrible moment when our world was overturned by the eruption from beyond, and all of them bear a generic character that marks them as belonging to this new proclamation, this New Testament, which we are not reading but living.

"And did you truly experience such a vision with a statue of Saint Jude?" the voice asks, still located behind him. Its tone is overlaid with a scummy film, like the surface of a thick and slow-boiling stew, and he maintains his reverentially averted gaze. After pausing to regain his bearings in the relatively solid surroundings of the chamber, he softly shakes his head.

"I don't think so. Or rather, I don't remember. Reading the documents is like reading the transcript of a dream that I never knew I had experienced. Every line feels like a half-memory of something I had forgotten without ever knowing it at all."

He considers the description of the demon-dragon, and imagines it transplanted onto the patron saint of desperate cases and lost causes. The apostle's beard is a nest of writhing gray-green tentacles. Their tips caress the image of Christ hanging at the figure's breast.

He asks, "And how did these papers come into the Church's possession?" hoping that maybe this time the answer will contain something new.

"By strange channels and unknown messengers," the voice replies, as if chanting a litany, "the writings of the new apostle came to the Church to illuminate the shadows of these dark days."

"But the timing is all wrong," he says, unable to restrain himself. "The author must have written these things *before* the cataclysm began. Weren't they delivered on the very day when the great face appeared in the sky and the cities erupted into madness?" The voice remains silent, of course, for these details have already been analyzed and discussed *ad nauseam* within the Roman episcopate. He considers for the hundredth time the ramifications of the fact that some unknown individual who shared the name of the last apostle had written of these things in the past tense, before they actually happened, and had addressed his dark visionary rantings directly to the Holy See in Rome. The Church's frantically launched investigation had been hindered at every turn not only by the fantastic events unfolding around the globe but by false and disappearing leads that appeared positively supernatural in their abrupt and strategic occurrences. No publisher knew of a book offering a blasphemous reading of Isaiah. Only the vaguest of hints spoke of a renegade theologian writing a self-described *magnum opus*. The papers had been sent via a route that looked impossibly circuitous when staked on a map. The trail dead-ended simultaneously at indistinct locations in North America, Central America, Pacific Asia—and Rome itself.

The more he ponders it, the more it sounds and feels like a narrative being altered and overlaid by multiple rewrites, each intended to accomplish a greater opening to an emotion compounded of equal parts bafflement and spiritual revulsion. In the latest revision, the letters are addressed directly to him, and their author is rendered fictional, to await complete obliteration in a version yet to come.

"Why me?" he asks, even though he is growing increasingly terrified at the thought that the specific identity of the New Paul may be supremely unimportant in one sense and all-important in another.

The voice responds to his unspoken fear: "In the beginning was the Logos, which speaks not only in the lines of Holy Scripture but in the lines of the real itself. Our new apostle's writings and their accompanying signs and wonders declare a great rewording in which the notions of 'me' and 'thee' may be forgotten."

A pen, formerly unnoticed, rests beside the pages on the desk. His hand begins to itch. The voice intones, "The Word is a living thing. Like a farmer sowing seeds, one sows the Word but knows not how it grows. If all were written down, the world itself could not contain the books."

The multitude gathered outside in the piazza emits a sigh of anticipation and agreement.

He watches with shock and fascination as his hand picks up the pen and begins to add to the words of the final page, defiling its inviolable sanctity, writing in clean, crisp, orderly lines that cut across the jumbled chaos like the bars of a cage.

ITS IMMANENCE: Jerusalem and R'lyeh—might they always have been interlaced with each other? The physical Jerusalem and also the mythic vision of its bejeweled celestial fulfillment—both revealed as mere shades, devolutions, abstractions of the primary reality of those crazy-slanted, green-dripping towers and slabs emerging like the archetype of a chthonic city from the subterranean waters of the collective psyche, like bony black fingers rising up from Mother Ocean.

Christ and Cthulhu—might they both be hierophanies of the same aweful transcendent reality? Christ as high priest in the order of Melchizidek, Cthulhu as high priest in the order of the Old Ones, both of them bridging the gap and healing the division between our free-fallen souls with their burden of autonomous, inward-turned selfhood and the greater, all-encompassing reality of God-by-whatever-name; both implanting their own deep selves *within us,* thus undercutting and overcoming our categorically contradictory attempts to heal the primordial rift through conscious effort. These psychic disturbances that have so terrified us of late, all the collapsing distinctions between thought, imagination, and physical reality, so that a stray wish or undisciplined notion may cause finned, clawed, and tentacled atrocities to appear, or may even alter one's own physical body in awful ways that some of us have been unable to undo afterward, as in a nightmare from which one cannot wake because one has awakened inside the nightmare itself—may these not be the fulfillment of Jesus' promise to send the paraclete to "guide us into all truth" and "convict the world of sin and righteousness and judgment," and of his promise that his followers would perform even greater miracles than he himself had performed, and of the apostle Paul's teaching that the divine spirit living within us will show us directly those primal mysteries which "no eye has seen, no ear has heard, no mind has conceived"? Surely these last words, quoted by Paul from the prophet Isaiah, aptly characterize the marvels and monstrosities we have recently witnessed.

Still writing, still horror-struck, he sees in his peripheral vision the Voice moving away from him in a swirl of smoky shapes. The new scriptural corpus is complete. The Church can now achieve alignment with that which truly is. What might be a wholesome human form dressed in liturgical vestments and wearing the papal mitre might also be a mutated manshape sprouting dragon's wings and surmounted by a head like a cuttlefish, and this dual superimposition of high priest might be walking on the floorstones or gliding above them.

The crowd assembled in the piazza might be a wild-eyed multitude of ragged and terrified survivors or a stalk-eyed horde of flopping fish and toads.

The vast visage painted across the dome of the twilit sky might be a white-bearded transposition from the nearby chapel ceiling or the imprint of an extra-cosmic monstrosity now burned eternally onto the face of heaven.

The granite obelisk planted in the piazza's center might be a skeletal black finger rising from Mother Ocean. The curved walls enclosing the crowd might be alien stone hewn into an architectural impossibility.

The incarnate voice emerges onto the balcony. The crowd roars, raising hands or fins or webbed claws and screaming in desperation or delight, singing a hymn of horror to the face in the sky.

The voice begins to speak, delivering its opening blessing: "*Iä! Cthulhu fhtagn!*"

Inside the ornate room he continues to write, binding the pages with a meaning that can only be known, not spoken.

The answer, Francis, must surely be found in the implicit order that lies buried in all this chaos. Embracing it is our salvation. God's ways are not man's. To Him a thousand days are as one, and one as a thousand. He is terrible to behold. Our religion, all the world's religions, may once have kept Him out, all unknowing of their true role, but now they, we, have become His conduit, again ignorant of our purpose until it is upon us to fulfill.

Gaunt faceless gargoyles hover on black leathern wings above the assembled multitude, showering whitefeather plumage as they beam benevolence from gold-glowing countenances.

The Lord God sits on His throne above the throng, towering above the basilica in a redblack inferno. His crown burns black. His beard coils green.

In these letters I intend to present you with the rudiments of a viable theological recalibration that will explore the avenues opened up by these shocking juxtapositions, and that, in doing so, will safeguard the possibility of our salvation, albeit in a much modified and, as I fear we shall be unable to keep from feeling it, far less agreeable form.

A Cherished Place
at the Center of His Plans

With Mark McLaughlin

1. THE HATCHLINGS

Where does it come from? The questioning voice echoed in Erik Thornton's mind for what felt like the thousandth time during that hot, endless night. It was past three, and the stifling atmosphere of his attic apartment pulsated with the maddening heat of his own creative energy. Or perhaps his nerves were just frayed after five solid hours of painting. He could not be sure. In the past, he had sometimes mistaken his weariness and its accompanying sensory distortions as inspiration. Not infrequently, he had deliberately interpreted it that way. Either way, the end result was always the same. His work unfailingly emerged, so people said, as brilliant, electrifying, and shockingly disturbing—a visual explosion of ferocious originality and dark visionary power.

He was pleased to agree with these assessments. For him, the most important fact was that each painting successfully channeled his soul onto the canvas. He had never faced a failure, never had to admit defeat. All twenty-seven of his works, produced over a ten-year span, were the perfect expression, the externalized quintessence, of his deepest self.

At the moment, he was in the midst of creating another one. He sliced the brush downward in a vicious arc, adding a black gash over the two humanoid figures embracing in a universe of chromatic chaos. They were separate yet one, these figures, these effigies. Their arms bled into each other's torsos, their faces melded one to the other, and they were joined in the middle where their hidden hearts, or rather a single heart between them, throbbed inside those shiny, oil-based breasts. As the scene had taken shape, he had fancied the two figures must ultimately share the same soul, since they were obviously two discrete expressions of the same transcendent self.

But he also knew, and he smiled at the thought, that this was merely his opinion. Gallery directors and art patrons found their own meanings in his images, and they paid handsomely for the luxury of taking his work home and contemplating it at their leisure, in private, where it could speak to them in whispers that might come to sound strangely similar to their own secret voices.

Where does it come from? The question echoed again in his head, and again there was no answer. It seemed that whenever he dwelled too long on the matter, his hand slowed and the work stalled, so he ignored the thought, refused to follow it, and simply let the painting continue to create itself.

He finished up around six, just as the first tricklings of dawn seeped through the wooden blinds covering the rounded window. He walked to the window, tilted the blinds with paint-smeared fingers, and peered down at the street below. The houses looked like tombs in the murky morning light. The manicured lawns of the tidy middle-class neighborhood were as pale and damp as freshly dug clay. With a grimace, he withdrew from the window, inhaled the creative solitude of his apartment, and vowed again that when he had enough money—perhaps earned from this latest round of work, soon to be on display with many of his other pieces at the Mondrago Gallery downtown—he would find different lodgings. This house in American suburbia was no place for a man with a mission like his.

Where does it come from? This time he cursed the echo before resolutely ignoring it again. His work was finished for now. He needed a long morning and afternoon of sleep before tackling his first meal of the day—dry toast with a pot of strong coffee.

As he settled onto his mattress, which lay uncovered on the

hardwood floor, he glanced back up at the painting and willed it to be his most powerful work, the one piece that would unlock the next stage of his life and show him where he was meant to go and what he was meant to do. The practical labor was done, but now came the most important part: the spiritual act of filling the painting with the charge of his soul. It was a culminating ritual that he had created for himself years ago, perhaps from some idea he had encountered in a book, or perhaps heard from a fellow artist. The memory was lost, but the ritual remained. He stared at the still-wet painting and willed his soul to enter it. He visualized a fiery ray emanating from his heart. He conjured the physical sensation of energy coiling and blazing within his core and leaping forth to penetrate and permeate the painting. The nebulous figures twined together on the canvas accepted this energy willingly, or so their wide eyes announced.

The name for the painting presented itself suddenly and incontrovertibly: *The Hatchlings*. This was a coveted moment of grace, one that did not always come, and he silently thanked whoever or whatever had delivered it.

When he had expended his last ounce of imaginative energy, he fell back onto the mattress with a heavy sigh. His muscles loosened and his consciousness began to blur almost immediately. His exhaustion was total. Within seconds, sleep had enveloped him like a soft blanket, like the warm waters of a cottony dark sea.

In a dream, he was walking through tall, wild grass. A black-velvet sky glittered with infinite stars. He approached a pool of dark water with an oily sheen swirling lazily on its surface. A coolness rose from it to press his cheeks and eyes with clammy hands.

The water stirred. The disturbance converged on a single point. A yellow-hooded head broke the surface and rose, cool and dry, to confront him with a faceless black emptiness. Two yellow stars ignited within the cowl, two ocular pinpoints of harsh golden light. They sought out his own eyes and peered into them with startling intensity. Without warning, his lungs seemed to deflate. He tried to gasp but his chest was paralyzed. The eyes inside that yellow cowl continued to stare at him, and into him, with an imperious malevolence so vast, so inconceivably ancient, it felt like a blast of hatred from the cosmos itself. And yet there was irony with the hatred, something like laughter, equally ancient and equally awful.

There was no sudden jolt out of the dream, no sudden springing awake and sitting up in bed with gasps of terror and relief. There was simply a torturous eternity of that silent exchange with the figure in the water, an eternity of suffocating under the scrutiny of those baleful eyes in their yellow cowl. Then there was a moment when he came to awareness in his attic, with his eyes already open and his breath rattling in his throat. The sight of his ceiling did not so much replace or displace the dreamworld as cover it up. The dream did not so much end as conceal itself, dipping beneath the surface of the room and taking up residence in invisible proximity.

Dazed, he turned his head in his supine position, saw the ceiling joined to the walls, the circular window with its blinds, the easel and the canvas, the physical normality of the room. But he still felt the dreadful gaze of that yellow-hooded head at the center of the pool. It was still there, still staring, as if lurking behind every shape, surface, and shadow.

It was many minutes before he could rise, first to his elbows, then to a seated position. Finally he crawled to his feet. He wobbled slightly, searching for balance. His body felt as if it had been motionless for years. His joints and muscles protested every movement; his head throbbed. Under normal circumstances, he would have reflected with pleasure on such a memorable dream with such vivid after-effects, since it was precisely this type of thing that often formed the fodder for his work. But he was categorically unable to feel that these circumstances were normal.

Still dazed and unsteady, he turned and found himself looking at his newest work. *The Hatchlings*. The title was still perfection, but the figures on the canvas had somehow changed. The colors, angles, textures, shapes, all the objective components, were unaltered, but now their true emotional coloration revealed itself as if for the first time. Looking at the intertwined figures encased in their maelstrom of colors, he now wondered how he could have missed their expressions of absolute horror.

2. The Exhibition

"Don't look now," said Powers, "but you're being watched." Bernard Powers was the director of the Mondrago Gallery on Equine Street. It was the opening night of Thornton's one-week exhibition, and Powers, ever solicitous and ever the salesman, was handling him.

It had been three weeks since the completion of *The Hatchlings*. Three weeks, with the memory of the yellow hood and the eyes and the pond gradually fading. He was surprised to find that he almost missed the electrifying terror that had accompanied him constantly for the first few days. Almost—but not quite.

He glanced around the gallery, pleased to see that the evening was turning out just as he had hoped. The exhibition had drawn all the hottest collectors in the city. There were even some new faces present in the crowd, posh and polished couples and individuals who were obviously major players, judging from their custom-tailored clothing, expensive haircuts, and designer jewelry.

His work adorned every wall of the multi-roomed gallery. As the crowd milled from painting to painting, he indulged in one of his favorite fantasies: that lines of fire lanced out from his works to fill the gallery with a glowing blaze. The guests were all trapped unknowingly in a web of his soul energy. He smiled at the delightful mental image.

"Watched?" he answered Powers indifferently, preferring to remain wrapped up in his daydream. "No surprise there. It's my show, after all. I imagine everybody will look my way, if they haven't already." He plucked a champagne flute from the tray of a passing waiter and took a sparkling sip.

"Yes, but this is someone *special*." Powers tilted his head slightly to the left. "He's over there by *The Ducklings*. Try not to stare."

Thornton choked on the champagne. In keeping with his usual custom, Powers had misnamed the latest painting in the most insulting way conceivable. Thornton refrained from correcting him, knowing it would be useless, and turned to see the person Powers had mentioned.

The gentleman standing next to *The Hatchlings* was handsome in a way that embarrassed the word itself. He was in fact a veritable Adonis: high cheekbones, square jaw, golden tan, thick black hair, and a trim yet powerful figure, clad immaculately in a tuxedo whose cost could have purchased a good portion of the art gallery itself.

But for all that, there was something disturbingly *wrong* with the man. Even from a distance, Thornton could see that he was cross-eyed. Other factors were more obscure but no less definite. The man's fingers seemed longer and thinner than one would have expected. Moreover, his tanned flesh had a glow to it that seemed out of place. It was more like the glow that might grace the features of a pregnant woman.

For a moment the contradictory cues in the stranger's appearance struck Thornton as cloyingly cute, like the unproportioned mess of a Siamese kitten or a fluffy gosling. But on continued observation, the setting of those misaligned eyes in that godlike face produced an impression that was not at all charming. If anything, it felt oddly revolting.

Thornton continue to stare until the man suddenly turned his face and eyes—or at least one of them—directly toward him and flashed a goofy, lopsided smile. Thornton gasped and whipped around to look at the floor tiles next to Powers.

"I told you not to stare," Bernard said, smirking. "He really should do something about those crazy eyes. He certainly has enough money to fix the problem."

"So who is he?" Thornton asked. "He looks like a male model with the brain of a village idiot."

"That, friend Erik, is Tony Anthony, and he is a legend."

Thornton lowered his glass, looked furtively at the stranger, and then back at Powers. "A *legend*? This guy looks about, what, twenty-five? Too young for a legend. You have to actually live and do things to earn that title."

"My friend," said Powers, "Tony Anthony is *forty-seven years old*. He's what people mean when they say 'well-preserved.' Those who know him say he must have formaldehyde in his veins. He's old money, too. Timber money, I believe. His family owns land in half a dozen states. And as for his legendary status—" Powers moved closer and touched the back of Thornton's arm in a motion that effectively drew the two of them into a private conference right there in the midst of the crowd. "He's a legend because he's a collector who grabs works by hot new artists just before they become hot. Some say he *makes* them hot. I think he used to be an artist himself. Can't remember what he did, though."

Thornton looked once more at the stranger. A cold shock, adrenaline mixed with nausea, washed up from his stomach. "Jesus, he's actually *staring* at me. Or at least I think he is. Hard to tell with those eyes. What the hell kind of name is 'Tony Anthony,' anyway?"

"'Tony' is short for 'Anthony,'" Powers explained with a smile.

"Are you telling me the man's name is *Anthony Anthony*? What kind of sadistic parents—? Oh, God. He's coming this way." Thornton stiffened and looked around for an escape route. "What should I do?"

"Just be nice. Or since this is *you* we're talking about, just be as nice as you can. At the very least, please don't mention his eyes."

There wasn't a waiter in sight, so Thornton had to hold his now-empty glass as Tony Anthony approached. The man's preternatural handsomeness vied for dominance with his crooked gaze as he exchanged perfunctory pleasantries with Powers. His nearness felt almost literally magnetic as he and the gallery director made small talk. Then Powers raised his arm and made a sweeping gesture of introduction. "Mr. Anthony, may I introduce Erik Thornton, the man of the hour!"

Thornton plastered on his best mask of polite indifference, a kind of blank pout worthy of a brooding artist, as he extended his hand. Up close and head-on, Tony Anthony's combination of stunning good looks and comic idiocy was even more unnerving. But it was outmatched by the touch of his hand, which felt oddly cool and flabby as Thornton shook it. Anthony's glowing flesh had a distasteful sponginess about it, as if the muscles beneath the skin were borrowed from some plump, chilly reptile. When the two released their mutual grip, Thornton fought down the urge to wipe his hand on his pants.

"Mr. Anthony," the artist said, "this is a real pleasure. I'm flattered you've come to view my work."

"I assure you," said Anthony, "I'm here to do more than just look." Almost predictably, Thornton thought, the man's voice was equally off-putting. It was both nasal and strangely muted, putting Thornton in mind—ridiculously, he realized, but the impression suggested itself and would not let go—of Peter Lorre speaking through a mouthful of oatmeal.

Powers, for his part, was instantly aroused by Anthony's words. "Do you mean that you plan to *buy*?"

"Oh, I most certainly *do*." Anthony nodded toward the wall across the room where *The Hatchlings* resided at the center of an array of five paintings, surrounded by *Dark End of the Spectrum*, *Four Figures Lost in the Inferno*, *The Illusionist's Noose*, and *Time Enough for a Scream*. "I plan to buy that entire wall. You've got a real treasure on your hands here, Mr. Powers." He put his own hands on his slim, tuxedoed hips as he sized Thornton up, raking his curious eyes up and down the artist from head to toe. "Erik Thornton is onto something. Something big." His smile widened and his voice lost some of its comical quality to become softer and deeper. "I wonder if he is not aware of just how big it might turn out to be."

The statement, delivered in that strangely altered tone, struck Thornton as containing some sort of veiled threat. Or perhaps it was a sexual come-on. Despite himself, he opened his mouth to respond with unplanned sharp words when faithful Powers butted in to save the moment.

"Ah!" he said. "Are you thinking, then, of launching the career of yet another budding young artist?"

"I think we all know," said Anthony, "including Mr. Thornton himself, that he is well past the budding stage. I think our young artist is quite ready to bloom." He looked directly into Thornton's eyes, and at once the room grew darker and quieter. Anthony's pupils and irises somehow righted themselves and swiveled into perfect alignment. They seemed to resemble gleaming crystals, with ebony pools of darkness embedded inside. Thornton heard the whisper of wind blowing through tall marsh grass. A hooded head rose from the depths of an oily pool, and twin points of yellow starfire flared into being. . . .

Then, as quick as a stroke of lightning, the yellow stars were replaced by the pupils of Tony Anthony's crossed eyes. Thornton shook his head to clear away his momentary flash into dreamspace. The gallery crowd murmured and chattered all around.

A waiter glided by with more champagne, so Thornton snatched a fresh flute. Powers remained alert, eager and obsequious.

"Do you know what you're doing?" Anthony was saying. "With your paintings, I mean. Did you deliberately paint those five pieces as a series? Or did they just come out that way?"

"I never ask my muse for too much explanation," Thornton said. "She and I have a working agreement. She provides the fire, and I provide the booze."

Powers, standing next to the two men, barked out a too-loud laugh. Anthony continued to stare at Thornton, as if awaiting more explanation. Thornton hefted his glass in a kind of salute. "No, I didn't paint them as a series. But they seemed to go together, so I had them displayed as a group."

"Yes," said Anthony. "Yes, they *do* go together. Your sense of your own work is well developed." He turned to regard the paintings again, and for a moment the three of them fell silent as they examined the wall. Male and female guests draped in expensive clothing, bearing fat pocketbooks, continued to mill about the Mondrago Gallery.

"I'm definitely buying all five works," Anthony announced. "And I would love for you to come see me at my house, Mr. Thornton."

Thornton blinked. Powers's eyes momentarily bulged, but he recovered immediately. "Oh, Mr. Anthony, I'm sure Erik would *love* that! Wouldn't you, Erik? I mean, Mr. Anthony doesn't invite just *anyone* out to see him."

"Yes, of course," Thornton said. "I'm thrilled."

"My card," Anthony said, holding out a cream-colored rectangle.

Thornton reached out and took it, carefully avoiding contact with the man's clammy flesh. He then handed Anthony one of his own cards.

"My personal secretary will call you," Anthony said. "He will set up a day and time. I'm dying to commission a new work from you."

With that, Anthony turned and walked toward the exit, not acknowledging any of the people who randomly blocked his path. As if by magic, like a miraculously parting sea of flesh, they stepped aside automatically to let him pass.

Powers clapping Thornton on the back and congratulated him for his amazing good fortune. The gallery owner laughed so hard that tears spilled from the corners of his eyes. Thornton, for his part, stood unmoving, staring after the departing Anthony, maintaining a deliberate inner stillness as the man stepped through the exit door. Once he was gone, Thornton turned his eyes in search of neutral space, seeking a place to look at nothing and reflect on what had just transpired.

He found his gaze coming to rest on his beloved Hatchlings, mounted on the far wall. It caused him no small amount of consternation, mingled with a curious dismay, to find that their horrified expressions now appeared to have gained an added nuance of pitiful, frightened bewilderment.

3. THE SECRET GALLERY

On any other morning, the misty forested vista of the mountain-side would have inspired Thornton's imagination with pleasurable intimations of new artworks to come. But today, as he motored steadily up the steep asphalt road in his old Ford Escort, on his way to Tony Anthony's mansion, he found himself preoccupied with forebodings about what he might find, and what he might be expected to do, when he reached his destination.

The previous night, as he'd slept in his attic cell, strange hunches and suspicions had suggested themselves in unnerving profusion. Now, a scant fifteen hours after having met Tony Anthony, he was headed for the man's house while listening to the sinister voices of his subconscious . . . lurid voices that whispered of wealthy lunatics whose money enabled them to enjoy secret lifestyles filled with sex parties and serial killing, either separately or in combination.

The call had come early that morning, at the unhallowed hour of seven o'clock. His phone had awakened him from another dream of the dark pool and the hooded head with the golden eyes. He'd nearly fallen off the edge of the mattress in his rush to answer it. Then, before he was really conscious, he had heard a coolly cultured male voice, strangely ageless and colored with an indefinable Eastern European accent, that inquired whether he was "the painter Thornton?"

Upon receiving Erik's sleep-blurred affirmation, the voice had informed him that Mr. Anthony would be able to receive him at eleven o'clock that very morning. Thornton had mumbled his acceptance of the invitation, or rather the summons.

Later, he found himself wondering if the cultured voice on the phone had in fact been Anthony himself. He'd heard before that rich eccentrics, as well as performers and politicians, did things like that. A curt phone presence helped to cut down on time-consuming small-talk.

Anthony's mansion was situated on a spacious shelf of land, located halfway up a pine-forested mountain north of the city. In fact, townspeople referred to that land-formation simply and uniformly as The Mountain. The capital *T* and *M* were always audible in the pronunciation. This striking geological singularity had been the first thing seen by Thornton during his initial drive into the city when he moved there three years ago. He had never bothered to learn its formal name, but in town he'd heard people talk from time to time about The Mountain with an odd undertone of reverence in their voices. The irony was not lost on him now, as he found himself summoned to ascend said Mountain on a mysterious pilgrimage to the lofty home of a distasteful god-figure.

On that particular morning, the city had been positively infuriating with its noise and traffic and fumes. When he'd finally broken free of its clamor, he had been seized with a sense of freedom that lasted until he began the long drive up The Mountain and found himself enclosed in a forest of ancient pines laden with milky mist. Instead of seeming cool and refreshing, the forest felt oppressive, and his sense of suffocation was augmented by the inner chatter of those worrisome suspicions about Anthony's intentions.

The drive soon began to feel like a dream. In the gloomy primal womb of the trees and fog, he could almost believe he had never really awakened, but was merely driving farther into a dream that had begun when the phone first rang. It was a disorienting feeling, and also, he feared, a decidedly unsafe one, in light of his recent encounters with involuntary waking dream-states.

Eventually the entrance to the mansion emerged from among the trees. The house itself was located half a mile inside the perimeter of a vast wrought-iron fence. Getting to it required passing through a similarly massive iron gate, which brooded over a misty gray lawn and a blacktopped driveway. The gate stood open, as if waiting for him. He braked to a halt and took a breath. He thought he saw a deer in his peripheral vision, but when he turned to look, he saw nothing but a swirl of mist. He pressed the accelerator and drove slowly through the gate, noting well his feeling of crossing more than just a manmade threshold.

When he reached the driveway's end, he stopped the car, switched off the engine, and spent a moment taking in the sight of the muted architectural wonder that was Tony Anthony's mansion. It consisted of multiple angles and planes, spires and finials, turrets and towers, lancet windows, pointed gables, and more, all fused together in a crazy cluster that was somehow Gothic and modern—chic modern, sleek modern, even in its disorienting randomness—in a way that Thornton could not pinpoint. Greenish-gray ivy was draped over most outer walls. Clearly, nothing was simple here.

He stepped out of the car to find himself enveloped in utter stillness. No bird sang; no breeze blew. The clammy mist hung motionless in the air. He searched the windows of the house for some sign of movement. As he made his way toward the massive front door, the silence and chill made him feel like a sleepwalker, lost somewhere between dreamland and reality. Up here the city seemed impossibly remote, tucked back down at the bottom of The Mountain in a dark, dank well that he called his life.

The front door opened before he touched it, swinging inward without a sound, and he stepped into the mansion without a moment's hesitation. Dreamlike trances could be useful, he reflected, for masking fears and inhibitions.

Inside, he discovered a large, richly decorated foyer with gleaming wood floors and walls. Rooms and corridors branched off all around him, but he had no time to investigate, for Tony Anthony was descending a curved, carpeted staircase to greet him.

"Mr. Thornton!" Anthony's voice conveyed real pleasure, reminding the artist—and again, a ridiculous thought presented itself with inconvenient timing and unshakable tenacity—of Peter Lorre speaking through a mouthful of sugary oatmeal on Christmas morning.

Anthony was dressed in a dark sweater and loose-fitting pants. At the foot of the stairs, he spread his arms flamboyantly like the wings of a raven, or perhaps a pterodactyl. "Thank you for coming! We have so much to talk about." Thornton offered his own thanks and waited for Anthony to make the next move. There was a subtle alteration in the man that he could not place. Anthony looked somehow different from the night before.

The difference became obvious as the millionaire stepped closer: his eyes were no longer crossed. Or at least, not as much as they had been at the gallery. The left one still looked a bit lazy and unfocused, but other than that, his facial appearance was normal. Or actually better than normal, for now he truly looked the part of a Greek god. The effect was literally breathtaking.

"Please," Anthony said, "come with me. I've put your paintings in the studio. I arranged for them to be delivered last night." He turned and walked toward the interior of the mansion, obviously expecting Thornton to follow him. Which, of course, he did. As he left the foyer, Thornton noticed the front door whispering shut behind him with no visible aid. Probably under the control of a mechanical device with an electronic eye.

The "studio" turned out to be located deep within the labyrinth of the house. Thornton followed his host through halls and kitchens and parlors so numerous and convoluted, he soon lost all sense of direction. Each room, hallway, alcove was decorated to a level of almost absurd opulence, with many striking works of art installed throughout. Eventually, they descended a long flight of stairs and emerged into the natural-light glow of a long, low-ceilinged, unfinished basement with a row of narrow windows set high in the far wall. Thornton breathed a sigh of relief and looked longingly at the glass panes, which seemed at this point like a welcome escape route. The house had begun to feel like a vast and terrible maw around him, cavernous and carnivorous. Then he noticed the tableau spread out before him, foregrounding the far wall and the windows, and thoughts of escape were eclipsed by something like wonder.

Spread out in a fantastic array across the length and breadth of the basement was a collection of mysterious figures draped in sheets of white linen. The figures were obviously human or humanlike statues. The telltale outlines of heads and arms were enough to make this plain. His astonishment was magnified when he looked at the gypsum walls on the right and left and saw that they, too, were hung with sheets, and that these sheets concealed what could only be paintings. A hundred or more of them lined the walls on either side. The whole space seemed to be held under a hush, like a church sanctuary.

"In here," Anthony said, shutting the stairwell door behind them, "I keep my most treasured collection. It is a room that I have devoted entirely to the power of art in all its forms. I believe art has the power to transform the world, to give us all a sense of widened perception and heightened consciousness. Don't you agree, Mr. Thornton?" His voice echoed with a dull reverberation against the cold concrete of the walls and floor. Without waiting for an answer, he led Thornton through the graveyard of shrouded forms. "I have hung your works in the back, where I put all my most recent purchases. Would you like to see?"

Thornton followed closely behind him. He was careful not to touch anything, for fear that he would disturb some deliberate arrangement whose logic he could not perceive. Pale shapes loomed on either side like mute guardians of some obscure secret. He fancied he could feel the pressure of restrained visionary power billowing outward from beneath the sheets, and he breathed a sigh of relief when he and his host left the shapes behind and came to the far wall.

Anthony turned to the right and pointed, and Thornton saw that they were facing an alcove in the corner where his paintings, the ones from last night's gallery encounter, had been hung. Unlike the others in the room, they were uncovered, and the familiar sight of his own work sparked a welcome sense of security. Their arrangement, however, was unusual, for Anthony had hung them next to each other in semi-interlocking fashion like the pieces of a puzzle, resulting in a kind of horizontal arc that resembled a letter "C."

Anthony waited a moment and then spoke. "I think you see what I'm needing, don't you?" He pointed to the empty space within the arc. "One piece is lacking. When it is finished and placed with the others, the series will be complete." He slipped his hands into his pockets and offered Thornton another of those lopsided grins. Thornton noticed that his voice was losing its mealy sound. Down here, surrounded by his secret, sheeted gallery, Anthony had begun to speak in an increasingly commanding baritone, rich and resonant.

"You must paint this final piece for me, Mr. Thornton," Anthony said. "Or at least, I *hope* you will. Despite appearances, I'm not an arrogant aristocrat who issues orders simply because I think I can buy people and manipulate them to my will. I'm seeking a true collaboration between the two of us, one in which the environment and financial backing that I can provide will enable you to create a masterpiece—the final painting in this important series."

He paused, and Thornton knew a response was required. He licked his lips before speaking. "Thank you for all this, Mr. Anthony, including the good words about my work. And my apologies, but I feel I need to remind you that I didn't paint those works deliberately as a series. I mean, look." He pointed to each painting in turn. "*Time Enough for a Scream* is over a year old. The next three I painted over the course of last winter. I only finished *The Hatchlings* recently. They're not a series, they're *individual* works. I created each one without thinking of the others. I wouldn't know where to start painting something to finish 'the series,' because there isn't any series to begin with."

"Strange, then," said Anthony, "that I knew how to line them up in chronological order. Wouldn't you say?" He waited for Thornton to see it, and when he did . . . by God, Anthony was right. Starting with the top point of the arc, the paintings were hung in the order of their creation. A moment earlier, when Thornton had pointed to each and recounted this order, he had not noticed that he was simply tracing the arc Anthony had created.

As he looked more closely, the artist began to recognize a distinct thematic consistency to the paintings' arrangement. For all the world, it was as if Anthony truly had found an implicit coherence that connected this recent string of work—an internal thematic logic that had been hidden from their very creator.

"Now, perhaps, you can see," Anthony said, smiling in a way that was not at all lopsided, "why and how I have come to be known as a nurturer of new talent."

Thornton smiled, nodded, blinked—and, in the nanosecond of darkness behind his closed lids, saw a cowled face staring at him with yellow glowing eyes.

"Perhaps I could," the artist finally said after a long pause, during which he kept himself very still, both mentally and physically. "Perhaps I could come up with something. Perhaps I could complete this series that I didn't even know I was painting. It would take time, though. I can't tell you how much. I never know." He hesitated and then forged ahead. "Not to sound crass, but there's still the matter of payment."

Anthony's smile was radiant. "Money is no object. Since you brought it up, am I to understand that we've now reached the negotiation stage of this transaction? And that you have, therefore, said yes?"

Standing there in Tony Anthony's subterranean gallery of hidden, hooded artworks, which was located beneath the immensity of his isolated, convoluted mansion, which perched halfway up the sloping expanse of The Mountain, which sat under a white sky that concealed a glittering infinity of star-strewn space, the artist parted his lips, drew a breath, and said, "Yes."

4. THE CRUCIBLE

Erik Thornton did not know what he had expected to happen as an immediate result of that crucial assent. The situation was unprecedented, so he had no context by which to judge the likely unfolding of subsequent events. He held no expectations about what the following weeks might hold. One thing he had not expected, however, was failure. Utter, abject failure of a type he had never before encountered. Desertion by his muse. Inability to make even an inch of progress. So when this very thing manifest-

ed itself, beginning the day after his deal with Anthony and continuing unabated for two weeks, he was thrown into creative agony, tipping over into outright, clawing despair.

It began the day after they closed the deal. Anthony sent him
home bearing a cash payment of a ridiculous sum, representing
only half the total amount to be paid, with the remainder to be
paid upon completion, and with Thornton agreeing to return in
twenty-four hours to commence work on the new project. That
was one of Anthony's conditions, and one so distasteful that only
the money could overcome it: "You must start tomorrow, and you
must paint your final picture right here, with the others in view."

Anthony had been serious when he'd referred to the basement
as the studio. Thornton was required to complete the work entirely in that environment. He was even prohibited from producing
any preliminary sketches at home. When he left and drove back
down The Mountain to spend the rest of that day and that night
brooding in his attic, he surprised himself by honoring Anthony's
request and refraining from conducting any "test borings," as he
customarily called his initial efforts when gestating a new painting. When he slept soundly that night for the first time in weeks,
with no dreams disrupting his rest, he took it as a good omen and
a sign of the rightness of his decision.

The next day he returned to the mansion and followed Anthony into the basement, and found that he had been supplied
with a new easel, a fresh canvas, and more paints and brushes
than he had ever worked with before. The easel was set up to face
the alcove where his paintings were hung, and he was expected to
start right away.

Anthony barely spoke to him. Yesterday's warmth and enthusiasm had vanished. The eyes of Thornton's new patron were
completely crossed again, and the smiling, encouraging, congenial
patron had been replaced by a cold and distant supervisor. Anthony showed him where a bathroom was located in the basement, referring to it in European fashion as a water closet, and he
showed him a digital wall panel in the main basement area by

which Thornton could order various coffees and teas, pastries and cheeses, even an entire meal if he wished. Anthony offered him lodging in one of the guest suites, but Thornton declined. His host did not acknowledge the refusal.

"Start now," he said. "Stay until at least five o'clock. You will not see me again today. Return tomorrow at the same time." Without waiting for a reply, he turned and walked back through the sheeted gallery of statues and paintings to leave Thornton to his work. When Anthony shut the door to the stairwell behind him, Thornton's heart lurched momentarily, and he waited to hear the sound of a lock being turned. But there was no such sound. There was only the shrouded silence of this subterranean madhouse, as he had begun to think of it.

He took a few minutes to collect himself. He examined the tools Anthony had supplied, admired the brushes and paints. He mixed a few colors experimentally. He primed the canvas with the provided gesso. Then he sat on the stool Anthony had left for him—no chair, no sofa, just a three-legged wooden stool in all that floorspace—to contemplate his finished paintings on the wall, and to stare into the blank canvas on the easel as if it were a window and he were waiting to see what walked past it.

That was the beginning of his agony. For *nothing* walked past the window. The canvas, it turned out, was not a window but a wall. It was a blank barrier, impermeable to creative sight. He had expected this at first, but when it persisted for half an hour, and then a full hour, he began to perspire. He shifted on the stool, rubbed his eyes, rolled his head and shoulders. Still nothing, no inspiration, no spark, not the faintest hint of the vaguest idea.

He settled back down into his inner seat of power, and *bore down* in the way that he had learned and practiced all these years, pressing down into the well of his soul where he and his muse lived in communion at the deepest level of their respective beings, where they were essentially a single entity. He had learned this trick, or rather this inner discipline, long ago, and had found from hard experience that, by means of this technique, inspiration could in fact be forced, at least to an extent. He could kickstart creation, and it had never once failed.

Until now. The psychic bucket that he cast down within himself hit the bottom of the well in his soul and seemed to strike dry ground. He felt it scrape across an unyielding surface, drawing up absolute nothingness. He gulped and gasped, and bore down again. This time the effort caused him an almost physical pain, as if a hand had seized his heart from within his ribcage and given it a violent squeeze. He almost cried aloud. Again, he was left with nothing, not a hint of soul fire or creative energy. For the first time in his life, the well was empty. He was flatly, starkly, helplessly becalmed.

When five o'clock rolled around, he had sat there for eight hours in a daze of wretchedness, trying and trying again, and failing each time, and finding himself weaker and more wretched after each effort. He departed the basement at five o'clock sharp, as if he were on a punch clock, leaving a blank canvas that terrified him with its emptiness, especially in the face of the finished works that glared at it from the alcove. The house, as before, was empty as he fled. He descended the mountain as if fleeing the scene of a crime.

That night, he slept dreamlessly.

*　　*　　*

The blockage continued the next day, and the next, until the days became a week. Several times during those interminable hours, he made a few exploratory strokes. He spent time mixing colors and visualizing scenes and shapes. Once he laid out a surreally distorted landscape in his mind's eye and then spent two hours attempting to reconstruct it on the canvas. But it was soulless and forced, an arbitrary act of desperation. He found it garish and awful, and actually horrifying in its spiritual emptiness. He wiped the entire thing away with a rag and linseed oil and then knocked the canvas to the concrete floor, where it lay the rest of that day. When five o'clock arrived, he placed the canvas back on the easel and climbed the stairs with legs that were numb and a heart that was heavy with desolation. He felt the Hatchlings watch him leave. Their eyes were filled with sadness.

*   *   *

The days rolled on. The meals were good, when he wanted them. All he had to do was make selections on the digital panel, like ordering in a restaurant, and they were provided via a dumbwaiter in the wall behind him. During the first week he had hardly eaten; but now, during the second, he tried to fill the emptiness inside him with three meals each day. Despite the food's high quality, it left him feeling bloated and sick. This did not disturb his sleep when he got home, though. He passed each night in his attic immersed in total unconsciousness, like lying in a coma at the bottom of a deep, dry well.

*   *   *

During the second week, the daily journeys up and down The Mountain and the basement stairs began to blur into an indistinguishable unity, as if he were perpetually ascending and descending at the same time . . . as if he were staring at the blank canvas in the basement while simultaneously lying comatose in his attic.

In time, he began to feel that a strange alteration was taking place inside him. For many years he had believed that, as an artist, he was in control of his soul. He had thought that through the exercise of his art, he had made a bargain with the dark forces of his unconscious mind and kept them from running amok, the way they did in other people's lives. Now he began to fear that he had been wrong about this, for there was a new force at work inside him that moved with unknown rhythms and made him feel a stranger to himself.

He could sense its presence at all times, whether ascending or descending, waking or sleeping, and yet he had no conscious access to it. It was alien to him, something independent and autonomous. He could not fathom its nature or motives. He only knew that it was there. It felt, he realized, as if he were literally haunted—not by some ghost or revenant that threatened him from outside, but on the inside, within or behind his own self. He found he could not even look at the Hatchlings anymore, for their wide eyes and rounded mouths were now unreadable, and the painting frightened him with the hidden meanings that it might signify.

*   *   *

At the end of the second week, Thornton did not return to his own house when he left Anthony's mansion. Instead, he drove straight to the Mondrago Gallery. He had not spoken with Bernard Powers since the exhibition, and now he needed more than anything to reestablish contact with a member of the wider human race—someone who was not Tony Anthony. In Powers's particular case, he also needed to connect with someone who represented Thornton's life before Anthony had come into it. He also needed to read Powers the riot act for failing to warn him about what he was getting himself into.

He found Powers alone in the main room of his gallery, walking from wall to wall with a clipboard in hand, cataloguing works by various artists. Some were Thornton's, and the artist ignored the imagined hints of visionary fire that he saw leaping out from them as he walked straight up to Powers. The man looked up from his clipboard, startled out of his concentration, and then a smile cracked his serious expression.

"Thornton! Where have you been? I thought you'd call after that night when Tony Anthony showed up. Have you spoken with him again?" His balding forehead gleamed in the glow of the strategically arrayed track lights overhead, contrasting sharply with the dark hair still clinging to his temples. As Thornton searched and struggled for words, Powers's smile faded. "Erik, you look *exhausted!* Aren't you sleeping?"

This pricked a bubble Thornton had not known was lodged in his chest. To both men's surprise, he burst out laughing. He laughed and laughed until Powers, who at first had joined in with him politely, stopped laughing and observed Thornton more closely. A line of concern creased the director's brow. "I gather we need to talk," he said. "Here, follow me." He led Thornton to his office, where they sat down on opposite sides of the director's rustic pecan wood desk. "Now," said Powers, "tell me what has happened."

By the time Thornton had finished describing all that had transpired since they last saw each other—except for his dreams and visions, which he'd never told Powers about anyway—Powers was chewing on a fingernail and staring down at the desk's woodgrain pattern. His clipboard was lowered to his lap and momentarily forgotten. He appeared to be deliberating over something.

"That's a strange story indeed," he finally said. "I just can't imagine how you must be feeling. But let me tell you, Erik"—he paused to lean forward, reach across the desk, and put a hand on Thornton's arm—"this sort of thing is not out of line, not unheard of, for Tony Anthony. You've probably already figured out that he's the very model of a modern lunatic. I suppose I may have, um, *downplayed* his eccentricity when I introduced the two of you." He pulled his hand back from Thornton's arm but remained perched forward in a posture of concern. "I'm truly sorry. I don't know what else to tell you."

"What else to tell me?" Thornton all but shouted the words. He was still riding high on the energy crest from his laughing fit a few minutes ago. It had felt so good to laugh, and he let the residual wave carry him along and lend force to his words. "I don't think you realize what you've gotten me into. I don't even think *I* fully realize it. You have to help me here. Tell me what to do. I can't back out . . . can I? I mean, Anthony has the power to make or break me, right? Will I even have a career left if I renege on our deal? Or will that be the least of my worries? Will I even still be *alive?*"

Powers held up his hands in frustration. "Erik, please! Dial it down, my high-strung friend! Don't get ahead of yourself. And *don't give up.* You're too close to the situation to see it clearly. Anthony may be weird, but he's not dangerous. He's crazy Tony Anthony, a category unto himself! And despite your recent close encounters with what truly does sound like some Category Five oddness, he's just an art collector. A patron of the arts. You've met his type many times. Anthony is just *more* of that type than anybody you've ever known. Put that together with his money, and it means his power to help—or hurt—your future prospects is accordingly amplified."

Thornton nodded as he sighed wearily. He wanted to believe, but he was still wavering.

"Listen to me, please." Powers pressed on, sensing that he was getting through. "Sure, you're stuck for ideas right now. But from the way he's structured your agreement, it sounds like the one thing you do have on your side is plenty of time. I recommend that you just do whatever you'd normally do when you're stuck. I've known you a long time, Erik. I know you have your little rituals. Just *do* them. Trust the process. Trust your muse. You'll be glad you saw it through." He raised his arms in a "Who knows?" gesture and asked, rhetorically and jovially, "Where the hell does inspiration come from, anyway?"

Just as it had happened in the first of the dreams, Thornton's lungs seemed to deflate. He struggled to gasp. Pressure gathered in his head like a throbbing volcanic seam. Then it let go, and he was calm. Calmer than he had felt in weeks.

"You know," he said slowly, "I'm not even sure why I came here. I don't know what I expected. But thank you, Powers."

Powers sat back in his chair and beamed. "You're welcome, Erik! Can I assume, then, that my weak words have struck some fire from you?"

"You can. I think I'm back on the horse. A little unsteady, but riding high in the saddle."

"This is delightful to hear," said Powers, smiling. "Cowboy metaphors and all." He suddenly started in his seat and checked his wristwatch, like a man coming to himself after an unplanned nap. "You know, closing time came and went fifteen minutes ago. Would you like to get dinner together? Or coffee? It strikes me that you'd be better off with some company."

Thornton shook his head. "No. I'd better get back to my attic and sleep. I have to be up there early tomorrow. I'll never finish if I don't devote myself completely to it."

Powers looked at him for a moment and then nodded. "Okay, then. I admire your dedication. You'll come and see me, won't you? Please don't let this much time go by again. You'll suffocate by yourself in that basement."

But Thornton had already checked out of the conversation. He was already retreating back into himself and into the new world he had come to inhabit. "Thanks again," he said, pushing his chair back from the desk and rising to his feet. "I'll update you when it's finished. Because I *will* finish." He was already out the office door and heading through the gallery toward the exit to Equine Street when he called back over his shoulder, "I *will* finish."

The words reverberated through the empty expanse of the gallery as though it were an underground cave.

*　　*　　*

Powers, standing in his office doorway, watched Thornton's receding form through the glass panes of the main door. He looked down and rubbed the toe of his polished black shoe idly on a floor tile. Then he began switching off the lights and preparing to leave for the night.

His path took him at last to Thornton's *The Luster of Yellowed Bones*. Before he turned off the ceiling row of LED can lights that illuminated the wall, he paused to study the painting, even though he'd seen it literally a thousand times. And for that thousandth time he wondered what could possibly compel a person, even someone with as gruesomely repulsive an artistic imagination as Erik Thornton, to paint a picture of such galling horror. It literally made Powers shiver to see the undefined shapes in the foreground, performing horrendous acts on an equally undefined additional shape, while in the background, an even more indistinct entity presided over the proceedings like a stage director, or a puppet master, or an emperor, or perhaps all three. Beyond those roles loomed some vague but tangible presence that not only combined and encompassed the others, but *transcended* them and thereby put the viewer of the painting in touch with meanings from a sphere beyond mere art.

That Thornton could, through his use of nothing but color, shape, texture, and compositional techniques both conventional and unconventional, imbue the master entity with such an aspect of transcendental significance was virtually miraculous.

No less cunning was the manner in which he somehow imbued the same figure, which lacked any concrete characteristics, with an aspect of infernal delight and delectation, suffusing the entire painting with a sense of overwhelming dread. And yet, the true anchor point of the whole work was the undefined shape in the foreground that was the receiver of all this awfulness, condemned to hang there on the canvas forever, unable to cry out, unable to escape, unable even to understand the nature of its own suffering and horror.

After a moment of considering all this, Powers switched off the lights and exited the gallery, still brooding as he locked the front doors.

Yes. Unquestionably *yes*. Erik Thornton would be able to satisfy the desires of Tony Anthony, no matter how outlandish or unpleasant they might ultimately prove to be.

Of that, Bernard Powers was certain.

5. THE OPENING

The next morning, Thornton—sequestered in the depths of Anthony's mansion—glanced yet again at his wristwatch. 11:06. The weak white glow of a cloud-covered sky spilled through the narrow windows above like ice water. The sheet-covered figures sat silent in their strange array, almost begging to have their shrouds lifted and their mysteries exposed. The alcove where his works hung resembled the darkened passageway to an alternate dimension, with Thornton's paintings positioned like panes in an other-worldly French door, beckoning entry to a kaleidoscopic nightmare on the other side. Thornton sat on his stool brooding over all these things, still mired in misery, still failing, still desperate and feverish and bereft of any clue about how to proceed.

But now he had a new companion, one who promised to see him through this impasse: anger. And another fine friend: hatred.

Anger and hatred for Anthony. For Powers. For all the fatuous aristocrats who had attended Thornton's recent exhibition and strutted like peacocks in mating season. Most of all, anger and hatred for himself, because of his stupidity in taking this job, and his foolishness in thinking that he had ever been an artist of professional standing.

Because of this universal loathing, he now possessed a limitless desire to silence and humiliate everyone, including himself, by proving them wrong. Not just wrong about him, but wrong about *everything*. Whatever it was, any and all thoughts and beliefs, attitudes and assumptions, he wanted to prove them wrong and himself wrong with them. He wanted to negate everything, to obliterate it all, to overturn the universe and see them all—including himself—gaping in horror as the stark glare of revealed reality annihilated their blinkered denials and the world they protected.

He had not eaten since the previous morning. He had not slept except for a couple of fitful hours, during which he had stared in paralyzed dread at the hooded figure rising from the black pool. The nightmare had returned, and though it horrified him, he also inexplicably welcomed it.

Sitting alone in the tomblike silence of Tony Anthony's secret gallery, he felt that he might shatter into a thousand pieces at the onset of any sudden noise or motion. The palette was in his right hand, the brush in his left. The canvas rested bare and dull before him. He raised the brush, then lowered it. In the background of his sight, behind the canvas, the Hatchlings watched in mockery, their open mouths howling with silent laughter.

In the foreground, with no warning, soundlessly, the canvas became a window. The barrier of its surface shuddered and dropped away, and the resulting rectangular aperture began to glow with the inverted light of a black sun, as blinding as a welder's arc. An iridescent outline formed itself there, and with an insight born from some obscure place within him—the place where his muse resided, the place whose real nature and location had always eluded him—Thornton realized that he was seeing the completion of the thematic vista portrayed in the other paintings. The canvas had at last become the final pane in the door. All he had to do was recreate with his paints the vision of otherworldly access that he was now seeing stenciled on the canvas. The knowledge was clear, immediate, and undeniable. He was being handed the greatest work of his life, as if someone were showing him a work already completed, and he had merely to put it into concrete form for the rest of the world to see.

"Hail and farewell," he murmured aloud, and then wondered what he even meant by it. Like a wayfarer dipping a torch into a slick, gleaming pool of pitch and setting it ablaze to light the way, he swirled the colors from the palette onto the brush and began to mark the canvas with the outlines of an impossible truth.

*   *   *

Elsewhere in the mansion, three floors above the basement, Tony Anthony sat alone in his study. Six video monitors squatted in a row on his massive oaken desk, displaying color images of Erik Thornton from six different angles. With one hand, Anthony delivered forkfuls of a delicate French pastry to his mouth from a gold-rimmed bone-china dish. With the other hand, he held a small remote-control device.

On the screens, the artist sat motionless and slumped, just as he had done for most of the preceding two weeks. But suddenly, for no visible reason, his posture shifted and his body language changed. He rose to his feet, standing ramrod straight, with his eyes blazing and his jaw set. Anthony set his fork on the dish and leaned toward the screens. He watched Thornton mix colors together and raise his hand, bearing a brush, to begin marking the canvas for the first time since his abortive experiment a few days earlier. Without taking his eyes off the screens, Anthony pressed a button on the remote to start the rack of video recorders on the wall beside him.

Thornton continued to move his arm and hand. Soon his movements became vivid and violent. He backed away and shouted at the canvas, then rushed forward to stab and slash it with the brush. The canvas rocked on its easel from the violence of the attack. The artist's motions became even more frenzied. He laughed wildly, the tinny sound of it spilling through the small speakers on Anthony's desk.

The ghost of a smile curled the corner of Anthony's lips. Clearly, he thought, the moment had arrived. The culmination was afoot. Still watching the monitors, he took a sip of wine from the glass before him, a rare red Romanian Muscat, and felt the liquid warm him all the way down. It was an effect he savored.

He tilted his face upward to gaze at the massive image that dominated the twenty-foot-high main wall of the study. His books had once rested on shelves there, many years ago, until they had taught him everything they could. He had then turned to other ways of gaining the knowledge he sought. On that wall was displayed a single painting, centuries old and awesome in both size and subject. It depicted a hooded figure with glowing yellow eyes, rising out of a pool of oily, vile blackness.

Anthony raised his glass to the figure. "Soon," he said. "Very soon now. You and I. Face to face." Taking another sip, he stared into the enormous yellow eyes in the painting, eyes that burned with a fire from beyond this world. After a moment, his own pupils dilated sharply. His left eye tugged inward even more than usual, and with his skewed vision, he saw the figure stir into motion and begin to rise, while the black pool seethed and bubbled.

6. The Wraiths

Thornton finished the painting in three days. He worked at a feverish pace, pausing only for the briefest of interims each night to
retreat back to his attic apartment and snatch a couple of hours of
fitful sleep before heading back up The Mountain. The dream had
once again disappeared, but as he had experienced on the morning after its first arrival, he could feel the hooded figure watching
him from behind every surface of the waking world.

For nourishment, he took only a hasty bite of leftovers from his
refrigerator each morning as he dashed out of his apartment to return to the studio, high on The Mountain and deep in the mansion.

It was the most glorious period of his life, and he was fully
aware of it. He also appreciated what a rare blessing it was to recognize such a thing as it was actually happening. He felt as if he
were balanced on the sizzling cusp between two worlds, one of
them a complex prison of meaninglessness, the other a shimmering realm saturated with color and consequence, a place where he
could extend his arm and watch multi-hued meanings flow effortlessly from his brush. It was this second world that he was access-
ing and materializing on the canvas, and he felt that his muse was
guiding him unerringly in his efforts. Never before had he felt
such a fulsome sense of precision and rightness in his work.

Nor had he ever known, with such certainty, the precise instant when the flow of inspiration stopped and a particular painting was finished. It happened at 5 P.M. sharp on the end of the
third day. One moment he was painting furiously, and the next,
the fire inside him had gone out.

His hand was still raised with a loaded brush, and it froze in
mid-stroke. It trembled. He watched it with alarm. The hand fell
to his side, a drop of russet-colored paint fell from the brush to
the floor, and he wavered in a moment of confusion. With an effort he raised the brush to apply another stroke, but this produced
such a violent sense of restraint, like a shock wave emanating
from the canvas to repel him, that he staggered back and nearly
lost his balance.

Finished. A voice whispered the word. He whipped around to see who was there in the basement with him, but then he recognized the source of the word. It had been spoken by the same inner voice that used to ask where his creativity came from—a voice that had gone silent during this new phase of life. Now it spoke again . . . *Finished* . . . like the wings of a dragonfly brushing his ear. In the silence that followed, Thornton scanned his inner world and discovered with horror that his sense of coursing vitality, which had remained constant these three days, had vanished. His sense of being guided by an unerring instinct had disappeared as well. In place of both was a sense of utter *lostness,* like being stranded in an arctic wilderness, accompanied by an aching hollowness in his chest and gut. The latter was so acute, he could almost imagine someone had stolen his inner organs.

He huffed a heavy breath, and it took all his strength to suck in the next one. His head threatened to loll back on his neck. If he had eaten any food in the mansion that day, he would have suspected that Anthony had drugged him.

The painting. He had to look at it, had to see what he had created, the image of the world that had so savagely possessed him. But his vision blurred when he tried to focus on it. He blinked, refocused, and looked again. But in place of his painting, he saw only a milky impression, as though his eyeballs were coated with a film of mucus. He pressed the heels of his hands against his eye sockets, blinked several times more, and tried yet again.

This time, not only was the problem still there, but it had actually grown *worse.* Now he was unable to see even the outline of the canvas. It was as though a wraith the color of old milk were hovering on the easel, rippling slightly like a roiling vapor. And beyond the canvas, in the alcove, he saw five more wraiths, five more rancid-yellow blurs or blanks that obscured his paintings.

At that moment, Tony Anthony came walking through the sheet-covered figures of his secret gallery.

"Erik," he said. It was his rich baritone voice, not his mealy, fiendish one. "My friend, how is it coming?" He looked unchanged from when Thornton had last seen him, more than two weeks ago. He even wore the same clothes. His eyes, however, were perfectly aligned.

Thornton looked at him, then at the herd of wraiths, and then back at his patron. He cleared his throat and attempted to control his mounting panic. "I think . . . I mean, I believe I've finished."

Anthony merely graced him with a stiff smile before turning to look at the new painting. He slowly ran his hand over his chin and then tapped his nose with his index finger.

Thornton's panic boiled within him while Anthony contemplated the picture. What was the mad millionaire seeing? What was the source of that sickly, milky optical phenomenon that partially clouded his vision? What was *going on* here?

"Hmm," Anthony said. Then he said it again: "Hmm." And then, "Ha!"

Thornton used the lull to press his hands to his eyes again. When he lowered his hands, he found that some of the yellow milkiness had now claimed Anthony himself. He face was suffused with a soft vaporish glow. Through it, Thornton could see that his eyes had crossed again.

"Yes! You are, indeed, *finished*," Anthony said. There was a tightness in his voice that suggested a fiercely restrained undercurrent of joy. "I judged you correctly. You'll be pleased to know, the painting is worth every penny I said I would pay you." He clasped his hands before him in a prayer-like gesture and shook them with his next words for emphasis. "Thank you, Erik. Thank you *sincerely* for your service. Now, come upstairs and I'll pay you the rest of what you are owed." With that, he turned and walked back through the shrouded gallery of statues.

Thornton followed automatically. He tagged behind Anthony like a child fleeing the dark. The shrouded shapes of Anthony's secret gallery seemed to stare down at him with malicious disdain. A thrill of terror washed through him at the thought of seeing those statues uncovered, with their colorless stone faces and empty eyes.

He found his host waiting for him at the top of the stairs. Tony Anthony led him to a cramped study located just off the foyer, where there was a signed check waiting on top of a cherrywood desk. Anthony removed a pen from a ceramic holder and wrote down an amount considerably higher than they had agreed upon. "For your troubles," he said as he handed the check to Thornton, who looked at the amount without expression.

"Thank you again," Anthony said. "It's been a pleasure."

He walked out to the entryway and up to the front door, which was opening on its own. Thornton followed. When he paused before Anthony, he saw that his host was smiling at him with the same crazy expression he had worn at the Mondrago Gallery, nearly three weeks ago. Thornton looked away and walked through the door. It whispered shut behind him. He stood alone on the front steps in the silence and mist. The mansion was now a secured fortress, and he was no longer welcome.

When he started the engine to his car, no birds fluttered from the trees. No leaf or needle blew on the branches lining the drive. As he motored slowly away, passed through the iron gate, and coasted down The Mountain toward the city, he had the sense that he was in the process of awakening from one dream, only to enter another. But the one he was now entering was merely his former life, seen through new eyes. Seen from the vantage point of emptiness.

7. THE ARRIVAL

Three months later, Bernard Powers held another showing of Thornton's works at the Mondrago Gallery. This was more a gesture of friendship than an act of artistic commerce.

Powers had noticed a distinct change in Thornton's manner in the weeks following the end of his association with Tony Anthony. It was the same change noticed by all who knew the young artist. Thornton was no longer so angry and intense. These qualities, which had previously defined him and his work, had left and been replaced by a brooding distance. Thornton often failed to respond when addressed directly in conversation. He spent a lot of time staring into space, out of windows, at the ceiling or floor, any direction that did not require him to focus on another person, to make eye contact or establish a direct line of human communication.

After his final return from The Mountain, he'd immediately started to paint again, but his latest works reflected his new temperament. The select crowd who had followed his early work were nonplussed by the steady stream of icy melancholy that now poured from his brush. They might have embraced the change, if there had been some spark of his earlier fire in the new work, but such was not the case. The new paintings were as spiritually empty and desiccated as the subjects they depicted: deserted corridors, empty park benches, hulking angular shapes like icebergs, and a mountain, repainted many times, with what might have been a house on top, only the structure was difficult to identify because it was obscured by a milky yellow cloud.

The number of viewers interested in Thornton's work dropped rapidly and sharply. The number of actual buyers dropped even more. This current exhibition, Powers knew, would be the last, though he lacked the heart to tell his young friend.

It was while Thornton was standing self-absorbed in a secluded alcove beside one of his new paintings—an abstract work entitled *Foaming Antarctic*, composed entirely of white and various shades of pale gray—that Powers decided to inject a bit of cheer into his friend's evening. A lovely blonde woman in a strapless red dress had been eyeing Thornton all night, but the artist had not noticed. He preferred instead to spend his time staring assiduously at the floor and into empty corners. The drinks were flowing freely. The crowd was loosening up. Someone, inspired by the sheer force of alcohol, would probably decide to buy something soon, and Powers was filled with a sense of compassion for his young friend. Midway through the exhibition, he edged his way over to Thornton and touched his arm.

Thornton turned and looked at the gallery director with eyes that would have appeared desperately sleepy if they had not been so starkly empty. Powers waited for a sign of recognition, an indication that Thornton recognized him and was aware of his surroundings. Receiving none, he almost abandoned his plan, but then decided to go ahead with it, on the grounds that there was nothing to be lost.

"Don't look now," he said, "but you're being watched." He nodded toward the woman in red, who at that very instant was looking at Thornton from across the room. She gave him a sly grin when their eyes met. Then she turned to examine one of his paintings.

"Are you trying to surprise me?" Thornton asked. His voice came out as a murmur. It was flatter and emptier than his painting of a polar desert, hanging across the room. "She probably wants to sleep with me. Maybe she thinks she can gain something by having sex with the artist."

Powers grimaced and groped for a response. "Well, there's nothing wrong with a little harmless pleasure, is there? You make it sound like it's pointless even to try."

"Isn't it?" Thornton asked.

Powers could not think up a reply, so he merely continued to hover beside his friend.

What happened next, Powers could never say. He tried for a long time afterward to piece together what might have caused his friend to exhibit such behavior with no visible provocation. He could never escape the feeling that some nugget of truth was concealed within the incident, and that if he could only uncover it, what he found might clarify what had happened at the final showing of Thornton's work.

Had he been able to see into the artist's mind, he would have known that Thornton had glanced at the blonde woman one last time. At that point, he'd been shocked to see a yellow hood take shape around her head. Of course, it was surely nothing more than the form of her coiffure that created the illusion. Still, as Thornton looked at her, a yellow cowl replaced her blonde hair—and then her face disappeared, giving way to pure darkness.

The fact that this thoroughly monstrous figure was planted directly beneath his recent painting, *The End of It All*, seemed prearranged somehow, as if it were the fulfillment of a prophecy. The two of them, the painting and the hooded figure, were like pieces of a puzzle in Thornton's eyes, fitted together to form a window onto another world.

Lines of fire began to jet from his paintings, hung all around the gallery. He staggered as they formed an interlaced pattern, ensnaring the guests in a flaming web. Burning yellow eyes flared within the cowl of the figure that had replaced the young woman. The paintings themselves shuddered as their surfaces tumbled inward. Each became a window onto a field of crimson and ochre, bathed in the rays of a black sun. Multiple figures in yellow cowls, all with blazing eyes, peered through each aperture. Within the frame of each former painting, the left eye of every pair trembled and then swiveled slightly inward.

Thornton screamed uncontrollably. The cries were ripped out of his throat and chest from a level of fear beyond conscious thought, a realm of pure terror that bypassed and transcended awareness, where screams were the sole reality. He slammed back against the wall and began to push against it, as if he could escape into the woodwork. The emptiness in his chest had become a bottomless abyss that would eventually swallow the rest of him, leaving only a hungering darkness in the shape of a man. He shook so violently that his teeth literally chattered.

Confused and frightened, Powers leaped away and gaped at Thornton. The guests froze in their places and tried not to appear horrified, an effort at which they unanimously failed. After a petrified instant, universal throughout the gallery, during which Thornton continued to shriek, Powers reached toward him and started to say something, anything. But at that moment, Thornton sprang away from the wall and tore through the gallery, out the front door and into the night, still screaming. The guests nearest the door heard Thornton's car start with a roar and then pull away from the gallery with a screeching of tires.

Everyone stared at everyone else. Over by *The End of It All*, the blonde woman in the red dress stood stiffly, immobilized by the same shock and confusion as everyone else. A middle-aged man in a white tuxedo laughed once, nervously, and then stopped.

Fortunately, the clever waiters realized that only booze could salvage the evening. They glided through the room with flutes of champagne, all eagerly snatched up by the rattled guests.

8. THE END

The drive up The Mountain was silent and smooth, like a sled sailing over the frozen surface of a polar desert. The night outside the vehicle's windows was pitch-black except for the stars, glittering overhead past the tops of the pines. Thornton again had the sense of exiting one dream and entering another. The cold light of the stars, gathered into constellations that seemed strange and alien, goaded him with pinpricks of silvery terror. The forest rushing past on either side was an impenetrable jumble of monstrous shapes.

The artist's throat and lungs were raw from screaming. His cries had stopped as soon as he had driven away from the gallery. The vision of the figure from his dream, multiplied in the frames of his paintings and manifest in the transformation of the young woman, had receded both physically and psychologically, the farther he drove away from the site of its occurrence.

Now he gripped the steering wheel with white knuckles and stared straight ahead at the ribbon of road, his mouth closed and his jaw set. He needed no visual confirmation, no additional apparition. Now he felt the eyes looking at him everywhere, from every direction, from the blacktop, from the trees, from the sky. He could barely bring himself to peer for even a second into the rearview mirror, for fear that he would see the physical presence of the intruder floating behind him.

In time, the iron gate of Tony Anthony's mansion came into view in the yellow beams of the headlights. It seemed perfectly natural that the gate should swing open, as if on cue. The mansion was lit with a pale yellow effulgence glowing in every window, giving it an appearance of warmth that it had never possessed before.

When he parked and approached the front door, it opened silently by itself. The stars prickled his back until he had stepped inside. It was then, as the door was closing behind him, as he stood alone in the vast foyer, that he wondered for the first time why he had come here, of all places. Here, to the mansion, the locus of the mental and spiritual sickness that had overtaken his life.

He did not have to wait for an answer.

Thumpings and scufflings begin to sound from somewhere in the mansion—whether from above or below, he could not be sure—and in a moment Tony Anthony came around a corner, somewhat abruptly, and stopped to face him. It was not lost on Thornton that around that corner lay the route to the basement.

The wealthy man was dressed all in black, with a platinum amulet dangling from a chain around his neck. The design on the amulet was almost impossibly intricate, so much so that it hurt Thornton's eyes to look at it.

Anthony stared in crazy-cat fashion at Thornton for a moment. His breathing was labored and his face was flushed. At last he leaned against the doorframe and shoved his hands in his pockets. "Erik. Didn't I know you'd come back?"

Thornton could see that he must have interrupted the millionaire in the midst of some sort of strenuous activity, but Anthony did not look the slightest bit irritated.

"I tried to make a point with the extra money," Anthony said. "But then you're an *artist*, aren't you?" He spoke the word scornfully. The Peter Lorre impression was nowhere to be seen. Anthony's rich voice boomed out clearly, and his eyes were perfectly aligned. "You take a sense of pride in your work, don't you? Perhaps you wonder just what I'm planning to do with your paintings, up here at the top of The Mountain."

Thornton had no voice. He merely stood and stared.

"I could take you down to the gallery, you know." Anthony removed his hands from his pockets and began to wander idly across the foyer. In Thornton's eyes, he looked like a snake charming its prey. "I've placed your last painting on the wall with the others. It's the pivotal point of my entire collection. Wouldn't you like to see how it all fits together?" His voice was thick with mockery. Before Thornton could answer, Anthony stopped moving and fixed him with a piercing stare.

"I've uncovered them all," he said. "All the pieces in my secret gallery. No more sheets. No more hidden wonders. They're all facing each other now. You should see it! All those lines of sight slicing through the air and weaving a web of fire. It's miraculous."

Thornton's throat worked. He tried to speak, but what emerged was only a strangled croak.

Anthony laughed. "Yes, I can see the fire, too. Don't worry, you're not insane. You've just been cursed with the unfortunate ability to see more than most."

As Thornton listened to these shocking statements, his mind began to turn corners faster and faster, trying to backtrack along the way to where he had been, just a few short months ago. But these attempts fell short. The pathways of his memory always doubled back on themselves and inexorably funneled him into the nexus of this impossible present moment.

"I suppose I should explain things to you," Anthony said. "If your life was a movie, I imagine I would be the villain—and the villain always feels the need to explain his wicked ways." He wavered slightly in Thornton's vision, like a reel of film skipping off its tracks. "Should I start by describing a figure in a hood that stares at you with yellow eyes?" He smiled at the effect his words had on his guest. "Don't ask who he is. That is a question without an answer. You can only know him by what he does. Did you know that everything you do serves him? Your ideas, your thoughts, your words, your actions—they all come from him and point toward him. This is especially true of all your *art*. It's all about him. There is nothing you or I or anyone else can do about it. You're either working for him, or else you're working for him. How's that for a raw deal?"

Anthony laughed long at his own words. When he had calmed

down, he studied Thornton's face before continuing.

"I pieced this collection together from all over the world. It was not easy, believe me. Often the owners did not part willingly with their investments. And when I couldn't buy what I needed, I commissioned new works from new artists. Which is, of course, where you come in." His lopsided smile no longer seemed to hint at idiocy, but at a deep-seated depravity. "You're not the first, you know, and you won't be the last. It's gone on for as long as there have been people to make art. It's all a big puzzle, but basically, it's about *creating* something. And about *opening* something—or should I say, somewhere? The whole process involves creating and opening a door to the visions I've longed to see for my whole life." His gaze grew wistful and distant, and his left eyeball began to tug inward. He appeared to be trying to focus on something, some object or vista, that was not perceptible to normal vision.

He continued to speak, even with his eyes fixed on an invisible horizon. "When you leave here tonight, close your eyes and see if you do not receive—like some sort of splendid yet horrific gift—a vision of a room filled with the most dazzling array of grotesque artwork you can imagine. A room where the atmosphere bleeds from the slicing wounds of a thousand lines of fire, and where the vague outlines of the impossible take solid shape at last. Then you'll know whether I'm right or not, and whether you should think of me as a lunatic or a visionary."

Anthony came back to the room suddenly, with a shiver like a dog shaking water from its pelt. His eyes focused on Thornton again, and he shrugged. "Or maybe it's not finished. It may well be possible that your work *isn't* the final piece of the puzzle. Perhaps it will require another search for another artist, and we will have to play the game again and wait just a bit longer to witness the fruition of this quest. In any case—and I want you to know this above all, so hear me well—*your* role here is played out."

He moved toward Thornton then, and raised his arm as if to drape it over the artist's shoulder. Thornton flinched and feared he might vomit.

"Erik!" Anthony said with a small, soft cry that might have been a laugh. He appeared genuinely surprised, and not a little hurt. "It's all right, I assure you. I won't do you any harm. You are simply . . ." He searched for the right word. Then he found it: "*Spent.* Yes, you are spent, my friend. You've got far deeper problems than any possible threat from some crazy, rich eccentric."

Anthony began to back away. "You know, it just dawned on me: you came all this way to see me this evening, and yet you haven't uttered a word! Just as well. Even if you had a question, I've already answered it for you. So, just go, and try to locate your muse again. Return to that primal question, and ask it deeply: *Where does it come from?* I promise you'll fail. You'll receive no answer. It's like a door that was always intended for you and you alone . . . but alas, it's locked from the other side."

Anthony had reached the doorway to the hall that led to the basement. His breathing, which had calmed during his monologue to Erik, was becoming faster and deeper again in anticipation of his descent into the depths of the house. "You've played your role well, Erik," he said, backing into the hallway with one hand grasping the frame of the doorway. "But it's over now. The one we both serve has had his fill of you, as have I! Everything you do for the rest of your life will still be from him by him and for him, but your cherished place at the center of his plans is a thing of the past."

A clock somewhere in a nearby room chimed midnight. The metallic tones only thickened and deepened the dreamlike atmosphere of the mansion. Thornton's legs felt rubbery, but they carried him well enough toward the front door in a backward stagger. The door swung open to let him out as he backed out onto the front steps.

The last thing he saw before the door closed was Anthony's face, dominated by those enigmatic eyes. The left one was turning inward again, perhaps in preparation for his descent into the gallery.

Thornton's imagination placed him momentarily in the center of that gallery. In his mind, he pictured lines of fire erupting from the dead eyes of countless works of art and lancing across the length and breadth of the basement to slice open its atmosphere with seething wounds. Something new was being created, or opened, by those wounds, something wonderful and awful to behold, something that would answer every question he had ever asked.

During the drive down the mountain, he thought more than once about testing Tony Anthony's dare. He thought about stopping the car, closing his eyes, and finding out if the vision the other man had described, the vision that he could almost, but not quite, conjure up through sheer force of will, was indeed waiting for him in the darkness behind his lids. Perhaps it would feel good to know that he was not crazy, that what he had experienced was real. Or perhaps it would make him feel even better to know that everything Anthony had told him was a lie, that the man was just a raving lunatic who preyed on the ambitions of talented young artists.

But there on the dark road, just past the blackened tree line, beneath a sky bristling with the silvery teeth of countless stars, he knew the answer would not matter either way. Truth, lies, sanity, madness—what did such things mean anymore? As Anthony had said, Thornton was *spent*. Used up. Hollowed out. The final answers were inconsequential, meaningless, worthless.

Driving at that late hour, deliberating over his fate, Erik Thornton felt for the last time as if he were suspended between two dreams. One lurked behind him at the top of The Mountain, where something new might be coming into being in the labyrinthine womb of Tony Anthony's mansion. The other stretched out before him like a barren wasteland of shattered ambitions and hollowed-out hopes. Neither seemed real.

He wished he could stay right where he was, forever. He wished he could remain suspended between the dreams of past and future, riding the crest of the present icy moment in the solitude of eternity, where nothing could touch him, where he could simply be *left alone*.

But of course, his journey had to end somewhere.

Acknowledgments

The author would like to express his appreciation to the following people for their roles in bringing this collection to life:

To the late Wilum Pugmire for his generosity in sparking the whole project to begin with by establishing a connection with Hippocampus Press.

To Mark McLaughlin for his wit and expertise as a collaborator, not to mention his patience.

To Jon Padgett for serving as a first publisher and editor for three of these stories in the misty past of the late 1990s, and for two decades of wonderful friendship and support.

To Thomas Ligotti for his valuable early feedback on some of the stories herein, and for many years of friendship and literary inspiration.

To S. T. Joshi for his editorial support, and also to Derrick Hussey and the rest of the crew at Hippocampus Press for their epic patience and steadfastness over a span of six years while they awaited the final story.

Publication History

"An Abhorrence to All Flesh," first published online at Thomas Ligotti Online, January 1999. Also in *Divinations of the Deep* (Ash-Tree Press, 2002). Also in *Allem Fleisch ein Greuel* (in German translation), edited by Eddie M. Angerhuber and Boris Koch (Medusenblut, 2005).

"The Basement Theater," first published online at Terror Tales, April 2000. Also at The Art of Grimscribe, 2000. Also in *Divinations of the Deep*.

"Blackbrain Dwarf," first published in *Dark Awakenings*.

"A Cherished Place at the Center of His Plans" (with Mark McLaughlin), first published in *Hell Is Where the Heart Is* by Mark McLaughlin (Medium Rare Books, 2003). It has been significantly revised and expanded for this collection.

"Chimeras & Grotesqueries," first published in *Dark Faith*, edited by Maurice Broaddus and Jerry Gordon (Apex Books, 2010).

"Desert Places," first published in *Alone on the Darkside*, edited by John Pelan (Penguin/Roc, 2006). Also in *Dark Awakenings*.

"The Devil and One Lump," first published online at Horrorfind, 2001. Also in *The Best of Horrorfind II*, edited by Brian Keene (Horrorfind.com, 2003). Also in *Dark Awakenings*, where it appeared in a significantly revised and expanded form (retained here).

"Divining the Darkness," first published in *Divinations of the Deep* by Matt Cardin (Ash-Tree Press, 2002).

"The God of Foulness," first published online at The Art of Grimscribe, 2002. Also at Terror Tales, 2002. Also published as Volume 5 of the *Dark Homage* series, edited by Shane Ryan Staley (Delirium Books, 2004). Also in *Dark Awakenings*.

"If It Had Eyes," first published in *Divinations of the Deep*. It has been significantly revised for this collection.

"Judas of the Infinite," first published in *Divinations of the Deep*. Also at The Art of Grimscribe, 2002 (in German translation).

"The New Pauline Corpus," first published in *Cthulhu's Reign*, edited by Darrell Schweitzer (DAW, 2010).

"Nightmares, Imported and Domestic" (with Mark McLaughlin), first published in *The HWA Presents: Dark Arts*, edited by John Pelan (Cemetery Dance, 2006).

"Notes of a Mad Copyist," first published online at Thomas Ligotti Online, January 1999. Also in *Divinations of the Deep*.

"Prometheus Possessed," first published in *Dark Faith: Invocations*, edited by Maurice Broaddus and Jerry Gordon (Apex Books, 2012).

"The Stars Shine without Me," first published online at Horrorfind in 2002. Also in *In Delirium II*, edited by John Everson (Delirium Books, 2007). Also in *Dark Awakenings*.

"Teeth," first published online at Thomas Ligotti Online, 1998. Also in *The Children of Cthulhu*, edited by John Pelan and Benjamin Adams (Del Rey, 2002). Also in *Dark Awakenings* (Mythos Books, 2010), where it appeared in a significantly revised and expanded form (retained here).